STAR TREK™
PROMETHEUS

IN THE HEART OF CHAOS

Also available from Titan Books

Star Trek Prometheus:
Fire With Fire
The Root of All Rage

STAR TREK™
PROMETHEUS

IN THE HEART OF CHAOS

BERND PERPLIES   CHRISTIAN HUMBERG

Translated by Helga Parmiter
This edition published by arrangement with Cross Cult in 2018
Based on *Star Trek* and *Star Trek: The Next Generation* created
by Gene Roddenberry, *Star Trek: Deep Space Nine* created by
Rick Berman & Michael Piller, *Star Trek: Voyager* created by
Rick Berman & Michael Piller & Jeri Taylor

TITAN BOOKS

Star Trek Prometheus: In the Heart of Chaos
Print edition ISBN: 9781785656538
E-book edition ISBN: 9781785656545

Published by Titan Books
A division of Titan Publishing Group Ltd
144 Southwark Street, London SE1 0UP

First Titan edition: November 2018
1 3 5 7 9 10 8 6 4 2

Did you enjoy this book?
We love to hear from our readers. Please email us at readerfeedback@titanemail.com or write to us at Reader Feedback at the above address.

To receive advance information, news, competitions, and exclusive offers online, please sign up for the Titan newsletter on our website
www.titanbooks.com

STAR TREK™
PROMETHEUS

IN THE HEART OF CHAOS

PROLOGUE
10,000 YEARS AGO

City of Hestaon, Iad

With the ardent passion of gods—their wrath easily provoked, their favor to be solicited anew time and again—the Ancient Reds looked down from the heavens above Hestaon onto the gathering of the Renao, their faithful worshippers.

Bharatrum, the Bringer of Doom, shone particularly brightly during this night. Radhiri felt chills running down her naked back, despite the oppressive heat that lingered in the city. Disaster was looming on the horizon when Bharatrum's eye glowed fiery within the mists.

It's good that we have gathered to make a sacrifice, the young woman thought. *An offering will surely propitiate the gods.* Only if they were appeased—her birth mother had taught her this canon when Radhiri was a little girl—would they spare the Renao from storms, white rot, and *Giaku* swarms.

Radhiri fixed her gaze on the broad, natural stone slab outside the Big Temple of Hestaon. Six high priests had gathered on the platform, all richly adorned in their robes. During rituals such as this, the priests wore the ceremonial masks that transformed them from ordinary mortals into avatars of the gods themselves: Bharatrum, as well as Acina, the Giver of Life, Coaraston, the Giant, and all the others. The priests walked as gods among the Renao, and their deeds, their words, and their bidding were binding.

The evening ceremony devoted to making sacrifices to the gods hadn't started yet. The high priests stood silently in the background while four strikingly handsome Renao were busy at the front of the stone platform. Two young women were sweeping the floor with long wooden sticks that had fronds tied to their ends. A pair of men held small bowls with incense in their hands, swinging them from side to side. Their joint task was to clean the site for the ritual—the floor as well as the air.

Slightly envious, Radhiri watched the four young people going about their work. Cleaning the ritual site was one of the most honorable tasks, but she had never been assigned it, although she was one of the most beautiful girls in the city. She believed that one of the high priests, Jamous, had his lustful eye on her. But Mheron, Hestaon's best sponge diver, had been courting her, and she had finally yielded. One year from now, when Radhiri reached maturity, they would become a couple. Even a mighty man like the High Priest of Coaraston wouldn't change that. However, the young Renao woman had to admit that she found Jamous's interest flattering, and the thought of being intimate with the man with the mask of the gods had provided her with two or three nights filled with frivolous dreams.

She felt a hand on her naked shoulder, startling her out of her reverie. When she turned her head she saw Mheron, who must have approached her from behind, and she felt a pang of conscience at her thoughts of another man.

"Mheron," she said, surprised. "What are you doing here? Weren't you supposed to dive for glowing sponges?"

He made a negative gesture. "We've given up on that. Yesterday's hefty tide has ripped most of the sponges off the rocks. There were hardly any left." Mheron's skin was dark red like that of most other men who worked outside all day. His broad chest and shoulders bore witness to the fact that he swam a lot in the nearby ocean. His black hair had been close-cropped, as was traditional among the sponge divers, and it was hardly more than a dark shadow on his scalp.

Looking at Radhiri, his golden eyes glowed brightly. "It's wonderful to see you."

The smile he gave her made her heart beat faster. "It's also wonderful to see you." Radhiri raised her hand, stroking his bare chest with two fingers. She forgot about Jamous and his mask of the gods. She wanted to spend the next few days with this man.

A gong sounded, opening the ceremony. The four chosen with their fronds and incense bowls withdrew humbly.

Muahadha, the High Priest of Bharatrum, stepped forward, raising her hands imploringly. The six high priests took turns to preside over these ceremonies, and today, it was hers.

"People of Hestaon," she began, "we have gathered here today to beg for mercy. The Six Brothers glow wrathful at the red firmament. We have sinned, oh yes, all of us. Each and every one of you knows your guilt. And even if you did not share your guilt with the community, the gods know your misdoings. Think about it!"

She paused briefly, to give those present the opportunity to remember all the things that they had done wrong during the past four ninedays since the last ceremony. Radhiri recalled her own sins. To her mind, they were negligible. She had lied to her creators a few times in order to meet Mheron. She had wished the white rot on one of her friends because she hadn't keep one of her secrets. And she had dreamed about Jamous one night with open eyes because

Mheron had stood her up in their hideout by the cliffs. All those couldn't possibly infuriate the gods, but who knew how the gods reached their judgment?

The gong sounded again, announcing the next part of the ceremony.

"In order to appease the gods," Muahadha continued, "we have to make a sacrifice to them. And which sacrifice could be greater than that of our own lives? The highest honor is bestowed upon those who give themselves to the gods for the good of the community, who carry our sins upon their shoulders, offering their body, mind, and their very existence to the Six in exchange for those sins. So I am calling upon the person among us who is without fear, and who will look the gods in their faces, submitting to them so they may forgive us for going astray."

This was an ancient ritual that had been handed down from generation to generation, repeated every four ninedays. The call for a volunteer was usually rhetorical, as the sacrifice had been selected beforehand. Oftentimes they were elderly citizens of Hestaon who felt their vitality dwindling. They didn't want to be a burden for their families, and in order to do the community one last service they would commit the ritual suicide. Sometimes, dishonored citizens would volunteer in an attempt to redeem themselves. There were also people who were disappointed in life in general, or those who tried to prove their worth to others with this selfless act. Convicted criminals tried to purify their souls, while escaping execution (if not death) at the same time. And if they couldn't find any volunteers to sacrifice themselves, prisoners from other towns would be led onto the stone platform. Due to incessant festering quarrels, there was never a shortage of those. They tended to appear with a silly grin on their face, caused by intoxicating herbs, which lasted until they had transcended from life to death.

"I wonder who it is going to be this time?" Radhiri mumbled. She had watched the creators of her creators, her male creator's sick brother, and a friend who had been eaten up by unrequited love all climb up to the sacrificial altar. Death didn't scare her anymore. Still, whenever she attended the ceremony, she was always excited when they announced the sacrifice.

The man climbing up to the stone platform was obviously of an advanced age. His shoulder-length black hair showed several gray streaks, his face and his bare chest that had been painted with the ritual body paint were full of wrinkles, and he walked with a stoop. But his violet eyes glowed with determination as he stood in front of the priests, straightening up.

"I, Hamadh, son of Ouras, am stepping forward, wanting to go to the gods. I will take on all sins of the people, and I will beg the gods for their mercy for all those living. I am willingly giving my body, my mind, and my very existence."

Those present, including Radhiri and Mheron, applauded him by hitting their right hand onto the left side of their chest. Some of them praised the old man verbally.

"Do you know him?" Radhiri asked. Personally, she'd never noticed Hamadh in Hestaon.

Mheron tilted his head. "My creator sometimes associated with him. He lives on the edge of the city, and he has been cultivating *basuudh*-tubers for years. Last winter his partner died. Since then, he has lost the will to live. I knew that sooner or later he would appear on that platform."

"Hail to thee, Honorable," Muahadha intoned. "Through your deeds you become a paragon for us all. Your sacrifice is our blessing, and your name will be engraved on the stone of Hestaon for all eternity." After the ceremony's conclusion, an acolyte would engrave the sacrifice's name into the stone platform. More than two thousand names had been immortalized there already. They told the story of several generations.

"Do you choose the old or the new way of sacrifice?" one of the priests asked Hamadh. He was Acina's avatar, and Radhiri didn't know him. This was yet another rhetorical question, as all volunteers chose the chalice with the quick-acting poison of the *rassaris* plant. Death by blade was usually only expected from Hestaon's enemies.

So a surprised murmur rose when the old farmer gave his reply. "I have always been a man of tradition. I choose the old way."

The priest hesitated, obviously not expecting that response. "Are you sure?"

But Hamadh merely straightened himself, and suddenly he didn't seem quite so fragile to Radhiri anymore. Undoubtedly they saw an old man standing there, but his spirit was unbroken, and he had the heart of a warrior. Which made his readiness to meet his death even more astounding. He must have loved his partner very much.

"I am," said Hamadh.

"So be it." The High Priest of Acina took a step back, turning towards one of his servants, who handed him an *Acouak*, a short double-edged blade with a penetrating tip and an extended hilt so it could be held with both hands. The priest handed this dagger to Muahadha, who walked into the middle of the platform where Hamadh waited.

Radhiri felt a chill going down her spine. Her respect for the old man grew. Strength and the willingness to endure pain was required if you wanted to sink an *Acouak* into your own heart. She doubted that she would dare to do so if she ever climbed onto that platform.

Clutching the blade with both hands, Hamadh turned it and pointed it towards himself. He looked up to the heavens. "Listen to me, Ancient Reds," he shouted with a surprisingly booming voice. "I'm coming to join you—me, Hamadh, son of Ouras. I'm carrying the sins of the community of Hestaon, and in the name of all those present, I'm begging you for mercy. My life will be yours. May you grant me the kindness to be reunited with my partner."

Muahadha also looked up, raising her hands into the air. "Listen to us, Ancient Reds. We're making this sacrifice to appease you. Take Hamadh, son of Ouras, in, and acknowledge his selfless bravery. Honor be with you for all eternity."

Radhiri and Mheron joined all the others by tilting their heads back and raising their hands. "Honor be with you for all eternity," they repeated. Above their heads, red fires glowed in the night sky—the eyes of the gods that saw everything.

At first, Radhiri barely noticed it, but the longer she looked up to the sky, the more it seemed as if the red glow above them increased. Did the gods come to claim Hamadh? Did his sacrifice executed in the old way impress them so much that they would come and claim him personally?

The gong sounded one last time. Everyone looked back at the ritual site. Hamadh took a deep breath; all the required words had been said. Now, all that remained to do was the act of the sacrifice itself. He fell to his knees. Muahadha stood behind him, placing her hands on his shoulders like a kind mother would. The grip of his fingers was so tight that his knuckles were white.

And then he stabbed the *Acouak* deep into his heart. His face distorted in a grimace of pain but he still managed to tear the dagger out of the wound. Blood colored his torso red as he fell sideways, the dagger still in his lifeless hand.

Everyone present drummed against their chests, praising the gods with loud voices.

Suddenly, the red glow that Radhiri had noticed in the sky was below them, scarlet mist enveloping the entire site, encroaching on the houses and streets like fog at high sea. It was a confusing sight, both wonderful and daunting.

Several Renao began to scream and attack each other for no apparent reason! Radhiri was horror-stricken. Her eyes widened while she stared at the stone slab that was only a few steps in front of her. Hamadh suddenly scrambled back onto his feet. His chest was covered in blood but his wound seemed to have closed. With an insane flicker in his eye, he raised the *Acouak* in the air.

"You wanted to force me to commit suicide," he shouted at the priests. "I should have died because of you, you false prophets. You will pay for that!"

Radhiri wanted to observe this incredible scenario unfolding before her eyes but suddenly strong hands grabbed her by the shoulders, turning her around.

"You lewd woman!" Mheron bellowed at her. Saliva sprayed over her, while his yellow eyes glowed menacingly. "Did you really think that I didn't know? Do you think I didn't sense that you were lying with another man?"

"What?" Radhiri exclaimed, horrified. "What are you talking about?" She was seething. "*You* are denying yourself to me. Did I not wait for you in the evenings while you were out, spending your hours with your friends?" A ludicrous thought struck her. "Or are *you* the dishonest one here? Isn't it you who has a secret affair? That's why you're avoiding my bed!" Now that she had said it out loud, it suddenly all made sense.

"Don't try to place your blame on me!" He shook her vigorously. "Somehow, I always knew that you wouldn't be faithful to me, but I was blinded by love. But now I can see clearly, and I'm telling you, you deserve the same punishment as any woman that cheats on her companion." He pushed Radhiri to the ground, reaching out for a club that was next to him on the floor.

Radhiri pulled a knife from her belt. For a brief moment she wondered why she was carrying a weapon, but then boiling rage washed over her. She leapt to her feet, emitting a deafening cry as she lunged towards Mheron. Enveloped in red mist, only one thought remained. *Kill him*, something screamed in her mind. *I need to kill this wretched rapist!*

One last time, she hesitated briefly, asking herself what, by the gods, was happening. But then she succumbed to the same violent frenzy that had taken hold of all Renao on the ritual site of Hestaon. The gods wanted blood? They would get blood!

1
NOVEMBER 25, 2385

U.S.S. Prometheus, in orbit around Iad
Souhla system, Lembatta Cluster

"We must bombard this being from orbit! It is our only option!"

Kromm, son of Kaath, rested his fists on the conference table of the *U.S.S. Prometheus*, staring across at Captain Richard Adams with dark eyes.

"No." Adams shook his head. "That is *not* our only option, Captain."

"It's the only reliable and safe one." The Klingon pointed at the semi-transparent holographic image that was hovering above the center of the table. It was based on the sensor analyses from both the *Prometheus* and Kromm's ship, the *I.K.S. Bortas*, depicting a region of the planet's surface. Iad, this mysterious world hidden under a veil of chaotic radiation, was orbited by three separated sections of the Federation's ship as well as the Klingon cruiser. All of them were protected by a joint defense shield.

The holoimage showed a city in ruins surrounded by a dense jungle. Only the foundations of the city's buildings still existed, but the surrounding trees were no more than a hundred years old. Less than fifty kilometers to the east lay the source of the devastation: the massive impact crater at the crash site of the Federation starship *Valiant*. The warp drive's explosion a century ago had leveled the planet's surface for several kilometers in every direction.

"This creature drove the *Valiant*'s crew mad, forcing their ship to crash," Kromm continued. "We cannot allow that to happen to us."

"I watched the same recording from the *Valiant*'s bridge that you did, Captain," Adams said testily. They had discovered a log buoy near Bharatrum, and the images they had been able to retrieve from the damaged data storage devices inside were disturbing to say the least. The crew went insane and tried to kill each other with weaponry that seemed to materialize from nowhere. Eventually, First Officer Edwards deliberately steered the *Constitution*-class ship toward the planet's surface.

Kromm's reply was just as testy. "Then you are fully aware of how dangerous this entity is. Your people's incompetence freed it then, and it's wreaking havoc now."

Quickly, Adams said, "We still don't know exactly how the Son of the Ancient Reds has been set free." Even as he said the words, however, he had to concede that the evidence pointed at Starfleet. According to an ancient Renao legend, a so-called White Guardian had imprisoned the Son of the Ancient Reds on Iad. Nine thousand years of peace ensued, before the *Valiant* appeared and was lost during a simple cartography mission in the Lembatta Cluster. Now, more than a century later, madness had spread throughout the region and beyond.

Waving his arm in front of his face, Kromm said, "It matters little *how* this being awoke. What matters is that our enemy is on Iad. Either we kill him, or he will force us to raise our weapons against each other and fight to the death… repeatedly, if Ambassador Spock is correct." He raised his gloved hand, pointing at the half-Vulcan diplomat who followed proceedings in the *Prometheus*'s conference room quietly and with a pensive expression. "Is that not correct?"

"I am reluctant to offer an assessment whether this entity is the same being that the *Enterprise* encountered many years ago," Spock replied slowly. "That life form was indeed dangerous. It destroyed the Klingon vessel *Voh'tahk*, contrived to imprison that ship's survivors on the *Enterprise*, and then fed on the hatred of both crews. Not only did that being influence our emotions and manipulate our memories, it was also capable of transforming matter to ensure that we had weapons available at all times and whenever we felt the urge to kill."

Next to Spock, the *Prometheus* security chief, Lenissa zh'Thiin, spoke. "No weapons have appeared on board here, so the defense shields that Commander Kirk modified are working."

Also present were science officer Lieutenant Commander Mendon, Adam's first officer Roaas, chief medical officer Doctor Barai, and the aforementioned Kirk, the ship's chief engineer, as well as Kromm's personnel, first officer Commander L'emka and security chief Rooth.

Spock nodded. "We have indeed remained protected from the entity's influence thus far, thanks to the cooperation among Commander Kirk, Lieutenant Commander Mendon, and Doctor Barai in modifying the *Prometheus* shields." The telepathic Betazoid doctor had guided Kirk and Mendon according to what he sensed within the crew, so they had been able to block the radiation's mental effects with the deflectors. Spock had also played an important role, but his typical modesty ensured that he neglected to mention that. He continued: "But that is not the only reason why I consider the current danger to both our ships as minor. Unlike the creature I and my crewmates encountered a century ago, the Son of the Ancient Reds is quite obviously trapped, as he has made no effort to leave Iad in order to reach us here in orbit."

"Unfortunately," Mendon said, "we remain unable to obtain accurate sensor readings thanks to the multiple radiations forming in chaotic patterns around the planet."

Kirk snorted. "It's easier to look out of the window with binoculars to get information about the planet's surface." She nodded towards the holoimage.

Kromm shook his head. "I have studied the log entries made by *Dahar* Master Kang aboard the *Voh'tahk*. The entity is malevolent. It will take advantage of every opportunity to make us fight—against each other, and against others." The Klingon hit his chest with his gloved fist. "Far be it from me to shy from a fight, but *I* decide who I'm pitting myself against."

"As if that matters," zh'Thiin mumbled.

"What is *that* supposed to mean, Commander?" Kromm glared at the Andorian woman.

Her antennae bent forward belligerently. "That you've spent this entire mission regarding anyone and everyone as your enemy. All we've heard from you is about making the Renao feel your wrath. You're simply dying to lay waste to a planet—like Xhehenem a few days ago."

"The Renao *are* our enemies!" Kromm shouted. "They erased Tika IV Beta! They laid waste to Korinar! You yourselves lost a starbase and a drydock! Yet you continually refuse to take proper action! But what do you expect from a weak league of bickering planets that—"

"Captain! Commander! Get a grip." Adams looked at both of them sternly. "We need to be extremely careful here. All of us have smoldering aggressions waiting to erupt. Our shields are tamping it down, but the entity is still working its influence, trying to draw strength from our fury. We *cannot* allow it to acquire that strength, or we'll never be able to defeat it."

The Klingon glared at Adams with ferociously glowing eyes, before taking a deep breath.

"Captain." L'emka put a hand on his shoulder.

He brushed it off. But then he visibly relaxed. "You're right, Adams. But that's proof how dangerous our true enemy is, sneaking into our minds although we are in the very heart of your ship." The Klingon glanced at the female security chief, and for a second it seemed as if he was about to say something. Instead, he just grumbled, nodding at her.

Zh'Thiin's antennae straightened, and she tilted her head.

That was about as much peace as Adams could expect between the two of them.

"So?" Rooth, who had remained silent so far, spoke up with his harsh voice. "Are we going to bombard or not? I'm all for it." The *Bortas*'s gray-haired security chief folded his arms in front of his chest.

"We should exhaust all other options first." Adams touched the intercom control that was embedded in the conference table. "Adams to Winter."

"Winter here, Captain," the communications officer's voice sounded over the loudspeakers.

"Have you been able to establish contact with the energy entity on the planet's surface?"

"Unfortunately not, Captain," the young human replied. *"I have tried all frequencies and all established forms of communications, including light signals with our landing lights and whale songs."*

The last one surprised Adams. "Whale songs?"

"From humpback whales," Winter said. *"That worked on Earth a century ago in order to establish contact with an exotic probe."*

"I can confirm the ensign's statement." The corners of Spock's mouth twitched slightly. "As chance would have it,

I was present during that incident."

"*I'm really grasping at every straw I can find, Captain,*" Winter said, "*but so far it's been to no avail. The entity doesn't respond, at least not in a way that I would recognize or understand. The radiation values don't change; there are no patterns, no peaks, no nothing.*"

"Thank you, Ensign. Keep trying. Adams out." The captain closed the channel.

"It would seem the creature doesn't share the Federation's obsession with *talking*," Kromm said with a snarl.

"Or it simply can't communicate with us," L'emka added. "It's entirely possible that the being is in some state of unconsciousness—at least by its standards."

Adams hadn't thought of that at all. Somehow, he had been certain that the energy presence was wide awake, acting deliberately. To think that everything they had been through might be the consequence of troubled sleep was even more disturbing.

"If that's the case I don't want to be around when it wakes up," Kirk mumbled.

"While the commander's hypothesis is intriguing, I do not believe that the creature is resting," Spock said. "I have sensed only purposeful actions from the presence. Wouldn't you agree, Doctor?" The Vulcan gazed at the Betazoid.

Barai wiped his brow with his hand; the doctor looked haunted by the stranger's influence. "Yes, I can sense a hunger that can't possibly come from someone who's asleep. A hunger for violence."

Adams looked at his science officer. "Mr. Mendon, is there any way to neutralize this entity without bombarding it? Is it possible to counteract the radiation now that we know where it originates and how it forms?"

The Benzite took two breaths from his respirator, contemplating. Mendon needed this inhaler to enrich the *Prometheus*'s standard atmosphere with gases that were vital for him. "I'm afraid not—at least, not yet. Once Ambassador Spock pointed us in the direction of the entity that he had encountered on Beta XII-A, I went through all available files in our databases. We might be able to establish a shield array enveloping the entire ruined city with mobile generators and projectors, and we could possibly configure them the same way as our ship's shields. But we still couldn't be sure that they would stop the being. According to the files, this species— that's if we're indeed encountering a species of sorts—is very powerful and can't be bound by matter and ordinary technology. Maybe one possible explanation is that the entity from Beta XII-A doesn't originate from our reality, and has instead crossed here from a parallel universe. And we still aren't sure that the entity on Iad is anything like the being on Beta XII-A. So far, we don't have any viable data about either of them. Our entire working theory is based on the feeling that Ambassador Spock had when we approached Iad."

"*Feeling* is not quite the accurate term, Lieutenant Commander," Spock said gently. "Rather, I sensed a familiar psychic energy pattern. However, I must agree that our knowledge base is limited. Although it feeds on hatred, fury, and similarly strong emotions, and has the ability to create matter, it still might be very different from the entity on Beta XII-A."

"We're not here to study this abomination!" Kromm growled. "We need to destroy it."

"I agree with Captain Kromm," said Roaas, Adams's first officer. "The Renao need to be healed from being possessed by the Son of the Ancient Reds, or there will be many more victims on our and on their side." He looked at Spock. "Isn't there a Vulcan proverb? 'The needs of the many outweigh the needs of the few.'"

"Or of just one," the thin-haired ambassador finished the sentence, nodding slowly. "Yes, such a proverb exists. And I have been acting according to this precept for decades. Even today, it is most difficult to fault the logic behind those words. But I cannot conceal the fact that I would not be here among you if it hadn't been for a certain Starfleet captain who felt that the needs of single persons carry a certain weight. Sometimes even so much so that many are willing to risk their own well-being for them."

"With all due respect, Ambassador, this is not the right time for philosophical excursions," said Adams. "Is there a certain point you are trying to make?"

The half-Vulcan raised an eyebrow. "I do indeed, Captain. I wish to volunteer myself to attempt to establish contact with the entity."

"How is that supposed to work?" Kromm frowned irritably. "The ensign at communications has already admitted his failure. Are you going to attempt a Vulcan mind-meld with that thing?" He guffawed—and abruptly fell silent when his gaze met Spock's. "You're not serious, are you?"

"My plan is to leave the ship in a shuttle, before trying to establish some manner of mental link using purposeful meditation. It is possible that I may be able to establish some kind of telepathic exchange akin to the mind-meld. At the very least, I might be able to gain some useful information about its goals and weaknesses."

Adams wasn't very happy with this plan. "Do you really believe that you'll be able to communicate with such a powerful spirit?"

The ambassador raised an eyebrow. "I have established telepathic contact with many extremely powerful entities over the decades, Captain, including a Kelvan, a sophisticated computer probe called Nomad, and more than one vast, destructive energy creature. While some of those experiences were overwhelming, I have grown stronger from them."

Kromm snorted. "You Vulcans have never suffered from a lack of confidence."

"Vulcans are able to self-assess with considerable accuracy, Captain Kromm."

"All right then, let's give it a try, Ambassador." Adams still felt uneasy considering that Spock would be subjected to the entity's full mental force. He saw what it did to Geron Barai, not to mention the Renao on sickbay—Kumaah ak Partam and Alai ak Yldrou. Strong sedatives were required, and even those only barely kept the madness at bay. On the other hand, his Starfleet oath demanded he tried everything in his power to avoid violence. And who was he to doubt the self-assessment of a great man such as Spock?

Adams added, "We will control the shuttle remotely from *Prometheus*."

Spock tilted his head approvingly. "A wise precaution."

"We can't configure the shuttle's shields the same way we did with those of the *Prometheus*," Kirk said. "They're not designed for that."

"I have no intention to activate the shields," Spock said, "as they would interfere with my attempts to make contact."

"In case of emergency we will beam you straight back aboard," Adams promised.

"And then we bombard Iad?" Kromm asked.

Adams nodded grimly. "Yes, Captain, if this fails—*then* we will bombard Iad."

2
NOVEMBER 25, 2385

Carefully, Spock steered the small spacecraft out of the shuttle bay in the upper secondary hull of *Prometheus*. The *Charles Coryell* was a small, sleek vessel, the latest shuttle design from the engineers at Utopia Planitia. It was capable of speeds up to warp five, and its shields were remarkably powerful for a spacecraft of its size, although they wouldn't be able to protect Spock from the Son's influence once he left the *Prometheus*'s protective shield bubble behind.

Only his experienced, focused mind would be able to achieve that. He trusted that would be sufficient.

The Vulcan part of his mind wondered why he exposed himself to the danger of a direct confrontation with this being. He had studied what little data was available in the files about the Beta XII-A entity as thoroughly as the short time had allowed. Captain Jean-Luc Picard of the *Enterprise*-E had also come across the creature, during one of his encounters with the entity known as Q, and his report matched what Spock had observed on the *Enterprise* a century ago: the being was purposeful and evil, and it pushed its victims into an endless blood rage. Assuming that this creature would act differently wasn't logical, considering it manipulated the Renao in a similarly destructive manner.

Logic is the beginning of wisdom, Spock recalled, *not the end.*

Thus, his human part hoped that understanding could evolve from hostility if only someone had the courage to risk their life in order to facilitate some sort of communication.

Spock's personal history alone was full of examples that even the most diversified cultures and life forms were able to come to a consensus. There was V'Ger, a violent force that Spock had managed to communicate with and stop its destructive swath. The mine workers of Janus VI had assumed that the Horta was a murderous monster that needed eliminating—but after Spock mind-melded with her, they discovered that she was a mother protecting her young, and soon an understanding had been reached.

Several frightened Starfleet senior officers had been convinced at the end of the last century that there wasn't a future for the Federation and warmongering Klingons. Spock and his old companions from the *Enterprise* had played a significant role in proving them wrong and cementing an alliance with the Klingon Empire that had been a cornerstone of the quadrant for the better part of the twenty-fourth century. He had prompted humpback whales to save Earth and Romulans to sit down at the table with Vulcans, their distant and much-hated relatives. Communication was the key to peaceful resolutions of conflicts.

Therefore, Spock had no other choice right now than to seek communication—anything else would have been illogical.

"Spock to *Prometheus.*" He swerved the shuttle past the arrow-shaped primary hull.

"We hear you," Adams's voice answered via the intercom.

"I am leaving the perimeter of the *Prometheus* shields and turning control of the *Charles Coryell* over to you, Captain."

"Understood. Good luck and may you be successful, Ambassador Spock."

He watched as the conn controls were taken over by Ensign Naxxa on *Prometheus*. Spock had only briefly met the Bolian woman serving as shuttle specialist, but she had struck him as a calm and competent young woman.

The shuttle penetrated the shield that Commander Kirk had switched to permeable for a brief moment. Behind the small spacecraft, the shimmering barricade that was constantly bombarded by exotic radiation sealed tightly.

Immediately, Spock sensed the increase of pressure on his mind. It was as if he had stood in front of a heavy door, behind which loud music was playing, and then he suddenly found himself in the room, bombarded with sound.

Interlacing his fingers, he closed his eyes and focused on his mental defenses. Spock's mind had suffered incredible agonies throughout his almost one hundred and forty years of service for Starfleet and the Federation, including death and resurrection. He had overcome each challenge, and they had all combined to make him grow stronger.

But it was still not sufficient.

Who are you? he asked into the entity's deafening mental roar.

Pain, hunger, and madness tore at him.

Spock raised his hands, pressing his fingers against his temples. A feverish wrath washed over him, briefly eliminating all rational thought. A cry formed in his throat, and it erupted with a feral howl. Leaping out of his seat, he staggered against the bulkhead.

"*Ambassador Spock?*" somebody's voice asked from the intercom. "*Are you all right? Ambassador Spock?*"

Doubling over, Spock groaned and kept his eyes shut tight, trying to keep out the screaming inferno that was engulfing his mind.

"We're going to beam you out of there, Ambassador!"

"No!" Spock shouted, still trying to fend off the Son's presence, while struggling with the vortex of chaotic emotions. It wasn't actually a response to the voice from the *Prometheus*. "No!" he repeated, agonized. "Must not fail! Must not..."

He opened his eyes wide and stared through the cockpit's front window. The multicolored flashes and the iridescence of the permanently changing energies swirling around Iad burned into his retina.

"Who are you?" he gasped, struggling against the assault of the ancient, enormous presence. "What drives you?"

Once again he closed his eyes, believing that he had detected some kind of fluctuating, pulsating center in all this chaos, directing his mind that way.

"Talk to me!" he cried hoarsely. With his agonized but by no means beaten mind, he probed into the alien being's conscience.

Then the Son of the Ancient Reds finally noticed him.

U.S.S. Prometheus

"Bridge to transporter room," said Adams. "Beam him out, right now!"

"Aye, sir," Chief Wilorin replied. *"Waiting for shields to be lowered."*

An inarticulate scream came from the intercom, a scream like no other the captain had ever heard from any Vulcan. The elderly ambassador seemed to be unable to withstand the onslaught from Iad's surface any longer.

"Shields are down," Commander Sarita Carson at ops said.

"Retrieving the *Charles Coryell*," said Ensign Naxxa. The pilot sat at the environment control station near the bulkhead to the right of Adams, which had been temporarily modified to a remote control console for the shuttlecraft.

"*Captain,*" Wilorin's voice came through the intercom, "*I can't lock on the ambassador. The radiation interference is too strong.*"

Adams felt an uncontrollable wrath well up inside of him. This useless Tiburonian was simply incapable of doing his job properly. "I don't want excuses, Chief! We need to save Spock from this monster on the planet surface."

"*I don't know how!*"

"Then find someone to relieve you from duty if you're incompetent!" Adams yelled. "If Ambassador Spock is harmed because of you, I'll have you in front of a firing squad!"

"Captain!" Roaas, sitting at tactical, glanced at him, warningly.

Adams met his gaze—and understood. *Keep calm*, he chided himself. *Pull yourself together. That anger isn't yours.*

Barai's voice sounded over the speakers. "*Sickbay to bridge.*"

"Go ahead, Doctor," Adams said.

"*I can sense an enormous increase in the aggression levels on board.*"

"We had to take the shields down briefly."

Naxxa at the shuttle controls cursed in her native tongue.

"Problems, Ensign?" Adams asked.

"These idiots from gamma shift closed the bulkhead to the shuttle bay. I'm unable to dock."

Adams immediately opened a channel to the current watch officer in the upper secondary hull's battle bridge. "Bridge to th'Talias. Lieutenant, what's going on over there?"

"They want to enter the ship, Captain." The Andorian sounded haunted. *"We mustn't let them in."*

"No one is entering the ship, Lieutenant. Now open the hangar bulkhead. We need to land Ambassador Spock's shuttle."

"I parked the *Charles Coryell* right alongside the ship's hull," Naxxa said.

Carson reacted instantly. "Raising shields again."

"The *Bortas!*" Roaas cried. "She's firing photon torpedoes."

Horrified, Adams asked, "At us?"

"No, at the planet surface. Four torpedoes, wide yield."

"On screen."

The image changed to show the glistening red of the projectiles that the Klingon battle cruiser had just fired. The torpedoes blended into the flashes of exotic radiation that surrounded Iad. Powerful explosions—recognizable from orbit only as sudden clouds of dust and soil—tore the landscape around the ruins open. They all assumed that the alien being was located somewhere in that area.

"Any effect?" Adams glanced at Lieutenant Commander Mendon at the science station. He noticed that the rage clutching his mind was abating. He took a deep breath, trying to push it aside completely.

The Benzite checked the displays on his monitors. "Negative, Captain. The radiation levels remain unchanged."

"Ensign Winter, get me Kromm on screen."

"Aye, sir."

"Transporter room to bridge," said Wilorin.

"Go ahead, Chief," Adams said.

"I was finally able to beam Ambassador Spock aboard. He's in pretty bad shape. Doctor Barai has taken him straight to sickbay."

"Understood. Thanks, Chief. Oh, and… Chief?"

"Yes, Captain?"

"Please excuse my earlier outburst."

"Already forgotten, sir," the Tiburonian replied. *"I'm glad I managed to prevent myself from saying what was on the tip of my tongue at that moment."*

"I've got Captain Kromm now, sir," Winter said.

The captain focused on the image on the bridge's main screen. It was split in two—one half showed the smoldering ruins on the planet, while the *Bortas* bridge appeared on the other half. Both were illuminated by red light, the former from the radiation, the latter from standard Klingon Defense Force lighting during an alert. Kromm sat in his command chair with ferociously sparkling eyes and his flowing shoulder-length hair, and greeted Adams: *"What do you want?"*

"You're firing at the being on the planet surface," observed Adams.

"It's attacking us," Kromm replied. *"It's trying to take over our minds. We will* not *allow that!"* He gave an order in Klingon. Again, gleaming projectiles sped towards the planet surface from the embedded torpedo ramps in the *Vor'cha*-class cruiser.

"You're wasting torpedoes," said Adams. "You won't achieve anything with your mindless bombardment."

Kromm snarled. *"You should help us instead of blathering. The ambassador failed. Now the warriors must take matters into their own hands."*

The captain glanced at his science officer again. "Mr. Mendon?"

The Benzite shook his head regretfully. "No noticeable effect, sir. But I wouldn't want to rule out the possibility that the *Prometheus*'s quantum torpedoes might yield better results than the Klingons' photon torpedoes."

The turbolift door hissed open. To Adams's surprise, Spock entered the bridge, with Doctor Barai at his heels. The ambassador's expression was disconcertingly haunted for a man who was generally calm and imperturbable.

"Ambassador Spock, shouldn't you be in sickbay?"

"That he should be," Barai said testily. "Unfortunately, I wasn't able to convince him of that."

Spock did not respond to the doctor's complaint but instead addressed Adams, speaking with a very uncharacteristic sense of urgency. "Captain, we must act immediately. The danger is more grave than we had assumed. The being on the surface is out of control."

"What do you mean?"

"I managed to glimpse into its conscious mind. The entity is…" He seemed to be grasping for words. "It is insane. Its mind is a chaotic morass of hunger and pain."

Roaas asked, "Didn't you say that you sensed some kind of purpose in the presence when we reached the system?"

Spock nodded. "Yes. There is a purpose to its greed. But I'm afraid I misinterpreted the cause. This being is driven not by malice, but by desperation."

"That almost sounds as if it's addicted to all the hatred and violence it causes," Lenissa zh'Thiin said, her antennae swaying back and forth.

"That assessment could indeed be correct," Spock said to the security chief. "The entity is addicted—and still very weak."

Adams couldn't believe his ears. "Weak? The Son is throwing an entire cluster into turmoil with his mental manipulations."

"Captain, if the Son does belong to the same species as

the Beta XII-A entity—and I am increasingly convinced that this is the case—he has barely begun to explore his potential. Thus far, he has only driven several million Renao to voluntarily meet their death, or to satisfy their own hatred. As yet, there have been no transformations of matter, nor has the being tried to leave Iad in an attempt to approach the inhabited planets of the cluster. According to Renao legend, the Son has been asleep almost nine thousand years after having been imprisoned by the White Guardian. To use an Earth metaphor, he has hardly rubbed his eyes and yawned within the last one hundred and twenty years."

"So you think we're dealing with an opponent who is completely exhausted on the one hand, and on the other he's waiting for his next fix of violence?"

"That is my best hypothesis given my exposure to its mind," Spock said. "However, that exposure was rather brief, and my own mind was under extreme duress at the time. I could, perhaps, be mistaken."

Adams's lip curled slightly, the closest to a smile he was capable of achieving these days. "But that's not very likely."

"No."

"Is that enough discussion for now?" Kromm asked, ill-tempered.

Adams straightened his uniform jacket. "It is indeed. Evidently, we don't have any other choice but to eliminate this being." He tried to convince himself—not very successfully—that they were basically finishing off a dog with rabies. "*Prometheus* out." Adams motioned for Winter to cut the link to the Klingon ship. He turned to face his tactical officer. "Commander Roaas, load quantum torpedoes and ready them. Full array."

"Aye, sir. Loading quantum torpedoes." The Caitian

faced his console, entering several commands. "Torpedoes loaded and ready to fire."

"Mr. Winter, relay the same order to the upper and lower hull sections."

"Right away, sir." Winter turned around, speaking quietly into a communicator. "Commander Senok and Lieutenant th'Talias are ready, sir."

The captain turned toward the bridge screen again. His expression hardened. "Fire."

Moments later, six gleaming blue quantum torpedoes streaked toward their target area.

The explosions tore the ground of the ruined city open and destroyed everything the Klingon photon torpedoes hadn't already devastated. The huge blast snapped trees, hurling rocks and soil hundreds of meters into the air.

"No effect, sir," said Mendon. "If anything, the radiation intensity seems to have increased marginally."

"Do you want me to fire phasers?" asked Roaas.

Adams shook his head. "Negative. It seems to be feeding off the energy of the torpedoes—phasers won't be any different."

Jassat ak Namur looked up from his console. The young Renao's golden yellow eyes glowed brightly. "Captain, I have an idea."

"I'm all ears, Lieutenant."

"We studied the Dominion War at Starfleet Academy, and I recall a mention of an energy dissipator utilized by the Breen."

Adams had read reports of that weapon, though he had never encountered it in person, as his former ship, the *U.S.S. Geronimo*, had been destroyed at Chin'toka, and he had spent the rest of the war assigned to planetary and starbase duty. But the dissipator had caused the Federation and its allies quite a lot of problems after the Breen Confederacy entered the war in 2375. The weapon drained all energy from ships it targeted, rendering them adrift in space. It very nearly was a turning point in the war inexorably in favor of the Dominion, until Starfleet had been able to capture one of the weapons and develop a countermeasure.

"It's a nice idea," said Roaas, "but *Prometheus* doesn't have such a weapon at her disposal. Starfleet never issued one."

"And we can hardly ask the Breen for help," Sarita Carson dryly interjected. "Mind you... they might swap an energy dissipator for one of our slipstream drives."

Adams knew that Carson was being facetious. The Typhon Pact in general, and the Breen in particular, had been trying for years to acquire slipstream technology from the Federation, as they perceived it as a dangerous disparity in the balance of power.

Ak Namur shook his head. "I know that we don't have access to an energy dissipator. But couldn't we reconfigure the main deflector dish to emit an energy blast similar to the characteristics of the energy-dampening weapon?"

"Interesting thought," Roaas said.

Adams rose from his command chair, turning to the engineering station. "Lieutenant Chell, your thoughts on that?"

"Give me a moment." The sturdy Bolian started to work his console.

Gently, Barai put his hand on Spock's shoulder. "Come, Ambassador. There's nothing we can do here right now, and you really need to rest."

To Adams's surprise, the elderly diplomat didn't protest. "Very well."

Apparently, even Barai hadn't expected that answer. "No backtalk? I'm surprised."

Spock's expression remained unchanged but there was a certain glint in his eye. "I have learned throughout the years that disputes with doctors should be limited to absolutely necessary circumstances."

The doctor gave Adams a knowing look. "Perhaps you should remember this wise insight, Captain."

"Right now, I really have other things on my mind," Adams snapped. It was meant to sound like an amicable rebuff, but the words came out sharper than intended.

Barai briefly stiffened before nodding tersely. "Aye, sir." He turned around, disappearing with Spock into the turbolift.

Adams stared after him with a certain sense of guilt. But he was tired of apologizing for every sentence, and remained silent. Besides, Barai knew better than anyone that everyone on *Prometheus* was acting irrationally.

"Good news, Captain," Chell said. "I believe Mr. ak Namur's plan might actually work. However, we will lose a part of our shielding as we would have to disconnect the main deflector dish from the array."

"Does that mean the radiation will pose a danger to us?" the captain asked.

"Difficult to say." With a hint of uncertainty in his expression, Chell looked questioningly at Mendon.

"We will lose one of the adaptive polarization filters that are required to stabilize the shield bubble we're in," said the Benzite. "So the shields will be a little more strained, that's true. But we will be able to compensate for that temporarily. Of course, we will also lose some of our sensor resolution. But again, I consider that limitation acceptable, considering we're much closer to our target now than we were when we first entered the radiation zone."

Adams nodded slowly. Mendon had been the one to

suggest separating the *Prometheus*, linking their three deflector systems with that of the *Bortas*. This enabled them to eliminate most of the destructive effects around Iad with the help of incoming data from passive sensors and a subroutine that he had written.

"Do it, Mr. Chell."

"Aye, Captain." The engineer turned back to his console. "Disconnecting main deflector from array and modifying it."

"Mr. Winter, establish a link to the upper hull section."

"Done, sir."

Adams addressed the commander of the other ship section. "Adams to Lieutenant th'Talias."

"Th'Talias here, Captain."

"We're reconfiguring the main deflector to emit an energy burst similar to the Breen energy-dampening weapon. Lieutenant Chell will send you the specifications. Be prepared to set off the deflector on my mark."

"Understood, sir. Ensign Quandil awaits your order."

"I'm done," Chell said. "Our temporary energy-dampening device has one major drawback, though: we can only emit an extremely short burst—otherwise, we'll be destroying the deflector dish. And even then, I'm afraid we will have to restart the deflector system. So we would need a few minutes for a follow-up burst."

"Well, one shot will have to suffice then," Adams said.

The engineer shrugged. "We'll see once we try it, Captain. In battle, the Breen only ever needed one burst in order to incapacitate our ships. Our energy burst should have ten times the intensity."

The captain nodded. *What other choice did they have?* "Understood. Carry on."

Chell turned back to his console. "Transferring

configuration data to the upper secondary hull."

Soon after, Adams received the all-clear from th'Talias. The Andorian sounded very eager to overwhelm their enemy.

"Activate main deflector," he said.

A glistening blue streak appeared on the main screen, stabbing at the planet for approximately one second. It hit the multicolored shimmer which hovered in the midst of the crater-strewn ruined landscape, penetrated it, and struck right in between the debris. Blue energy fingers branched in all directions, dancing between stones and piles of dirt, and licking up into the incorporeal fog the Son was comprised of.

Adams turned to Mendon. "Any effects?"

"One moment, sir. I..." the Benzite trailed off. He hesitated, and his eyes widened. Defensively, he raised his blue- and gray-flecked hands. Adams didn't need to ask what was wrong with his science officer. He could also sense it: an unbelievably disconcerting feeling, best described as the horrifying, irrational dread that people sometimes felt in nightmares just before they were torn from their sleep. This feeling built up in Adams like an offshore tsunami... no, it built up in everyone. Carson gasped in horror. Zh'Thiin's antennae bent down until they lay flat on her white hair. Chell whimpered quietly.

And then, the *Prometheus*'s shield bubble was suddenly struck by an enormous blow.

3

NOVEMBER 25, 2385

I.K.S. Bortas, in orbit around Iad

Raspin huddled over his console when chaos broke out. The red light on the bridge flickered, and a sound similar to heavy rainfall could be heard from outside the armored battle cruiser. The calm sea the *Bortas* had been smoothly sailing through, protected by the shield bubble of the Federation starship, had transformed into a stormy ocean. The ship shuddered, and pressure built up inside Raspin's head.

The Rantal with the white skin and the jet-black eyes looked at his captain in confusion. He wanted to ask what had happened, but he swallowed his words when he noticed how the faces of the other crew members had distorted. He wasn't Klingon, he was *jeghpu'wI'*, a member of a species that the Empire had conquered. Less than a citizen, more than a slave, Rantal were permitted to serve on Klingon Defense Force vessels in crew positions.

"Starfleet is attacking us!" Second Officer Chumarr cried out, standing at the gunnery console in the back of the bridge.

Rooth, standing next to him, shook his head so vigorously that his white hair flew in all directions. "That's not Starfleet, you fool! It's that beast on the planet."

"And Adams does *nothing*!" Kromm furiously pounded his command chair's armrest with his fist. "He dares to call himself a warrior? He allows the Renao to do as they please and attack us. And now, he wishes to *talk* to that creature down there."

Resting his hands on the front of the gunnery console, Chumarr bent forward. "Adams must *go*."

"Yes, Captain," Klarn said eagerly, working his comm console on the port bulkhead across the bridge from Raspin. "Let us destroy *Prometheus* and then destroy Iad—once and for all!"

The pressure inside of Raspin's head increased to the point that the Rantal feared his head might explode. He turned back to his console, and to his horror he realized that all the displays had gone mad. *The* Prometheus *shields have collapsed,* shot through his mind. *We are completely unprotected against the energies emitted from Iad, and against the influence of this being on the planet surface.*

He knew that the legendary Son of the Ancient Reds had been influencing the entire cluster mentally. In all likelihood, the Renao had been exposed to this exotic radiation for years. But their worlds were far apart, which had probably kept the irrational fury caused by the Son at bay. The *Prometheus* crew had found a way to neutralize most of the radiation with their shield modifications, but now those shields were down, and disaster had struck.

Once more, Raspin glanced at the Klingons on the bridge, anxiously awaiting their next move.

Strangely enough, while the alien presence seemed to be giving him a pounding headache, that was apparently the only effect it had on Rantal minds. He wasn't feeling the same anger that everyone around him was experiencing.

"Separate the *Bortas* from the formation," Kromm said. "We're going to attack."

"Captain, no!" L'emka, his first officer, turned away from

the helm. She was piloting due to her being better qualified to fly in close formation than Toras, the usual pilot. "This is the being on the planet retaliating against our attack. You're not thinking straight."

"Be silent, Commander," Kromm shouted, "and obey my orders. Or would you like to continue our duel here and now?"

Raspin almost felt sorry for her. L'emka was an intelligent officer, far too good to serve under a fool like Kromm, who took a predictable, conservative path to dubious honor and glory. During the entire mission in the Lembatta Cluster both senior officers had clashed time and again. Above Xhehenem, they had been ready to slit each other's throats.

"Oh, I'm ready to fight, believe me, Captain," L'emka answered sharply. "But not while our ship is in danger." On cue, the lights on the bridge flickered again, and the pattering sound on the hull turned into pelting.

Kromm leapt from his chair. "You're a coward! That's why you won't fight me! You are a disgrace to the Empire!"

L'emka whirled around, the light of the damaged ceiling lamps reflecting furiously in her eyes. "You are the disgrace, Captain! A drunk, brawling, bawling disgrace! Your entire life is a feeble attempt to achieve glory and forget that you are *not* the hero of the *Ning'tao*."

Furious, Kromm cried out, "Be *silent!*"

Shaking her head, L'emka said, "Oh no. It's about time someone held a mirror in front of your eyes and took your delusions away. The High Council cares not a whit for whatever pathetic deeds you might accomplish. You were not given the former flagship of Chancellor Gowron to honor you but because it was already scrap! You were consigned to the outer edge of the Empire in the hopes that you wouldn't do *too* much damage."

Klarn took a step back from his console, and moved toward L'emka, snarling. "The captain told you to be silent!"

Rooth approached Klarn. "Take your station, Klarn. You're out of line."

The communications officer pulled his *d'k tahg* from his belt and let out an incoherent growl as he ran toward the gray-haired security officer. But L'emka intercepted him, thrusting her knee into his stomach.

Again the *Bortas* shuddered. Raspin gasped, his head pounding harder, as if he'd drunk an entire barrel of bloodwine, though he hadn't touched a drop.

"The Federation wants to kill us!" shouted Chumarr. "Firing disruptors and photon torpedoes." Glistening streaks of energy appeared on the bridge monitor, cutting through the swirling radiation zone around Iad.

Kromm shouted at the top of his lungs, pounding the comm controls on his chair's armrest. "Security! Kill them all! Kill them all!"

They're all losing their minds, Raspin thought. Haunted, his gaze flickered from left to right, watching violence break out all around him. *I have to do something.* But he didn't have a clue what he *could* do.

U.S.S. Prometheus

"Evasive maneuvers!" Adams clutched his command chair's armrests while the primary hull shuddered under the disruptor hits from the *Bortas*. An energy conduit to his left burst with a loud bang. "Defense status?" The barrage from the radiation zone made it sound as if *Prometheus* was located under a giant waterfall.

"Ablative hull plating holding," Sarita Carson shouted above the din. "Shields down to forty percent and weakening. The strain is simply too much."

"Reroute emergency power to the shields and initiate the polaron modulator."

"Aye, sir."

The *Prometheus* was hit by a photon torpedo and shuddered.

"Shields down to twenty-seven percent," Carson said. "The regeneration circuits can't cope with the fluctuating radiation."

"Sir, do you want me to return fire?" Roaas asked from tactical.

"Negative, Commander." Adams was sweating. He had to almost physically force himself to remain passive. Everything inside of him was screaming out to discipline this wretched barbarian on the *Bortas* who had been nothing but trouble since the beginning of the mission. But he knew that this was the Son's influence speaking.

Pull yourself together.

"Status of the *Bortas*?" he asked.

"She was under our protective shield bubble until it collapsed from the first attack," Carson said. "Our automatic emergency measures kicked in, raising the regular shields. But the Klingons are without protection from the radiation."

"I was afraid of that." He cursed under his breath. Kromm in full command of his mental faculties was difficult enough to deal with. If he had gone into a frenzy he would not listen to reason at all. "Tactical defense mode theta two, Mr. ak Namur. Evade the attacks as best you can."

"Understood, Captain." The young Renao's hands danced across the console, and the glimmering mists suddenly dropped to one side when he took advantage of the *Prometheus* section's superior agility to evade the Klingons' mindless raging.

The captain glanced at the comm station to his left. "That goes for all sections, Mr. Winter."

"I'll let the others know, sir," the dark-skinned German hastily acknowledged.

"Shouldn't we try to hail the *Bortas*?" Roaas asked. "Maybe we can get them to listen to reason."

"I doubt it, but you're right, we have to try. Mr. Winter, hail the Klingons."

Winter nodded. "Right away, Captain." He operated his instruments for several seconds before finally saying, "Here we go. No response, but I managed to establish a link to their bridge."

"On screen." What Adams saw after giving him that order did not give him hope for a rational conversation. There were several figures wrestling, illuminated by the bridge's dark red light and the erratic flickering of a console. He heard growling and roaring, interrupted by inarticulate words here and there. A disruptor shot screamed, striking one of the panels on the wall, sending sparks flying in all directions.

"Captain Kromm?" Adams leaned forward in his command chair. "Heavens above, Kromm, can you hear me? Commander L'emka? What's going on over there?"

A pale face with large black eyes came into view, slowly rising up in front of the viewscreen pickup. After a moment, Adams recognized Raspin. It looked as if the Rantal had been hiding under the console.

"*They're all insane,*" he whispered frantically. It was the first time that Adams had heard him speak at all. "*They're killing each other.*"

A Klingon stumbled into the image from one side—one of the soldiers Adams didn't know. He bared his crooked teeth, his mouth and chin smeared with blood. Someone must have punched him in the face. Or he might have bitten someone... Adams couldn't tell. The Klingon growled something unintelligible, staring into the pickup, before pushing himself back furiously and disappearing.

Raspin returned. He appeared to be completely terrified, but amazingly he wasn't in the least bit aggressive. Did the Son not have a hold over him?

"Listen," Adams said. "We're under massive attack from the alien life form down there on the planet surface. The *Bortas* is firing at us. That needs to stop. We don't want to shoot at you, but we won't have any other choice soon."

"*There's nothing I can do,*" Raspin said. "*I'm only a* bekk—*worse, I'm* jeghpu'wI'. *Nobody will listen to me.*"

The *Prometheus* shuddered under another direct hit. Adams believed he heard triumphant laughter over the comm line.

"Shields down to twenty percent, Captain," Carson said. "We need to retreat—or fire, sir."

Fury hammered in the captain's chest. How dare this brazen woman interrupt him during a conversation, trying to give him orders? "Leave the decision of what we do or don't do to me, Commander!" As soon as the words left his mouth, he realized what he had said, and he forced himself to calm down. "Thank you for the warning, though, Carson." He focused his attention once more on the chaos on the bridge's main screen. "*Bekk* Raspin, it's in your hands. We can't let the *Bortas* back into a shield bubble as long as she's firing on us, unless we incapacitate you, and that would have dire consequences for the entire mission. Can you fly the cruiser?"

Hesitantly, the Rantal nodded. "*Yes, Captain.*"

"Do it. Plot a course to the periphery of the system, beyond the chaos zone. Your people should regain their senses then."

"I can't do that..."

Adams got up and stepped forward. "Yes you can, dammit! Get to the helm and save your ship, *Bekk*. That's an order!"

The white-skinned alien winced, and looked like a beaten dog. Adams took pity on him. It wasn't his place to get involved in another captain's internal ship procedures, but no crewmember should be as petrified as this young *bekk* was.

"Sir, I will do—"

A disruptor beam blinded the pickup, and the image vanished. The computer switched back to exterior view, where the olive-green cruiser orbited high above Iad.

Horrified, Adams stared at the screen. "Damn," he mumbled.

"I guess that's it as far as the *Bortas* goes," Carson said. "No one can save her now." The *Prometheus*'s primary hull took another direct hit, and she added, "Shields down to twelve percent."

The energy storm's pelting increased in volume. Adams imagined the worm-eaten roof of an old wooden house that was torn to shreds by hailstones as big as golf balls. He returned to his command chair and sat down. "Mr. ak Namur, head to the edge of the system. Take us away from here. Full impulse. Mr. Winter, all sections retreat."

Both men acknowledged the orders. The Renao's fingers danced across the conn. "Course set, Captain. Full impulse."

The *Prometheus* suffered another hit, which almost threw everyone out of their seats. Ensign Naxxa was startled, and screamed, while Adams heard a racket and a thud behind him.

"The shields have collapsed!" shouted Carson. "Regeneration routines are failing. Those damn bastards got us!"

Adams once again felt fury welling up inside of him... No, not just fury—it was pure hatred! Was he surrounded by idiots? He felt like throwing them out of the nearest airlock. The computer navigated *Prometheus* better than any human, Bolian, or Renao anyway!

"And now it's time to get them!" Furious, Adams leapt from his chair, raising his voice to a thunderous shout. "Kromm! I'm going to kill you!"

Paul Winter started to tremble. Beads of sweat appeared on his bald head as he stared into empty space. "No... they want to kill us. That's all they ever wanted to do."

The exotic energy's roar was deafening, and the bridge lights began to flicker. Adams heard a hiss behind him.

"Get away from my weapon systems," Roaas said in a low, menacing tone.

Mendon was whining. "I didn't do it on purpose. I had no intention of falling onto them."

"If you don't want to do something, don't do it."

Sarita Carson faced Jassat ak Namur. "You! It's all your fault. We're only in this situation because of you and your people of fanatics and terrorists."

"Oh really?" The young Renao's yellow eyes sparkled as he rose from his seat, neglecting the controls. "Get out of the cluster, then. That would be for the best, anyway. No one wants you here. Sphere defilers!"

The upper secondary hull came into view on the bridge's screen. Glaring amber beams stabbed at the massive hull of the *Bortas* when Lieutenant th'Talias retaliated, using the Mark-XII phaser arrays.

Through the blood-red haze of anger, Adams thought, *It's happening, just like it did on the* Bortas *and the* Valiant. *We're going insane with rage.*

"Computer," he started. "Attack mode Alpha…" He trailed off, pressing his lips together. He wanted to destroy the *Bortas* so bad, the urge was overwhelming. It would be so easy. *But it's wrong! Wrong! WRONG!*

"*Please repeat your last command,*" the computer's calm voice intoned.

Adams plucked up all the self-control he could muster. Carson began hitting ak Namur while Winter screamed attack orders at the comm station. Chell covered his ears with his hand, whimpering.

"Ignore command," Adams shouted. He realized that they had but one last chance. "Computer, activate Emergency Medical Hologram."

Trik materialized in the center of the bridge, animated by the holoprojectors that were embedded in the bulkheads.

"Please state the nature of the medical emergency." He realized what was going on, and his eyes widened. "Oh dear, oh dear."

"Doctor!" The captain beckoned the EMH over. Trik hurried to his side.

"Sir, what's going on here? I—"

"Shut up and listen, Trik." Adams spoke faster than he intended and sounded haunted. He hated himself for that. No captain should ever lose his calm. "You need to take over the ship. Seal all consoles with your medical override code. The crew is suffering from a severe case of mass psychosis. Take the *Prometheus* away from here."

Trik pulled out his tricorder that he always carried on his belt, which had led to his nickname. "Captain, I—"

"Right now!" Adams yelled, making a menacing move toward the hologram.

Alarmed, Trik backed off, tucking his tricorder back into

his belt. "As you wish. Loading standard command routines."

After a second Trik straightened himself, and his long face became more serious and confident. His uniform flickered briefly, the blue trim of the medical and sciences department replaced by the red of command. The medical programming took a back seat while command functions gained priority. This was a direct consequence of when the *Prometheus* had been captured by Romulans during her maiden flight. The kidnappers, who had killed the entire crew, had only been stopped because the EMH of the starship *Voyager*—which was still missing in the Delta Quadrant at the time—had appeared by pure fluke, and relayed himself through an antiquated communications network to the other end of the galaxy in order to establish contact with the Alpha Quadrant for the first time. *Voyager*'s EMH had displayed remarkable initiative and flexibility in the usage of his program routines, and some of those traits had been programmed into Trik.

"Computer," he said, "this is the Emergency Medical Hologram. I declare the entire crew unfit for duty and assume command. Override code Omega-178-Z."

"Override code Omega-178-Z of Emergency Medical Holographic program accepted," the computer said. *"Please state your orders."*

"Block all consoles aboard the *Prometheus* for manual or voice control. Restart shield systems. All sections: heading 270-Mark-10. Full impulse. Initiate reintegration sequence."

"Acknowledged."

Adams's temples were pulsating, and he was pounding his command chair's backrest. *Kill, kill, kill,* echoed through his mind.

"Not today," he whispered hoarsely, watching both

secondary hulls passing on the main screen, swerving and speeding up. "Not today."

Raspin crawled on all fours across the rusty deckplates on the *Bortas* bridge. Blood covered his bald head, trickling down his face. All around him, his Klingon crewmates wrestled with madness and with each other. Chumarr fired every weapon that the attack cruiser had to offer, and Rooth tried to reason with Kromm, who was flanked by two bodyguards—one of them was trying to restrain the captain, and the other one wanted to club the first one for that. On the far end of the bridge, Klarn and Toras pummeled L'emka, but she hissed and gave as good as she got. It was utter chaos.

Fortunately, nobody cared about Raspin, as usual. Besides, a Rantal crawling along the floor provided much less of a target than a belligerent Klingon.

Still, his heart hammered wildly. If one of them actually took notice of him, he was dead. Raspin had no doubt about that whatsoever.

Breathing heavily, he pushed past the smoldering corpse of *Bekk* Koddoth. The soldier had tried to restore order on the bridge with a disruptor and he had laid waste to large parts of the bridge until Rooth shot him in self-defense, more or less. Although the body had been burnt to a nauseating crisp and had been definitely dead a minute ago, his arm suddenly twitched slightly. Raspin averted his eyes, horrified.

He had witnessed something similar a few minutes ago when L'emka had slit open Toras's throat with her *d'k tahg*. The pilot's blood had gushed out of the wound all over Raspin, but only moments later Toras returned from the dead with renewed fury in his dark eyes. Sto-Vo-Kor *has closed its gates*, Raspin thought, *and we're living in a dimension of pure madness.* These horrific images would haunt him until the end of his days, he knew that much.

He reached the empty niche containing the helm. A black singe was visible across the base, but the console and the displays seemed to be intact. They indicated that the *Bortas* was still in high orbit around Iad.

Quickly, Raspin looked around one final time. Toras had slumped onto the floor again with a *d'k tahg* in his chest, but not much else had changed during the past few seconds. Furtively, the Rantal made the necessary course adjustments. But when he reached for the button to confirm them, he hesitated.

Bekk *Raspin, it's in your hands.* The Starfleet captain's voice echoed in his mind. He had the opportunity to bring Kromm, Klarn, and everyone else who had mistreated him during the past few months to justice. All he had to do was to wait and do nothing. The Klingons would just keep killing each other. Or he could do as Adams had asked—as Adams had ordered—and plot a course to the periphery of the system. Then everything would return to normal.

Was that really what he wanted? Did he want them to come to their senses so they could continue to treat him like a leper, although he had never asked for anything and had done everything to live up to the proud heritage of the former flagship? Didn't he deserve better?

Save your ship!

He gazed over to L'emka, doubled over after being hit by Klarn, and he looked at Rooth, who at least had treated him somewhat decently and had punished violations against his dignity and privacy. There were beings aboard who hadn't forgotten what honor really meant. *There is me,* he thought. *I might be* jeghpu'wI' *but I know what honor is.*

He would save the *Bortas*. Because it was his duty as officer of the Klingon Defense Force. Besides, the knowledge that he had saved them all would be far more uncomfortable for his crewmates than the eternal fight on the brink of delirium. This revenge for all the physical and mental abuse would be much more rewarding.

Raspin confirmed the heading before activating the engines. The *Bortas* left the orbit of Iad, and the humming of the engines increased when she lurched into warp.

It's done, the Rantal thought, satisfied.

In the next second, Klarn whirled him around. His face was in ruins. One eye had swollen up and closed, the nose was broken, and blood covered the grim features. The other, good eye was screaming for murder, and his split lips formed a bloody grin. "And now it's your turn," Klarn said, and stabbed his *d'k tahg* into Raspin's stomach.

"This is all your fault!" Evvyk ak Busal screamed furiously at the other Renao who occupied the same cell on the *Bortas*. "If you hadn't gotten mixed up with that preacher with his nonsense about dragging the galaxy into war, we wouldn't be here getting tortured! We'd be safe and sound in Konuhbi if it wasn't for you."

"Safe and sound?" Moadas ak Lavoor rose from his metal bed and angrily pointed an accusatory finger at Evvyk. "There's no place safe and sound. The sphere defilers took that away from us. Their ships are flying between our stars, their crews are violating the purity of our home. They even corrupted Konuhbi itself! The fight against them is not only just, it's our duty!"

"Look where your wretched duty has taken us!" Evvyk was furious, overwhelmed by the urge to kill him. "We have been abducted, imprisoned, questioned, and tortured. We've been treated worse than animals! If it wasn't for the Vulcan and the first officer, we would have died an agonizing death. And you're still talking about fighting?" Clenching her fists, she spat at him with all the contempt she could muster.

In truth, their situation had improved some. After the first officer and the Vulcan diplomat had seen them, they had been provided with fresh clothing, medical treatment, and food. But Evvyk was unable to feel gratitude for their improved circumstances as her mind was entirely overwhelmed by her anger at Moadas. He was gullible enough to believe false prophets and to plunge headfirst into disaster—dragging her down with him.

Slowly, the man whom she had taken as her companion two years ago in an apparent fit of madness wiped the saliva from his face. His expression changed to pure hatred. "You selfish piece of dirt. All you can think about is your worthless excuse for a life. You can't see the big picture!"

Evvyk laughed derisively. "You don't even *have* your own life, worthless or otherwise. You just do what others tell you to do. 'Stand on one leg, little Griklak. Dance for me, little Griklak. Die for me, little Griklak.'"

Screaming incoherently, Moadas hit her face with the back of his hand, sending her sprawling.

Evvyk cried out in pain as she fell to the floor. Her cheek stung, and tears of pain and fury shot into her eyes. The hatred burned hot inside her, and she thought the fire would evaporate the tears. Her hand clutched a club that had suddenly appeared next to her.

"I'm going to kill you," she whispered. "You destroyed my life, and I will destroy yours."

"Oh really?" He looked down on her mockingly. "I'd like to see you try." He took a step back, beckoning her as a challenge.

Growling, she lunged forward, swinging her club. But Moadas blocked the blow with his left arm, before planting his fist into her face.

Evvyk staggered backward, her head colliding hard with the cell bulkhead. Colorful specks danced before her eyes, and the metallic taste of blood filled her mouth.

Squinting, she raised the club again, but Moadas knocked it aside and then closed his hands around her throat. "If you're not with me," he uttered with clenched teeth as he throttled her, "you're against me. And I have to kill those who are against me."

Evvyk groaned, gasping for air and trying to wriggle out of his grasp, but he was too strong. Black mists encroached on her vision, and the fear gripped her.

Suddenly, she felt a piece of metal in her hand. Looking down, she saw an old-fashioned projectile weapon of a type that hadn't been used on Onferin for more than five decades. Without thinking, she pressed the muzzle against Moadas's lower abdomen.

And suddenly, it was all over. Just like mist at sea that had been blown away by strong winds, the red veil of fury dissipated. With a terrified gasp, Moadas released his grip on Evvyk, staring at his bloodstained hands in utter disbelief. Finally, he looked up into her face, and his eyes widened even more.

"E-Evvyk…" he stammered.

Struggling for breath, she slid down the wall to the ground. Her neck hurt, and when she wanted to wipe her lips with her left hand, she found blood all over her fingers. In her right hand she still held the gun, and she quickly dropped it.

"Moadas," she croaked.

"By the spheres, Evvyk." Shocked, he fell to his knees, brushing her neck with his fingers. It was a gentle, caring gesture, but instinctively she backed away. He withdrew his hand instantly. "What was that? What happened to us?"

Without a word, she shook her head. She remembered everything, but she didn't understand any of it. The dispute, the unforgiveable words, the physical violence. *I was prepared to kill him*, she thought, mortified. *I wanted to kill him—and he me.*

It didn't make any sense. They had had good times and bad, but they loved each other!

Again, tears welled up in her eyes. She tried to meet his gaze. "Moadas, I'm scared."

Shifting close to her, he embraced her. This time, she didn't pull away.

"Everything will be all right, Ev." He spoke in a soothing tone meant to reassure her, comfort her—but all Evvyk heard was desperation.

4

NOVEMBER 26, 2385

U.S.S. Prometheus, on the periphery of the Souhla system

The three segments of the *Prometheus* hovered in space on the edge of the Souhla system, outside of the Kuiper belt. Parts of the ablative plating showed some disruptor-fire damage, but overall the ship was none the worse for the encounter with the Son of the Ancient Reds and the Klingons.

The same could not be said for the crew. Adams's gaze wandered around his ship's bridge. Nurse Chu walked from one station to the next with her medkit, attending to the wounds his people had sustained during the brief moments of unbridled fury.

Mendon had been hit hardest because he had been unfortunate enough to clash with Roaas. The Caitian had clawed across the Benzite's chest with his strong hands, leaving the scientist's uniform in tatters. Long, bloody scratches showed on the Benzite's thick, smooth amphibian skin. All these details were proof of the fact that the usually placid and level-headed Caitians were a force to be reckoned with during a fight—especially at close range.

Right now, Mendon—who didn't have his own seat on the bridge—sat waiting in the chair at the environment controls, while Chu methodically moved her dermal regenerator over the injuries. Roaas stood next to them, looking chagrined.

"I'm so sorry, Mendon," he said for the third time. "I really didn't want to harm you in any way."

"I already told you that there's no need to apologize, Commander. You weren't yourself." Mendon shifted slightly and grimaced.

"Please sit still," the nurse said.

"Still, it shouldn't have happened," Roaas said. "A Starfleet officer should be in better control of himself. *I* should be in better control of myself."

"It just proves how dangerous our opponent really is," Adams said. "And how powerless we really are…"

"Lieutenant ak Namur's idea to use the energy-dampening beam was excellent," Mendon said quietly. "However, it's unfortunate that it failed so miserably."

The captain gazed at the conn, where Jassat ak Namur sat, crestfallen.

"What's even more unfortunate," Mendon continued, "is that I have absolutely no alternative ideas how to defeat the Son."

Adams put his hand on the Benzite's shoulder. "We'll find a solution. We simply have to—not just for the benefit of the Renao, but for the benefit of the entire galaxy."

"Yes, sir."

"Sickbay to bridge," a female voice came from the intercom. It belonged to Doctor Calloway, the deputy chief medical officer.

"Adams here," he said.

"Captain, it might be a good idea if you could make some time to come down here."

"What's the matter, Doctor?"

"The empaths and telepaths among our crew are not doing so well, sir. I need to confer with you about their condition."

Adams's query as to why the chief medical officer wasn't making this call died on his lips upon hearing the term *empath*. "Is Doctor Barai among them?"

Calloway hesitated long enough that he knew the answer before she gave it. *"Yes, sir. And he's in critical condition."*

"I'm on my way." He turned to his first officer. "Mr. Roaas, you have the bridge. Keep patching up whatever damage has been done. And try to find out what happened to the *Bortas*. If we lost it, I need to dispatch a communiqué to Headquarters."

"I'll do my best." The Caitian made his answer sound as serious as a sacred oath. Maybe it was for him. Adams suspected that his old friend would engage in this mission with even more zeal than before, just to make up for what had been a brief moment of failure in his eyes.

In sickbay, Adams was confronted by a horrific scene. He hadn't seen sickbay so full since the Borg invasion four years ago, after the desperate battle to defend Vulcan. Admittedly, the outcome above Vulcan had been a lot bloodier. Even the *Prometheus* with her reinforced shielding and ablative armor had suffered enough damage from the Borg to leave dozens of crewmembers severely injured. Crewman Sears had lost his left leg beneath the knee when a duranium beam had crashed down on him, and Lieutenant DeCandido—gamma shift's chief engineer—had almost died from radiation poisoning after the polaron modulator's containment field had failed.

Today's suffering was less physical, but no less devastating for that. And the victims were more specific in terms of species: Vulcans, Napeans, Deltans, Betazoids. Lieutenant Commander Senok, Lieutenant T'Shanik, Crewman Uardo Nama, and the others had no injuries to their bodies.

Their minds were another story. Some were screaming and wailing. Others stared at the ceiling with glazed eyes. Several tried fighting off an invisible enemy with such ferocity that they had to be restrained.

A large percentage of the medical staff were among the patients. Adams saw doctors Oana Pena and Casserea and Nurse T'Sai. And right at the back of the room he found Geron Barai.

The only ones still standing were the human personnel and Trik.

Maddy Calloway approached Adams, a grave expression on her face. "Captain, thank you for coming." She had joined *Prometheus* from the *Enterprise*-E five years earlier.

"How bad is it?" Adams looked at Barai, who rested with a feverish red face and twitching limbs on his biobed. Trik attended to him.

Calloway took Adams aside into the small office allocated to the doctor on duty.

"As you can see, the influence of that alien being has been traumatic for our telepathically gifted crew members. One bit of good news is that the Vulcans are all showing signs of recovery, and should be fit for duty again before too long."

"I didn't notice Ambassador Spock," Adams said.

"He's in his quarters. We treated him there, and he's currently meditating. I must say, his mental resilience is remarkable. His body may betray his age, but his mind is able to cope with a lot more strain than you would expect."

"And what about the others?" The captain made a vague gesture towards sickbay.

Calloway stared at the floor, grimacing. Finally, she looked up again and met Adams's gaze. "I don't know, Captain. Medical science can do wonders for the body, but the mind remains a difficult field. Of course, we're doing our best. Unfortunately, Geron has been hit particularly hard because, unlike Vulcans, Betazoids embrace the emotions of others. Of all patients the only one who is in worse condition is Doctor Casserea."

Adams wasn't the least bit surprised that the young Deltan woman had taken the brunt of the Son's assault. She was not only renowned as one of the most sensual people aboard, but as one of the most sensitive. He knew several of his crew preferred to turn to Casserea with their problems rather than Counselor Courmont. Now, the bald woman with the dark brown eyes lay motionless and quietly whimpering on the biobed, saliva dribbling from the corner of her mouth.

"However," Calloway continued, "that isn't why I asked you to come down here. I would like to ask your permission to relocate them to their quarters. Our primary sickbay is small and designed for short-term treatment, and the med bays in the secondary hulls are even worse. Tending to a dozen mentally impaired patients whose recuperation might take weeks will put a strain on our capacity, especially given how many of our medical staff are ill."

"Do you consider it safe to leave them to their own devices in their quarters? I don't want anyone to injure themselves inadvertently." Adams thought of the Renao who were sometimes completely out of control. Also, the movements of both Napean crewmembers, Uardo Nama and Oana Pena, seemed to be motivated by panic—despite sedatives and fixation.

"I have already spoken to Lieutenant Tabor from engineering. He thinks it's possible to surround their bunks and beds with containment fields. We will use the holoprojectors, which are installed in every room."

"And you can treat them just as effectively in their quarters?"

"Yes, Captain. Sedatives can be applied in any location, and we can hook them up to bio-monitoring. That's all we can do anyway. We need to rely on the mental self-healing powers that most telepathic species have."

Adams mulled the suggestion over, and an idea came to him. "Listen, Doctor, would it help if we rendezvoused with one of the other ships on the edge of the cluster and transferred our personnel there? The *Venture* and the *Bougainville* are patrolling the outer cluster." Both the *Galaxy*-class ship and the *Nebula*-class ship were significantly bigger than the *Prometheus*.

But Calloway shook her head. "I doubt that, sir. The *Venture* and the *Bougainville* may have more space, but our equipment is more modern. Besides, xenopsychology happens to be my specialty. They won't get better treatment anywhere else, except at a starbase. That said, a couple of days won't make any difference in these cases, and our mission is subject to a time restriction, if I understood that correctly. Didn't the Klingons issue an ultimatum?"

Adams sighed. "Yes, they did, Doctor. But right now I couldn't care less about the High Council's wishes. If we need more than one hundred hours to solve this problem, we'll take it." He straightened his uniform jacket. "Still, you're right—this crisis needs to come to an end, sooner rather than later."

"In that case, it should be sufficient to send all patients who don't show improvement to a rehab facility on Earth after our return."

"All right, Doctor, I trust your judgment." Adams

avoided the unspoken phrase, *if we return to Earth*, that was implied by her tone, and inferred by Adams regarding this entire insane mission. "Do whatever is necessary to help your patients. But if anyone's condition dramatically deteriorates, I want to be informed."

"Absolutely, Captain."

He started to depart the office, then stopped and turned back around. "Oh, Doctor, how are our Renao patients doing?"

"They were heavily sedated at the time of the onslaught. I haven't had time for a full exam yet, but according to the bio-sensors, their brains didn't take any further damage."

"That's something, at least." Adams nodded. "Thank you, Doctor." He stepped back into the main sickbay.

Casserea, whose biobed was next to the office, extended her slender fingers pleadingly in his direction. "Captain…" Her voice was nothing more than a whisper.

"Lieutenant." He took her hand. It felt moist and cold.

"The horror…" she whispered. "I've seen pure horror." A tear rolled down her cheek.

"I know," Adams said soothingly. "I saw it too." In a clumsy attempt to comfort her, he gently squeezed her hand. "But we will prevail, Lieutenant. I promise."

When he left sickbay, he was only too aware that he didn't have the faintest idea how to keep that promise.

I.K.S. Bortas, on the periphery of the Souhla system

The first thing Raspin saw when he regained consciousness was a metal sky with a glowing red sun. It took a while before he realized that he was still aboard the *Bortas*, staring at a light in the ceiling. But he was no longer on the bridge's grid deckplates, but rather a solid slab of metal, and he was closer to the ceiling than he would have been had he been lying on the deck.

"He's awake," said a voice to his right. A head came into view, slender, grim, framed by dark, thick hair that had been tied into a bun at the back of his neck. It was Drax, the *Bortas*'s doctor.

I'm in the medical bay, Raspin realized. He was both relieved and surprised. Relieved because it meant that he had managed to steer the ship away from Iad successfully—otherwise all those who had been fighting wouldn't have calmed down sufficiently to waste any thoughts on injured crewmembers. And it surprised him that such thoughts had been extended to the *jeghpu'wI'*.

An explanation was offered a moment later when Commander L'emka's face came into view. The first officer's attractive face sported several cuts and bruises that had been briefly treated. They probably hadn't had the time to do more; the ship must be full of injured crewmembers.

L'emka said brusquely, "You may leave, Doctor."

Grumbling, Drax turned away.

Carefully, Raspin moved his head. The biobed he was resting on stood at the back end of the small medical bay. All the other beds were occupied by Klingons with stab wounds, bruises, and disruptor burns.

Whatever had instantly healed the deadly wounds of the fighters in orbit above Iad had lost its effect as soon as the *Bortas* had gone into warp. Raspin wondered how many crewmembers had died during those last seconds of fighting, before common sense returned.

L'emka studied him silently for a moment. Her face showed an expression he had never seen on her before—at least not when she'd looked at *him*. He wondered whether his eyes were deceiving him, or whether he was imagining it, but even after he blinked, the expression was still there: respect. For the first time since Raspin had come aboard, the Klingon woman saw him not only as a pale figure at ops but as a valued crewmember, maybe even an equal.

No, that's laughable, Raspin thought.

But L'emka didn't laugh. Instead, she opened her mouth and said something remarkable. "You were extremely brave, *Bekk* Raspin. And you have acted honorably. None of us could have done what you did above Iad—and you would have had every reason not to do it after the manner in which you have been treated. But you have shown true courage. Once I regained my wits, I saw the adjustments you made at the helm. You saved the *Bortas*, as well as each and every one of us, and you have prevented the ship and its crew from meeting a disgraceful end. However, don't expect that fool Kromm, or anyone else, to acknowledge that in any way."

Raspin wanted to answer but his throat was too dry to talk. He cleared his throat before managing to say, "But why are you here, then, Commander?"

"Because honor demands it," L'emka said earnestly. "Because you deserve to know that you were successful. Because I, as I have found out in the past few days, don't think like most others here." The corners of her mouth curled upwards. "And because I'm the only one who can make sure that you get the best available medical treatment. The *Bortas* needs her ops officer back as soon as possible— knife wound or not."

Her words finally prompted Raspin to inspect himself. Below the chest he practically felt nothing of his body. The painkillers did their job well. Warriors generally preferred to go without them, but they had been applied to the Rantal. Perhaps they didn't think he could bear the pain. It was yet another subtle humiliation, and he probably should have been offended. But right now, he was glad not to feel his injury. Raspin's wound had been treated but remained open, a cloth spread over it. Drax would, he presumed, eventually find the time to complete the treatment.

"So I guess I was lucky, eh?" Raspin asked, facing L'emka again.

"Very lucky, yes. Klarn's *d'k tahg* was stuck in your stomach up to its hilt. I had you beamed to sickbay along with Chumarr and Lieutenant Woch."

Raspin swallowed. He would have preferred not to ask the question that was on the tip of his tongue, but he had to. "How many casualties were there?"

The Klingon woman shook her head. "We don't know yet. We only dropped from warp half an hour ago at the edge of the system. Besides, that shouldn't be your concern. You shouldn't count those who died while you rescued us but those who survived. Their number is far greater."

Reluctantly, Raspin had to agree with her. The casualties weren't his fault—the Son of the Ancient Reds was to blame. Hopefully the others aboard would also see it that way. Klingons excelled in placing the blame rather than being grateful, that much he had learned during his time among them.

Raspin had another thought. "What about Klarn?"

The first officer's features hardened. "He will be punished for his attempt to murder you. The being's influence was a mitigating circumstance up to a point. However, he was still stabbing you once the *Bortas* had gone into warp, and he didn't even attempt to hold back. It is my hope that Kromm will not simply ignore that." Uncertainty swung in her voice during her last sentence. Both Raspin and L'emka were quite aware of Kromm's ability to overlook injustice and make questionable decisions.

"Don't worry about it," he said quietly. "He failed in his attempt to quench his hatred with my life, and I saved the ship—and thus him. I believe that knowledge is enough punishment for him."

L'emka gazed at him skeptically. "Are you sure? As a soldier in the Defense Force you have the right to vengeance, even as *jeghpu'wI'*."

The Rantal nodded. An inner peace that he hadn't even dreamed of a few days ago washed over him. Forgotten were the self-loathing and the self-doubts. He had proven his worth, and none of the Klingons could deny him that without becoming dishonorable liars.

And even if they did deny it, at least two people knew it—Raspin himself and L'emka. That was enough.

"Yes, I'm sure, Commander," he said. "Klarn is not worth it."

She tilted her head. "You're an extraordinary man. It's a shame that nobody aboard has noticed that yet." She smiled thinly. "Nobody *else*, in any event."

He briefly hesitated, then dared to smile back. "Thank you, Commander."

5
NOVEMBER 26, 2385

U.S.S. Venture, outside the Lembatta Cluster

The *U.S.S. Venture* was renowned as a ship that was always on the frontline when things got rough. Unlike many of her fellow *Galaxy*-class ships, which had been used for deep-space exploration missions lasting several years, Captain Bjarne Henderson's ship was usually deployed on diplomatic missions: shipping ambassadors, admirals and other high-ranking dignitaries from world to world.

To that end, the *Venture* frequently crossed the core regions of the Alpha Quadrant. She therefore worked well as a rapid reaction force whenever a crisis was imminent. During the short war between the Federation and the Klingon Empire in 2373, she had defended Deep Space 9. During the Dominion War, the *Venture* had helped retake both that station and the Chin'toka system from the enemy. During the Borg invasion, she had defended Andor. After the destruction of Deep Space 9, she had been one of the first ships on location to offer help. Now, she was here, patrolling space around the Lembatta Cluster as part of a fleet consisting of almost twenty ships.

Starfleet Command had labeled this deployment a sector blockade. They were supposed to prevent the fanatics of the Purifying Flame from committing any further suicide attacks on innocent worlds or space stations. Considering the Renao terrorists had at least one ship with experimental solar-jump technology at their disposal, which allowed them to cross up to thirty light years in zero time, Captain Henderson felt that this blockade was pretty porous, if not virtually useless.

Still, he suspected Starfleet was not here for the Renao alone. They wanted to take a stand against the Klingons who had amassed their own fleet beyond the border to Federation space with the full intent to invade the Lembatta Cluster, if that was what it took to eradicate the Purifying Flame.

Although he dismissed that notion as far too radical, Henderson had to agree with the Klingons in one respect: it was definitely easier getting down to the root of trouble than trying to catch all the spores drifting through space.

But maybe that was the reason why Admiral Gepta had just arrived aboard the *Capitoline*—to provide new orders.

"Captain, we're being hailed by the *Capitoline*," Lieutenant Andreas Loos reported from ops at the front of the bridge.

Henderson combed his thick brown hair with his thin fingers. He tended to ensure that his appearance was impeccable, even more so since he had celebrated his fiftieth birthday. His unruly hair often defied his efforts but he was proud of its fullness—which still grew without the aid of any hair restorer—and he refused to crop it to military length, as he looked much more attractive with fuller hair. Having to go the extra mile to keep wayward strands at bay was something he was willing to endure.

"On screen," he ordered, screwing on an expectant smile.

The image on the bridge monitor changed. The streamlined *Vesta*-class ship hovering in space beside them—Henderson secretly called the *Capitoline* and her sister ships the "slipstream taxis" because they had to ferry even more VIPs around the quadrant at high speed than the *Venture*—was replaced by the pleasant appearance of its commanding officer. Captain Roberta Holverson—her friends called her "Bobby"—was several years younger than Henderson and had chestnut-brown hair. Although she was quite sophisticated, she wasn't above a good evening of poker with like-minded colleagues, which made her one of those fellow captains with whom Henderson would have loved to spend shore leave, or at least have a drink in a cozy bar on one of the starbases. Unfortunately, their busy schedules had prevented that from happening so far.

"*Bjarne.*" Holverson greeted him with a warm smile.

"Bobby." He tilted his head. He had been wondering for a while whether Holverson had noticed his interest in her and was toying with him somewhat. For more than a year now, there had been this subtle undertone in their conversations—merely the hint of a flirt. It was so indefinable that others might have regarded it as cordiality among colleagues, especially if they didn't know that they hadn't met for more than a few minutes at a time yet. "Have you had a pleasant journey to us out here in the wild?"

"*It was short, as expected,*" Holverson replied, rubbing his nose in the fact that the *Capitoline* was much faster than the older *Venture*.

Henderson laughed. "I can imagine. Space is alarmingly small when you race through it at high speed, don't you think?"

She shrugged. "*I prefer slowness for all things that I should enjoy,*" she replied suggestively. "*But if there's a job to be done, I detest unnecessary waiting time. Admiral Gepta is the same, by the way.*"

Henderson took the hint and straightened. "Then we

mustn't let him wait. The *Venture* is ready to beam the admiral aboard."

"Very well. I will inform the transporter room."

"Affirmative. Oh, and, Captain Holverson?" Henderson leaned forward. "We need to have an in-depth discussion about commanding a quantum slipstream spaceship—as soon as there's a little more time."

The corners of her mouth twitched. *"Absolutely, Captain Henderson. Capitoline out."*

Two minutes later Henderson stood along with First Officer Di Monti, his Tellarite security chief Kraalbat, and a four-person honor guard in the *Venture*'s main transporter room. The captain nodded at the Bajoran transporter chief. "Energize."

The chief obeyed. Shimmering energy columns appeared above two of the transporter pads when Admiral Gepta and his female adjutant materialized. Henderson had already met the admiral several times, whose reputation as an uncompromising crisis manager preceded him. Still, his presence never failed to impress Henderson. Gepta was a Rigellian Chelon. To the casual observer he appeared to be an upright-walking turtle the size of a human. Instead of a shell he wore a polished breastplate made of duraplast. His skin had an olive-green hue and was covered in scales, his deep-set eyes had a piercing gaze, and his powerful ocher-colored jaws had an oily shimmer.

"Admiral on deck," Di Monti announced in a loud voice, following protocol. Everyone snapped to attention, and one of the crewmen blew a boatswain's whistle.

Gepta waved his gloved hand dismissively. "As you were. We're in the field here, no reason for a parade. At ease." His voice was rumbling and deep, as was often the case with Chelons.

Henderson nodded at his crew, and everyone relaxed a little.

"Captain Henderson?" Gepta should have known that, but Henderson overlooked the question. If Gepta had half the difficulty telling humans apart that the captain had with Chelons, he should count himself lucky that Gepta hadn't addressed the blonde and curvaceous Crewman Miners.

"I'm honored, Admiral," said Henderson, shaking his visitor's hand. The admiral wore protective gloves, as in stressful situations the Chelon skin produced a very potent contact poison. Despite the protective measures, Henderson hoped that Gepta carried neutralization tablets with him— just in case.

The captain introduced his officers.

"Delighted to meet you, gentlemen. My adjutant, Commander Deveraux."

She and Gepta complemented each other perfectly, thought the captain. They both looked as if they needed a refresher course in smiling.

"Would the admiral like to go to his quarters first to freshen up from the journey or…"

"From the *journey*?" Gepta emitted a cackling noise that could have been interpreted as laughter, but sounded more like gasping for breath. "The flight aboard the *Capitoline* from Earth to here was barely longer than a transfer by shuttle to Mars. This slipstream technology the *Voyager* brought back from the Delta Quadrant is truly a miracle weapon."

Henderson noted with some concern that the admiral called the propulsion system a weapon. This assumption— that the Federation might use the slipstream technology in order to gain a strategic advantage over the Typhon Pact powers—was mainly responsible for the four-year-long tensions between Federation, Klingons, Ferengi, and Cardassians on one side, and Romulans, Gorn, Breen, Tzenkethi, Kinshaya, and Tholians on the other.

"I understand," he said, trying to conceal his sentiments in this matter. "Let's go to the conference room and I will bring you up to speed."

"That's exactly what we're going to do." With those words, Gepta marched out of the transporter room toward the turbolift as if he owned the ship.

Don't fool yourself, Henderson pondered as he followed him with a resigned expression. *Chances are that he will take over the* Venture, *making her the flagship of this operation.*

They took the turbolift up to the bridge. Upon their entrance, Henderson's second officer rose from the command chair, making way for the captain. Di Monti said, "Admiral on the bridge."

"Nothing to report, sir," Commander Makzia said. The Saurian woman with purple skin blinked with her big eyes and took her station at conn, relieving the ensign who had filled in while she commanded the bridge.

"Before we get to work, I'll need a shipwide channel," Gepta said. "And record my words so they can be distributed to all other ships in the vicinity."

I knew it, shot through Henderson's mind. He nodded at Loos, who had turned around, gazing at him quizzically. "You heard the admiral, Lieutenant."

"Yes, Captain." He was just about to enter the necessary commands when the ops console alerted them to an incoming message. Quickly, he called up more information. "Captain, the *Bougainville* is hailing us. Audio only. The message is urgent."

Henderson briefly glanced at Gepta, but the admiral merely folded his arms in front of his chest. "Your ship, Captain. Do your job."

Nodding tersely, Henderson said, "Let's hear it."

A brief crackle came from the hidden loudspeakers of the intercom before a female voice spoke. *"This is the* U.S.S. Bougainville, *on patrol in mission sector seven-four. We are in the Theris system close to the Klingon Empire and have encountered three Klingon battleships illegally crossing the border: a Vor'cha-class battle cruiser and two B'rel-class Birds-of-Prey. Demands to withdraw have been ignored. We're requesting reinforcements. I repeat: we're requesting reinforcements."*

"Ha!" Gepta said. "That was bound to happen sooner or later. The Klingons have kept calm for far too long." He rubbed his gloved hands. "Very well. I guess we'll have to chase them back behind the border. This is still Federation space, and if anyone will conduct patrols here, it'll be Starfleet." He turned to Loos. "Lieutenant, what's your name?"

"Loos, sir."

"Which ship is closest to be of assistance to the *Bougainville*?"

"One moment, sir." Loos checked his console. "We are, sir. At maximum warp, we're sixteen minutes away from the Theris system."

Snapping his jaws, Gepta then said, "Reply to the *Bougainville*, and let her know that the *Venture* is on her way. Have them keep an eye on the Klingons, but they mustn't let themselves be provoked. If memory serves we diverted the *Bougainville* from a cartography mission, which means that she's probably flying with a sensor-pod configuration. She won't be a viable opponent for three Klingon battleships." He briefly tilted his head to one side, apparently reconsidering his last words. "Come to think of it, she wouldn't be anyway. *Nebula*-class ships are no battleships. Unlike a fully fledged *Galaxy*-class. Captain?"

Henderson straightened in spite of himself. "Admiral?"

"Head for the Theris system. Maximum warp." Gepta marched to the command chair in the center of the bridge, and sat down.

"Yes, sir."

Henderson forlornly relayed the order to Makzia, amazed and appalled at how quickly he had lost command of his own ship.

6
NOVEMBER 26, 2385

U.S.S. Venture, Theris system

The Theris system consisted of an extraordinary seventeen planets orbiting a most ordinary white dwarf of the main sequence. Those planets were either too close or too far from the star to support any life beyond a few single-cell organisms, and were unsuitable for colonization.

It wasn't completely empty, however. Several years ago, an industrial consortium under Tellarite leadership had discovered that the higher atmospheric layers of the system's largest gas giant contained rare isotopes. They installed a mining platform into orbit around in order to collect and refine those gases.

The crew consisted predominantly of Tellarites and several humans, as well as a Pakled chef. They were ill-tempered men and women, doing their jobs with as little effort as possible, and they didn't care about the rest of the galaxy. During their spare time, they enjoyed playing *Kera & Phinda*—a card game owing its name to two Tellarite moons—or they would sit by one of the panoramic windows, staring silently out into space with Theris XI in the foreground and the glowing nebulae of the Lembatta Cluster in the distance.

Galactic political affairs were of little interest. Who cared about the problems of people who lived light years away when a gas-phase separator got stuck, or one of the super-isolated transfer conduits leaked? Due to this severe lack of interest, the screens in the three staffrooms hardly ever showed newscasts from the Tellarite news agency or the Federation News Service that the mine operator had dutifully subscribed to. So when a full shift of tired workers ascended on their atmosphere lifts from the lower collector platforms to the living area of the complex and saw four starships—three Klingon and one Starfleet—circling each other in close proximity, they were completely taken by surprise.

"Are we at war with the Klingons?" one of the foremen asked his neighbor, scratching his beard in confusion.

"Nonsense. The Klingons and the Federation are allies," his neighbor replied.

"Doesn't look like it if you ask me. This seems more like…"

"…two brothers picking a fight." Admiral Gepta snapped his ocher-colored jaws twice, which was a gesture of affirmation and self-assurance, as Henderson had figured by now.

Unless he's got nervous twitches, the captain thought sarcastically.

The red alert klaxon was sounding, the *Venture*'s shields had been raised, and weapons had been readied.

Long-range sensors put the *Bougainville* and the three Klingon vessels close to a gas giant. But the *Venture* was approaching at maximum speed, and it was only a matter of seconds before she would arrive at the eleventh planet of the Theris system.

"Computer, identify Klingon ships," Henderson said. Along with Gepta, he stared at the main screen on the bridge, where a tactical view of the four ships and the gas giant was being displayed.

"*The* I.K.S. Drovana, *the* I.K.S. Chong'pogh *and the* I.K.S. Nukmay." The ships' names appeared next to the symbols of the attack cruiser and both Birds-of-Prey.

"The *Nukmay*?" Gepta leaned forward in the command chair. "Commander Koxx. Which means the Fifth Fleet under General Klag has arrived at the border. And I thought they were going to get there tomorrow."

Clearing his throat, Loos turned around to face him. "Begging the admiral's pardon, but the *Nukmay* is currently serving in the Seventh Fleet under General Akbas."

Slowly, Gepta rose from his seat. His large, gloved hands stroked his chest plate, while he stared at Loos as if he wanted to devour him.

Henderson saw the young officer go pale and snap to attention in his chair.

"Sir."

"Thank you, Lieutenant, for correcting me," the Chelon grumbled. Henderson really didn't want to be in the shoes of the staff member who had transferred the erroneous data to the admiral's padd.

"Leaving warp," Makzia said. "Distance to our destination: five hundred thousand kilometers."

"We're within visual range," Loos added.

Gepta nodded grimly. "On screen."

Four ships came into view, moving through the space over a giant orange and brown planet. The *Bougainville* was in the center of the quartet, desperately trying to avoid any angle where the main disruptor of the *Vor'cha*-class cruiser could fire at her. Both *B'rels* circled around the larger ships like vultures waiting for carrion.

"Open a channel to the *Bougainville* and the Klingons."

"Aye, sir." Loos quickly attended to his console.

"The Klingons have spotted us," Kraalbat said. He stood by the curved tactical console at the back of the bridge. "The *Drovana* is on an intercept course."

"Let them." Gepta put his hands on his plated hips. "Lieutenant Loos?"

"Link established, sir."

"This is Admiral Gepta from the *U.S.S. Venture*. Klingon vessels, you are trespassing in Federation territory. I demand you withdraw immediately to your side of the border."

"No response, Admiral," Loos said.

"The Klingon weapon systems are hot," Kraalbat said, "but they haven't targeted us or the *Bougainville* as yet."

"Keep us in motion, Commander Makzia," said Henderson. "We don't want to give the *Drovana*'s crew any opportunity to aim at us with their main disruptor."

"Disregard," Gepta snarled. "We're not going to prance about like an Antedian pond skater. We're boasting twice their mass, and we're much bigger than the *Drovana*. Klingons only respect strength—and strength we will display. Head straight for the attack cruiser. Load phaser banks and torpedo launchers."

"Admiral—" Henderson wanted to object but Gepta cut him short.

"Trust me, Captain. I know what I'm doing."

Henderson swallowed. He fervently hoped this to be true. The *Venture* might be bigger than the *Drovana*, but the *Vor'cha* class was a battleship and, as such, much more heavily armed. *On the other hand, Klingons are not very apt poker players*, the captain mused.

"I repeat, this is Admiral Gepta from the *U.S.S. Venture*.

Klingon vessels, you are trespassing on Federation territory. I demand you withdraw immediately to your side of the border. Otherwise, I have been authorized by the Federation president and the Federation Council to destroy you."

"The *Bougainville* is assuming a flanking position to the *Drovana*. The Birds-of-Prey are pursuing her." Was it just Henderson's imagination, or did Kraalbat sound less grumpy than usual thanks to the prospect of battle? He made a mental note to have a chat with the tactical officer later.

"Warning shot across the bow, Mr. Kraalbat," Gepta said.

Kraalbat obliged. Silently, a golden beam cut through space, crossing the *Drovana*'s path.

"They're hailing us," Loos said. His tone of voice betrayed a broad, knowing smirk.

"On screen."

The image of the maneuvering spaceships disappeared, and an agitated Klingon commander came into view. *"How dare you fire on us! We fight the same enemy! You would attack us just because we entered your space?"*

Gepta planted himself in the center of the bridge with spread legs, his fingers interlaced in front of his barrel chest. "If you don't cooperate, I absolutely will. You've no business here right now, Commander... Koxx, I presume?"

"How do you know my name?"

"I'm a great *admirer* of your former superior, General Klag." Gepta stressed the word *admirer* in an odd way, and Henderson wondered whether there was some kind of hidden irony behind the Chelon's words. "So I made it my business to familiarize myself with the commanders of the Fifth Fleet as well. I know, for example, that you used to command the *Nukmay*. Congratulations on your promotion, by the way. When did you take over the *Drovana*? A month ago? Two?"

"What does that matter, Chelon?"

"Oh, I'm merely trying to point out to you that you have virtually no experience fighting aboard large and sluggish vessels. And a *Vor'cha* is more sluggish than a Chelon egg keeper. I, on the other hand, am extremely familiar with ships of the *Galaxy* class. So you should probably think twice before challenging me." To emphasize his words, he made his jaws snap.

The view seemed to vex the Klingon, and he made a dismissive gesture with his hand. *"We do not wish to fight our—our honorable allies. We're here to assist in patrolling the systems that might be future targets for these Renao fanatics."*

"Yes, you already told the *Bougainville* that... and her captain informed you that we don't require your help. Stick to patrolling along your own border. I'm sure there will be ample endangered systems within reach of a—"

"Captain, Admiral, the *Bougainville* is hailing us!" gasped Loos.

"Excuse us a minute, Commander." Without further ado, Gepta had the channel muted. "Patch the *Bougainville* through. Audio only." The admiral faced away from the screen just like Henderson would have done, so Koxx wasn't able to draw any conclusions as to the nature of the message from his reaction.

"This is the Bougainville," the familiar female voice spoke again. *"Venture, we have located a ship at the magnetic north pole of the sun. It just appeared, and it's attempting to hide behind the sun now."*

"What kind of ship, *Bougainville*?" Gepta asked.

The woman's voice sounded nervous. *"According to the configuration it's one of the Renao's so-called solar-jumpers."*

The Chelon's jaws snapped several times, an indication

of his surprise. Suddenly, his eyes showed that he was burning for action. Henderson wagered that Gepta would have grinned grimly if he had been physically able to do so.

"Intercept course, *Bougainville*. We're going to capture the ship. No, wait. Disregard. I have a better idea. Mr. Loos, give me Koxx, pronto."

"Yes, sir."

The channel to the Klingon commander was reopened.

"Listen, Koxx," said Gepta before his counterpart could even open his mouth. "We have located a Renao solar-jumper. It's hiding around the magnetic north pole of the sun. Clever, but not clever enough to escape our sensors. We will capture it—and as you're already here with your people, you might want to participate in the operation."

"*Absolutely.*" Koxx bared his teeth.

"Excellent. I have a plan." Clasping his hands behind his back, Gepta began pacing up and down in front of the monitor. "If we have been correctly informed, the Renao need at least a day to recharge their drive. Which means we have all the time in the world. But we should refrain from making them nervous by heading straight toward them. So, what we're going to do is this…"

Solar-jumper *Coumatha*

"Did they spot us?" Manouk ak Lovaal ran from one sensor console to the next. The young Renao felt his blood rush through his veins in anticipation. A voice inside his head screamed at him to confront these wretched strangers, these sphere defilers! He wanted to release the *Coumatha*'s lethal cargo in order to destroy these five enemy ships.

But he restrained himself. They had a more important target: a place that was forced to endure millions of reprehensible souls—colonists who had left their ancestral home sphere to conquer space. The thought was enough to make Manouk's stomach turn.

"No, the sphere defilers are still circling each other at the gas giant." Jalal ak Nourmi pointed at the display. "They didn't notice our appearance." He cackled almost hysterically. "They are so busy with each other that they don't even see their own doom coming."

"I say we attack them," Houma ak Nourmi said urgently. She was the third person in their confined bridge and Jalal's sister. She clenched a red hand into a fist, and her yellow eyes glowed like stoked firewood.

Manouk gave her a stern look. "No, remember our task. This isn't about a mere few ships."

"They are not just ships! Two of them are capital ships with thousands of sphere defilers on board! And they are threatening to attack our home spheres. They've said so on several occasions."

Houma's passion had always been attractive to Manouk, albeit in secret. He admired her zeal and shared her desires, but they needed to stay on their mission. "You don't eliminate weeds on the fields by picking off some leaves. You need to pull out the roots. *That's* our sacred mission. Our enemies mustn't see us here. We need to hide. Otherwise, they will stop us before we can take our brethren to their destination."

He was referring to the pilots aboard the *Coumatha* with them—fearless fighters for the cause of the Purifying Flame. They were waiting in the cargo hold that had been converted into a hangar. Ten young men who each had been assigned to one of the small black and lethal *Scorpion* attack fighters stowed there. All of them had been stuffed with a highly explosive mixture of blasting agents, and they were waiting for their deployment.

"I don't think we'll have to worry about that." Jalal gesticulated like a madman at the sensor console. "Look, the Klingons and the Federation are fighting each other. They're shooting at each other and chasing each other through space."

Incredulously, Manouk moved to stand next to him. *It's true*, he realized in amazement. The larger of the three Klingon ships fired at the larger Federation ship. The smaller one appeared to escape to the other side of the gas giant, followed by the two smaller bumphead ships.

During the *Coumatha*'s jump from its secret base deep inside the Lembatta Cluster to this position, he had feared the worst. They had come upon five hostile ships, and they would have found it difficult to deal with a fleet of that size, even if they had successfully launched the ten *Scorpions* at short notice.

Fortunately, the Son of the Ancient Reds watched over them and their sacred mission for the restoration of harmony to the galaxy's sphere order.

"They are blind," Houma realized. "The Son has struck them with folly. These fools surely think they're fighting us, when in truth they are killing each other. Serves them right. He who wears a weapon in our home spheres must die by that weapon."

Her words sounded like a quote from one of the scripts about the sphere harmony, although they were unusually aggressive. Manouk wasn't familiar with them.

"We're losing the three smaller ships from sight," Jalal said. "They're behind the gas giant now."

"And the large ones?" Manouk asked.

"Are still firing. By the stars, I wish I could command their weapons. Our righteous battle would be over swiftly."

"We have all the weapons we need for a victory," said Manouk. "And the Son is with us. His fire can't be doused."

Although he said it to convince Jalal, Manouk knew it to be the truth. The fire burning within all of them was hotter than a thousand suns. Nothing would be able to stop them... ever. Victory was merely a question of time.

"Jalal, keep an eye on the sphere defilers," he said. "Houma, activate the antimatter converter to recharge the jump drive. We should see to it that we get out of here as soon as possible."

"On it, Manouk," she replied, sitting back down at the engine control.

He marched past her to the massive hatch separating the cockpit from the rest of the ship. "I'll be in the hangar," he said. "I want to see how our pilots are doing after the jump." Some people felt very nauseous during their first solar jump. Manouk, who had completed almost two dozen journeys aboard the ship, had gotten used to it by now.

The Renao went down a short corridor, and then took a lift down into the belly of the box-like solar-jumper. Soon after, he arrived at the ship's former cargo hold. The small black attack fighters had been lined up in two rows of five spacecrafts. They didn't have any tractor beams or docking clamps at their disposal so they had secured them with steel nets. With their elongated windshields and curved stabilizing fins they looked pleasantly aggressive. Unfortunately the enemy usually didn't get to see them, as they darted toward their target cloaked and at maximum speed.

Manouk turned left toward the makeshift jump harnesses

that had been fastened on the hangar wall. Ten men were just unstrapping, stretching their hurting limbs; another side effect of solar jumps.

"Everything all right?" Manouk asked. He was barely older than them but somehow he felt responsible for them as captain of the *Coumatha* and a Purifying Flame veteran.

The pilots all nodded. One of them looked pale, but none of them had vomited.

Manouk was proud of these warriors who were willing to make the ultimate sacrifice for the cause, for their sacred mission. *You will enter into eternal harmony*, he thought. *And the Son will reward you.*

"How many of these jumps do we have to endure?" asked Nadash, the leader of flight one. He was a young man who had shaved his head for the mission, adorning it with golden jewelry and symbols.

"Five, if everything goes to plan." Manouk permitted himself a grim smile. "But don't worry, brothers. It will. We will reach the world that the Federation calls New France, and we will burn away the cancerous colonists who have spread all over its surface. And the Son will smile upon us, because we are restoring the harmony of the spheres. That's how it will be." He had inadvertently raised his voice, and now he was shaking his fists.

The ten attack fighter pilots mirrored his gesture, cheering enthusiastically. "That's how it will be! For the harmony of the spheres! Death to all sphere defilers!"

Suddenly the proximity alert went off. The cheers died down, and Manouk looked up in surprise.

Confused, Nadash and the others stared at him. "What's that?"

"I have no idea," Manouk said.

The *Coumatha*'s hull suffered a direct hit, and soon after, a second one. The ship shuddered. Manouk's stomach tied into a knot. *Oh no, please don't*, he thought.

"Be prepared," he said to the pilots. "The enemy is here!"

"The enemy?" Nadash asked, incredulous.

"No time for explanations." Manouk darted toward the cockpit.

"They just appeared in front of us," Jalal shouted instead of a greeting. "Just like that! I didn't see them coming." He pointed desperately at the narrow cockpit windows.

Manouk rushed to the controls, gazing through the plated windshield. Below them, the sun's photosphere bubbled with intense brightness, which was only bearable because the windows were equipped with strong polarization. This polarization allowed him to detect two dark figures in the shape of predator birds approaching steadily. The weapons mounted on the tips of their curved wings hurled green energy charges toward the *Coumatha*.

"The shields are failing," Jalal shouted. "This is the end!"

"No!" Manouk ran to Houma who sat at the controls, adjusting settings frantically in an attempt to speed up the recharge process. "Houma, we need an emergency jump, no matter to which sun."

"We won't make it," she answered in desperation. "We don't have enough energy."

"Overload the systems, I don't care. The *Coumatha* must not fall into the hands of our enemies."

Another blast, and the solar-jumper was jerked to one side. Both Manouk and Houma lost their footing. He crashed into a cockpit wall, and she collapsed into his arms. Under different circumstances he would have enjoyed this moment of unexpected closeness. Now he just pushed the young woman away, stepping up to the controls himself. Warning lights flickered everywhere.

Manouk groaned in desperation. "The engines are failing. We're stuck here."

Jalal rose from his seat. An ominous fire burned in his eyes. "That leaves only one thing." He looked at his sister and Manouk gravely.

Manouk nodded in understanding. "Self-destruction. We allow the sphere defilers to come close, and then we blow ourselves up." Due to the ten attack fighters on board, they had more than enough explosives to achieve that.

"I'm going dark," said Houma. "That way, they'll figure we're defeated and easy prey for them." She joined Manouk at the controls, flicking several switches. Darkness fell over the bridge. Manouk imagined the pilots in the hangar, who didn't know what was going on and might start to panic, but he couldn't help that.

Suddenly they heard an unfamiliar, ethereal chime. Three columns of red light appeared on the confined bridge. And it dawned on Manouk that he had forgotten something essential.

"Transporters! The sphere defilers are beaming aboard." Instinctively Manouk's hand went to his belt, but the holster with his weapon wasn't there. He had left it in the closet in his cabin. Why would he need a weapon on board his own ship?

"Retreat!" Jalal shouted. "To the hangar!"

All three scrambled to the door, impeding each other. Behind them they heard an animalistic howl, before the whine of an energy weapon.

Houma screamed.

Manouk's eyes widened when he realized that the woman for whom he would have given his life had collapsed next to him. She had been hit in the back by one of their attackers.

He whirled around. Anger welled up inside of him, bubbling like lava. He glared at the three Klingons who had materialized in the center of the *Coumatha*'s bridge. They wore martial clothing made from heavy leather, and stood there with raised weapons.

Without thinking, just filled with a hot desire for vengeance, Manouk tore a fire-killer from the wall next to the hatch, hurtling the heavy metal cylinder towards their attackers. It hit the Klingon in the center of his body, sending him sprawling.

One of his comrades fired at Manouk, narrowly missing him. The Renao fighter hardly noticed the heat that whizzed past his upper arm. With a guttural scream he launched forward. Ramming his shoulder into the Klingon's stomach, he pushed him back two steps, and he hit the controls.

Manouk's fingers fumbled around the Klingon's belt for something he assumed to be a knife. In the dim emergency light he hadn't been able to identify it properly. Closing his fingers quickly around the hilt, he pulled the weapon from its sheath. His opponent hit him in the neck with the butt of his rifle, and Manouk collapsed on the floor. Although he felt dizzy, the anger made him spin around instantly, attacking while he was still on his knees. Howling, he stabbed the knife into the Klingon's abdomen. The man screamed in agony, dropping his weapon. He brought one hand up to the hilt of the blade that stuck in his stomach. With his other hand he dealt another devastating blow to Manouk, throwing him off his feet. Again the Renao jumped up, fire in his eyes and foam on his lips. His head was pounding, and he tasted blood, but he didn't care.

Manouk focused his attention on the final opponent, who was just about to raise his energy weapon. Manouk leaped towards him.

The Klingon fired.

A green energy blast, glowing hot like the sun, sped towards Manouk, hitting him straight in the chest. He was stopped dead in his tracks and whirled around. His torso cramped when a wave of agony sped through his entire body, searing his nerves. His agonized scream filled the narrow bridge, before the emergency lights went out and blackness engulfed Manouk—eternal blackness.

U.S.S. Venture

"My warriors have captured the solar-jumper, Admiral," Commander Koxx reported to Gepta with audible pride.

"Excellent." Gepta, standing next to Henderson in the center of the bridge, nodded at the Klingon. "It's extremely satisfactory when a plan is so smoothly executed."

He was hinting at the fight in orbit of Theris XI that the *Bougainville* and the *Venture* had staged along with the *Drovana*, the *Chong'pogh*, and the *Nukmay*, during which the *Bougainville* had drawn both *B'rels* behind her around the gas giant until they could be sure that the Renao sensors didn't pick them up any longer. The *Chong'pogh* and the *Nukmay* had cloaked, darting at maximum speed towards the sun. With the element of surprise, it had been easy to incapacitate the Renao ship and board it—just like Gepta had predicted.

"It was not entirely smooth, *as you suggested,"* Koxx said. *"These Renao fought like berserkers. Five of my crew are dead and two others are severely injured."*

"No war is without casualties," Gepta said. "But your men have achieved honor through our victory."

Henderson raised his eyebrows in surprise. So far, he hadn't been aware of the fact that they were at war with the Renao. Hadn't the president of the Federation repeatedly stressed how important it was to regard this as a peace mission? Still, he decided to remain silent. This was neither the right time nor the right place to point out politely but firmly to a superior officer that war was exactly what they all were trying to avoid—hopefully. *I'd rather have this conversation in private in my ready room*, he mused.

Koxx, on the other hand, didn't seem to be on the same page as Gepta, which was not surprising. He laughed.

"You almost sound like a Klingon. Maybe there's hope for Starfleet after all."

The Chelon admiral dismissed the dubious praise. "How many prisoners did we take?"

His counterpart's expression darkened. *"None. They fought to the death. The last two took their own lives to avoid capture."* A grim smile crept onto his face. *"But we captured something else that should be deeply interesting for you…"*

7

NOVEMBER 26, 2385

U.S.S. Prometheus, on the periphery of the Souhla system

Sarita Carson looked up from ops to the main screen on the bridge where a blurred shape emerged from the red nebulae. "Captain, we found the *Bortas*."

"What's their condition?" Adams asked.

Roaas checked the tactical display. "The ship took some damage to the outer hull. Th'Talias didn't fire long enough to affect any important systems."

"She had a lucky escape if you ask me," Carson mumbled.

"Mr. Winter, hail our allies please," the captain said dryly.

He stifled a yawn. It was almost 0900, but he hadn't had much sleep during the previous night. The repairs to the ablative armor and the damaged systems, as well as the worry about his people laid up in sickbay, had kept him on his toes. He had only spent three hours in his quarters before the quiet but insistent alarm called him to alpha shift. But Adams knew that most of his crew shared that pain with him.

Kromm's face appeared on the bridge's screen. The Klingon looked as if he had just returned from a bar brawl on one of the outer worlds of the Empire. His right eye had swollen shut, and blood trickled from a cut on his left cheek. A wiry Klingon woman was tending to his injuries but Kromm growled and waved her off with an impatient gesture. The nurse responded with a hiss that the universal translator wasn't able to translate. She disappeared from view.

"*Adams. Your ship looks as if it has taken a beating.*" Kromm's lips parted in a gap-toothed grin.

"The damage is superficial," Adams said. "You look pretty well beaten yourself, Kromm. Who did that to you? Commander L'emka?"

The other captain frowned.

Adams knew he was provoking the Klingon by insinuating that a woman had overwhelmed him. He also knew that their permanent bickering was foolish and childish—now more so than ever, as they were facing an imminent threat. He still found it agonizingly difficult to treat Kromm in the objective and professional manner that was appropriate between two allied spaceship crews. Part of that could be blamed on the Son, but the simple fact was that Adams and Kromm didn't see eye to eye—on much of anything.

Quickly Adams raised his hand to forestall further comment from his counterpart. "Let's leave it at that, Captain. We have more important things to do than score points with insults. What I meant to say was: we need to talk about what we have learned. And then we should ask ourselves in what way we should proceed against the Son of the Ancient Reds."

Gritting his teeth, Kromm nodded. "*As is the case with annoying regularity, Adams, you are correct. Give us time to wipe the blood off the furniture, and then you and your crew will be welcome aboard the* Bortas.*"

Adams was tempted to insist on a meeting aboard the *Prometheus*, but he had to admit that they had always convened on his ship. Kromm had every right to play the host for a change. And if this little triumph of playing a home match made him a little more bearable, Adams was ready to pay the price of hard metal chairs, reddish lighting, and bloodwine for refreshment.

"We expect your invitation."

An affirmative growl was the answer, before Kromm terminated the link.

"Mr. Winter, please inform ambassadors Spock and Rozhenko and Lieutenant Commander Mendon about the briefing. They will accompany me to the *Bortas*—if they are up to it."

"Aye, sir," the dark-skinned German replied.

The captain got up and walked towards the turbolift. "I'll be in main engineering. Commander Roaas, you've got the bridge."

The Caitian confirmed the order as Adams passed him, getting up from tactical; zh'Thiin hurried over to relieve him.

Adams arrived at the main engine room on deck twelve shortly after, and walked into bustling activity. Jenna Kirk stood by the main engine controls. A technical drawing of the *Prometheus* had been brought up on a large display. Several sections flickered yellow, while two red dots were visible in the aft sections. Kirk studied the damage notifications, deploying technical teams to the repair sites.

Behind her the slim warp core shimmered. The column, consisting of several separate sections, spanned the entire secondary hull. The three sections were interconnected matter–antimatter reaction chambers. The main chamber ran in standard mode, while the upper and lower reaction chambers would come into use with the help of additional matter and antimatter conduits during the ship's separation. Adams knew that his ship's core was a delicate piece of technology which didn't exist in any of the other ship classes in Starfleet. That made for complicated repair schedules.

The same could be said for the softly flickering globe construction in the adjacent room, which was visible through a hatch. The newly installed and independently operating quantum slipstream drive was currently the crème de la crème of modern propulsion systems. Admiral Kathryn Janeway had brought this technology home from the Delta Quadrant, and it had been only four years since ships had been equipped with it. Sometimes Adams had the distinct feeling that no one really felt safe flying with it. It was like speeding through a busy city center doing a hundred kilometers per hour. The tiniest mistake in the complex calculations required to keep up the slipstream could have fatal consequences.

Of course, the control programs were improved every year, and during their pit stop at Deep Space 9 almost a month ago, the *Prometheus*'s software had been updated. Still, Adams only ever used the drive in emergency situations. His ship didn't belong to the *Vesta*-class that had been constructed especially for quantum slipstream travel.

"Captain." Kirk had spotted him and was looking at him in surprise. "What brings you to us gearheads?"

"I just wanted to talk to you about what happened to us in orbit around Iad, Commander."

The chief engineer put her hands on her hips. "If you're referring to the failure of our shields, sir... that was an extreme situation by anybody's standards. We were inside this chaos zone, and a Klingon attack cruiser decided to fire on us, while none of us were able to think clearly."

Defensively, Adams raised his hands. "Nothing was further from my mind than to blame you, Jenna, or anyone else. There was no way that we could have anticipated any of what happened. But that means we have to consider how we can avoid similar incidents in future. We have no other choice but to return to that chaos zone if we want to stop the Son of the Ancient Reds."

"Understood, sir." Kirk nodded. "We... Hey, Bottlinger, Na Bukh! Where are you going with those bio-neural gel packs? We need them here. Go and get some from the cargo modules." The petite human woman and the Triexian with the orange skin confirmed her order, lowering the transport box that they had intended to carry out of the room.

"Begging your pardon, sir," said Kirk when she turned back to Adams. "You're right, of course. The *Prometheus* must be able to deal with any challenge. She failed in this case. So we need a few good ideas. I'm just wondering whether I'm the right person to talk to. Commander Mendon knows much more about this permanently fluctuating radiation than I do."

"But you know much more about this ship's technology than he does," Adams said. "Go through all the data that we collected about this chaos zone. If you need help, request anyone from the science department you need. Commander Mendon and I need to go to a meeting on the *Bortas*, but when we get back he will join you to assist."

"Does this take priority over the repairs?" Kirk asked, motioning to include everything around her.

"I'd appreciate it if you could deal with both, Commander," Adams replied earnestly. "Concentrate on the question of how to enhance the shield regeneration routines so that they can withstand radiation impact. The defense shield in combination with the adaptive radiation filter seems to have worked very well. However, it didn't regenerate after the *Bortas* took a shot at us. We need to find the reason for that, and we need to close the gap in the system."

Kirk nodded. "All right, Captain. I'll hand the repairs over to Tabor, and I'll start working on that problem right away." She did try to hide her lack of enthusiasm, alas not very successfully.

Adams gave her a sidelong glance. "Is there a problem, Commander?"

"No, sir. Not really."

He regarded his chief engineer in silence before taking her aside and lowering his voice. "We've served together for eight years, Jenna. You're one of my longest serving officers, and you know that I appreciate honest words. So, out with it… What's the matter?"

Sighing, Kirk's shoulders slumped slightly. "Well, it's this cluster, Captain. The cluster in general, and Iad in particular. I don't mind challenges, that's for sure. The Borg, the Typhon Pact, the Klingons—you name it, I'll do everything in my power to get *Prometheus* ready for battle and to make sure that we survive. But these… inexplicable space phenomena… they're getting to me. The permanent anger that this being on Iad is whispering to us, the radiation interferences of this cluster, and most of all this chaos zone around Iad itself… it's wearing me down." She snorted bleakly. "I looked at the sensor records. That chaos zone defies all known science. Something like that shouldn't even be possible. But hey, I'm a Kirk. I should know better than anyone that nothing is impossible in this galaxy. My ancestor has undertaken journeys through time into the past, travelled to a parallel universe, and added at least half a dozen god-like entities to Starfleet's first-contact database. This would probably just be another day in the office for him."

Gently, Adams put his hand on her shoulder. "That

was a different time. Many things were new and hadn't been encountered before. James Kirk and his crew from the *Enterprise* matured to heroes during their careers, without a doubt. But even if they cast their larger-than-life shadows on each and every new class of Starfleet cadets, we mustn't forget that they were all people, just like us. They did their jobs, and they did their best. We're doing exactly the same. And I wager that even your ancestor had his doubts on occasion, that even he lost the belief in being able to overcome certain challenges. Still, he never gave up. He got up after every setback and pulled through. And that's what we're going to do right now, Jenna. At the end of the day, we will triumph, I'm sure of it. You're one of the best engineers that Starfleet has to offer. Doctor Barai is one of the most renowned doctors, Roaas is an outstanding tactician, and on and on. We have an exceptional crew, and we're going to prove that to the Son of the Ancient Reds. Trust me." He patted her on the shoulder, smiling at her reassuringly.

Jenna Kirk smiled back, straightening her shoulders. "I trust you with my life, Captain."

"Let's hope I'm worthy of it, Commander." He nodded at her. "And now, back to work. Get our shield regenerator routines up to scratch."

"Yes, sir. And forgive my doubts, sir."

Adams sighed. "Don't worry, Commander. It happens to the best of us." *Including me.*

Lenissa zh'Thiin didn't trust the Klingons. She had had her reservations about the *Bortas* crew right from the beginning, and they had steadily grown every time she had encountered Kromm.

With very few exceptions—namely Ambassador Rozhenko, Commander L'emka, and the engineer Mokbar with whom she had been captured by Renao fanatics— Klingons only ever thought about themselves. They didn't seem to have any kind of sincere intentions to end this conflict without glorious battles. What's more, they had severe problems with the chain of command, they were not very keen on any kind of cooperation, and most of all they seemed to keep secrets from the *Prometheus* crew. The latter had been proven to be the case recently when the two captured Renao had been discovered aboard the *Bortas*.

Moadas ak Lavoor and Evvyk ak Busal—both sympathizers of the Purifying Flame from Konuhbi on Onferin—had been reported dead to Adams. Instead, Kromm had kept them prisoner under degrading conditions and had tortured them to gain information he could use to show off to Adams.

There was no love lost between zh'Thiin and the Renao— not since her ordeal in the hands of the terrorists—but there were rules civilized people should adhere to, even during a war. On the other hand, it was probably grossly exaggerated to claim that the Klingons were civilized.

Their ship, the *Bortas*, did not really convey that impression. Looking at her from the outside, the slender, furcated front part and the rear end with the wide curved aft section relayed some sort of martial elegance. On the inside, however, dark metal corridors, heavy support struts along bulkheads, and metal grating on the deck dominated the scene. Everything was dimly lit in red. The *Vor'cha*-class was undoubtedly sturdy, yet it felt like being in the entrails of a metal dragon.

Apparently this dragon suffered from irritable bowel

syndrome. Traces of vandalism were visible everywhere—crushed monitors, bent tubes, grating plates that had been ripped from the walls and floors. In some spots, zh'Thiin's experienced eye spotted patches of fabric and leather. At a junction, she found an abandoned boot. She saw plenty of splatter-stained conduits, struts, and ceiling panels—dried Klingon blood that hadn't been wiped down yet.

The internecine battle seemed to have spared the conference room. The Andorian woman didn't believe for one second that Kromm had had their meeting point cleared up. Just like the rest of the ship, the room was very constricted. She saw no chairs, just a long octagonal table that stood waist-high in the center of the room. Two terminals were embedded in the table's surface. A screen was mounted at the front wall of the room.

Kromm was already present when zh'Thiin, Adams, Mendon, Spock, and Rozhenko arrived. He was flanked by Rooth and Nuk. The absence of First Officer L'emka was conspicuous. Adams also seemed to notice it, and exchanged a knowing look with Spock and Rozhenko.

"How is your crew, Captain?" asked Adams. "I hope you didn't have any casualties."

Kromm frowned. "Let us not discuss that, Captain. This is a dark hour."

But Adams was insistent. "How many?"

"Fourteen, one of them my comrade of many turns, Toras, our pilot. He wasn't even supposed to be on the bridge when all hell broke loose, as L'emka had taken over his station during the formation flight with the *Prometheus*. It was she who killed him…"

"Your people weren't themselves," Rozhenko said. "You can't blame anyone."

"My head knows that," the Klingon replied, growling. He hit his chest with his fist. "But tell that to my heart."

"How is Commander L'emka, if I may ask?" Spock interrupted. "Is she well?"

Kromm glowered at the ambassador. "Yes. She's on the bridge, coordinating repairs."

"If you need assistance, the *Prometheus* crew is at your disposal," said Adams.

Zh'Thiin assumed that it couldn't be easy for him to make this offer, considering Kromm's recent actions, not to mention that their own people were spread thin. But they were still allies, and Starfleet would help anyone who was in need.

"Unnecessary," Kromm replied. "Doctor Drax and his staff have everything under control, as does Nuk's engineering staff."

"Good. Then let's turn our attention to the main problem." Adams let his gaze wander across all those present. "What are we going to do to deal with the danger that the Son of the Ancient Reds poses, and to free the Lembatta Cluster?"

"Violence doesn't seem to be the solution," said Mendon. "Neither phasers, nor disruptors, nor photon or quantum torpedoes were able to harm the energy life form. Even the attack with the modified deflector dish only resulted in angering the being."

"Is that your opinion, or do you have hard facts to prove that?" Rooth asked.

The Benzite tilted his head affirmatively. "I studied the sensor recordings earlier. They provided fairly useful information up until the point when the formation flight was abandoned shortly after the energy-dampening impulse. They don't show any noteworthy signs of the Son weakening.

Additionally, I have scrutinized the radiation zone around Iad once more. There are also no significant changes."

"But we don't know whether the intensity of the radiation cloud is directly related to the being's condition," Rozhenko said. "We can't even say with any kind of certainty whether he does indeed emit it, or whether it is part of his prison."

"No, that's true," Mendon admitted. "There are a great many coherences we are not aware of. We lack the sensor equipment for such extensive research. A proper research vessel would be helpful."

"The issue is not merely a lack of equipment, Commander, it's also the lack of time," Kromm said. "We cannot *watch* a space phenomenon for months while fanatics attack our worlds. If we can't destroy the evil at the source, we need to contain its excesses. If we cannot subdue the Son, we have no other choice but to declare the cluster a no-flight zone, and to put all Renao worlds under quarantine."

Zh'Thiin hated to admit it, but she had to agree with the Klingon captain.

"Perhaps there is yet another solution." Spock, who had been listening with a pensive expression, looked up.

The Vulcan still looked slightly pale after the mental assault he had endured at Iad, but his posture was straight and his gaze clear. Zh'Thiin admired him for his mental strength. She wished Geron had Spock's abilities. Thinking about the doctor who lay in his quarters with a collapsed mind stung. *I really must visit him*, she thought. Despite having the excuse that things aboard the ship had been frantic since the Son's attack, in truth she knew that she was afraid of seeing Geron in his diminished condition.

Kromm's growling brought her back to reality. "Well, let's hear it then, Ambassador."

The half-Vulcan folded his hands in front of his stomach. "We have learned much on Xhehenem and Bharatrum about the ancient Renao legend of the Son of the Ancient Reds. Ten thousand years ago, he came to Iad where the ancient Renao lived. We learned how he was responsible for an era of fury and desperation, and that he was finally defeated and bound by a being called the White Guardian, who subsequently resettled the Renao on Onferin."

Adams frowned. "Are you going to suggest that we chase after that legend? That we search for this White Guardian?"

Spock raised his eyebrows. "Indeed I am, Captain. Consider—we also deemed Iad to be a legend, just as many of the modern Renao do. Yet we discovered the ruins of an ancient civilization there, as well as a being that fits the description of the Son so precisely that we use that name for it. Many details that this legend tells us appear to have a plausible historical background. Thus it is only logical to assume that the White Guardian also exists."

"But according to the legend he disappeared some nine thousand years ago," zh'Thiin said. "Even if we assume that he belongs to a similarly long-lived species as the Son does, we have no idea where to search for him. The galaxy is pretty damn big."

"It pains me to say this, but it might also be conceivable that he—just like the Beta XII-A life form—comes from another dimension," Mendon added. "Possibly one where radiation zones such as the one around Iad are part of the laws of nature, unlike in our own universe."

On the other side of the table, Nuk emitted a croaking, cackling noise. "Traveling through dimensions searching for a mythical being? I'd really like to see us try selling that one to the High Council."

"We won't," said Kromm. "The notion is absurd."

Spock raised a wrinkled hand defensively. "If I may continue?"

"Go on, Ambassador," Adams said. "How are we supposed to find the Guardian?"

"With the help of the sensor data from the radiation zone that Commander Mendon has collected. We agree that the hyper-physical fluctuation status in that zone is highly unusual, considering the laws of nature that we are familiar with."

Everyone nodded silently.

"Then our next step would be to turn to Memory Alpha, the largest database in the Federation."

Mendon, standing next to zh'Thiin, dragged hectically on his respirator, which he usually did when he considered a plan particularly fascinating. "Outstanding idea. If we send all recordings of the entity's energy patterns and the radiation zone to Memory Alpha, the computers there might find similar recordings in one of the more obscure databases in the library's memory banks."

"Precisely," said Spock. "And that might provide a clue as to the whereabouts of the White Guardian."

"As long as the Son and the Guardian originate from the same region," zh'Thiin said.

"I consider that to be highly likely," the ambassador replied. "The Guardian was not only able to defeat the Son, he also displayed an interest to do so and to effectively imprison the energy life form afterward. The term 'guardian' suggests that the second being had been sent deliberately in order to set bounds to the first one."

The security chief nodded in understanding. "Like a law-enforcement officer catching an escaped prisoner."

"Correct. In the meantime, I suggest we return to Bharatrum. It was there where we met the majority of Renao believing in Iad and the Son. Perhaps we might uncover more details pertaining to this legend that might be useful."

"That's better than sitting around here twiddling our thumbs." Adams nodded, pleased. "Right, sounds like we have a plan. Kromm, any objections?"

The Klingon shook his head. "Send your data to your archives, for all the good it may do. You have only twenty hours to make considerable progress in the fight against the Purifying Flame and to stop it from being a clear and present threat to the Empire."

"*We*, Kromm," Adams said calmly, "*we* have twenty hours. Once the ultimatum has come and gone, we all will have failed. You will have forfeited your opportunity to gain honor through this mission. Or do you seriously believe that the generals waiting at the border with their fleets will share their honor with you once they have invaded the Lembatta Cluster?"

The captain was rewarded for his words with irritated silence. Zh'Thiin almost burst out laughing.

Obviously Kromm had finally figured out that they were all in the same boat. A very small boat in the vastness of space.

8

NOVEMBER 26, 2385

Palais de la Concorde, Paris
Earth

Nothing was worse than the nights. Kellessar zh'Tarash had been president of the United Federation of Planets for three weeks, and she had learned more about this office than she had ever expected to learn. But one lesson definitely stood out from the others: nothing was worse than the nights. Outside the windows of the Palais de la Concorde, the seat of the Federation government in Paris, another night was about to conquer Earth—and zh'Tarash's mind.

19:00. The large city on the Seine was smartening up for the night. Cafés and brasseries were closing, bars and clubs were opening for business. Some night owls were already prowling the quaint streets, and the Tour Eiffel was illuminated in blue artificial light. Night was approaching, zh'Tarash sensed it.

And during the night her concerns weighed down on her even more than during the day.

Not if I can do anything about it, the president vowed to herself. *Not this time.*

"Your visitors have arrived, *Zha* President."

Turning around, zh'Tarash tore herself away from the view. "Thank you, Dimitri," she said to her deputy chief of staff who had appeared to fetch her. Dimitri Velonov smiled encouragingly, but he was tense. "Has our... *special* guest also arrived yet?"

Velonov shook his head. "I'm afraid not, *Zha* President. To be honest... To be honest, we don't even know whether he received our invitation."

Zh'Tarash nodded. Velonov was doing his best to conceal his thoughts, albeit not very successfully. He didn't expect their "special guest" to make his way to Paris. No one here did. Except the president herself.

"He will come," zh'Tarash said gently but with steadfast conviction—and with the courage she would need to defy the night. "When he does, will you please send him in straight away?"

"Of course, *Zha* President." Velonov nodded. "If you're ready...?"

Together, the two so vastly different government members—the bearded man from Earth and the Andorian woman with blue skin—walked down the corridor. They were heading for the Wescott conference room on the fifteenth floor.

"*Zha* President," Admiral Leonard James Akaar greeted zh'Tarash as soon as she walked through the doorway. The Capellan with silver hair rose behind the conference table where he had been sitting with his back to the window. "Good evening."

"The same to you, Admiral," she replied, walking to the front end of the long table where Velonov had already put down a cup of steaming Andorian *katheka* and a padd for her. She nodded gratefully at her human staff member, who left the conference room, closing the door behind him. Once he was gone, she turned to her second guest.

Ambassador K'mtok sat across the table from Akaar.

While the Starfleet admiral and commander-in-chief appeared polite and calm, the representative of the Klingon Empire seemed to be seething—and apparently he wouldn't keep it inside for much longer.

"Ambassador," she addressed him, not shying away from a certain sharp edge in her voice. "How nice of you to make the time. After our last encounter I wasn't sure whether you would grant us another audience."

K'mtok snorted. His long hair and beard were both graying, and he wore a warrior's armor under his long and loose-fitting cassock. He was clearly furious, and all too happy to take the bait. "Spare me the snide remarks, zh'Tarash!" he snapped at the president with a dangerous, not at all diplomatic glint in his dark eyes. "Considering the circumstances I have no choice but to speak with you, whether it's important to me or not."

"And these circumstances are…?"

Akaar answered this question, and suddenly zh'Tarash's night threatened to become even darker: "The ambassador is referring to the Renao shipyard."

"Damn right I am!" K'mtok hit the conference table with his flat hand so hard that some of the *katheka* spilled over. His words were like a predator's low growl, and his broad shoulders twitched belligerently. "General Akbas reported to me about it moments ago, *Zha* President. And I promise you, my rage is nothing in comparison to that of the High Council back home on Qo'noS!"

Zh'Tarash didn't hesitate. "I understand your displeasure, Ambassador, but—"

"Displeasure?" he interrupted her. Little drops of saliva sprayed from his mouth, raining onto the table's surface. "I can assure you we are far beyond displeasure. The High

Council has been watching this bizarre conduct for far too long. Not a second longer! Qo'noS will—"

"Qo'noS will adhere to our agreements set forth after the events at Xhehenem!" It was her turn to interrupt him, and each word was as sharp as the blade of an *ushaan-tor*. "Nothing has changed about the goals of our mutual mission. The *Bortas* and the *Prometheus* believe they have found the source of the Renao threat. Currently, they are working on putting an end to this threat."

"Iad is completely irrelevant right now!" K'mtok's roar echoed from the walls in the Wescott Room. The Klingon had jumped to his feet, and he had completely lost control. He had never been a particularly controlled diplomat in the first place. Several times his stubborn, unreasonable manner had strained the political relations with Qo'noS rather than improving them. "The danger does not stem from Iad," he continued, slightly more restrained—but no less furious. "Iad is just a pathetic world. We can take care of it when the time is right."

"And where do you see the biggest danger?" Akaar asked tersely.

"All over the Lembatta Cluster!" K'mtok shook his head. "If you still can't see that you're an even bigger fool than I thought. No wonder that your oh-so-virtuous Federation has been stumbling from one crisis to the next during the past few years. Even if someone presses a *bat'leth* against your throat, you still want to negotiate instead of fight." Akaar raised both hands in protest but K'mtok hadn't finished yet. "The Renao are the problem. Each and every one of them is a ticking time bomb. You saw the hate message. You saw how many suicide fighters the Purifying Flame have at their disposal. Stopping them is of the utmost importance right now. Let Iad be the root of all evil, but it's the fanatics who threaten our worlds. We must come down on them with all our might. And since we don't know who has been affected by Iad's madness, we have to assume that the entire region is dangerous."

"According to the *Prometheus* some members of this species are withstanding the radiation longer than others," zh'Tarash said.

"So what? Is that supposed to be some kind of consolation? Can you tell by looking at the red-skins whether they will become assassins today or next week? No, you *can't*!"

"And that's why they are all your enemies?" Akaar said, furious. "You consider that a justification for genocide? With all due respect, Ambassador, that is despicable!"

"Urgently required, that's what it is," K'mtok said. "And it has been right from the onset. This hate message full of fighters capable of cloaking proves that point."

Zh'Tarash wasn't prone to emotional outbursts. She was inclined to consider sobriety and foresight much more productive than short-sighted actions, but K'mtok just managed to push her over the edge. She jumped to her feet and cried out, "That's enough! Ambassador, we're running around in circles. We're not getting anywhere—and we didn't the last time we met. And the time before that." She looked at K'mtok sternly. "Tell Chancellor Martok that the Federation doesn't see any reason to negate the Xhehenem Resolution. What was valid yesterday is still valid today. Innocent lives are innocent lives, and warriors of the Empire hungry for glory and revenge who shoot first and ask questions later are the last thing the farmers on Xhehenem and the fishermen on Onferin need right now."

The ambassador laughed dryly. "There are lives at stake,

Madame President—*Klingon* lives. The High Council is obligated to protect them, and it will do just that, no matter what the Federation thinks about it."

"Once the agreed ultimatum has passed," Akaar said.

But K'mtok didn't seem to care about that. "Right *now!*"

Zh'Tarash took a deep breath. She had been worried that their talks might take this turn, and therefore she had one last ace up her sleeve. But would it be enough?

"I'd like to suggest a compromise, if I may," she said, sitting back down. As quickly as she had allowed her anger to flare, she was able to conceal it again. "As of now, I will open the borders—*our* borders, not the Renao borders. If Qo'noS wants to mobilize its war fleet, they may enter Federation space unhindered and advance to the edge of the Lembatta Cluster. They may patrol the ship routes in the area and keep an eye on the cluster; guard it, if you want. Get in position. That's what you want, isn't it?"

Suspiciously, K'mtok eyed her. "Compromise means that you want something in return. What is it?"

Zh'Tarash interlaced her fingers on the table surface. "I want the ultimatum off the table. The *Bortas* and the *Prometheus* are currently making considerable progress in their investigations. It wouldn't be beneficial if our and your fleet invaded the cluster now as it would unnecessarily inflame the situation. You want protection for the Empire. I'm offering to give you access to all systems near the cluster that are relevant for your security, so you can position your ships there. But you must give captains Kromm and Adams more time. We don't want a local crisis to endanger the alliance between our nations now, do we?" Her voice was quiet, but the unspoken threat was unmistakable.

K'mtok stared at her in silence. His fury hadn't subsided

but her offer had taken the Klingon by surprise, and it got him thinking. "I can promise nothing," he finally said, proving that there had to be a tiny fragment of an actual diplomat hidden somewhere within him.

"Of course not," zh'Tarash said with a nod.

"And I doubt the High Council will agree to it."

She nodded silently.

"But I will at least talk to Qo'noS. We will see…"

"Thank you very much, Ambassador." Zh'Tarash got up. "Let us know what Martok decides."

He snorted, complying with the unspoken request and rising to his feet, then walked to the door without another word.

Right at that moment the door was opened from the outside, and another man entered the room. He wore gray clothes, and his hair had been combed straight.

K'mtok stopped dead in his tracks, staring at the newcomer—before bursting into laughter. "Well, if *that*'s your idea of solving problems, *Zha* President," he said, pushing past the person, "nothing will surprise me anymore." With these words, he closed the door behind him.

Kalavak had stopped, nonplussed, and looked at zh'Tarash and Akaar. "An… interesting welcome, really," said the Romulan.

"That was a farewell." Zh'Tarash stepped toward Kalavak. "*This* is a welcome. *Jolan tru*, Ambassador."

"Former ambassador, I thought." Akaar had also gotten up. He looked just as surprised as he sounded. "I'm glad to see you, Mr. Kalavak."

The corners of the Romulan's mouth twitched slightly. "A sentence I don't hear very often from your mouth, Admiral." He nodded at him in greeting. "But I understand what you're attempting to say. I am now... what do you humans call it? The lesser of two evils."

For years Kalavak had been the Romulan Star Empire's diplomatic representative on Earth. The relations between the Federation and the Romulan senate had been difficult, and for the most part the negotiations with Kalavak hadn't been easy either. But zh'Tarash had invited him to this meeting nonetheless—and not his successor, the Tholian woman Tezrene, who spoke for the entire Typhon Pact, although her attendance at this meeting would have been much less doubtful.

Since the Romulan Star Empire had become part of the Typhon Pact along with avowed adversaries of the Federation such as the Breen, the Kinshaya, and the Tholians, relations between Paris and the Romulan capital, Ki Baratan, were even more fragile than ever before. Just like her late predecessor Nan Bacco, President zh'Tarash tried her utmost to keep the peace with Romulus, and she made every effort to reunite both people—or better still, the entire Pact and the Khitomer powers—at the round table. Bacco had already made considerable progress. But time was of the essence, and zh'Tarash knew that the Pact would deliberately delay giving her the urgently required information, and presumably they would be much more reluctant to pass on that information to her than, as Kalavak himself had put it, the lesser of two evils.

"You are here," stated the Andorian emphatically as if those words said everything. She pointed at K'mtok's vacated chair at the conference table. "And I hope you've got some answers for us."

The former ambassador sighed, settling in the chair. Akaar and zh'Tarash also sat down. Kalavak rested his forearms on the table, looking at the president, and nodded. "I do indeed, but I suspect that they do not correspond with your hopes."

"Believe me, Mr. Kalavak," Akaar said quietly, "our hopes are miniscule indeed."

A hint of a bitter smile played around the lips of the visitor from Romulus, and he folded his hands. "Right then. I've asked around with my former contacts. Discreetly, of course, and through unofficial channels. I can assure you that my homeworld does not have any business relations with the Renao or the Purifying Flame. Least of all in the weapons export sector."

Zh'Tarash leaned back in her chair, thinking. Kalavak's words underlined the official statement of the Romulan senate and Praetor Gell Kamemor, who had an open and liberal mindset. That was reassuring, but did it change anything?

"The Purifying Flame does have these attack fighters with cloaking ability," the president said. "That's a sad fact."

"And their design is very much like that of your *Scorpion* fighters, Kalavak," Akaar added. "The same as the wreckage that the *Prometheus* discovered near Starbase 91."

"But just like then, my government doesn't have anything to do with it," Kalavak said. "We don't make deals with these terrorists."

"Achernar II does."

The Romulan regarded Akaar with a tired, reproachful gaze. "Oh please, Admiral. Achernar II was many things, but not a branch of the current Romulan senate. Besides, we have already arrested the members of the smuggler ring that was active there." He looked at zh'Tarash. "If the Flame has ships of this design at their disposal they must build them somewhere else."

The president grabbed her cup but the *katheka* had gone cold in the meantime. Cold as the night. "You're talking about your government, Mr. Kalavak," said zh'Tarash. "But what about the Typhon Pact? Are you also speaking for your allies?"

This time the Romulan laughed quietly, shaking his head. "The Pact, *Zha* President, acts on behalf of its members. They wouldn't sell any Romulan products without Romulans' knowledge."

"And you're absolutely sure about that?" Akaar sounded skeptical. "You'd vouch for the Breen, the Kinshaya, the Tholians?"

"I *understand* the Pact," Kalavak said firmly and didn't let himself be provoked in the slightest. "Can you say the same, Admiral?"

The Capellan stood his ground. "The Pact is probably very interested in destabilizing the quadrant. A strong Purifying Flame might soon lead to a weak Klingon Empire or a weak Federation."

"You forget that we are also targets of these terrorists."

"Allegedly."

"Actually," the Romulan stated quietly but sternly, "I repeat, Admiral: we—Romulus as a sovereign political entity, as well as the Typhon Pact—do not maintain any kind of business relations with the aggressors from the Lembatta Cluster." With this, he rose. His gaze was fixed on Akaar but his words were quite obviously also addressed to zh'Tarash. "Whether you believe this statement is entirely up to you. I do not care either way. But *you* asked *me* to be here, not the other way round, to give you this answer. Now you must decide whether it was worth your efforts."

"It was," said the president. She rose to her feet, nodding respectfully at the Romulan. "You have our thanks, Mr.

Kalavak. It… it's always worthwhile maintaining old contacts."

The visitor tilted his head once, but zh'Tarash was unable to determine whether this was a nod, a confirmation, or something else entirely. Then he left the room.

"No Romulans," said Akaar. He sounded only semi-relieved. "And no Typhon Pact, either."

"But also no Klingons," she added quietly. A deep sigh escaped from her throat as she left the table to stand by the window. Paris had grown darker but the night appeared less dark to her than it had done earlier. "At least something."

"Let's hope so, *Zha* President," Akaar whispered behind her back. "Let's hope so."

9
NOVEMBER 26, 2385

Kharanto, Xhehenem
Nuari system, Lembatta Cluster

Dawn painted the little town by the sea in a warm glow. Some sun beams reflected from the glass façades of the arcologies, and a pleasant breeze blew from the east across the sea. It smelled of algae and vastness, and, most of all, stability.

Brossal ak Ghantur knew that the wind was lying. He saw it in the faces that passed him by, and in those of his own young family.

Nothing was stable anymore.

"Why do we have to go there in the first place?" asked Hiskaath, Brossal's firstborn, behind him, not for the first time. "They made it perfectly clear during Iad's Awakening that—"

"This is not about Iad's Awakening," Brossal sternly interrupted his cheeky offspring—also not for the first time. "It's about the Harmony of Spheres. As always. And you know that full well, Hisk."

Hiskaath remained obstinate. "Iad's Awakening is about the Harmony of Spheres. That's my point. We have to wander new paths if we want to protect the spheres, and—"

That was enough. Turning on his heel, Brossal stared at his child. He didn't even try to hide his anger. "Are you going to talk back for a while to come yet, or are you done now?"

Both Hiskaath and Brossal's other child, Hiskaath's sister Alyys, winced visibly. So did Brossal's partner Kynnil. All three of them walked the customary two steps behind the family patriarch.

Brossal continued sternly: "We're going to the evening prayer." Why didn't they understand him any longer? Where did this terrible disobedience come from? "As we do every day. Because we are Renao, and our ways hold value for us. They give us strength, just like they give our spheres strength. We honor the spheres in the same way as our fathers and forefathers have done. That's the way it is."

All of them had stopped in the middle of the road. Aly looked insecurely at her mother, Hisk met Brossal's gaze and held it—defiantly, but with silent obedience. From the corner of his eye, Brossal noticed other inhabitants from the arcologies on their way to prayers. He saw men in festive dark robes similar to his own, followed by their kin.

The father of two noted that, apparently, an unusual number of discussions were taking place this evening, if not protests.

But it's not just the women and children. There are also men calling into question the use of prayers, or am I wrong? They are doubting the benefits of consistency.

His concern was growing, as he had been observing this phenomenon for weeks now—and not just within his own small family. More and more citizens of Kharanto seemed to be breaking with their old ways. It all had started relatively harmlessly with a symbol of the Purifying Flame scribbled on a house wall here, and a mentally disturbed— in Brossal's eyes, anyway—young Renao woman who tried to engage passers-by like himself in conversations about the "aggressors from beyond the borders" and "the resistance of our brothers and sisters from the other cluster worlds."

These occurrences had bewildered Brossal, but he

had been able to ignore them, dismiss them as isolated incidents. But it hadn't stopped there. That first Renao woman was followed by others, and within a few weeks there had been a seemingly endless stream of speakers and agitators. Preachers who spoke of Iad and sphere harmonies being destroyed and the power of the many. Youths who distributed flyers in the streets and parks. People in the *ley*-taverns and in public places in Kharanto who spoke not of their everyday business or home lives, but instead about Klingons, Cardassians, humans, Romulans, Vulcans, Ferengi and other strange aliens. They talked about spaceships from foreign star powers traveling across the spheres of the Renao, as if they hadn't caused enough trouble in their own spheres. People clenched their fists in anger when talking about them.

Frequently, someone would call openly for violence. Preachers and speakers encouraged the people to take up arms, and to stop the deluded beings from beyond the cluster whose actions disturbed the Harmony of Spheres. The more they talked, the more their efforts seemed to come to fruition.

Every day Brossal witnessed it anew. In the streets of his harbor town, within the corridors of his home arcology, and even on the offshore algae growth station where he worked, he saw Kharanto's citizens increasingly agreeing with the assertions of these radicals. He had even heard of violent altercations during the mass rallies called Iad's Awakening, which were held by the self-proclaimed preachers traveling the lands. Renao attacked Renao! There had even been casualties! And the situation on other cluster worlds was supposedly similar.

Brossal shuddered inwardly. What did he care about other worlds? Since when did a Renao care for incidents that happened outside of his home? And how was it possible that Renao—proud and reverent Renao, of all people!—could be enticed to employ violence against outworlders and even their own neighbors?

It didn't make any sense. It defied everything that Brossal deemed normal, important, and right. The preachers said that the outworlders were dangerous malefactors, but even if that were true, wasn't it a sacrilege if a Renao's sight went into the distance rather than in front of his own feet? Wasn't that also a sin against the harmony and the old but incredibly valuable traditions?

But no one seemed to care about that. Not even in Brossal's family.

"*We* are weakening the spheres," Hiskaath mumbled grimly, but he walked the path towards the temple like a good boy, trotting behind his father. "Because we stand idly by while strangers abuse them."

For a brief moment Brossal was tempted to chastise his child, but he would not teach nonviolence by employing violence. So he kept quiet, setting one foot in front of the other. He didn't turn back again and didn't stop until they reached the temple atop a small rise west of the settlement. He opened the door for Kynnil and his two children.

"We will pray," he repeated quietly. Kharanto's citizens were pouring into the temple from everywhere, and he had no intention of having this conversation in front of an audience. "Anything else would be a sin against harmony. A Renao knows their place, and this is ours—whether you like it or not, Hisk."

And why don't you like it? Brossal didn't like to admit it, but his family's changing attitudes presented him with a horror that welled up inside him. That horror was colder than the air inside the temple. His neighbors and work colleagues were one thing. They displayed appalling stupidity, but that was their problem. But Hisk and Aly and Kynn were his family. *The most important home I have, and I don't understand them anymore.* Worse, he was scared for them. The violence that lingered in Kharanto like an as-yet-unspoken curse made him fear for their safety.

Would he be able to protect them if things boiled over? Would they *let* him protect them? Or would the three people with whom he shared his life want to stand in the front line when fists began flying?

Is my entire world doomed to descend into madness, and I'm the only one immune to it?

Filled with concern and fear and regret, Brossal closed his eyes and began to pray.

The brief evening ceremony was about to come to an end when the sirens began wailing. Confused, Brossal looked around. Not many of Kharanto's inhabitants had turned out today—their numbers dwindled daily—and wherever he looked, he saw confusion and bewilderment that matched his own.

And then he heard the fire. It began quietly—a gentle sizzling and crackling sound reached his ears from behind him—and increased in volume with every passing second.

Brossal whirled around. At first, he doubted his senses. Dark specks had appeared on the back wall of the small temple and they grew as fast as lightning. Small but steadily growing flames ate their way through the wooden entrance door while black smoke billowed underneath into the temple.

The vestibule is on fire!

Seconds later, the broad and colorful mosaic window to the right of the visitors' seats shattered, shards flying everywhere, broken by a narrow tube the size of a forearm that had been thrown through it. It hit the temple floor, rolling a bit before lying still and flickering.

"Explosives!" someone yelled.

Immediately, panic broke out. Brossal felt Kynn's hands on his arm, and he heard Aly's frightened gasping. The small lamps on the tube flickered faster than before.

Horrified, he grabbed Hisk's and Aly's hands, dragging them with him. Kynn clutched his arm as if the world was an ocean and she was about to drown in it. They reached the door in no time.

Another attendant of prayers was already attempting to kick the door down. He was successful but his robe caught fire. The people around him had to roll the panicking man around on the floor in order to extinguish the flames.

Brossal glanced into the vestibule… or what was left of it. An inferno raged there, the entire entrance engulfed in flames. The algae farmer had never before experienced heat like this on his skin. They would not be able to escape this way.

Still, they had to try. They couldn't go back, so they had to risk going forward.

"Stay close to me, all of you," Brossal shouted. "Kynn, Hisk, follow me. Aly, come here." Grabbing the horrified little girl, he cradled her in both arms, leaning forward to shield her with his upper body as best he could—and darted forward.

Just as soon as he stepped into the vestibule, the temple exploded.

The night was pleasantly cool, which was at least something. But Brossal ak Ghantur hardly noticed it. It seemed to him as if he would never be able to feel anything ever again.

"Kynn." Devastated, he knelt beside the body of his partner. Hiskaath and Alyys had miraculously made it out without sustaining any noteworthy injuries. He himself had received several burns, but nothing fatal.

Kynnil on the other hand… "Kynn."

After the blast of the detonation, the temple roof had caved in. Debris had buried several people who had been trying to escape. Kynn had been one of them.

Brossal had noticed it too late when he was outside. When the rescue forces arrived to fight the fire, survivors had been sitting by the wayside, suffering from shock. They had cried, hoped, and despaired. The rescue teams had doused the flames eventually, but they could only recover dead bodies.

Like Kynn's.

And they had uncovered who was responsible for this atrocity. Now that most of the smoke had dissipated, they could see it clearly: a head-high scarlet symbol had been painted by hand on the outside of the temple wall.

The emblem of the Purifying Flame.

"Because we didn't do anything," Hisk mumbled. Brossal held him in his arms, just like the sobbing Aly. But although Hisk's tone of voice indicated sadness, he didn't cry. "That's the reason why this happened. Because, otherwise, we wouldn't have changed anything."

That's the reason why this happened. Brossal looked at his eldest child. Incredulity mixed with consternation when he realized how matter-of-factly his offspring spoke about what had happened here. How detached and insightful. *That's the reason.*

Action and reaction, guilt and atonement, sacrilege and tenet. Kynn was dead—and three other Renao along with her—because people with the same mindset as Hisk believed they should send a message to people with Brossal's mindset, to make their point clear. Misguided people who might even have lost their minds and probably felt that their assassination was necessary and justified. The sphere was everything, after all, and every Renao knew that. And the bombers of Kharanto apparently considered the protection of the spheres more important than an individual life—or four. If the result hadn't been this horrific, Brossal would have almost understood them.

Helpless, he hugged his children even closer while the night surrounded them. Kynn, his beloved Kynn, had fallen victim to the madness that had infested his home. That realization was too much for him, and he closed his eyes.

He had no idea how much time passed. Eternities, moments, or something in between. It didn't matter. Time didn't exist any longer… not in this new reality without Kynn. Brossal felt the warm bodies of his children next to him and Aly's salty tears on his chest. He smelled her scent, and that was all that mattered. The now. The past had just become too painful to bear, and the future looked to be even worse.

Eventually, Brossal looked up. Mounim ak Hazzoh, Brossal's shift colleague from the growth station, approached him from the crowd and stood by Kynn's lifeless remains. Behind him was the smoldering debris of the temple. Brossal had no idea why Mounim was here.

"All this is your fault," Mounim said in a scathing whisper. He had a glint in his eyes that was brighter than the earlier fire and told of unfathomable fury and outrage. "All of you. You brought this upon yourselves. You refuse to face the truth. Instead of fighting back and defending the harmony, you're clinging to yesterday." He shook his head.

His hands were clenched to fists, twitching uncontrollably. "Bross, you shouldn't be surprised that today is trampling all over you. None of you should."

Brossal opened his mouth but was unable to say anything. Licking his lips, he tried again. "Wh… What are you saying?"

Mounim glanced over his shoulder and watched the rescue teams work among the debris, the other mourners, and the gawkers, then turned back to face him. "Join us, Bross. Come to your senses. You're in the way of the sphere if you reject today. You stand in the way of safety. And we can't and won't have consideration for the likes of you anymore. The enemy is right within our spheres, Bross! They have thrown their worlds into chaos, and now they come to destroy ours as well. And our governing bodies stand idly by!" Mounim spat on the ground contemptuously. "No, you hear me? We won't let that happen! We need to act now in order to prevent things from getting worse. We need to take a stand. We need to make sacrifices. Listen to me, Bross: the time for compromises and waiting is finally over. Not just in Kharanto, right? Everywhere! On Xhehenem, on Onferin, on Acina and Catoumni—everywhere. Because there's no other way. Because we need to get involved if we—and all living beings in all other spheres—don't want to lose everything. The flame must purify, my friend. Else we will suffocate in dirt. So you should be smarter in future, Bross. Do me that favor. Do it for your offspring. For the good of home, of harmony—and for your own good."

With these words Mounim turned away and disappeared into the crowd.

Take a stand. Make sacrifices. The phrases bounced around in Brossal's mind like echoes in the caves down by the sea.

Act in order to prevent things from getting worse. Everywhere. And suddenly, it dawned on him who had hurled the explosive charge through the window.

It was true—the perpetrators deemed their actions to be the justified means to a vindicating end. Renao attacked Renao and called it self-protection. *Sphere*-protection. They didn't even see the error of their ways, the terrible disgrace they brought upon themselves.

"Do you understand now?" asked Hisk. Tears had welled up in his son's eyes. He looked at his father with a trembling lower lip. Not just from mourning, realized Brossal, but from regret.

And Brossal nodded. "Yes, son," he whispered with a heavy heart. "Yes, I understand."

There was only one way out. He needed to leave his home sphere.

10
NOVEMBER 26, 2385

U.S.S. Prometheus, en route to Bharatrum

"The packet for Memory Alpha is on its way, Captain," Winter reported.

"Thank you, Ensign." Adams glanced around the bridge. They were on their way back to Bharatrum along with the *Bortas*, where they would arrive in the late afternoon, ship time. The repairs had almost been completed, Kirk and Mendon were pondering an improvement for the shield regeneration routines, and Doctor Calloway tended to the sick telepaths of his crew. There wasn't much for him to do at the moment.

"I'll be in my ready room," he announced, getting up and leaving the bridge. He crossed a short corridor to reach his room at the back of bridge deck. After he entered, he went straight to the small replicator in the corner. "Coffee, special blend Adams-02."

With a shimmer, a coffee mug containing steaming dark brown liquid appeared. Lifting the mug with both hands and bringing it to his nose, Adams deeply inhaled the wonderful aroma. He sighed appreciatively.

Of course, every replicator on the ship was capable of making coffee; the special blend Adams-02, however, was only available from this device. He had had Kirk build in a special sample buffer where he had stored some of the quadrant's finest coffee blends, straight after grinding them with his manual coffee grinder, producing the desired fineness. It took a certain degree of decadence to drink a Jamaican Blue Mountain coffee—of which barely twenty thousand barrels were harvested each year—while being in the middle of a war zone, but Adams had decided very early on that a captain was allowed to entertain at least one guilty pleasure.

He had just settled behind his desk and taken one sip when the door chime sounded. Adams briefly closed his eyes, before placing the mug in front of him on the desk and straightening himself up slightly.

"Come."

The door slid open, and Roaas stood in the doorway. "Captain, do you have a moment?"

"For you, Roaas, always. Come in."

The Caitian entered and the door hissed closed behind him.

"Coffee? I still have some of my Blue Mountain blend in the replicator."

Roaas shook his furry head. "No thanks. You know that I don't have any appreciation for good coffee. It doesn't taste any different than the brew they serve in the mess. It would be a waste of your special blends."

"It was worth a try," Adams replied, smiling. "At least take a seat." He gestured toward the chair across the desk from him, before grabbing his coffee mug and sipping from it. "What can I do for you?"

Roaas sat. His ears were twitching the way they always did when something bothered him and he didn't know how to handle it. He sat silently for a moment, seemingly gathering his thoughts before speaking up: "Captain, I'm not here for myself, but for you."

"Am I giving you reason to be concerned, old friend?"

"Let me put it this way—I'd like to prevent you from making a wrong decision."

"Explain."

"Captain, I know how much you dislike Kromm's behavior. I feel more or less the same way. He's hungry for glory and a warmonger—even worse than usual for a Klingon, and they aren't good traits while we're in the position we're currently in."

Adams grimaced. "Tell me something I don't know." He took another sip from his coffee. The Blue Mountain blend was truly a culinary delight, but the reminder of Kromm's narrow-mindedness had somewhat spoiled it.

"I also know," Roaas continued, "that you want to bring the situation within the Lembatta Cluster to a peaceful end under all circumstances, just like Admiral Akaar and President zh'Tarash do."

"Who doesn't? Except for a few hardliners inside the High Council. The Renao as a people are not our enemy. At best, only a handful of misguided fanatics in the shape of the Purifying Flame are, and even that is questionable, considering our latest discovery on Iad. Are those fanatics really culprits? Or are they just victims of a creeping horror that the Son has instilled into them?"

Roaas nodded. "All that is true. But we must not lose sight of the facts. Thousands have already died on Starbase 91, Tika IV, and Cestus III. We must prevent another attack at all costs."

"That goes without saying. What is your point?"

"My point is that we shouldn't sink our teeth too deeply into the problem of the Son. We thought that Iad was the key to this crisis. That may be the case, but defeating the energy entity on Iad should be a long-term objective. Isn't it much more important to find the headquarters of the Purifying Flame first? The place from where they launch their solar-jumpers and kamikaze fighters?"

Adams looked at him, thinking, *If we can't destroy the evil at the source, we need to contain its excesses.* Those had been Kromm's words during their meeting. "You think I'm throwing myself enthusiastically on the mystery of the Son because I don't want to accept that fighting the Renao directly might be our only realistic chance to guarantee the safety of the Federation and the Klingon Empire?"

His first officer nodded gravely. "I don't like this situation either, believe me. I prefer a clearly defined enemy, like the Borg were. There was no room for hesitation or doubt. The Borg wanted to eliminate us, so we had to eliminate them first. This time, it's all much more difficult—at least where the ethical side is concerned. But we still mustn't forget that we're a warship, and we have been sent to the cluster by Admiral Akaar in order to eliminate a danger for the Federation. We have been tracing this danger for almost a month now. We're getting closer to our goal. Can we afford to be distracted by some scientific anomaly?"

"An extremely dangerous scientific anomaly," Adams said. "We haven't heard from the Beta XII-A entity for years, but I'm sure there have been enough wars to satiate its hunger. Only the creature knows how many battles during these wars were caused by it. But one thing is certain—under no circumstances must another being of the size and potential power of the one we discovered on Iad become strong enough to roam freely in the galaxy. It would lead to chaos and destruction of unprecedented and horrific proportions. And to be perfectly honest, I don't want to rely on the Q Continuum to come to the rescue of us mortals. After all, they stood by during the collapse of the Tkon Empire before intervening, according to that report Captain Picard made a while back."

The Caitian's whiskers quivered. "Yes, I haven't forgotten that, or that one of the Q rescued the *Enterprise*-D from first contact with the Borg."

Adams's eyes focused on his first officer over the rim of his mug. "You don't have to worry, Roaas. I'm still keeping my eye on the big picture. Yes, I'm irritated with Kromm. Yes, the Son is influencing all of us, and not in a good way. And yes, I'm well and truly sick of war. That may all be getting me off-track, but I still have you, Spock, Rozhenko, and maybe even that damn Klingon captain to offer me new perspectives and focus my senses on the things that need to be done. So I thank you for your concern, my friend, unnecessary though it may be."

"I guess it's my duty as first officer to be concerned." The corners of Roaas's mouth twitched slightly.

"Absolutely. And I think we're on the right track. The Purifying Flame has been very active on Bharatrum. So by going there, we're combining our search for the White Guardian with the search for the core of the fanatics. Apart from that, we should wait for the data from Memory Alpha before deciding how to proceed. And if necessary we can separate *Prometheus* and be active in several places at once."

The communications system on his desk sprang to life. *"Carson to Adams."*

Adams saw that Roaas wanted to get up, but gestured for him to wait. Activating the intercom, he set his mug down. "What is it, Commander?"

"Captain, we're receiving a message from the Venture.

Admiral Gepta demands to speak with you."

Adams and Roaas exchanged surprised glances. The deployment of the Chelon with rigorous military mindset to the Lembatta Cluster from Starfleet Command was a clear indication of just how concerned the decision-makers back home on Earth really were. He got to his feet.

"I'm on my way to the bridge." As Adams walked around his desk, he longingly stared at the hot drink standing there. The crisis within the Lembatta Cluster didn't even permit him to have a good cup of coffee in peace.

"Captain, we have good news for you." The turtle-like Chelon stared intently at Adams from the main screen. *"A battle group consisting of Federation and Klingon ships were able to capture one of the Renao solar-jumpers within the Theris system on the periphery of the Lembatta Cluster. Annoyingly, we couldn't capture the crew alive, and their navigation computer is encrypted, though we're working on decrypting it. But we also managed to secure ten brand-new Scorpion replicas, and our specialists are examining them thoroughly as we speak. It's only a question of time before we find out where the Purifying Flame get their materials from, and where they put them together."*

"The *Prometheus* and the *Bortas* have been following a lead regarding a potential shipyard, as you probably know," replied Adams. "So far, all leads point to Bharatrum. Before we could engage in further investigations there our mission was derailed by finding the *Valiant*'s log buoy, which led us to Iad."

Gepta snapped impatiently with his ocher-colored jaws. *"I am up to date on your mission reports, Captain. In fact, you have not found a shipyard or a base anywhere in the Bharatrum system or the Souhla system, isn't that right?"*

Adams felt like a schoolboy whose performance had been lacking and who was facing a dressing-down from his principal. "Unfortunately that's correct, sir. The locals are extremely uncooperative, and our mandate doesn't give us much leeway when it comes to ignoring the wishes of the governing bodies within the Lembatta Cluster. However, we gained important new insights on Iad regarding the source of the entire crisis. The report was submitted to Starfleet Command last night."

"Mhm, must be still lying around somewhere in Headquarters." Gepta let out a disgruntled growl. *"Send a copy to me on the Venture."*

"Right away, sir." Adams signaled Winter with his eyes to forward the relevant log entries.

"What is your position?" the admiral asked.

"We're en route to the Bharatrum system for further investigations. Iad is a dead end for the time being. You'll find all the details in my report."

"Very well." Gepta nodded. *"Patrol the Bharatrum system. Find further clues regarding the Purifying Flame. And expect our call just as soon as we have determined the origin of this solar-jumper. Oh, and, Captain…"*

"Sir?"

"Presumably Admiral Akaar will get in touch with you about this, but just so you know—the ultimatum of one hundred hours imposed by the High Council has been lifted."

Adams heard some of his bridge officers gasp in surprise. "How did that happen, Admiral?" No sooner had he finished asking the question when it dawned on him that he might not like the answer.

"An agreement was reached between Ambassador K'mtok and

the president. Qo'noS dropped the ultimatum, but in return the Klingon Defense Force now has full access to Federation space around the Lembatta Cluster. We're tightening the noose around the Purifying Flame's neck, Captain."

"Not too tightly, Admiral," Adams said. "These solar-jumpers supposedly have a range of up to thirty light years."

"We are well aware of that, Captain." Gepta's usual snippy tone intensified. "We're prepared for that. I mention it to you mainly because some Klingon captains may decide to achieve extra glory by entering the cluster, even though they don't have permission to. So be on the lookout."

"Understood, Admiral. How should we proceed if we do encounter any Klingon ships?"

"Tell them to leave the cluster immediately."

"Very well, but we won't be able to verify their departure—we can't be distracted by escorting Klingon strays out of the cluster."

"Just report any such incidents to the Venture, and then I will demand a report from General Akbas. He's leading the Klingon operations in the sector. Still, at the end of the day, the Klingons only pose a minor problem for us out here."

Adams found the admiral's statement to be dangerously dismissive. "With all due respect, sir, I'm not so sure about that. The captain of the Bortas has proven himself to be just as militant as the worst fanatics of the Purifying Flame. If it were up to him, all planets within the cluster would have gone up in flames already—as a warning to all Renao not to trifle with the Klingon Empire. More warriors of Kromm's temperament would be counterproductive in the cluster right now."

"We'll keep an eye on our allies," Gepta said. "See to it that you focus on what our enemies are up to."

The barely concealed reprimand almost made Adams wince. This time the admiral really was in a bad mood. He probably had hoped for better results from the captured solar-jumper than just a few makeshift attack fighters and an encrypted system.

Nodding, the captain straightened himself. "Aye, sir. We're on it."

"Excellent. Gepta, out."

The Chelon's image faded and was replaced by the red swirling cluster nebulae at warp speed.

"Who put a scratch in his shell?" Carson mumbled.

Adams shot her an admonishing look. "Commander!"

"Sorry, sir."

He stood next to ops, putting his hand on the backrest of her chair. "I'm surprised at your knowledge of Chelon idioms."

Carson looked up at him. "I used to have a Chelon crewmate on the *Lexington*, sir. He was very talkative—and rather, ah, profane."

In spite of himself, Adams grinned. "I understand. But next time, I suggest you keep your voice down a bit more when mocking an admiral."

"Aye, sir."

The door to Geron Barai's quarter was closed but not locked to allow the medical staff access to their patient at all times. But Lenissa still hesitated when she arrived at his room.

Part of her was afraid of crossing that threshold. How many nights had she spent with Geron behind this door? They had eaten, joked, made love, and shared hours completely losing themselves in passion.

Now, the man she had taken as her lover when she had

arrived aboard the *Prometheus* was lying in his bed once more. But this time, he didn't wait for her. She wouldn't join him, he wouldn't take off her uniform with his nimble, gentle fingers, and they wouldn't make love. This time, he would probably barely notice her presence because his mind—according to Doctor Calloway—had shattered under the onslaught of the monster on Iad.

Her antennae swayed back and forth insecurely, while she considered walking away again. What was she doing here, anyway? If Geron didn't perceive her, she was wasting her time. There were more important things for her to be doing. For example, she should schedule a boarding drill, just in case they found the Flame's shipyard.

Coward! she chided herself. All those thoughts were merely excuses. In truth, she didn't want to see Geron vulnerable and broken. If her memory served, Paul Winter had told her once that humans—when they committed to a relationship—promised to be there for each other during good times and bad times. Maybe that was the reason why Lenissa shied away from relationships. She wasn't good at dealing with bad times.

Lenissa heard quiet footsteps coming down the corridor. Someone would soon be here and find her standing outside this door glued to the spot. *You have fought space pirates, Borg, and Tzenkethi! Now face this opponent as well!*

With a resolute motion she touched the control panel beside the door, which obediently slid open. Lenissa went inside.

The room was not very large. The *Prometheus* was not a *Galaxy*-class ship, offering luxurious and spacious cabins to their senior staff. There was a bed—which, admittedly, was wider than the bunks of the non-commissioned crewmembers—a small table with two chairs, a workstation, and a separate sanitary niche. The room had no windows. The *Prometheus* was a warship and thus had considerably fewer windows than many other Starfleet ships. Instead, one wall was covered by a large viewscreen that would show space or any other environment as required. Those displays had a soothing effect and made the room seem larger, despite the virtual nature of the imagery.

Right now the screen was switched off and the lights dimmed. Lenissa also noticed the silence. Geron loved music played by the Betazoid *Khitarr*—a quiet, emotional instrument that suited his personality well. He had often played a selection of his extensive collection as ambient music when they were in his quarters. Lenissa generally preferred more lively music, but now she found herself missing the gentle sounds. The only noise in the room came from the mobile diagnostic unit that linked to sickbay.

Lenissa approached the bed. In the past, she'd do so with joy and pleasure, but now she felt only apprehension and caution. Everything felt wrong. Geron lay flat on his back under the sheets. His arms and legs twitched slightly, although he was heavily sedated. Lenissa saw his eyeballs moving rapidly behind his closed eyelids. Apparently Geron's mind was still in a state of unrest, despite the medication. She didn't even want to know what kind of nightmare he was currently trapped in.

She stood next to his bed, wondering whether she should say anything. Sometimes it was helpful for patients in a coma to hear the voices of a familiar, *loved* person. At least that was what Geron had told her some time ago.

And you do love me, don't you? she thought. Of course he loved her—or if nothing else, he had fallen in love with her. That had been undeniable ever since their return from the patrol near the Tzenkethi border. At first, everything had been good and carefree. Lenissa had been transferred to the *Prometheus*, and she had looked for a man to have fun with, as she usually did. In the doctor she had found not only a fantastic lover but also some sort of soulmate.

They had had so much fun, because they had found the perfect outlet for the pressure that their everyday duties entailed. But then, their relationship had gradually changed.

Oh, Geron, why did you have to develop feelings for me? Sighing, Lenissa wanted to sit down on the edge of the bed next to him, but she felt an increasing resistance. *Right. The restraining field.* Reaching out with her arm, she switched off the small field projector underneath the diagnostic unit. It was supposed to prevent Geron from injuring himself if he experienced a fit of madness and fury. As long as she was by his side, he didn't need it. Lenissa was convinced that she would be able to control him if he went mad. After all, she had always been in charge when they had been in bed together.

The only thing I couldn't control were your feelings. In that respect you were always the stronger one. Quietly sighing, she settled down on the edge of the bed, holding Geron's left hand in hers. It felt unusually warm, and when she briefly touched his forehead, she noticed that he felt extremely feverish. For a moment she considered calling Doctor Calloway. But one glance at the diagnostic unit told her that all vital signs of the Betazoid were within normal parameters. Geron's life was not in danger, but he was quite obviously sick, nonetheless.

Sympathetically she pointed her antennae at him. "I should have known better," she said quietly, talking more to herself than to the restless man on the bed. "A relationship with a Betazoid, with someone who's able to look into the heads and hearts of others, can only lead to emotions. But, well, you know, you were my first Betazoid. I wanted to have a fling with a Napean on the *Lexington*, but he proved to be fairly demure." She giggled. "I have to be careful what I tell you. You can hear me after all, and that will be pretty embarrassing when you get better."

If he got better… They had no idea what long-term effects the Son's mental onslaught would have for his victims. The Renao seemed to be driven into a lethal fanaticism by the subtle, constant influence. But their minds had been poisoned for years. The *Prometheus* crew had received an extraordinary overdose of this poison within a few moments. It seemed unlikely to Lenissa that Geron's mind and character would significantly change because of that. But he might never regain a clear mind, and that was just as bad.

Maybe I should talk to Doctor Calloway or Counselor Courmont, she pondered. *If anyone knows the answer to the question of what's going to happen to Geron and the others, it will be them.*

The Betazoid shifted restlessly and groaned. His eyelids fluttered and closed again.

Gently, Lenissa squeezed his hand. "You will get better, do you hear me? You must." She noticed her vision blur. With a short and desperate laugh, she wiped away the tears. "Look what you're doing to me! I'm an Andorian *zhen*. I have a heart of ice. Never have I wanted more from a man than just a little fun. If anyone came close to me, I pushed them away."

She had also pushed Geron away, she knew that. She had tried to, anyway. After her abduction by the Purifying Flame, he had seemed a little too caring, and the unspoken love had changed into something that went too far in Lenissa's eyes.

He had been constantly concerned about her well-being, and that had collided with her urge to remain independent.

Her natural reaction had been to distance herself, at least on the inside. Her self-imposed lack of compassion had hurt Geron—both literally, when she almost broke his pelvis during a night full of passion by being reckless and using the full force of her Andorian physique, and figuratively, as it broke his heart. Now she regretted her behavior. He was a good man; gentle, friendly, caring on one side, while unbridled and eager to try out new things on the other. It wasn't fair that his mind had lost its orientation, maybe even forever, during their personal crisis. What was there to support him now? How should she let him know that she didn't feel as indifferent towards him as she had let on?

She bent forward, pressing her cold forehead against his warm one. She felt a glow as if an unholy fire burned within him. Her antennae swayed gently back and forth.

"I'm sorry," she said with a choked voice. Her vision blurred again. "I'm just so sorry about everything. If you're still somewhere in there, please, listen to me very carefully. Listen, because I want you to know this, and I want you to cling to it."

Lenissa brought her lips close to his ear, lowering her voice to an almost inaudible whisper. And then she said something she had never thought she would ever say out loud—and maybe she wouldn't have done if Geron had been conscious.

"I love you."

11
NOVEMBER 27, 2385

Memory Alpha

The day when Kosinski had started working as a data analyst on Memory Alpha was the day when he had given up completely. His career had finally reached an all-time low. He contemplated quitting, but he loved working in space far too much to retire.

In his youth, he had been a rising star. Specializing in propulsion systems, he had worked for the Starfleet Corps of Engineers, and always dreamed about revolutionizing warp travel. For a while it had even looked as if his dream might come true.

With his assistant—an engineer from Tau Alpha C—he had developed methods to increase the performance of warp drives. They had even successfully been installed on several ships.

But on a fateful day in 2364, his life had taken a terrible turn. Kosinski had conducted a warp experiment aboard the *U.S.S. Enterprise*-D when disaster almost struck. During this incident, two things had come to light: one, Kosinski's assistant was in truth a highly developed life form calling itself "the Traveler"; and two, Kosinski's concepts were nothing more than nonsense, and the improvements to the other ships' engines were all a result of the Traveler's superhuman abilities.

A child, of all people—a boy genius named Wesley Crusher, who had permission from Captain Picard to roam freely about the ship—had figured Kosinski out in the end. That moment in the engine room couldn't have been any more embarrassing.

Starfleet insisted that they would not hold Kosinski's failure against him, and he received no reprimand. However, from that moment on his career had stalled as his competence was called into question. It didn't help that his attitude could charitably be called self-confident—though more accurately he was an arrogant ass. The colleagues he'd been dismissive of and rude to before could barely conceal their glee at his downfall.

Eventually, he had left the S.C.E. and had transferred to the Utopia Planitia Fleet Yard's development department, but that hadn't improved matters much. No one trusted his judgment after what happened on the *Enterprise*.

When his superior officer showed him the offer to work as a data analyst on Memory Alpha—"a new beginning, you know"—he had jumped at it, becoming a staff member of the Federation's biggest library.

It did sound impressive, at least: the complete knowledge of all Federation member worlds was archived in the databases of Memory Alpha. There was a database for astroculture, a department on the history of Starfleet, and a cartographic archive. The department for antiquity boasted, among other things, a two-thousand-year-old map of the Vulcan systems, as well as one of the three existing copies of the Andorian *Liturgy of the Temple of Uzaveh* from the third century. And the collection of the fine arts brought tears of awe to experts' eyes.

How anyone could have come up with the absurd idea

to establish this epicenter of knowledge on a tiny, lifeless planetoid was way beyond Kosinski, even after two years. Without the huge atmosphere domes or the subterranean gravity generators, working or leading a normal life on Memory Alpha would have been impossible. Of course, there were records about the construction of the galactic library, but Kosinski hadn't found any reasons for choosing this location.

"Good morning, Ezra," he greeted his colleague from the night shift. "What's new?"

The hairy Xindi-Arboreal, who reminded Kosinski of an upright-walking sloth, burst out laughing. "Really, that joke doesn't get old, Kosinski." Ezra shook his head, which was framed by a white and gray mane.

Kosinski sighed quietly. Ezra might be a walking database, but his sense of humor was awful. "I'm serious, Ezra. Did anything happen within the galaxy while I was asleep that I should know about?"

"Hmm, let me think." The Arboreal tapped his rubbery lips with the index finger of his clawed hand. "The Federation has received an invitation from the Typhon Pact to a power summit in a place called 'Embassy of Distance.' A planetwide epidemic is spreading on Rigel VIII, and the world has been placed under quarantine. The *U.S.S. Berlin* caused a diplomatic incident at Evora, and the planet is threatening to break with the Federation. And the Lembatta crisis is heating up. The president has given the Klingons permission to patrol in the systems around the cluster." Ezra's face lit up. "Talking about Lembatta. A few minutes ago, a Doctor Mandel forwarded a task from the *U.S.S. Prometheus*. They are looking for an extremely weird space phenomenon."

"Why didn't they link with the database themselves?" Kosinski asked, frowning.

"How should I know?" Ezra shrugged. "Maybe the connection from the Lembatta Cluster is too weak." He pointed at the terminal. "I have already entered the data in the query screen. But now that you're here, you might as well continue."

With these words, the Arboreal pushed himself out of his chair. Picking up his cup and a plate covered in crumbs, he nodded at Kosinski, before stomping past him towards the exit. "Good luck. I'll see you tonight."

"Yeah, see you later." Kosinski sat down at his workplace, bringing up the query that Ezra had prepared for him. "Priority one, of course." Kosinski sighed. That meant many lives were at stake, and he needed to find the required answer as soon as possible. Apparently, the situation in the Lembatta Cluster was critical.

He took a closer look at the inquiry. Captain Adams was looking for clues regarding a certain stellar phenomenon described by his science officer as a zone with variable radiation.

Kosinski didn't consider himself to be an astrophysicist but he knew a little about radiation phenomena. The reference data in front of him didn't seem to make any sense whatsoever. He was tempted to contact Ezra in order to ask him whether he had mixed up data while entering the query into the system. But despite his jovial demeanor, the Arboreal was usually the epitome of accuracy.

"Computer, check data packets from the *Prometheus* for transfer errors," he said.

"No errors found in the data packets."

Kosinski stared again at the radiation patterns he had been sent. "This is impossible. This is physically impossible."

But then he remembered the mission on the *Enterprise* that had derailed his career. The Traveler, whom Kosinski in his arrogance had believed to be a mediocre engineer from Tau Alpha C, had also been traveling with his ship to a place that shouldn't exist according to physics. Space, time, and thought had been one in this place. Whatever someone thought about became reality, and the limits of travel were defined by the limits of your imagination. He hadn't even begun to understand how all that could be consistent with the concepts of the fundamental laws of nature within the universe. But he had realized one thing back then: certain wonders existed among the stars that were seemingly not possible. And this appeared to be just one of these wonders.

Kosinski shook his head. "Not my problem. I'm just here to find another one of these phenomena."

He accessed the central archive, feeding it with the necessary search parameters. The database's answer came fast: *"No matches found."*

He spent the next two hours accessing every data collection within the various departments of Memory Alpha without success.

Eventually, Kosinski began to lose patience. He had tried approximately ninety-five percent of all listed knowledge bases within the library. The only ones missing were the physical collection items in the showrooms and storage facilities. But he couldn't imagine discovering information about chaotic radiation zones on ancient tapestries from Tellar or a burial urn from Bajor.

"Perhaps on some ancient maps in the cartography archive," he mumbled. Then he raised his voice. "Computer, requesting access to cartography archive."

His request was confirmed with an electronic chirp. *"Access granted."*

A gallery of images with several thousand photos of historic maps waited to be scrutinized by him. Just looking at the sheer number of images made him dizzy. *It's impossible for me to sift through all of them. I need to narrow down the selection.*

"Computer, eliminate all maps with planet surfaces or sections of planets."

Two-thirds of the material disappeared. Kosinski wiped his mouth with his hand. "Now eliminate all maps with only suns or planets. Keep only maps with unusual space phenomena."

"Please specify unusual space phenomena."

"Radiation zones, space rifts, anything like that."

This time, only a quarter of the images remained. The number of images was considerably more manageable, but it would still take him hours if not days to sift through all the pictures.

Perhaps he should trust the heuristic analysis function of the central computer after all. "Computer, apply parameters of the currently running query, and correlate them to the information on the remaining space charts. List probable matches."

"Checking data." After a pause, the computer continued, *"Two matches found. Maximum similarity, sixty percent."*

"On screen," Kosinski said.

Two photos of historic space maps stored on Memory Alpha as a permanent loan from the Vulcan Science Academy appeared on the monitor. Kosinski had no idea how to interpret the peculiar manner of representation.

Grumbling, he pressed the call button of the intercom. "Kosinski to Cartographic Archive."

"Cartographic Archive, Lokmay here."

Kosinski didn't recognize the name, which wasn't at

all surprising. More than six hundred people worked on Memory Alpha, and most departments kept to themselves. At the end of the day, it didn't matter who was on the other end of that connection, anyway.

"I need your help," he said. "I have received a query from the *U.S.S. Prometheus*, and they are looking for a specific radiation phenomenon. According to the computer, it's possible that this phenomenon can be found on two ancient Vulcan maps. Unfortunately, I don't recognize anything on them. Can I forward that query to you?"

"Of course. Send it to my terminal. We'll take a look."

"Thanks. Transmitting data." He typed the commands into his terminal. The channel remained silent for a while. Kosinski asked himself which species Lokmay might belong to. The name didn't sound human. The pitch suggested a male being, but even that wasn't certain. There were quite a few Klingon women who sounded more masculine than any man from Risa. He decided that—like so many other things around him—it didn't really matter, anyway. He didn't have any intention to invite Lokmay for dinner, after all.

"That is... an extraordinary radiation zone," Lokmay said after a few seconds.

Tell me something I don't know, Kosinski thought, but managed not to say aloud.

"I can tell you with some degree of certainty that the radiation phenomena on the maps from Vulcan are of a much more common nature."

"I was afraid you would say that," Kosinski replied. "Thank you for your help."

"Don't mention it." Lokmay finished their conversation.

Kosinski cursed under his breath. Presumably there wasn't another chaos zone like this one in the galaxy.

His research results so far, in combination with physical probabilities, indicated as much. He should simply finish the query with a negative answer and turn to his next task. But this was a priority one. No self-respecting member of Starfleet would push aside such a query without doing their utmost to find an answer.

Sighing, he got to his feet. "Oh, this is just brilliant." There was one more chance to find an answer. It was minute, but it existed.

The listed inventories of Memory Alpha didn't contain the full extent of knowledge data that was being stored on the planetoid. No one liked to talk about it, but there was the so-called Gray Storage. That term referred to data storage devices of all sorts—hard drives, microchip cards, isolinear chips—that had reached Memory Alpha via obscure routes. Some may have been donated by private explorers, while others could be part of the knowledge base of some insignificant planet on the periphery of the Federation.

Since the data analysts' daily business kept them more than busy, these new admissions had been treated with low priority. So they had been stored in boxes deep within the archives of the complex, waiting for someone with a few months' time on his hands to add them to the general storage listings.

Kosinski had only been living and working on Memory Alpha for two years, but even he knew that this would probably never happen. Which didn't mean that this knowledge was lost forever. It was possible to go down into the archives on the lower levels, and to read the data storage devices on special terminals. But that was a bear of a job. Finding something specific down there was more difficult than discovering the proverbial needle in a haystack.

Still, he had to try his luck. The *Prometheus* was counting on him!

Hours later, Kosinski sat at a terminal with a holographic interface, and he was about to despair. Not only had his shift finished hours ago, it was way past his bedtime as well. He had connected and searched at least one hundred different storage devices with promising labels. He hadn't achieved anything—apart from a headache and a stiff back.

Tired, he rubbed his eyes, staring at the shelves full of boxes and crates in the dimly lit basement room deep inside the planetoid. *One more memory chip*, he said to himself, and his gaze wandered to the small black storage device that lay next to him in an open box. *Just one more.* Sighing, he picked it up.

"No, this isn't getting me anywhere. I'm giving up."

"Hello, Mr. Kosinski."

The voice made Kosinski jerk. He lost his grip on the memory chip in his hand, and it clattered to the floor. He scanned the barely illuminated storage room with his eyes. "Is anyone there?"

"Yes, I'm here." A figure emerged from the shadows between two shelves, approaching him. This looked to be a young man. He had a very juvenile face, and wore the plain overall of a civilian who didn't really care for fashion. He looked somewhat familiar to Kosinski, but he wasn't able to place his visitor.

"Who are you?" Confused, Kosinski looked from the entrance to the shelves at the other end of the room. "And how did you get in here?" He hadn't seen anyone come through the door.

"Don't you recognize me?" his visitor asked, without acknowledging the second question. An amused smile flashed across his face. He came a little closer.

Suddenly Kosinski's tired mind clicked. "You were that boy on the *Enterprise*! Wesley Crusher, right?"

His counterpart nodded. "You do remember."

"But what are you doing here?" asked Kosinski. "Are you also working on Memory Alpha now?"

Again, the young man smiled, shaking his head. "No, not quite. I'm just visiting."

"Visiting?" Kosinski squinted in confusion. "What in the world could make you visit me after twenty years?"

"Has it been that long? Sorry, but time doesn't really work the same for me as it used to."

The young man's cryptic words confused Kosinski even more. "I don't get it."

"Let me explain," said Wesley. "Do you remember your assistant, the Traveler?"

"Of course. He disappeared that day when…" Kosinski hesitated. "…when he got the *Enterprise* back to normal space."

"He reappeared a couple of times after that, including when I was a cadet at the Academy. It was then that I realized I wasn't destined to become an officer like my parents had been. Instead, I joined him—and became like him."

Stunned, Kosinski stared at the young man. "You… what?" He burst into loud laughter. "Forgive me, but are you really trying to tell me that you're a Traveler?"

To his surprise, Wesley just smiled. "You don't have to believe me—as long as you're prepared to let me help you."

Kosinski frowned. "What do you mean?"

"You're looking for a specific location in the universe, but you can't find it. I have the solution to your problem."

Bending down, he picked up the memory chip that Kosinski had dropped and handed it back to him.

The data analyst accepted it warily. "Are you saying that I'll find another location with a radiation zone on here?" Wesley nodded. "That would be an incredible coincidence. I've been searching storage devices in this storage room for hours."

"No, it wouldn't be a coincidence. I took the liberty to complete the data that you will find on here."

"You? But how…?"

"I've seen many things during my travels, Mr. Kosinski," said the young man. "Terrible things. Beautiful things. And helpful things, such as an energy sphere where all thinkable variations of radiation appear and disappear… a zone in permanent hyperphysical fluctuation."

That did indeed sound like the phenomenon Kosinski was looking for. "Let me check."

Wesley made an inviting gesture. "Be my guest."

Sitting back down at the terminal, Kosinski placed the memory chip on the holointerface and selected a suitable slot. Finally, he read the data on the small black card.

"Match found," the computer announced. *"Similarity ninety-four percent."*

"I don't believe this," Kosinski muttered. He accessed the data packet, and the research area of a deep-space exploring mission appeared. Kosinski had never heard of this expedition, nor of the species that had undertaken it.

He looked up, staring at Wesley. "This isn't a trick, is it? Some kind of belated revenge for me mistreating you twenty years ago."

Wesley grinned. "No, Mr. Kosinski, the data is real. I genuinely do want to help you."

"But why?" Kosinski still struggled to understand what was happening here.

"For one, because I don't want the quadrant to end up in another war. But also because I think you've suffered enough. You deserve some success."

"Success..." Kosinski's gaze wandered to the report that also contained the exact coordinates of the radiation phenomenon. Slowly it dawned on him that he had really made it. The answer for the *Prometheus*'s query was on his screen. And Wesley Crusher of all people had helped him find it. He blinked.

"I... I don't know what to say," he began, turning back to his mysterious visitor.

But Wesley Crusher was gone.

"Hello?" said Kosinski. "Wesley?"

No answer. Kosinski was alone again.

He swallowed. "Thank you," he whispered into the emptiness of the cellar archive room.

12

NOVEMBER 27, 2385

Upper hull section of the *U.S.S. Prometheus*, Bharatrum system

"Nothing. No life signs. No signs of artificial structures. This moon is as dead as a dodo."

"Thanks, Ensign." Lieutenant Krish Iniri nodded at Vogel at ops, then turned to the conn. "Let's fly to the next moon. Ensign Naxxa, set course for Bharatrum VI-Delta. Half impulse."

"Aye, Lieutenant." The female Bolian pilot's fingers danced across the navigation console.

The ocher-colored moon VI-Gamma veered off to the left of the small main screen, before the upper hull section accelerated towards their next destination.

The young Bajoran woman didn't have command of one of the *Prometheus* sections often. Generally, she was only in command of a stand-in crew for alpha shift, but now many of the senior officers were on Bharatrum engaged in diplomatic talks, or they were in their quarters, unfit for duty. This had led to one of these rare occasions.

Captain Adams had separated the *Prometheus* in order to deal with several tasks simultaneously. While the primary hull and the *Bortas* continued to orbit Bharatrum, the lower secondary hull with Lieutenant Aduviri in command searched the inner of the eight uninhabited system planets for traces of the Purifying Flame. Krish flew with her crew in the upper secondary hull from one outer gas giant to the next.

It was a boring and tedious task, since they had to check four planets and thirty-six moons in all, then proceed to the Kuiper belt. It was like searching for a hara cat in the Bestri Woods. *At least our sensors work better here than above Iad,* Krish thought.

She leaned back in her command chair. They had been crawling from moon to moon for almost three hours now, and they hadn't found anything, except an ancient and long-since-abandoned mining facility on Bharatrum V-Beta, which the Renao called Meenoud. If Krish had been anywhere other than the command chair, she would probably have yawned loudly. But being in charge gave her ample satisfaction, so she could easily overlook indignities such as a boring search mission.

Besides, the mission was important. Imagine if they actually were the ones who found the Purifying Flame…

She turned to the tactical officer at the station to her left. "Bhansali, are you picking up any Renao or Klingon ships? Or any other vessels?"

"Negative, Lieutenant," the bearded man from Deneva replied. "Space within five hundred million kilometers is completely empty."

"Very good."

"*Good*, Lieutenant?" Bhansali snorted. "I wish we could get our hands on one of these spaceships of the Purifying Flame so I can personally thank these fanatics for their attacks on Starbase 91 and Cestus III. I lost a lot of friends in those attacks."

"You're not the only one," Krish said gently, aware that Bhansali had also lost most of his family when the Borg destroyed Deneva. "Still, this is not a vengeance raid. We didn't come into the cluster to hunt down Renao. This is about justice for the dead and the protection of the living. Don't forget that, please."

"Aye, Lieutenant." But Bhansali was still snarling.

In her heart of hearts, she could understand him; she even sympathized with his point of view. She had been born on Bajor during Cardassia's occupation of the world. As an adolescent, she had seen friends die at the Cardassians' hands. She was familiar with the desire for revenge—including taking revenge on an entire species. It had taken years before she had been able to gain enough inner distance from the past to recognize that individuals had been responsible for these atrocities, and that the majority of Cardassians had never even set foot on Bajor. Today's generation of Cardassians didn't have anything to do with the oppression that had ended fifteen years ago, just like the common Renao farmer on Xhehenem had nothing to do with the Purifying Flame's terrorist attacks.

Besides, she remembered when the Jem'Hadar made their retaliatory strike on Cardassia Prime at the end of the Dominion War, killing billions of Cardassians. Krish would have thought that would have satisfied her need for vengeance against her people's oppressors, but instead she found herself mourning the innocent lives lost because the Cardassians had rebelled against the Dominion just as Bajorans had rebelled against Cardassia.

She put her reminiscences aside as Bharatrum VI-Delta, the largest moon of this particular gas giant, appeared in front of them. The Renao called the planet Shoraoun, and the moon Calidhu, but Krish preferred to stick to the nomenclature of the early Starfleet expeditions that had initially charted this system. Strictly speaking, the moon was called LC-14-VI-Delta in the fleet's databases, but Krish found that a bit too technical.

VI-Delta was a gray and yellow rock with a diameter

of approximately three and a half thousand kilometers. It orbited the gas giant once every ten days. There was no water down there, but the enormous tidal forces of Shoraoun caused amazingly active volcanoes, leading to numerous calderas, some of which were incredibly large.

Vogel read off the results of the scan: "The temperature is around minus one hundred and forty degrees Celsius. The atmosphere consists predominantly of sulfur dioxide, and it's extremely thin. It's not a place where you'd like to spend your shore leave."

"How many places in space exist where you would actually like to spend your shore leave?" Krish asked.

"As far as I'm concerned: two," Vogel replied, grinning over his shoulder. "Casperia Prime and Risa."

"Not Risa anymore," Sh'rar muttered. The Caitian was the fifth person on the bridge, and he operated the engineering station. He shot Bhansali a look then turned back to his station. Like the tactical officer's homeworld, Risa had been devastated during the Borg invasion.

"The Federation is rebuilding Risa," Vogel said. "It'll be even more sensual than ever before."

"Risa's best times are over," Bhansali said. "Wrigley's Pleasure Planet—that's where you spend your leave these days. *Again*, I should say. The world was pretty rundown for a while."

"*Thank you*, gentlemen," Krish interjected. "I believe I have heard enough ideas for my next free fortnight. Could we turn our attention back to the matter at hand?"

"Aye, Lieutenant." Vogel turned back to his console, as did Bhansali and Sh'rar.

Naxxa reported: "We've reached orbit."

"Initiating surface scan," Vogel announced.

It was quiet for a minute on the bridge while everyone focused on their instruments, and Krish stared at the image of the moon with its yellow, jagged landscape. No one expected to find anything there, but they needed to remain vigilant, Krish knew. If it turned out later that she had overlooked anything, that would lead to a nasty reprimand in her Starfleet file. Not to mention the possibility of more people dying that she could have prevented from being killed.

"I'll bet ten pieces of gold-pressed latinum that we won't find a base anywhere around here," Bhansali announced suddenly.

"Where did *you* get gold-pressed latinum?" Vogel asked.

"I played *dabo* on DS9," the security chief said. "That was a good deal for me."

"Would you *please* concentrate on your work!" Irritated, Krish rubbed her ridged nose with her thumb and index finger. "I'm aware of the fact that we're not pursuing the most exciting of tasks in the world—"

"Lieutenant!" Vogel interrupted her, excited. "I'm picking up something on the moon's surface."

Krish sat up straight. "On screen."

The moon's surface shifted and zoomed in. A tactical triangular marker was placed over a massif in the center of the bridge screen.

"Here, Lieutenant. I'm definitely picking up artificial structures inside this mountain range. There are subterranean vaults."

"Any signs of life?"

"Difficult to say. Ores inside the rock are interfering with sensors. I'm reading geometrically shaped caverns with smooth surfaces, which can't be of natural origin, but I can't make out what's inside of them."

"Check the records for mining facilities on VI-Delta."

"Right away." Several seconds after the stocky man had typed the query into the computer, he said, "No settlements or plants are registered here."

Krish turned to the security chief. "Bhansali, tactical analysis."

The bearded Denevan peered at his console. "No energy readings of any kind, as far as I can tell. But as Vogel said, readings from inside the mountain are not conclusive."

"In that case, we're going down there with an away team," Krish said. "Vogel, find a good access point. Bhansali, take two security personnel and an engineer, and prepare for an away mission. Environmental suits and personal shields. We don't want to take any risks."

"Aye, Lieutenant. I'll take Meuer, Swallow, and Ensign Loanaa with me." The security chief got up and strode out of the bridge. After a minute, the turbolift returned and deposited Ensign Elisa Flores onto the bridge to relieve Bhansali at tactical.

Not long after, Krish received Bhansali's confirmation from the transporter room that they were ready.

"Excellent," the Bajoran woman responded. "Ensign Vogel will give you the coordinates to beam down to. Look after yourself, Lieutenant."

"Always," came the laconic reply.

"Bhansali's team is transporting now," said Vogel. "Transport successful—sensors are detecting the combadges in their suits. The lieutenant is hailing us."

"Put him through."

"Bhansali to Prometheus." The Denevan's voice sounded tinny, and he breathed heavily inside his EV suit helmet.

"We can hear you, Lieutenant."

"We're directly outside the massif. Above us, we can see several holes in the mountainside. They look like entrances to hangars, but if any ships are parked there, they can't be any bigger than shuttles."

"Are there any ships that you can see?"

"Negative, Prometheus. Everything here seems dead and abandoned. No energy readings, no lights, no atmosphere shield protecting the hangar entrances. Ensign Loanaa found a way in that is on a slightly lower level and easily accessible. We're going in now."

"Understood. Keep this channel open."

For about a minute, all they heard was panting and some quiet curses.

"The floor here is very uneven," Bhansali said. *"And there is this yellow dust everywhere. Looks pretty poisonous to me."*

"Presumably sulfur deposits," Vogel said. "They don't pose a danger to the EV suits."

"We've reached the side entrance now. There's a locked door. Loanaa thinks she can get it open."

The humming of a piece of equipment—probably a P-38, which engineers like Loanaa referred to as a "can opener"—was audible, followed by a clicking noise.

Bhansali said, *"The door's open. We're going in. Meuer, you take point. Swallow, you bring up the rear. Dammit, it's dark in here. It's like the inside of a grave. Activate your spotlights. Loanaa, you keep an eye on the tricorder. If this is a trap, I want to know about it before it springs."*

Krish felt her heart rate increase. She wished that she was leading the away team. Being tied to the command chair while others advanced boldly into the unknown sat poorly with her. However, Starfleet regulations were clear: captains had to remain aboard ship if their presence wasn't urgently required on site. At the end of the day, a captain's responsibility toward their ship and crew was much more important than the individual's desire for adventure. *Things used to be much better in the old days*, Krish thought wistfully, remembering her history lessons at the Academy about Jonathan Archer, Garth of Izar, Christopher Pike, and James Kirk.

"It really is a base," Bhansali said. *"The corridors and rooms have been carved into the rock. And there are Renao symbols on the walls."*

"Any indications that someone is home?" asked Krish.

"Negative, Lieutenant. There's no readable energy or atmosphere in here, except for the thin moon air. I'd be surprised if we found anyone here. It looks as if the base has been abandoned."

Someone said something that Krish didn't understand.

"True," replied Bhansali. *"Loanaa just noticed that the inhabitants can't be long gone. We found dirty dishes in the crew mess hall. There are open supply crates here, as well. It seems as if these guys made a hasty exit. Besides… Hey, now look what we've got here."*

Alarmed, Krish sat up straight. "What did you find, Bhansali?"

"A few posters have been put up here. I can't read what they say, but the symbol is unmistakable: the Purifying Flame! I'd say we hit the bullseye."

Krish wasn't so sure. "If the base was abandoned, it's doubtful whether we'll find anything to help us make any significant progress. The fanatics will have covered their tracks."

"If they had the time to do so," Bhansali said. *"There are all sorts of belongings here in the living area, where we are now— clothes, food, tools. They must have left in a hurry. We'll advance further. There must be a command center somewhere around here."*

"Be careful. These fanatics might have left behind surprises for any intruders."

"Aye, Lieutenant. We'll keep our eyes peeled. But the EV suits and the illumination in these corridors don't make things easy for us. And the tricorder doesn't seem to get on very well with the ore inside the walls. Our detection radius is almost zero."

Krish turned to ops. "Ensign Vogel, try to boost our sensor performance. Focus on the massif. If you register any strange increases in energy, we will beam our people out immediately."

"I'll do my best, Lieutenant," the German replied. "But that won't be easy. I'm not even sure if our transporters are able to lock on the away team through the rock."

Krish hit the sensor button on her armrest, activating the intercom with her fist. "Bridge to transporter room."

"Transporter room here." The Saurian crewperson S'arkee spoke with a slight lisp.

"Are you still locked on the away team?"

"Yes, Lieutenant. The lock is somewhat unstable but I can compensate for that. That said, if the team moves any deeper into the mountain, maintaining the lock will become difficult."

"Understood. Thank you." She slightly raised her voice: "Did you hear that, Bhansali?"

"We did," the Denevan answered on the open channel. *"We can't advance much deeper anyway, since we seem to be moving upwards now. We're just reaching some kind of an armory."* He whistled. *"I'll be damned… These pieces of…"*

"Enlighten us, Lieutenant," Krish ordered.

"The chamber has been pretty much emptied. But there are a few old cargo crates, which appear to have been holding guns and explosive charges. Romulan military, Cardassian forces… These guys have purchased ordnance from all over the quadrant. And they call us sphere defilers. Two-faced bastards."

Someone shouted something that sounded remotely like "command center" to Krish.

"On my way," said Bhansali. *"Apparently we've discovered the command center, Prometheus. Yes, there are scattered computers here. Ha, dabo! I'd say. Hey, what's that?"*

"Report, Bhansali!" Krish asked when he didn't continue.

"The tricorder is picking up a sign of life on this level. It suddenly appeared. Down there. Hey, who are you? Freeze, and don't move! On behalf of Starfleet, I'm asking you to... Oh no! Beam us up, Prometheus. Right now..."

They heard a sudden heavy thud, before the connection was terminated.

On the moon, they saw a minor conflagration on the outer mountain wall. And then, half of the mountain blew up.

"According to our analysis, large quantities of explosives had been stored in this specially protected room that our sensors couldn't detect due to the ore inside the stone," Lenissa zh'Thiin said, pointing at the holoimages of the almost completely destroyed mountain range that her staff had taken. "Apparently, the assassin stayed behind waiting for us, then blew himself up, which delivered the initial spark for the larger explosive charge. The blast of the explosion amounted in strength to approximately four standard photon torpedoes. The base has been completely destroyed; our away team didn't survive."

Adams listened to the report with a stony face. But behind the mask of professionalism, he was seething. It had finally happened. The *Prometheus* mourned her first victims of this mission.

Captains always had to be prepared for the deaths of people under their command, and Adams had lost numerous people during the past few years—especially during the Dominion War and the Borg invasion. Even in times of relative peace, a battle ship like the *Prometheus* would frequently suffer casualties, because Adams and his crew were usually deployed to dangerous locations. Although the captain had accepted death as a permanent companion in his life, that didn't make it any easier to bear the loss of crew members.

It never got any easier.

"Did we find clues in the ruins of where the fanatics fled to when they abandoned the base?" Roaas asked. He was in Adams's ready room with Adams and zh'Thiin.

The Andorian woman's antennae lowered. "None whatsoever. Then again, there's half a mountain burying these chambers. We have only gained access to a fraction of them."

"In which case, we will continue our search the way we started it," said Adams. "We don't have any other choice." Their investigations on Bharatrum proper had proven to be less than fruitful. The hard-line attitude of Custodian Goraal ak Behruun hadn't changed, either. He had only allowed them the bare minimum of freedom of movement, and the Federation's regulations forced Adams to comply with the wishes and whims of the locals.

The only thing the planetary space flight control had confirmed for them was the fact that the solar-jumper captured by the *Venture* had been flying to and from the system several times during the past few weeks. Before they had been able to follow up that lead, they had received word of the incident on Bharatrum VI-Delta.

Sighing, Adams put his hands on the desk. "Thank you for your report, Commander zh'Thiin. Dismissed."

"Aye, sir." Nodding briefly, the security chief turned on her heel and left.

Once the door had closed behind her, Adams looked at his first officer. "How is Lieutenant Krish?"

"She's feeling guilty, sir," Roaas answered. "She's asking herself whether she made a mistake. I tried to talk her out of it. No one could expect the Purifying Flame to leave a suicide bomber behind in an abandoned base. Believing that would have been bordering on paranoia."

"Apparently you can't be paranoid enough," Adams said. "Have Counselor Courmont talk to her. I want to know whether Krish is fit for duty or whether I should hand over command of alpha shift's interim crew to Commander Carson."

"I'll let her know, sir."

"I'll leave the reassigning of Meuer's and Swallow's duties to zh'Thiin, and Loanaa's to Kirk. Any suggestions as to who should take over Lieutenant Bhansali's shifts at tactical?"

"I'd suggest Ensign Flores, Captain. She's doing excellent work, and, so far, she hasn't expressed any questionable views regarding the Renao—unlike several other possible candidates for this post I could think of."

"Right. Flores it is then. I'll let her know personally."

"Very well, sir." Roaas hesitated before adding: "About the condolence messages, Captain—would you want me to take them off your hands? I knew Loanaa fairly well."

Adams shook his head. "Thank you, Commander, but I'll see to that myself. It's not a pleasurable duty but it's important and it's one of the tasks of a captain."

The intercom signal sounded, and they heard Sarita Carson's voice. *"Bridge to Captain."*

"What is it, Commander?"

"We have just received a message from Memory Alpha." Carson sounded excited. *"You're not going to believe this, Captain. They really did find a second chaos zone."*

13

NOVEMBER 27, 2385

U.S.S. Prometheus, in orbit around Bharatrum

"The Taurus Dark Cloud?" Kromm asked skeptically. "I do not know of it."

The Benzite science officer brought up a star chart on the screen of the *Prometheus* conference room for Kromm's benefit. "It's a region of approximately one hundred and fifty light years in diameter beyond the Pleiades Cluster. Due to its high molecular density, it absorbs the light of stars behind it and appears in the visual spectrum of black on telescopic records. Since it's located within the Taurus Constellation as visible from Earth, it derives its name—"

"If I wanted to listen to lectures, I'd have stayed at the Academy on Qo'noS." Kromm snarled and pointed at the screen with his gauntleted right hand. "This Pleiades Cluster... I assume it is more than two hundred light years away?"

"That's correct."

Kromm shook his head. "Even at maximum warp, we'd take..." He trailed off, looking questioningly at Nuk, seated next to him.

"Almost thirty-nine days," the engineer said after a moment of thought. "But you can forget that, Captain. The *Bortas* won't last two days at maximum. She might be tough but she's growing old. No ship could last that long at those velocities, not even *Prometheus*."

Adams, sitting at the head of the table, nodded grimly. They had convened on his ship in order to make plans and talk, instead of taking action. People from Starfleet loved talking. But they were in charge here, so Kromm had no other choice but to comply whenever Adams called for yet another session of babbling into the air.

This time, there were nine attendees. Adams's group consisted not only of Mendon, but also Roaas, Kirk, and Ambassador Rozhenko. Kromm had brought Nuk, Rooth, and Spock along. L'emka was still first officer aboard the *Bortas*, but he had banned her from the inner circle of his trusted advisors. It was his right as captain to leave her behind in charge of the ship. Excluding her from all important talks and decisions was his revenge for her constant second-guessing of his authority. He would have loved to execute her in orbit around Iad for the murder of Toras. Unfortunately, he had also killed a warrior in a rage of madness whose brother was a *QaS Devwl'*, one of the troop commanders. In order to protect himself from a challenge from the warrior's brother, he was forced to class all actions under the Son's destructive influence as involuntary, and all casualties as victims of ill-fated accidents.

"So," Kromm said, "what does the knowledge about this dark cloud do for us? It's too far away to just drop by. In the meantime, fanatics of the Purifying Flame could devastate ten worlds."

"Not quite," said Jenna Kirk, leaning back in her chair with folded arms. "It's too far away for the *Bortas*, but not for the *Prometheus*. We can cover that distance in one or two days with our slipstream technology."

"Ah, the Federation's mighty quantum slipstream drive." Kromm laughed bitterly. "How could I forget this technology that everyone craves and you don't share?"

Adams gave him a rebuking look. "Kromm, you know full well that the design of Klingon ships is not suitable for our slipstream technology."

"Of course." Kromm made no effort to conceal his doubts regarding the official statements of Federation scientists.

"Captain," Rozhenko cautioned, "this is not helping."

Before Kromm could upbraid the upstart ambassador, Rooth spoke up. "It's useless honing your blades over this, anyway. *Prometheus* has a slipstream drive at her disposal, *Bortas* doesn't. What does that mean for our mission?"

"I know *my* mission," Kromm said firmly. "My orders are to find the location of the Purifying Flame. Nothing is mentioned of spending weeks trying to hunt this mythical White Guardian. Our work is here, inside the cluster."

Quietly, Spock said, "I agree with Captain Kromm."

The Klingon captain didn't believe his ears. Had the geriatric pointed-eared diplomat just taken his side?

The ambassador continued: "Despite all the hope we may harbor to end this conflict peacefully, we must not lose sight of the task at hand. The White Guardian may be the key for victory against the Son of the Ancient Reds but the *Prometheus* and the *Bortas* are currently the key to ending the threat of the Purifying Flame."

Adams nodded slowly and looked at everyone in turn. "We'll split up. The *Prometheus* will use our slipstream to investigate the Taurus Dark Cloud in an attempt to find the White Guardian. Meanwhile, the *Bortas* will continue the search for the Purifying Flame."

Kromm burst into laughter. "That, Captain Adams, is the best proposal I've heard from you this entire mission." Let the people of Starfleet chase their myths with their heads in the clouds. That would give him free rein to solve the crisis in the Lembatta Cluster like a Klingon.

Rozhenko seemed to have read his thoughts because his face showed slight concern. "Shouldn't a part of the *Prometheus* remain in the Lembatta Cluster in order to continue the search for the extremists together with the *Bortas*?"

Adams looked at Kirk and Mendon.

"I wouldn't recommend it, sir," said the former. "We needed the deflector dishes and the computing capabilities of all three sections of the *Prometheus* in order to penetrate the chaos zone around Iad. According to Memory Alpha, the radiation readings inside the Taurus Dark Cloud match those of the Souhla system, so we'll need all three again." She shook her head. "It's all or nothing, Captain."

"There's your answer, Ambassador," said Adams.

Kromm sneered at the son of Worf. "Don't worry, Ambassador. We won't start a war while our friends from the Federation chase phantoms at the edge of the galaxy."

Rozhenko responded to Kromm's sneer with a grim smile. "I'll be here to make sure of that."

"What?" asked Kromm. "Are you staying here in the cluster?"

"Yes," the young Klingon said. "As Ambassador Spock would say, this decision is only logical. His telepathic abilities would be much more useful during the search for the White Guardian. My status as a member of the House of Martok will undoubtedly be of more use here." He looked at Spock. "Wouldn't you agree, Ambassador?"

Spock raised an eyebrow, nodding approvingly. "Indeed, a most logical decision."

For his part, Kromm didn't like the idea in the least. He also didn't appreciate the little upstart throwing his status as a member of the chancellor's House in his face.

"We could ask the *Venture* to take over from us in the cluster," Roaas said. "Two crews can achieve more than just one—no offence, Captain Kromm."

Kromm growled. Did they all think him a helpless fool? Adams, Rozhenko, L'emka, Roaas... they all seemed to believe that he required a *ghojmoq* to mind him. The thought infuriated him.

To his shock, it was Spock again who came to his rescue. "I'm afraid that it is not as simple as that. The negotiations with Onferin to obtain permission to enter the cluster were extremely complex. The Renao government will be reluctant to allow another ship into their space, particularly one as large as the *Venture*. In addition, I fear that Admiral Gepta's diplomatic sensitivity would not be sufficient to the task of dealing with the Renao."

Kromm snorted at the ambassador's euphemism. For his part, Gepta sounded like someone he might actually like.

"This decision is not ours to make," said Adams. "Starfleet Command needs to clear that with the government on Onferin." He turned to Kromm. "You now have the command over operations within the cluster, Captain Kromm. Prove yourself worthy of this honor."

"When you return from your excursion to nowhere with the *Prometheus*, I will welcome you in the government seat on Onferin with a celebratory drink for our victory," Kromm said.

Adams tersely said, "We'll see, won't we?" He glanced around. "Any more comments?"

No one said anything.

Adams nodded, satisfied. "Which means we've got a plan. I will inform Admiral Akaar immediately. You, Kromm, should contact the High Council. Let's get to work." He rose from his seat, ending the meeting.

When Kromm returned to the transporter room with his people, he mulled over the meeting. Having Rozhenko back aboard was definitely a nuisance, but it was a small price to pay to get rid of Adams and the *Prometheus*.

Finally, my time has come, Kromm thought, and his mood lifted with every step. *Now is the time for glory for Kromm, son of Kaath.*

I.K.S. Bortas

Spock strolled leisurely through the dark corridors of the *Bortas*. He was dressed in dark gray clothes and carried a small bag tucked under his arm, where he had packed what few personal belongings he took with him during his journeys. A *bekk* had already taken the rest of his luggage to the *Prometheus*. Before he transferred back to the Federation ship, he wanted to pay one last visit to L'emka.

He stood outside the first officer's cabin and touched the door alert, but there was no reply. Frowning, Spock wondered whether he had just missed her. Only a few minutes ago in his cabin, the ship's computer had informed him that the young female officer was in her quarters.

Logically, either L'emka was absent or she was inside her quarters and didn't want to see anyone. Spock dismissed the notion that she hadn't heard the electronic chime. His exceptionally sharp ears didn't pick up any audible noises behind the door—in contrast to Chief Engineer Nuk's quarters, where he heard the blaring sound of a Klingon opera.

Spock's thoughts were interrupted when the door opened

abruptly. L'emka stared at him with widened eyes from the doorway, a curse obviously already on her lips. But when she realized who had been disturbing her—she was only half dressed—she winced and swallowed her unspoken words.

Blinking, she looked at Spock. "Ambassador, I was not expecting you."

"Evidently," Spock replied.

She looked down at herself, clearly realizing now that she wore little more than her underwear while standing in front of a living legend. "Forgive my attire."

"No, it is I who should apologize," the old half-Vulcan replied. "I quite clearly chose an inopportune time to visit. However, it is not possible for me to postpone, as I am on my way to transfer to the *Prometheus*."

"In that case, come in. I was almost done, anyway." Stepping aside, she let him pass.

Spock entered the room filled with curiosity. The first officer's cabin was similar to the other accommodations aboard the *Bortas*. It was only about a quarter of the size of senior officers' berths on comparable Starfleet ships. A terminal was mounted beside the door, a metal *QongDaq* that served as a bed was in one corner, next to a door to the bathroom.

An unusual feature was an elaborate, obviously handmade tapestry depicting scenes of farm life on a Klingon world. Spock knew that L'emka came from a family of farmers. He assumed that the tapestry was there to remind her of her roots. Even more remarkable was the extensive collection of Klingon weapons adorning the walls. Spock counted at least twenty different knives and swords of Klingon origin. Some of them appeared to be museum exhibits, while others were more along the line of the current fashion of weapons within the Empire.

The only illumination came from several thick candles that L'emka had spread around the cabin, the artificial light completely dimmed. Spock noticed several drops of blood on the floor, and a stained *d'k tahg* on the chair.

"Please excuse me a minute," L'emka said, heading toward the bathroom. When she turned her back to Spock, he saw an irregular stab wound on the back of her bare left thigh. A trace of blood ran down her leg.

"You're hurt," Spock said.

"I know," replied L'emka without turning around. She disappeared into the small bathroom. Soon after, Spock heard the humming of a medical tissue regenerator. He wondered what exactly the Klingon woman had been doing when he had disturbed her.

The rustling of clothing was audible in the bathroom, followed by the sounds of the sonic shower. Spock clasped his hands behind his back and began inspecting the exhibited Klingon weapons.

Three minutes later L'emka emerged, freshly showered and clad in wide cloth pants and a comfortable brown tunic. Her hair, which had been tied up before, hung open over her shoulders like a dark waterfall framing her slender face.

"I apologize for making you wait, Ambassador."

"There is no reason to apologize," Spock said. "May I inquire as to the nature of your activities when I arrived?"

She smiled. "Not at all. I was busy with combat training." The young Klingon woman went over to the chair, picking up the *d'k tahg*. With a cloth she wiped off the blood.

"But why did you injure yourself? I trust I am right in assuming that your wounds are self-inflicted."

"Yes. That's part of my personal training." Carefully, L'emka placed the double-edged blade back in its rack on the wall, then turned back to face the ambassador. "Lust, fury, and pain—those are the three strongest emotions that a Klingon experiences during battle. The lust for fighting, the fury toward the enemy, and the pain of injuries. If you submit to them, you will fight like a wild animal. But if you learn to control these emotions, to push them aside and ignore them, you can defeat any enemy. So I'm not only practicing deftly wielding the *bat'leth* or the *tajtIq*, I also practice controlling lust, fury, and pain."

Spock raised an eyebrow. "Fascinating. Although our measures are far less drastic, the approach is similar to that taken by Vulcans while learning to control our emotions."

L'emka laughed. "Don't let the captain hear that. He's looking for an excuse to remove me from the ship, and being like a Vulcan would be just the thing."

"Indeed. I have observed that your relationship has altered within the past few days, and not in your favor. Since the events in orbit around Iad, Kromm has kept you at arm's length."

"Presumably because we've already made two attempts to kill each other. Computer, increase brightness fifty percent." While the cabin was bathed in golden ambient light, L'emka walked through the room, blowing out all the candles and collecting them.

"I regret that your status aboard the *Bortas* is so precarious," Spock said. "You are a fine officer."

L'emka stopped, looking at Spock. A shadow darted across her face. "Perhaps. Perhaps too fine an officer for the *Bortas*. My recent actions have turned not only Kromm but many other officers against me. I spoke out in favor of *jeghpu'wI'* and alien prisoners. I have been called weak, and I have been called a traitor. But what should I do? I live for the glory and the protection of the Empire. Wherever they send me, I will serve."

"There are many ways to serve your empire," Spock said. "I have come to remind you of that. I have observed you closely during my time aboard this ship. In that time, I have observed a woman of great strength, sharp wit, and a keen sense of honor. While some on board may beg to differ, it is my considered opinion that you are what a Klingon should be: a fearless fighter with a sense of compassion for the weak."

For a brief moment, L'emka stared at Spock with widened eyes, before a smile slowly appeared on her face. "I thank you, Ambassador. That is high praise from anyone, least of all someone of your accomplishments."

"Captain Adams and Ambassador Rozhenko also hold you in high regard," Spock said. "I therefore urge you not to be deterred, and not to allow your talents to wither away on a ship with a captain who does not appreciate what he has. I am confident that a post that is more suited to you will present itself in due course. And if you need an advocate in the Empire, I have no doubt that Ambassador Rozhenko would provide support if you requested it. And should you follow in the footsteps of another very remarkable Klingon by working within the Federation, you would have my support as well."

L'emka tilted her head humbly. "You are very generous, Ambassador. I know not how I may express my gratitude."

Spock permitted himself to display the faintest hint of a smile. "There is no need to thank me, Commander. My Vulcan forebears would say that it is only logical to support your abilities, but I believe it is more appropriate to speak as my human forebears would, and simply say: my pleasure."

14

NOVEMBER 27, 2385

Secret shipyard of the Purifying Flame
Somewhere in the Lembatta Cluster

Deep within the Lembatta Cluster, a dead planetoid drifted in space. It measured only a few kilometers in diameter, and it was surrounded by thousands of other similar celestial bodies. These conditions made it the ideal hiding place for the secret shipyard of the Purifying Flame. This was the location where they converted old freighter models into solar-jumpers, and here where they churned out an increasing number of *Scorpion* attack fighters to fill them with highly explosive cargos consisting of trilithium, tekasite, and protomatter.

At least that had been the plan of the Inner Circle and their leader, the Honorable Commander Hamash ak Bhedal. It was a plan that had become increasingly difficult to put into action.

"What do you mean you can't deliver any more protomatter?" Furious, ak Bhedal glared at Kluzh, the alien standing across from him.

"Is your universal translator malfunctioning?" Kluzh snarled. "What's there not to understand? Our sources have dried up."

Kluzh was a very large alien, and his face looked like a half-melted skull, framed by a wild shaggy mane of black hair. The smuggler wore heavy leather clothing, with a nasty-looking energy weapon holstered at his side. Ak Bhedal had no idea what species he belonged to, not that it mattered.

What *did* matter was Kluzh had been supplying them with resources and stolen weapons technology from the space of the sphere defilers. But now that the Purifying Flame's fight was gaining momentum, the smuggler had become increasingly unreliable.

Ak Bhedal exchanged a quick glance with his right hand, ak Joulid, who looked just as unhappy at Kluzh's words as he was.

"If this is an attempt to renegotiate prices, you're playing a dangerous game," ak Bhedal said as he turned back to the smuggler.

The pirate's companion, a stocky Orion man, growled threateningly, placing his hand on the rifle that was dangling in front of his stomach from a belt. The light from the ceiling lamps reflected off his bald head as he jutted his chin belligerently.

Kluzh stopped him with a wave of his hand. "What you're paying is fine, it's not the issue. Our supplier of protomatter within the Romulan Star Empire has completely dried up. The rumor is that the Federation gave the Praetor a subtle hint. And believe me, my friend, I'm just as furious about that as you are. That was one of my best sources, not just for protomatter."

Pressing his lips tightly together, ak Bhedal remained silent for a moment. They needed the protomatter. Without this highly volatile and reactive element, the bombs in the cloaked fighters wouldn't discharge enough explosive energy to devastate their targets. "Can't you find another source?"

Kluzh spread his arms. "I'm searching for one, but it'll take time. We're not talking about a crate labeled 'Medical

Supplies' that you can then fill with disruptors. Protomatter is difficult to find and is handled with extreme care due to its volatility."

"Which is why we need it," ak Bhedal replied. "It's dangerous. And we pay you royally for the acquisition."

Kluzh grunted. "I know that." He looked from one Renao to the other. "I'm doing my best to find a new supplier. As soon as I have one, I'll be in touch through the usual channels."

"You do that," ak Bhedal said with a frown.

The smuggler nodded at ak Bhedal one last time, before he and his Orion companion turned and walked through the cave hangar back to his sickle-shaped abomination of a ship.

After the smuggler took off into the red nebulae that engulfed the asteroid base, ak Bhedal regarded ak Joulid with annoyance. "I hope we won't receive any more bad news today."

The pair of them marched down the base's corridors toward the command level. They were met by a frenzy of activity. In the training area, ak Bhedal saw young people sitting in front of old flight simulators that had been decommissioned by the Romulan military. Others knelt in rows on the floor, listening to the lectures of a teacher who prepped them for the battle against the powers of the Alpha Quadrant.

From the dockyard halls in the lower levels of the asteroid, the screeching and hammering of machines reached his ear. They were churning out ever more attack fighters. Workers shouted advice or orders at each other. And very quietly, the driving rhythms of traditional Bharatrum music lingered in the air.

It was slightly more quiet on the command level. Men and women sat at computer terminals, watching the environment controls for the asteroid and the sensor grid that would warn them of unexpected visitors. When ak Bhedal appeared, everyone jumped to their feet, saluting him smartly. Walking past them, he made a dismissive gesture.

Ak Mahda, who was in charge of communications between the various Purifying Flame cells, stepped in front of him. "Forgive me, Honorable Commander, but I have news that…" She hesitated, before handing a padd to ak Bhedal. "Perhaps you should see for yourself."

Frowning, ak Bhedal grabbed the reader, scanning the collection of the latest news from all over the cluster. The members of the Purifying Flame on Xhehenem had started to punish the ditherers and laggards. That was good, because there were only two factions in war: those on your side and those against. On Bharatrum, support for the Flame had been steadily increasing. Even the planetary custodian, Goraal ak Behruun, openly sympathized with ak Bhedal's movement.

But then his gaze fell upon the next two news items, and he cried out, "No!"

"What happened?" ak Joulid asked.

"We have lost one of our solar-jumpers, the *Coumatha*. She was intercepted while she was on her way to one of the sphere defilers' colony worlds by ships of the depraved. According to the distress call, Captain ak Lovaal saw no chance to escape. He intended to destroy the ship so it wouldn't fall into the hands of our enemies, but was stymied."

Ak Joulid looked shocked. "Now we only have two active solar-jumpers left."

"We need to convert other ships, and quickly. Without the jumpers we're unable to carry our deadly seed into space." The commander turned to his communications officer. "Ak Mahda, summon the Inner Circle to the briefing room. We need to hold a war council!"

"Yes, Honorable." The woman hurried off.

"It gets worse," ak Bhedal said to ak Joulid as they continued their walk. "We have lost our base on the moon Calidhu. Our brothers and sisters had to flee when the sphere defilers' attention focused on the Bharatrum system."

They entered the briefing room. A large circular table dominated the room that had been carved into the rock. The walls were bare, save for a two-dimensional paper map of the Alpha Quadrant attached to the north wall. Seven chairs stood around the table—one for each inhabited Renao world.

Ak Bhedal took his place. With a furious growl, he threw the padd onto the table. "These wretched strangers! May Iad devour them!"

Picking up the padd, ak Joulid read the news for himself. "At least it would seem that some of them died when ak Lhamad sacrificed himself and blew up the Calidhu base."

"Yes, let's have a celebration," ak Bhedal snapped. "We killed a small handful of sphere defilers—and it only cost us our best listening post."

The remaining five members of the Inner Circle appeared at the entrance. Ak Bhedal motioned for them to sit down. He quickly informed them about the recent setbacks and defeats.

"We need to strike again immediately," he finished, full of anger. "These attacks on our people mustn't remain unpunished. We need to hit them where it hurts, more painful than ever before."

"Let's attack the homeworld of these humans, and strike into the heart of the Federation," ak Sahoon from Catoumni suggested.

"No," ak Bhedal said with a dismissive gesture. "We won't be able to do that. The humans' home system is far too well protected."

"How about a place where no one even considers war?" said ak Joulid. "A world where even seasoned veterans let their guard down?"

"Ah, now that sounds like an idea." The commander got up and walked over to the map. The borders of the large empires as well as hundreds of inhabited star systems were charted here. Several pins in different colors showed the locations of the latest victories of the Flame and marked future targets.

"Isn't there a world somewhere where they pursue their leisure activities the whole year round?" he mumbled, glancing at the map. "The sphere defilers meet there and relax after their expansion raids. Yes! Here it is." His finger poked at the map. "Risa." He whirled around, facing the members of the circle. "Risa is our next target."

"That all sounds fair and well," said Yssab's representative, "but with an attack here and an attack there we won't get very far. And what if the solar-jumper we send to Risa gets intercepted like the *Coumatha* was?"

"What are you getting at?" ak Bhedal asked.

"We need to think bigger!" the other Renao replied. "The next attack has to shake these tainted empires of the sphere defilers to their very core. And just how do we achieve that?" His glowing eyes wandered from one man to the other. "By not just attacking one planet, but seven simultaneously. One world of theirs for every world of ours!"

His words were followed by nervous murmurs. The plan was certainly ambitious—dangerous, but bold. Ak Bhedal liked it.

"We won't make it," Golaah ak Partam said. He was Xhehenem's representative and the shipyard's leading engineer. "We don't have enough ships."

"Well, let's build more ships then," ak Bhedal said. "We will speed up our workflow. And we capture two more freighters and convert them into solar-jumpers. With the three already in our shipyard, and the two active ships, we would have exactly seven."

Ak Partam stared at ak Bhedal incredulously. "That's absurd. We don't have enough workers. The ones I have are already being taxed beyond their abilities. I'd need twice as many people, maybe more."

Resting both his hands on the table's surface, ak Bhedal stared at ak Partam with burning eyes. "We will simply have to recruit more! There are enough people within the arcologies of Xhehenem, Lhoeel or Acina III. Let's strike there and take whomever we need."

Eyes widening, ak Partam asked, "You want to turn against our own people, Honorable Commander?"

"Not against *our* people," ak Bhedal said. "Not against those who are truly loyal sons and daughters of the Home Spheres. Only the cowards and ditherers who are not willing to participate in the holy mission should be our targets. Because whoever doesn't want to fight, whoever submits voluntarily to these sphere defilers, might as well be our slave."

15
NOVEMBER 28, 2385

U.S.S. Prometheus, in slipstream

Isabelle Courmont had been aware that things would be radically different for her when she gave up her successful practice in San Francisco and signed up with Starfleet. She was, after all, a civilian who had only left Earth's solar system once during the previous forty years of her life, that being a trip to Vulcan.

She had been driven by two different motivations. Since her separation from her husband two years ago, she had finally felt the old familiar wanderlust again that she had experienced as an adolescent and as a young woman. Back then, she had satiated that hunger with journeys all over Earth, to the moon, to Mars, and finally to Vulcan. Living with Max, a holoartist who was entirely satisfied with living in San Francisco, this wanderlust had dwindled and had been replaced by journeys into the world of virtual arts.

But then he had left her for a terribly dumb ginger-haired Orion starlet, and throughout the following months, Isabelle had realized that the biggest part of her life on the west coast of North America had been Max's life, and not her own. Without him, she had only her work as a psychiatrist with neurotic members of the arts and entertainment industry, and an apartment that was far too big for her with empty walls and an amazing view of the

San Francisco Bay and the grounds of Starfleet Academy.

After the Borg attack in 2381, the heartfelt urge to help others added to her wish to change her life around and to get away from the confines of San Francisco. She had followed the news and learned about the suffering of both the devastated planet populations and the uprooted refugees. She had also learned about the numerous war traumas that men and women aboard Starfleet ships had suffered while fighting against the relentless Collective.

One thing had led to another, and Courmont found herself on Starbase 22, where she initially helped station counselor Brian Ellis with tending to the *Prometheus* crew after their battle for Vulcan. That was how she had met Captain Richard Adams, who had been a broken man at the time. Not only had he lost a quarter of his crew, but also his wife Rhea. She had been the captain of the *U.S.S. Red Cloud* and had also fought above Vulcan.

Courmont had helped Adams—who had been an ill-tempered and difficult patient to say the least—to accept the gap in his life, and to continue in spite of it. One year later, after the *Prometheus* had undergone a complete overhaul, she had been surprised to receive Adams's invitation to transfer to his ship.

Her travel lust had been sufficiently satiated by then. She had visited Betazed, New France, and Denobula Prime; she had spent her shore leave on about a dozen unknown worlds on the Tzenkethi border, and finally, she had been allowed to see Bajor for herself and to marvel at the famous wormhole from the Promenade on Deep Space 9.

But helping others had become increasingly difficult. Starfleet officers were trained to be professionals. They had been indoctrinated with command structures and efficient thinking. It was extremely difficult for many of them to admit to individual weaknesses, let alone seek professional help. Right after the Borg invasion, horror had been widespread, and consultations with therapists of all kinds had been commonplace aboard ships. But as the crisis moved further into the past, the willingness to speak about fears and problems had lessened. Too many people felt that being haunted by past problems was a knock against their professionalism, and so they would not admit to such issues. It was foolish, but not unusual.

So Courmont was more than a little surprised when Lenissa zh'Thiin of all people suddenly stood in the doorway to her office. If anyone aboard the *Prometheus* was almost overzealous in her attempt to appear professional and her refusal to admit to weakness, it was the young Andorian woman.

"Commander... Lenissa—please, come in." Usually, Courmont didn't turn to first name terms with someone she had hardly had more than two conversations with in the past. But something told her that zh'Thiin would never open up to a ship's counselor, but rather to a friend—even if her intimacy was just pretense.

Hesitantly, zh'Thiin entered the room, glancing around as if to make sure that Courmont was alone. The counselor had set up her office to convey relaxation and comfort. A desk with a terminal stood by one wall, but the majority of the room was taken up by a comfortable seating area with a sofa, two armchairs, a low glass table, and a replicator. The windowsills, walls, and a shelf were decorated with exquisite pieces of art from Earth, Andor, Tellar, Vulcan, Bolarus IX, and other homeworlds of crewmembers. Her collection was not yet complete—she had yet to locate works of art from Delta IV, Trill, and Cait that she liked—but there was enough to see or comment on for every visitor, should they require an opener to their conversation.

Courmont stood up from her seat by the desk. "Please, Lenissa, come in, sit down. I was just about to make some tea. Would you like some?" She walked to the replicator. The skirt of her civilian clothing rustled. She had always refused to wear a uniform, as she didn't want to be perceived as a senior officer or as a female soldier but as the civilian that she was, even though she had been granted the rank of lieutenant when she enlisted. Besides, she had found that her casual dressing style sometimes helped withdrawn crewmembers connect with her more easily.

Zh'Thiin's antennae wavered. "No, thank you, Counselor. I… Are you sure that I'm not intruding?" She sounded like she was desperate for an excuse to escape. Courmont could tell that the young Andorian woman was in dire need of a counseling session.

"Absolutely not, Lenissa," she replied, touching zh'Thiin's shoulder gently and gingerly steering her towards the seating area. "I'm glad you're paying me a visit. And please, call me Isabelle." Gently but firmly she pushed zh'Thiin down onto the sofa before stepping to the replicator. "If you don't want tea, how about a *katheka* for you?"

"Sounds good," said zh'Thiin, stroking the soft cushions with her hands.

Courmont gave her a genuine smile. "In that case, I'll have one myself. I heard it's almost like coffee from Earth but with its very own taste."

"*Katheka* is much more tart than coffee," zh'Thiin said. "You should dilute it with milk."

"Thanks for the tip." Courmont ordered the two hot

drinks, placed one of them in front of zh'Thiin and settled into one of the armchairs. "May I ask you something, before you tell me why you're here?"

Zh'Thiin nodded. "Of course."

Crossing her legs and leaning forward, Courmont held the cup of *katheka* in both hands in her lap. "I heard that you have received lessons in Caitian motion meditation from Commander Roaas recently."

"That's correct. Why?"

"Would you recommend that meditation method to a human? A crew member has sought my advice because they are suffering from increasing insomnia since we entered the cluster. Now, I know some relaxation exercises but I had an inkling that this person might prefer ritual movements, rather than focusing on themselves in silence and motionlessness."

Zh'Thiin shrugged. "I can't speak for others. The routines are not too difficult for people with standard fitness if that's what you're asking."

"And do they work?"

"They do for me—for the most part." The Andorian grimaced.

Courmont took a sip from her *katheka*. She had to agree with zh'Thiin—the drink was fairly bitter. She should have ordered three units of milk instead of just two. But she concealed her discomfort. "For the most part? That sounds as if you have a lot on your mind. Is that why you're here, Lenissa?"

"Yes. No. Perhaps. I think." Nervously, zh'Thiin tucked her chin-long white hair behind her ear. She stared into her cup of *katheka*. A crease appeared above the ridge of her nose while she seemed to contemplate how to put her problem into words.

Finally, she looked up, and Courmont saw a deep insecurity in her blue and gray eyes.

"I'm concerned about the telepaths aboard the ship," zh'Thiin finally said after a long pause. "I paid Geron—Doctor Barai—a visit earlier today. He might be medically monitored, but there doesn't seem to be anything else happening. He's just lying there, haunted by inner demons, and I don't even see the tiniest attempt at therapy. Sedatives will only suppress the symptoms but they won't do any healing. Isn't there anything else we can do for the doctor and the others? Isn't it our duty to do more?"

Courmont thought about it and nodded. "You're right. I—like Doctor Calloway—think that the healing process of an overloaded mind can only begin with calmness and silence. However, we should probably take a more active approach, even if it's only for those who are still in full command of their faculties. Idly standing by while someone who means a lot to us is suffering is the most difficult thing to do." She paused, searching Lenissa's face. "He does mean a lot to you, doesn't he?"

"The doctor?"

"Geron."

Zh'Thiin's antennae raised defensively. "What gives you that idea?"

"It's my duty to look closely at people aboard the *Prometheus*, Lenissa. That's something we have in common. You look after the physical well-being of our crew, while I take care of the mental side of things. And I haven't missed the way you two look at each other." Courmont smiled again.

The blue hue of the young Andorian woman's cheeks darkened in a blush. "That wasn't supposed to be obvious to anyone."

"Don't worry, Lenissa. You've been very discreet. I doubt that anyone else but me would have noticed it." Courmont leant back in her chair, taking another sip of *katheka*. She decided that she could get used to this drink. "Don't fret over it, Lenissa. You are both adults, and you're not violating any Starfleet regulations as you both work in different departments and hold virtually the same rank. Nobody would hold your relationship against you."

Zh'Thiin snorted. "If only it were that easy."

"What do you mean?" Courmont raised her eyebrows.

The Andorian jumped to her feet. Clutching the *katheka* cup with both hands, she started pacing. "It's not a relationship. At least, it's not supposed to be. I wasn't after that, I just wanted a friendship—with certain benefits, so to speak. But no emotional strings. Now, though, there *are* emotions. Suddenly, he falls in love with me." Zh'Thiin steadily raised her voice, and her antennae pointed forward like belligerent snakes.

Courmont leaned back and let zh'Thiin continue at her own pace.

"I never wanted that," she continued. "I never wanted a relationship, just a bit of fun. All the *other* men understood that. But Geron didn't, Geron of all people. He's a Betazoid; he should understand me better than anyone else."

"Maybe he understands you all too well," Courmont suggested gently.

Zh'Thiin stopped dead in her tracks, staring at her. "What do you mean?"

"Please sit down, Lenissa. It'll be easier to talk openly that way. I assume that's why you're here, because you finally want to talk. Nothing of what's being said here today will leave this room. If you wish, I won't even put it on record that you visited me."

The security chief remained silent for a moment. Finally, she slumped back onto the sofa. Sighing, she put her *katheka* cup down and stroked her hair and her antennae with her hands.

"All right," she said quietly.

Courmont waited another moment but when zh'Thiin didn't begin to speak, she prompted her. "When did this begin—this reluctance to have a relationship? At the Academy?" If so, zh'Thiin was probably another sad example of Starfleet's method of grooming the perfect officers, while the humane side of things was increasingly forgotten. The enormous pressure to accelerate education, in order to compensate for the recent staff losses in combat, didn't help either.

Zh'Thiin stared into the distance. "I don't know. Maybe. No, probably much earlier. I've always been someone to pursue my goals with a burning ambition, even during my youth on Andor. Friends were all right. People I could surround myself with to let off steam. I never wanted more. I didn't have the time for a serious relationship, and I didn't want all the mess that comes with it. Responsibility, arguments… It's bad enough with a two-person couple, but for us Andorians? Four personalities clash when serious emotions are involved. I couldn't be bothered with that. And why should I?" She looked as if she wanted to say something else, but remained silent.

Thoughtful, Courmont took a sip from her *katheka*. "So you built walls inside, to prevent anyone from getting too close to you. And whenever someone threatened to even scratch at these walls, you got rid of them. That was always easy. A few hurtful words, maybe a flirt with another colleague, and the unwelcome admirer was gone."

Zh'Thiin gnawed at her lower lip, nodding quietly.

Courmont continued: "But it didn't work with Geron. He's a telepath. He knows what it looks like inside of you, and he knows that you didn't erect these walls because you don't want to love, but because you're scared."

"What should I be scared of?" zh'Thiin asked defensively.

"You tell me, Lenissa."

The trembling antennae betrayed her. The young Andorian woman knew full well what the core of her problem was, even though she had shut it away deep inside of her, and it had taken quite a while and the quiet hours of a slipstream flight to make it surface again.

"Tell me," Courmont repeated gently. "Why are you scared to love? Why are you scared of allowing emotions to come close to you? I can see that you have emotions. Otherwise, you wouldn't be this worried about Geron. What are these walls supposed to protect you from?"

Instead of answering, zh'Thiin got up again. Slowly, she walked towards the shelf next to the office door and picked up one of the items—an adorned goblet made of blue crystal. Four blue figures were arranged around the drinking vessel, sitting next to each other and holding hands, like a circle of solidarity. The figures were naked, and if you looked very closely, you could make out the slender antennae protruding from their heads. Deep in thought, the security chief stroked the glass with one of her fingers. She turned back to Courmont.

"Do you know what this is?"

Courmont also got up and joined zh'Thiin. "Not really. I bought the goblet two years ago in a small shop in the Kaybin District on Denobula when the *Prometheus* made a stop there. The merchant said it was an Andorian fertility goblet." He also said that the goblet would bring luck in love to its owner, which was probably silly... just like her impulse to purchase the trinket. But she had simply felt lonely that evening, on the fourth anniversary of her separation from Max.

"That's not entirely wrong," said zh'Thiin with a rare smile. "It's a *mashka*, a... well, okay, fertility goblet is probably the best translation. In some of the more traditional areas of Andor it would be circulated among the bondgroup before the *shelthreth*. Everyone would drink from it, thus creating a bond." The Andorian woman tilted her head curiously. "You know about Andorian reproduction?"

Courmont nodded. "I know what just about every Federation citizen knows." She knew that there were four genders—*zhen*, *shen*, *thaan* and *chan*—and that they lived in so-called bondgroups. The *shelthreth* was some kind of ritualized mating with the intention to sire offspring. Because four different gene pools were required, and the fertility time frame was not very large, these bondgroups were extremely important on Andor—now more than ever because they had barely overcome their reproduction crisis.

It suddenly dawned on Courmont that Lenissa zh'Thiin had maneuvered herself into a more than awkward position with regards to her culture. She had refused to return to her homeworld during the reproduction crisis to do what she could as a *zhen* to produce offspring. Instead, she had sought her pleasure with non-Andorians—an act that the term *rebellion* didn't even begin to describe.

"In which case, you probably know that the bondgroups are virtually sacred on Andor," said zh'Thiin, turning the crystal goblet in her hands. "The group is more or less an arranged marriage. Some of them are already arranged during childhood. The bond is tied before the twentieth year of life. Our society has always been obsessed with that. But the events of the last twenty years, when it became obvious that fewer and fewer children were being born, have only made things worse. In the end, Andorian adolescents were taught to put this bond above their individuality. The *shelthreth* became a ritual, if not a religious service, and the birth of a child was celebrated as a miracle. It all revolved around this one thing—and yet, we are still doomed."

The Andorian looked up, and her eyes met Courmont's. Her antennae trembled. "I didn't want that, you know? All this madness. I wanted to live, not for some bondpartners who were forced onto me, not for Andor, but for myself! So I fled. Did you know that? No, how could you, it's not even in my records."

"You left Andor and joined Starfleet," said Courmont. "I can't see anything wrong with that."

"Maybe you can't. But then, you're human—there are plenty of you in the galaxy. You should try talking to my bondgroup." Zh'Thiin laughed bitterly. "Yes, I'm married according to Andorian law, at least I was fifteen years ago—that's also not in my files, because I withheld that information. I fled from Andor during the night after the bond had been tied. I abandoned my bondgroup, because they didn't mean anything to me. Space meant something to me, the never-ending vastness out there. Andor wanted to take my freedom away, but I didn't stand for that. So I committed the sacrilege of disappearing. I, as a *zhen*, was supposed to help by bringing children into the world. But I didn't care. Andor didn't matter to me. And when those idiots left the Federation three years ago, I cared even less about them."

Zh'Thiin pressed her lips together, shaking her head. Tears shimmered in her eyes, and she wiped them away with two fingers. "I'm sorry," she whispered, put the *mashka* back on the shelf, and started to leave.

But Courmont put a hand on her shoulder, holding her back. "No, don't be sorry. You've done what your heart told you to do, Lenissa. And that was the right thing to do." Gingerly, the counselor led zh'Thiin back to the seating area and sat down on the sofa with her. She handed the young Andorian woman the *katheka* cup, and Lenissa took a sip.

Courmont gave her time to regroup before asking: "Did you ever regret it?"

Zh'Thiin glanced at her from the corner of her eye. "Leaving my people to join Starfleet?"

Courmont nodded.

For a moment, the security chief considered, and Courmont believed that she was truly confronting that question for the first time in a decade and a half.

"No. Never," she finally said. "I was happy in Starfleet, still am. The service is a challenge, but I like giving everything I've got to be worthy of it. And even when Andor called its citizens home, when so many of us left the fleet... that was never an option for me. Never. I just can't see myself as a mother and the loving center of a bondgroup—but that would have been my role on Andor. Besides, it was all so useless, so desperate. I wouldn't have been able to bear the mood on my homeworld."

Finally, it all made sense to Courmont. "So you pushed everything away from yourself, built walls and denied yourself all emotions beyond casual pleasure."

Zh'Thiin shrugged. "Looks like it. Pretty cowardly for an Andorian warrior, isn't it?"

"I'd call it… human, if you pardon the term. Your people's suffering during recent decades is a tragedy, something that wouldn't leave any Andorian cold. Some resorted to compulsive proactive ways, others to deep desperation, and yet others pushed everything away. All those are natural reactions to a tragedy. In your case, being afraid of the restraints of a relationship was added to the equation." Courmont looked at her, full of compassion. "But now you don't need these walls anymore, Lenissa. The reproduction crisis is over. Andor rejoined the Federation, and things are looking up for your people. It's only a matter of time. If you want my advice, try to look into the future with hope. Leave the burdens of the past behind you. And if you really have feelings for Geron, and you know that he also has some for you, you shouldn't make your life unnecessarily complicated. Just let everything take its course."

Zh'Thiin smiled woefully. "It would be the first proper love in my life. I don't know if I can do that."

"Take it slow," said Courmont, "step by step, cautiously. And believe me—you couldn't have a better partner for your first love than a Betazoid."

The security chief's smile vanished. "That's assuming he recovers. I wish I could do more for him than just sit by his bedside."

"Maybe we can." Something crossed the counselor's mind. "I will speak to Ambassador Spock. He was able to overcome the Son's attack relatively quickly and without lasting damage. Maybe his strength could aid the other afflicted patients."

"But how?" zh'Thiin asked.

"By conducting a therapeutic mind-meld."

"Do you think that would work?"

"I have no idea," said Courmont. "Therapeutic mind-melds are not unknown in Vulcan medicine. But I couldn't say whether they are helpful for members of other species or, in this special case, a mental overload. It's definitely worth a try, though. I will get in touch with the ambassador about it."

"Please do," said zh'Thiin. "And please let me know if this treatment is in any way successful." She got up from the sofa. This time, Courmont didn't hold her back. "Thank you for the *katheka*."

The counselor watched the young woman reactivating her shield. Lenissa turned back into Lieutenant Commander zh'Thiin, the *Prometheus* security chief, a professional through and through. She took two steps towards the door, and it slid open. But suddenly, zh'Thiin hesitated, turning back one more time, the door closing again. For a moment her face softened.

"And for everything else as well," she added. "Thank you, Counselor... Isabelle."

"No, thank you, Lenissa," replied Courmont, "for coming to see me and trusting me. It means a lot to me. And if I can do anything else for you... or even if you just want to have another cup of *katheka*, come and visit me, anytime."

Zh'Thiin nodded briefly. "I will."

She stepped again toward the door, which opened and let her out into the corridor.

Isabelle Courmont leant back on the sofa, staring pensively through the window into the blue swirl of the slipstream. She raised the cup of *katheka* to her lips, drinking the last sip. Somehow, the Andorian brew didn't even taste all that bitter anymore. *I could really get used to this stuff*, she thought.

16
NOVEMBER 28, 2385

U.S.S. Prometheus, in slipstream

"You and your uniform… Here, let me help you." Chuckling good-naturedly, Moba handed the man on the other side of Starboard 8's counter a cloth.

Jassat ak Namur took it gratefully, dabbing at his black uniform jacket where a wet speck was visible. He had toppled over a Q'babi juice glass with a careless movement of his hand.

"Thank you," he said to the Bolian barkeeper who was wiping his counter dry with another cloth. "That's so embarrassing."

Moba made a dismissive gesture. "Don't worry about it. That happens to someone every other day. It was even worse when we were in that damn cluster. They didn't just knock the glasses over accidentally, they threw them on purpose." The Bolian shook his head. Finally, he realized who stood in front of him, and his eyes widened. "Oh, Lieutenant, I'm so sorry. I didn't mean that about the cluster. Well, not quite. But you know…"

Now it was Jassat's turn to raise his hand dismissively. "It's all right, Moba. I know how difficult the journey through the home spheres was. I must admit…" He hesitated, before he continued, lowering his voice. "I must admit that I'm almost glad to leave the cluster behind, even if it's only for a few days." Downcast, he handed the cloth back to the barkeep.

Moba took the cloth, throwing it and his own into the recycler. He placed his hands on the counter, looking at Jassat sympathetically. "That wasn't quite the homecoming you had in mind, eh?"

"No," said Jassat. "Not quite."

"If you want to talk about it..." Moba poured a new glass of Q'babi juice and placed it in front of Jassat. "I'm not Counselor Courmont, but how does the old Bolian proverb go? Whatever bothers you during the day, you should tell your head massager; whatever bothers you at night, you should tell your bartender." He nodded encouragingly at Jassat.

"Thanks, Moba, but there isn't much to talk about." The young Renao cautiously picked up his glass, turning it between his hands. "You saw yourself what it's like within the home spheres. And you witnessed the mood swing aboard the ship."

The bartender mumbled affirmatively. "True, true. Here in Starboard 8 where people didn't have anything better to do than drink and think, it was probably even more obvious than at the stations." He sighed. "Luckily, things are improving now. With every passing light year we get farther away, things can only get better."

"I really hope so," Jassat said. It was this hope—and Jenna's perseverance—that had brought him to Starboard 8 today. Actually, he had intended to stay away from the club since he had been the victim of seething xenophobia twice in there. But Jenna had convinced him that he needed to take a stand against idiots like Lieutenant Björn Jansen and Ensign Ricat Na Bukh. If he hid in his quarters because of them, they had won, and they didn't deserve that.

While he waited for Kirk, whose steadfast friendship and support meant more to him with every passing day, Jassat sipped his juice, glancing around the dimly lit room. Most of the people here were crewpeople or ensigns from alpha shift security: Goran Tol, Pradnya Mandhare, and several others. A few of the science staff were huddling in a corner. Lieutenant Krish Iniri sat at the next table, staring out of the window at the hypnotic blue flow of the slipstream. The few who spoke did so quietly.

Jassat had noticed that during the past few hours, since they had left the Lembatta Cluster behind at slipstream speed, the mood aboard the ship was incredibly quiet. After the shields had failed in orbit above Iad, and artificial rage had overwhelmed many crewmembers, they had verbally abused their comrades or hurt their friends. Now that everyone was finally rid of the Son's terrible influence and they were able to think clearly again, they became aware of their actions, and regret and embarrassment had taken over. Apparently it had dawned on many of them that Iad had only been the painful climax of an insidious disease that had had a hold over them for quite some time.

The door to the club hissed open. Expecting Jenna, Jassat turned around. Instead, three people walked in. Jassat's heart rate increased. He didn't know the human man and the female Tellarite, but the third person was the three-legged, three-armed Na Bukh.

The Triexian joked with his colleagues, before turning his bald red-brown head to look around—and noticing Jassat. His slender legs stumbled briefly. A strange expression darted across his bony face.

Oh no, thought Jassat. *Not again.*

But Na Bukh looked away, walking to one of the tables

with his colleagues. While the human and the Tellarite sat down, the Triexian remained on his feet. His torso swayed slowly back and forth.

"Maybe I had better leave, after all," Jassat said to Moba, who was still standing behind the counter, as he wasn't needed elsewhere.

"No, you're staying here, Lieutenant," the Bolian said firmly. "You've been abused twice in my club. That's not going to happen a third time. Captain Adams might be in command on the bridge, but this is my domain. And I've watched people misbehave for the longest time. Na Bukh might have had an excuse in the cluster, but if he picks another fight now, he's history." Just to underline his words, Moba took two sidesteps, pulling out a handgun phaser from a compartment and placing it behind the counter.

Jassat stared at him incredulously. "You would shoot him?"

"Let me quote one of our finest thinkers: a smile is the strongest weapon—but it doesn't do any harm to have an alternative at hand." Moba grinned wearily. "My father was a wise man, that much is certain. Don't worry, though, the weapon isn't charged."

Na Bukh turned around. Determination showed on his face. Jassat placed his glass on the counter as he didn't want Moba to have to mop it up a second time. Jassat braced himself as Na Bukh strode towards him.

"Lieutenant," the engineer said. His voice had a sharp edge, but that was normal for his species. "I'm glad to run into you."

Jassat didn't know what to say, since all he could think was that the feeling was not mutual.

"Ensign, don't cause any trouble," Moba said quietly.

"Be quiet, Moba, I need to say something," he snapped. He stood next to Jassat, and suddenly hit the counter with his middle hand. He raised the other two arms, demanding attention. "Hey, listen up, everyone!"

After a moment, all eyes were on him. Some were astounded, others worried, still others confused. Almost everyone on board knew about Na Bukh's last encounter with Jassat in Starboard 8, after all. Krish Iniri looked as if she was prepared to physically intervene if necessary. She was also the ranking officer in the bar.

But Na Bukh's words surprised his audience, most of all Jassat. "I was an idiot. Worse, I was an idiot in front of *everyone*. And because I have been so public an idiot, I want to put things right in front of everyone, as well." He pointed at Jassat. "This is Lieutenant Jassat ak Namur. Most of you know him. He came on board several years ago as an exchange officer, went to Starfleet Academy and returned from Deep Space 9 about a month ago. He's Renao, and what's more, he's the only Renao in Starfleet, if I'm not mistaken." Na-Bukh looked at Jassat for confirmation.

All Jassat could do was nod. He was far too astounded to utter even one word.

"I won't lie—I always found him to be a bit strange. The red skin, the black hair, the glowing eyes… There are monsters in mythology of Triex that look somewhat like him. It's nonsense to judge a stranger's character by their looks, but that weakness resides deep within us. Usually reason is stronger than that. But sometimes it isn't."

His yellow eyes looked straight at Jassat.

"I got carried away by prejudice and the atrocities committed by some fanatics that happen to look like you, and accused you, Lieutenant—and not only you, but your entire species. I said some very despicable things that I wish I hadn't voiced. I shouldn't even have *thought* them. My behavior was completely inappropriate, not only towards a superior officer, but also towards a comrade from my crew. I sincerely apologize, Lieutenant."

"Hear, hear," came from the corner where the security people sat. Two or three people applauded Na Bukh's words.

Jassat couldn't believe what he was hearing. He wasn't surprised that some of his crewmates were ashamed of their latent aggression, which had been put on display of late. There was no room for xenophobia within the fleet. Tolerance and the curiosity for the diversity of cultures within the galaxy were not only classed as virtues, they were expected from everyone wearing the uniform. So once they were no longer under the Son's influence, they must have been devastated at the realization of how easily they had been manipulated. That someone would actually apologize to him as eloquently as this and in front of so many witnesses, however, he hadn't imagined in his wildest dreams.

"I'm not one to bear grudges, Ensign," he replied, because he had the feeling that he needed to say something, although he was barely able to think clearly right now. "You were under the influence of the Son of the Ancient Reds, just like everyone else."

"Wrong," said Na Bukh, and his bony head wobbled from side to side on his thin neck. "*Not* like everyone else. I have insulted and offended you; I allowed my fears and prejudices to get the better of me. I was weak. I expected more of myself. I really thought I was better than that." He genuinely seemed crestfallen at the realization of his failure.

"Not all is lost, Ensign." Moba grinned, putting his phaser aside. "At least you had the courage to stand up in front of everyone and admit your mistake. I would call that a sign of strength and character. Come here. You two are going to have a drink now. And you'll find that as the only Renao and the only Triexian aboard this ship, you have much more in common than you think."

Na Bukh tilted his head. "I need to eat something before my shift. But let me suggest something else, Lieutenant. If it's not beneath you to sit around a table with some Jeffries-tube scrubbers, join us, and we'll have a drink over there."

The club door opened again, and Jassat saw Jenna Kirk enter the Starboard 8. He made a grateful gesture, nodding at Na Bukh. "I'm sorry, but my date has arrived. We'll catch up some other time, I promise you."

The Triexian turned around, recognized the chief engineer, and his sheep-like face broke into a grin. "Some other time, then, Lieutenant. Have a nice evening." And with that, he returned to his table.

"Have I missed anything?" Jenna asked, approaching the counter with raised eyebrows.

"I suppose you could say that," Jassat said dryly. Pensively, he stared after the Triexian. *With every passing light year we get farther away, things can only get better*, Moba had said earlier. Apparently, he had been right. Maybe, just maybe, things *were* slowly getting better.

U.S.S. Venture, on patrol near Lembatta Prime

"This is getting worse and worse."

Glowering, Captain Bjarne Henderson stood in front of the five *Scorpion* replicas that had been lined up in Cargo Hold 3 aboard the *Venture*. One of the fighters had been almost completely dismantled save for its framework, while all the parts were scrutinized by the ship's engineers and scientists.

All other vessels had at least been opened up to remove their dangerous explosive cargo and disarm it. Afterward, three teams had focused on separate aspects of the replicas: the propulsion, the armament, and the defense mechanisms. During these inspections, Commander T'Eama, the *Venture*'s Vulcan chief engineer, had discovered something very unpleasant.

"I always thought the Renao were backward farmers," Henderson continued. "And now you're telling me they not only managed to recreate Romulan *Scorpion* fighters, they even improved them?"

"I would not describe the modifications to the attack fighters as improvements," T'Eama replied. "The engineers of the Purifying Flame have neglected all safety protocols in order to construct starships that will result in certain death for their pilots. Maintaining a cloaking device and shields simultaneously causes an energetic oscillation effect that gradually increases until the reaction overloads the drive and tears the ship apart."

Kraalbat, the Tellarite security chief, said, "If you have bombs made of trilithium, tekasite, and protomatter aboard, it probably doesn't really matter whether you're abiding by the usual safety specifications."

"That is a logical assumption," T'Eama said tersely.

Henderson shook his head. "So, let me get this straight— we are now dealing with enemy vessels that are not only extremely agile and flown by pilots with a death wish, but they also feature cloaking devices *and* active shields."

The Vulcan nodded. "That is correct, Captain."

Henderson wiped his brow with his hand, exhaling

noisily. "Fantastic. When I report that to Admiral Gepta he's going to dance with joy."

Next to him Kraalbat chuckled at the captain's sarcasm, no doubt envisioning the anger of the ill-tempered Chelon admiral.

T'Eama naturally remained stoic, her hands clasped behind her back. "The situation is not completely hopeless."

"How reassuring," said Henderson. "Let's hear the good news, then."

"These fighters appear to have been built in great haste. That has in turn led to deficiencies in both security and functionality, most notably in two aspects. First, the drive shielding has not been installed properly on any of the vessels, which means they will leak drive plasma when active. This drive plasma can be located by accordingly calibrated sensors. Furthermore, while the shields remain active while cloaked, they are of poor quality and are likely to collapse after one direct hit from a ship's phaser, according to my calculations."

"They'll still be difficult to fight," Kraalbat said. "They still have impressive speed and agility. In his debriefs, Captain Adams mentioned a fight against fanatics in orbit around Onferin. The fighters attacked the *Bortas*, and attempted to fly straight into her. The Klingon ship was badly damaged. And those fighters were neither cloaked nor protected by shields."

Henderson shook his head in resignation. "Brilliant. Just brilliant." He straightened himself, smoothing his uniform. "Very well, I guess I'm going to give the admiral the good news."

"We should also warn all the other ships in the fleet," T'Eama said, "as well as the Klingons. They need to adjust their sensors or they will always target the traces of the cloaked fighters and never the ships themselves."

"Thanks for the advice, Commander. I will see to it." The captain nodded at the Vulcan woman. "And despite everything—good work. Keep it up, and if you discover any more weaknesses of the replicas let me know right away. We need all the advantages we can get in the fight against these madmen."

17
NOVEMBER 28, 2385

Xhehenem

The hives were burning.

Brossal ak Ghantur saw it, but he still couldn't believe it: two of Kharanto's proud arcologies—these buildings of glass, stone, and metal that reached for the sky—stood in flames. Red and golden flames licked at the façades, dark smoke billowed from broken windows and open entrances.

Here and there, pieces of rubble rained down from collapsing upper levels, searing the carefully cultivated plants. The air was hot and smelled of destruction.

Wherever Brossal looked, all he saw was madness. In the streets, on the plazas... chaos everywhere. What had begun with the temple's destruction two days ago had now mutated to an insurrection, if not a civil war. But this war didn't know any front lines or parties, just death.

What has happened to us?

It wasn't the first time that Brossal had asked himself this question, and if he was brutally honest, he had known the answer for a while. The rumors were true—there was no other way. His people were losing their minds—no, they *had* lost them ages ago. The burning buildings, all the hatred, and the increasing number of casualties bore witness to that. Renao murdered Renao and called it a necessary resistance, or saving the Harmony of Spheres.

"Where are we going?" Brossal looked at Alyys. His little second-born girl seemed to have a fever; her brow was sweaty, her glowing eyes glazed over, her voice weak. Hiskaath, Brossal's son, carried in his arms because she was too small and weak to keep up with her brother's and father's walking speed as they fled from the flames. Again.

"To the harbor." The travel bags he was carrying on his back and in his hands hampered his movement more than anticipated. He considered leaving them behind so they could move faster, but they contained everything he had left—apart from his children. "We've already waited too long."

That was it, wasn't it? The worst thorn in his side, his biggest guilt. He had hesitated for far too long while holding out hope. Even when they had killed Kynnil, his beloved partner, even when Hiskaath had spouted radical nonsense, even when Alyys had been shouting and flailing in her sleep uncontrollably—Brossal had hesitated, although his bags had been packed a long time ago. He had hoped against hope. Clutched at straws. Because a Renao didn't give up his home. That was unthinkable. Where else did he belong? How did you leave a place that was part of yourself, as much as the nose on your face and the red of your skin? Just the thought was preposterous. Still...

I've waited too long. An epiphany, bitter as rotten *ley*. *Let's hope we won't pay the price for that.*

"Harbor?" Hisk was panting, but he persevered bravely. "Why are we going to the harbor? What are we supposed to do there? We are needed *here*, Father."

Brossal stopped, dropping one bag and grabbing his son by the shoulder. "What are we needed here for, eh?" he asked sharply, turning Hisk around so he could see the burning arcologies behind them. "To die?"

"To fight!" Hisk wrenched himself free. "The fire cleanses, Father. Don't you understand that? It brings about a glorious new beginning—for us and the Harmony of Spheres. Iad has awakened, and the Son will come to bring his salvation. He comes to us through the fire!"

Tears welled up in Brossal's eyes. For twelve cycles he had shared his life with this boy, but he barely recognized Hisk these days. The words that came out of him now were not those of the carefree child he had raised. Someone else's thoughts seemed to have taken root in Hisk's mind, putting words in his mouth that were not his. It broke his heart.

He wanted to scream and shake the boy until reason returned to him. But it wouldn't have changed anything.

Hisk seemed to interpret Brossal's silence as doubt, and he continued speaking. "The sphere is everything, Father. You taught me that. So don't be a foolish coward. Let's protect it like true Renao!"

A deafening noise made Brossal look up. The upper four levels of the arcology to the right succumbed to the insatiable hunger of the flames and collapsed. Burning debris crashed down to the ground, reflecting in the glass façade and smashing into burning shards.

Alyys cried quietly in Hisk's arms. She had closed her eyes, hardly noticing the world around her due to her fever.

"Do you call that protection?" Brossal's hand trembled as he pointed toward the destruction. "Was it protection when they came to set fire to your home? Was it what true Renao do, when they murdered your mother?"

Hisk remained silent. His eyes were defiant, proud— but mentioning the dead Kynnil had stirred up another emotion: pain.

"You're right, Hiskaath. I *was* a coward and foolish, and I will regret that for the rest of my life. But I'm not anymore." Brossal picked his bag up again. "Not a second longer."

He grabbed his son and ran forward, away from the ashes of their yesterday and down to the harbor, toward the ocean and the hope of tomorrow.

The plan was simple: they would take one of the *Kranaals* that flew for Brossal's employer to the offshore algae growth stations. He was hoping that they would make it to a large transport there in order to leave Xhehenem. The Renao didn't care much for space travel, so they didn't have many space ports on their worlds. But imports and exports of resources among worlds required that some of the algae stations had such ports at their disposal. Brossal's workplace—a huge offshore plant—was one of them.

This is our best chance, he thought when they arrived at the harbor. He had tossed aside the heavy travel bags somewhere along the way and had taken over carrying Alyys. *Our only chance.*

Chaos reigned in the harbor as it did everywhere else. Brossal saw smashed windows, burning fishing boats, and two corpses floating in the water, face down.

Even this, his familiar route to work, had become a frightening reminder of the horror of what his people had become.

"There!" Brossal pointed at a fence for Hisk's benefit. "This way, son. Behind the workshops. Do you see the high fence? There's the *Kranaal* landing area for my growth station."

They were not the only citizens from Kharanto banking on this escape route. Brossal saw dark silhouettes here and there between the huts in the harbor.

The last remaining sensible people, he thought, and that certainty hurt more than his overexerted lungs. *The last cowards leave the ship. Late. Too late. Just like me.*

And then the workshops exploded! The blast knocked Brossal off his feet. He hit the dock's stone floor hard as a wave of incredible heat washed over him. A terrible roar and hiss, similar to those of predators roaming the wilds of Xhehenem, deafened his ears.

Where was Hisk? Alyys was still cradled in his arms when he regained his equilibrium. She was fast asleep, despite all the horror. At least the fever was merciful that way.

But where was the boy?

"Hisk!" Brossal's wailing, panicked scream was drowned out by the roaring fire, but still he screamed, fueled by his anguish. "Hiskaath!"

Nothing.

Brossal saw gigantic columns of smoke rise from the remains of the workshops, felt the heat of the flames on his face and arms, saw terrified figures darting from the shadows. Some of them were burning like the huts up front and hurled themselves into the water—if they made it that far. Others seemed to withdraw into the dark as if someone was dragging them there. He didn't see his son.

"Hiskaath!"

Suddenly, he saw Kynnil in his mind's eye on the day Hisk had been born. He remembered the happiness in her face, the promises they had made to each other, and the hopes they had shared. Hopes for Hiskaath's future. For the start of their first-born's life, his family had been his sphere.

And suddenly he realized how much he had really betrayed Kynn and their time together. His dithering, his waiting, his hoping. There was no future, not here where this madness ruled and a life was worth less than an unfulfilled dream. Brossal had broken the most important promise that he had ever given by clinging to the familiar against all reason, when the familiar had become something twisted and horrible. He had trusted people he thought he knew over his home—and now they were all paying the price with their burning dreams, their dying wishes, and their blood.

"Hiskaath!"

Sobbing, he slumped to the pier floor. He pressed the sleeping Alyys against his chest, tears running from his eyes, his open mouth uttering a silent scream. It was over, here and now, because *everything* had come to an end.

And then he felt a wet hand on his leg. "Father."

Hisk! The boy pushed himself up onto the stony pier. Panting, he looked at Brossal. Salt water dripped from his hair and his clothes, and despite the heat of the fire columns behind them, he was trembling all over. But he was alive.

"I must have fallen into the water, Father," he said. His gaze wandered to the burning workshops. Stunned, he stared at them. "Were you looking for me? What… what happened?"

Brossal touched him, stroked his wet cheek with the back of his hand, almost incredulously. Was he dreaming? Was he also suffering from a fever that made him delusional? But this couldn't be a dream. Dreams didn't feel so real, so alive.

"Did the terrorists do that? Did they want to stop us from leaving our home?"

"Yes, son," Brossal whispered, grateful, oh so endlessly grateful. "Exactly."

Hisk looked at him. Big eyes, pale face. "But that means we can't get away from here!" He sounded scared. He sounded—for a moment—like the Hisk from the past who hadn't been blinded by madness. And Brossal realized that he did have a chance after all. The future awaited, and with it the promise he had given Kynn.

"We won't know if we don't try, son." Brossal scrambled to his feet—a little shaky but determined—took Hiskaath by the hand, and walked forward towards the flames and the fence behind them.

There was indeed one *Kranaal* left. Just one, because the rest had been crippled by the exploding workshops. One of the small passenger transporters had been impaled by a piece of debris through its roof; the metal rotors the *Kranaals* relied on in order to fly had melted from the heat of the conflagration. Just one was left standing. It was parked at the back of the station-owned landing pad.

In front of it stood a man, shooting at anyone and anything that came close to him.

Mounim ak Hazzoh had obviously lost his mind. The once proud face of the algae cultivator was covered in sweat, his eyes darting around. His lips were trembling, just like his shoulders. Only his arms with the black energy weapon moved purposefully.

"Come here then!" Mounim shouted. His once low and steady voice broke with every other syllable. "Come on, if you dare! Traitors! Enemies of the spheres! Come and get what you deserve!"

The handful of remaining escapees were driven by fear. Panic fueled them as they darted out of the shadows of the burning workshops toward this one last *Kranaal*. From the cover of the impaled transporter, Brossal could see them: stumbling, crying, pleading. And once again he felt as if hands reached out from the shadows, dragging some people back.

Did he just imagine that? It *had* to be an illusion.

He could also see Mounim, indiscriminately shooting at fleeing people without questions, without warning, without mercy.

Twitching bodies on the floor. Neighbors, dragging themselves forwards, bleeding. They looked around and were stunned, while the last remaining spark of life dissipated. Reason died on the cobbles of the harbor, and madness laughed at it.

"Anyone else?" Mounim shouted, shooting into the night air in celebration. Madness had taken over once and for all. "Was that it? No more who have come to betray the sphere? Or is there still anyone here refusing to save home? Come here, if you dare. The *Kranaal* is already on autopilot, the course has been plotted. All you need to do is climb in—if you can make it."

We're done, Brossal thought. But then he figured that they had been done for weeks. And nothing would change if he didn't act now.

"I'm here," he shouted, and he handed Alyys to Hisk, who looked at him in utter confusion as he left the cover of the destroyed *Kranaal*. "Here, Moun. Do you recognize me?"

Mounim obviously hadn't expected any more people and winced. But then he realized who was talking to him, and a broad smile appeared on his feverish and confused face. "Bross!" He laughed, half snorting. "Didn't I tell you that you needed to smarten up?"

"You did indeed," Brossal answered calmly—*no matter what, keep talking, don't panic, don't get excited*—and took two more slow, steady steps toward his colleague. "I remember it well."

"And you're still here?" Incredulity and mockery made

Mounim's voice sound shrill. To him, Brossal was the biggest fool ever, that much was obvious. Bewildered, he shook his head. "You still haven't understood anything, my friend, have you?"

"Oh, but I have, Moun. I understand perfectly well."

"You do?" Again, Mounim fired into the air. Every single shot shook Brossal to the core. With every report, Brossal imagined the energy discharge would hit Alyys or Hisk. He had to resist the urge to flee. *Whatever it takes. I'm doing all that's left for me to do. I'm hoping.*

"Doesn't look like it, Bross." Mounim spoke with feigned regret. "Doesn't look like it at all, you know?" He aimed the black energy weapon right at Brossal.

But Brossal continued his slow, cautious, calm approach. "You think?"

Another snort. "Don't you?"

Now! Brossal knew instinctively that this was the moment of his final chance. The algae cultivator tensed his muscles, launching himself forward and knocking Mounim over. Panting, both men fell to the ground, Mounim's head striking the stone pier with a hollow thud. The energy gun fired, but Brossal managed to grab the barrel and turn it away. Anywhere but in his direction.

Mounim now had a gaping head wound that was bleeding profusely. He writhed, kicked, and hit Brossal like a wild animal.

But Brossal had always been strong. He managed to wrench the weapon from Mounim's grasp, although he didn't get a proper grip on it. It fell from his hands, sliding away and disappearing into the darkness, out of sight.

Suddenly, Mounim's fingers dug into his face, fingernails of one hand scratching his cheeks, fingertips of the other trying to squash his eyes. Screaming in pain, Brossal punched Mounim in the abdomen and then grabbed at his opponent's wrists, yanking at them with all his might to get the digits away from his face. Once he was successful in that, Brossal tried to deliver another punch, but Mounim was faster. Brossal felt Mounim's thigh press against his hip and his hand press against his shoulder, pushing him down onto his back.

Suddenly, Mounim was on top, knees pressing onto Brossal's thighs. Grinning, Mounim held a razor-sharp piece of debris, waving it near Brossal's neck. "It's the end of your journey, old friend." Blood continued to run down Mounim's cheek from his head wound, and Kharanto's fires burned behind him. "Give Kynn my regards when you see her." With these words, he lifted the makeshift weapon over his head, intending to plunge it into Brossal's chest.

But he suddenly winced, froze, and fell sideways. Motionless, he lay on the stone floor next to Brossal, who stared in disbelief. Mounim's eyes were wide open, but there wasn't any life left in them.

He turned his head and saw the reason. Less than five steps away stood Alyys with the energy weapon in her tiny hands.

"Aly." Brossal scrambled to his feet, running towards her. A horror even greater than his apprehension at what his people had become, even more intense than his overwhelming fear of death, had gripped him. He sensed that more than just an insane colleague had died just now. Much more. "Aly, no…"

But the child barely noticed his presence. Her eyes were feverish and empty, her strength almost gone. Without paying attention, she dropped the gun.

"Aly." Brossal began to sob. Repeatedly, he stroked her head with his hand. She didn't respond. "Aly, where... where's your brother?"

"Gone." Her voice was hardly more than a whisper.

He hesitated. "What do you mean, gone? Where is he?"

She looked at him. Her smile was a mad mirror of her illness. The strange glow in her eyes went right through him.

"He's with the Son, Father," she whispered, half proud and half feverish. "With the Son of the Ancient Reds. Iad has awakened. Aren't you happy at all?"

Again, Brossal was horror-stricken. "Hisk!" he shouted, pressing one child against him, looking for the other. "Hisk!"

But there was no one else there—only the two of them, the dead, and their old home going up in flames.

Brossal ak Ghantur searched for his first-born until the sun rose above the ocean. That was when he realized that he had lost him to the shadows. Maybe even weeks ago. Not everything you believed you saw was an illusion. And good intentions weren't good deeds by a long margin.

Grabbing his daughter, the algae cultivator climbed into the *Kranaal* and took off toward the sun, the offshore station, and an uncertain future.

18
NOVEMBER 29, 2385

U.S.S. Prometheus, near the Taurus Dark Cloud

Confusion, fear, fury, pain… Spock encountered these and other emotions in Geron Barai's turbulent mind when he placed his long fingers on the Betazoid's face. The younger man's mind was in complete disarray. He was in a state of constant agitation, although there were no external impulses to cause it.

But something *is making him ill.* Spock closed his eyes, and his fingertips moved gently while he deepened the mind-meld between himself and Barai.

The doctor still lay on the bed in his dimly lit quarters, shifting restlessly and moaning quietly. Spock sat next to him on the edge of the bed.

He believed he knew what to look for. The Son's psychoactive radiation contaminated his victims' thoughts similar to the manner in which radioactivity affected the body. Long after the actual onslaught on the mind was over, disharmonious echoes of the unfathomable hunger for violence continued to reverberate.

Spock had freed his mind from this poisonous and glowing residue during meditation sessions by isolating each and every thought fragment that stood for fear or fury. It had been an arduous task. He was uncertain as to the efficacy of his being able to do the same for Barai's mind.

But Counselor Courmont had requested his aid, and he intended to at least make the attempt.

Cautiously, Spock advanced into the chaos of Barai's thoughts. As a trained telepath, the doctor could have put up strong barriers against him. But the Son's mental vortex had torn down his resistance. A kaleidoscope of horrific images flitted about his thoughtscape: the red glowing eye-lasers of menacingly approaching Borg... the shimmering, drop-shaped spaceships of the Tzenkethi... the long, deadly fall of an Andorian woman looking curiously like Commander zh'Thiin... a sneering Doctor Calloway.

Had he been prone to giving up easily, he probably would have withdrawn from Barai's soul after a quick glance, discouraged. But Spock had always taken pride in his patience. *Take heart, Doctor*, he projected reassuringly into the chaos. *I will aid you in returning to yourself.*

"According to our calculations, we're approaching the outer regions of the dark cloud," ak Namur reported. "Dropping out of slipstream in three... two... one. Exit."

In awe, Richard Adams watched the blue shimmering tunnel that had taken the *Prometheus* two hundred light years across the Alpha Quadrant with immense speed collapse. The ship's computer initiated an automated deceleration routine as the sensors would only function reliably in normal space. Nobody wanted to risk hurtling into an asteroid field or another stellar obstacle waiting at their destination.

"*Prometheus* answering all stop," ak Namur said soon after.

"All stations, report," Adams said.

"No damage reported," Chell said from the engineering station. "All systems are go."

"No traceable energy signatures," Roaas said from tactical.

"Affirmative," said Winter, cycling through the standard frequencies at the comm station. "No communication on any of the standard frequencies."

"Sounds as if we're all alone out here," Adams said. "Lieutenant ak Namur, could you confirm our position?"

"Yes, sir. We're in the outer regions of the Taurus Dark Cloud."

"Which, evidently, deserves its name." The captain gazed at the large screen, which displayed nothing but blackness.

"This is an optical phenomenon, Captain," Mendon spoke up behind him. "The high density of complex molecules absorbs the starlight from beyond the cloud."

Adams turned to face the Benzite. "Thank you, Commander. I know what dark clouds are." He smiled mildly at his science officer to reassure him that he appreciated the disclosure of information, nonetheless. Focusing his attention back on the screen, the captain continued: "I'd rather know if there really is a zone of chaotic energy somewhere around here, Mr. Mendon. Is this the right place, or has someone on Memory Alpha misinterpreted some obscure data?"

"One moment, sir." Tense silence fell over the bridge for several seconds, until Mendon spoke up again. "Captain, I'm indeed picking up a radiation zone similar to that around Iad. It's about one light year away and... it's enormous."

"On screen," Adams said.

"Switching to multi-spectral view to make the zone visible." The image on the bridge screen changed as Mendon spoke; strictly speaking, only the spectrum of the sensor readings changed. The blackness disappeared and was replaced by gray space dotted with dark spots that represented stars. Right in the center was a gigantic cloud-like accumulation of energy. It reminded Adams of a huge storm front, a mountain of clouds building up on a humid summer night on Earth. The edges of the radiation zone frayed, and lightning flickered deep inside it.

"Simulating visual spectrum," Mendon said. The gray space turned black again, but this time the stars remained visible, just like the cloud. It was a billowing, permanently changing, and multicolored flickering zone in the core of the dark cloud. Fields emitting polaron, tetryon, verteron, and other ultraviolet radiations formed and disappeared continuously. The incoming quantities of data were so large that the sensor readings scrolled with unbelievable speed down the side of the screen.

"Looks like a gate into chaos," Sarita Carson mumbled at ops.

Adams had to agree with her. The zone indeed made a disconcerting impression. "How big is this... this cloud?"

"The visible diameter is twenty light years," Mendon replied. "I have no data indicating its depth."

Nervously, the captain wiped his chin with one hand. Given half a choice, he would have stayed well away from this location. But they had a mission. "Commander Mendon, based on the data we have gathered above Iad: could the *Prometheus* withstand this zone?"

"Let me run a few simulations, Captain."

Adams glanced over his shoulder at the science officer, nodding. "All right. In the meantime, we'll approach the edge of the chaos zone. Lieutenant ak Namur, plot a course to the periphery of the phenomenon, warp nine point five."

"Aye, sir." The Renao's fingers danced across the navigation console, and then Adams observed the more familiar image translation on the viewscreen of the stars stretching as the *Prometheus* went to warp.

* * *

"There's a remaining risk, sir." Jenna Kirk shook her head in frustration. "I never thought I'd say this, but we could use the *Bortas* right now. Strictly speaking, we could do with its deflector dish and on-board computer. The three systems of the *Prometheus* might not be enough. If the spontaneous fluctuation rate of the radiation zone remains the same, we'll be all right. If the chaos increases inside the zone, our three computer cores might be unable to cope."

"Without the adaptive radiation filter we're in danger of being exposed to probably lethal doses of highly damaging radiation," Mendon added.

Adams nodded. "Which means that we have to advance very carefully, keeping a close eye on our environment."

"Yes, sir," Mendon said.

They sat in the large conference room, while the *Prometheus* sped towards the chaos zone. Mendon had successfully finished his simulations, and Kirk had added data from her readings. The result was at best disillusioning, at worst frightening.

Adams turned to the deputy chief medical officer who sat to his left. "Doctor Calloway, I want you and your team on standby so you can treat various radiation afflictions quickly."

"Understood, Captain," the brunette woman answered. "I'd like to point out though that sickbay is still understaffed. If the entire crew suffered from multiple radiation disorders, we wouldn't be able to cope."

"It won't come to that," the captain said. "As soon as we see signs of grave problems with the adaptive radiation filter, we will withdraw. Just in case, I will reassign some personnel from security to assist you."

"Thank you, Captain."

"Make sure that all three medical bays are equally staffed. We may not be able to conduct ship-to-ship transport once we have entered the chaos zone with the separated *Prometheus* sections."

"I will divide personnel up accordingly," Calloway said.

"Very well," said Adams. "Let's talk about the scenario that we're hopefully going to experience—that we can enter the zone unharmed and encounter beings matching the description of the White Guardian. How do we establish contact with them?" Again, he looked at Calloway. "Doctor, are any of our telepaths fit for duty again?"

"Our Vulcan crewmembers are making good progress. The Napean, Deltan, and Betazoid, however, are still in critical condition."

"Captain," Ambassador Spock spoke up at the other end of the table. "My experience with the Son and similar beings is unmatched. It is only logical that I should attempt to establish contact."

"Considering your last attempt, I'd like to avoid sending you out again," Adams replied. "You almost went mad."

"As you said, Captain—almost. My mind remains healthy. I was also able to retrieve some very important clues as to the nature of the Son." The ambassador gazed at Adams knowingly. "In addition, I believe the White Guardian to be much less aggressive than the Son of the Ancient Reds, whose mind is damaged and ill."

"As you said, Ambassador—you believe."

"I would call it a calculated probability."

Adams sighed. "I don't like it, but you're right—you're our best chance to get in touch with these beings. But I would like to have Ensign Winter attempt to find a less risky method of communication. Perhaps you could assist him, Ambassador?"

"I would be glad to."

"Excellent." Adams gazed at his officers. "Anything else we need to consider?"

Roaas, sitting to his right, looked thoughtful. "Captain, I've been wondering whether we shouldn't leave the majority of the crew behind outside the zone. The *Prometheus* is highly automated. Even separated, ten people per section would be enough to operate the ship. Why should we risk a hundred and forty-four crewmembers going mad? We could leave some security personnel and all scientists, civilians, and stand-in crews behind in shuttlecraft. If all goes well, we retrieve them as soon as we leave the chaos zone. However, if all *doesn't* go well... I'd say the fewer lunatics running through the corridors the better."

"In principle, I agree with you, Commander," Adams replied. "But no. We'll stay together. Our team spirit is our strength. Besides, I have no intention to turn this into a suicide mission. We couldn't afford that considering the situation in the Lembatta Cluster. I know that we're advancing into the unknown here—literally where no one has gone before. But we have precautionary measures in place. And the *Prometheus* is a good ship with an excellent crew. If we encounter a problem, we will overcome it—or we will withdraw."

"Aye, sir." Roaas nodded.

"All right." Adams looked at everyone. "That'll be all. You've got your tasks. Now let's find this White Guardian."

Solar-jumper *Coumatha*, Theris system

"Dammit!" Lieutenant Mika Niskanen from the *U.S.S. Venture* hit his fist against the brown casing of the station where he stood. "This coding drives me nuts."

The two Bynars who were on the solar-jumper's bridge with him stopped their work, turning around to face him. They were specialists from the *Bougainville* who had come over to the captured ship of the Purifying Flame in order to crack the encoded computer system.

"Could we…"

"…be of assistance?" asked 01001010 and 01010100.

"Not if you don't know any bigwigs inside the Cardassian government. Why did these guys have to buy encrypting routines off the Obsidian Order? Obtaining override codes for Klingon programs would have been much easier."

The bald humanoids with the small bodies came from the planet Bynaus in the Beta Magellan system. They turned their pale lilac faces towards each other and briefly communicated in their native tongue that sounded like twittering. Niskanen knew that they could transmit enormous data quantities within a very short time that way, and he wondered whether they were seriously discussing his remark that had been meant as a joke.

His question was answered when they faced him again.

"We are…"

"…sorry, but we are not…"

"…able to oblige," the two Bynars replied, obviously concerned. Their voices had a slightly metallic sound, which kept reminding Niskanen that these fragile beings had cybernetic implants and were half computers themselves.

"That's okay, I didn't expect you to." He sighed, staring at the small monitor where endless lines of code were displayed. Niskanen considered himself the best computer specialist aboard the *Venture*—that was the reason why he was working here alongside the two Bynars from the

Bougainville. But these program routines made him despair. *The Renao may be backward in our eyes,* he thought, *but you have to hand it to them—they only purchase top quality stuff for their terrorism campaign.*

"Perhaps you should…"

"…talk to your captain," 01001010 and 01010100 said.

"Why?" Niskanen asked. "So he can talk to Admiral Gepta, who can speak with Admiral Akaar to inform President zh'Tarash so she can ask Castellan Garak? You don't seriously believe that that will achieve anything, do you? Besides, it'll take forever. Not to mention the fact that it would ruin my reputation as a code wizard." He grinned warily at the inseparable pair. "You know, I come from a small village in the north of Finland on Earth. In Nuorgam, a man doesn't have anything but his salmon during the summer, alcohol in the winter and his good reputation for the months in between. Starfleet will only serve this synthehol crap, and the replicated salmon tastes terrible. So there's only one thing left for me, if you know what I mean."

Again, the two Bynars had a quick quacking exchange.

"We regret that…"

"…your career depends on…"

"…this task. We're doing…"

"…our best to…"

"…circumvent the encryption."

"Thank you." Niskanen put his hands on his hips, thinking and staring at the monitor. "Maybe our approach is all wrong." He glanced at the two Bynars. "Has anyone searched the captain's cabin yet?"

The two looked at each other, confused.

"No, not that we…"

"…know of. Why?"

The lieutenant licked his lips. "This is completely new territory for the Renao. The encrypting routines from the Obsidian Order demand very long password sequences. If I was a country bumpkin who didn't know anything about all this technology, I'd jot things down and hide them somewhere." The more he thought about it, the more logical his assumption sounded. He nodded. "Okay, you two carry on working here. I'm going to take a peek underneath the mattress in the captain's bunk."

"As you…"

"…wish."

The two focused on their work as Niskanen left the bridge, following the narrow corridor of the Renao solar-jumper. The captain's quarters were close to the command center, as they generally were in cargo space vessels.

The cabin was very small. The bunk was mounted on the wall across the room. Next to it was a locker that was also built into the wall. A sink, a small metal table, and a chair completed the spartan furnishings. The bed was neatly made, the sink was clean, and he couldn't see any clothes or private belongings lying about. Either the captain had been an extremely tidy person, or he hadn't spent a single night in this room.

First, Niskanen lifted the pillow and the duvet, discarding them without care. He also lifted the mattress, pulling off the sheets. Nothing. He looked underneath both the table and the chair, but there weren't any pieces of paper or padds glued to them.

Next, he turned to the locker. Inside hung a few coveralls and a holster containing an outdated projectile pistol, while a padd and a codex book lay on a shelf. Quickly, Niskanen checked the clothes pockets, before searching the coveralls for secret seams or something hidden between layers of fabric. He didn't find anything.

Ignoring the pistol, he took the padd and the book, and sat down at the table. The padd was made on Andor, and Niskanen had no problem overriding the password. Once he had done so, he programmed a small search routine to find anything that looked even remotely Cardassian. While the program ran, he turned to the book. It was written in a foreign language and lettering, and it seemed to be ancient. Maybe it was some kind of heirloom.

Niskanen shook the book but no piece of paper dropped out. He flicked through the pages, but there weren't any obvious markings. He noticed that the book jacket wasn't attached to the cover and removed it. A piece of paper the size of his palm fluttered towards the floor. Excited, he bent down, picking it up. Much to his disappointment, he didn't find any scribblings. It was the photograph of a Renao woman, smiling into the camera with glowing eyes. Somehow, she looked familiar to him. Had she been one of the dead bodies earlier? It didn't really matter. He placed the photo on the table.

That concluded his search of easy hiding places. Now, things became more difficult. Niskanen got up, glancing at the walls. Could there be a secret compartment anywhere— be it only a slot between two of the metal wall panels?

"Come on, Captain. You don't know anything about Cardassian software. You must have left a hint of the code sequence somewhere."

He thoroughly searched the walls, knocking at the panels looking for hollow spaces, peeking into gaps with the small handheld light that dangled on his tool belt. Nothing. This was infuriating.

Suddenly, the search routine came back with a pinging noise. "Last chance saloon," Niskanen mumbled. He picked up the padd. NO MATCHES FOUND.

With an annoyed growl, he threw the padd across the room. It hit the wall, ricocheted off, and fell to the floor. The plastic cover on the back snapped off and slid away, and Niskanen saw a small data disc that was stuck inside.

"Well, hello there, and what do we have here?" Crouching, he picked up the back cover, and removed the disc. Quickly, he grabbed the padd again, reactivating it. Lucky for him, Andorian technology was robust. The device hadn't sustained any damage except the missing cover on the back.

Cautiously, Niskanen inserted the data disc into the appropriate slot on the bottom of the device. *Please don't let this be a collection of soppy poems that he wrote to the woman in the picture*, he pleaded silently.

The data disc contained just one file. The padd couldn't read it, but when he took a closer look at the data structure, his heartbeat increased. "Cardassian code," he whispered.

Hectically ejecting the disc, he dropped the padd and ran back to the bridge.

"I found something," he announced to the two Bynars.

They curiously turned around to face him.

"And would you…"

"…care to…"

"…let us know…"

"…what it is?" 01001010 and 01010100 inquired.

Niskanen inserted the data disc into an appropriate slot at his station. He opened the file that he had found. The Obsidian Order's lilac and gray emblem and the silhouette of a menacingly cloaked figure appeared on the small screen. Finally, status reports of unlocking memory banks appeared.

"The key, my friends," Mika Niskanen said, and a broad grin appeared on his face. "I found the key."

19
TIME: UNKNOWN

Location: unknown

A flicker, followed by a crackling noise. Finally, an image—a close-up: a Renao man looking straight down the camera. He is the same man who has sent messages before, when he stood in front of the seemingly endless rows of black shimmering *Scorpion* replicas. Now he's in some manner of briefing room, a map of the galaxy on the wall behind him. Someone has ripped it in half, and one half is dangling.

"Your small victories are irrelevant," he says to his invisible audience. "Forcing us to give up our base on Calidhu and capturing our solar-jumper changes *nothing*. We have other bases, and we have other solar-jumpers. You won't stop us! You will *never* stop us! Because our mission to restore the Harmony of Spheres in the galaxy is sacred. And we're prepared to give everything, sacrifice everything. Are you as well?"

He leans forward, and his face, distorted with fury, fills the entire picture. His eyes glow with the fires of madness.

"Are you really ready for this fight? Think about it, long and hard. If you're smart, you will withdraw back to your home spheres. Give up your colonies—these boils on the face of formerly pure worlds—and scrap your spaceships that cut through spheres like knives. Cease your mocking of the natural order of things."

Slowly, he shakes his head, and the corners of his mouth turn contemptuously downward.

"I feel pity for you, for your inability to recognize the Harmony of Spheres. I despise you for your desire to explore and conquer ever new worlds. And I hate you for your arrogance that makes you believe you're doing it for the good of the galaxy. I swear, there will be no peace and no mercy for as long as your sacrilege continues. We will fight. We will be victorious. And for you, there will only be death."

NOVEMBER 29, 2385

U.S.S. Venture, Theris system

"They're scared," said Admiral Gepta.

Captain Henderson stared incredulously at the admiral, who stood at the center of the *Venture* bridge after the Purifying Flame's latest hate message played on the viewscreen. "With all due respect, sir, he seems fairly determined to me."

The Chelon turned to face Henderson. "He's doing his best to appear that way, yes. But I see that naked fear in his eyes. We're getting closer to the Purifying Flame, and they're beginning to flail like a cornered animal."

Henderson wondered whether Gepta really understood what Captain Adams and the *Prometheus* had uncovered on Iad. If the fanatics of the Purifying Flame had been influenced by this entity, they were unable to feel fear. They would be dominated by hatred and pure lust for violence, and that was all the captain had seen in the eyes of this madman. But he knew better than to argue with Gepta about that. In one respect he agreed with the admiral, though: the fanatics were cornered, and they were starting to flail. He was quite concerned about that prospect. If the Purifying Flame really did have several solar-jumpers at their disposal, they could cause immense damage before their movement could be quashed. Henderson hadn't forgotten the armada of menacing fighters that had been lined up in the background of the last message. These cloaked fighters with their deadly cargo must be prevented from leaving the Lembatta Cluster and reaching the adjacent systems.

Grimly, Henderson stared at the bridge screen where the Renao's furious visage had been frozen. "Switch that off, Mr. Loos," he said to the ops officer.

"Aye, sir."

The fanatic disappeared and was replaced by an image of the Theris system's sun. The small solar-jumper that had been captured by the Klingons hovered above the blazing gas globe. Commander Koxx had left with his ships.

The president of the Federation had given them permission to patrol around the cluster. The *Bougainville* had also left. Only the *Venture* waited for all investigations of the alien spaceship to be completed. At the same time, she guarded the system just in case the Purifying Flame were to come looking for their people.

"I'll be in my quarters," said Admiral Gepta, striding toward the turbolift. "Call me if there's any new trouble brewing."

"Of course, sir," Henderson replied, walking to his command chair and sitting down. He could have retired as well but First Officer Di Monti was in the engine room with Commander T'Eama to discuss possible countermeasures against the cloaked fighters of the Purifying Flame. Besides, these days Henderson enjoyed the few moments when he was permitted to be master of his own ship. Gepta stalked the bridge far too often, seizing the reins.

He asked a yeoman for a padd with the latest status reports when Loos spoke up. "Captain, Lieutenant Niskanen is hailing us. Audio only."

Henderson straightened. "Open channel."

"*Venture, this is Niskanen,*" the computer specialist's voice came from the comm system.

"We can hear you, Lieutenant," Henderson said. "What's up?"

"*Captain, I've got good news. I managed to crack the encryption code. We have read all data from the on-board computer. According to the log, the ship spent a considerable amount of time in the Shaool system, which we have listed as LC-6.*"

Henderson gazed at the Saurian woman at flight control questioningly. "Isn't there an inhabited world, Commander Makzia?"

"Yes, sir," she replied. "LC-6-VI, called Yssab by the locals."

"Yssab…" Henderson repeated slowly. "Sounds as if we've got a lead." He raised his voice. "Good work, Lieutenant. Copy all data and return with your team to the *Venture.*"

"*Aye, sir. Niskanen out.*"

Henderson looked straight ahead. "Mr. Loos, hail the *Bortas*. We need to inform Captain Kromm." The captain didn't particularly like being dependent on the Klingon to pursue the lead. Captain Adams's reports described the *Bortas* shipmaster as stubborn and hungry for glory, and willing to put his own interests before those of the mission. But the *Prometheus* was on the other side of the Alpha Quadrant right now.

They were negotiating with the government on Onferin about accepting a replacement Starfleet ship, but if they managed it at all, it would be the *Bougainville*, as she was a science vessel, underlining the peaceful character of the Federation's politics. But the Renao were concerned that a third or a fourth ship would follow soon. The two fleets that had tightened the circle around the cluster made the deciding bodies in Auroun very nervous. Henderson couldn't blame them.

"I've got Captain Kromm, sir," said Loos.

The captain nodded. "On screen."

One second later the young Klingon commander appeared. He sat on his throne-like chair with spread legs, his arms casually resting on the sides. His eyes glinted irritably. *"What do you want?"* he said by way of greeting.

"To help you, Captain," Henderson said with a smile.

"Help from Starfleet. How very exciting." The Klingon actually rolled his eyes as he spoke.

Henderson was tempted to terminate the connection there and then. Kromm was even worse than Adams had described him. *The mission*, he reminded himself. *Remember the mission.* "We have analyzed the data from the computer aboard the captured solar-jumper. All evidence points to the fact that they operated from Yssab, one of the Renao colonies in the cluster."

Kromm sat up straight at that. *"Yssab... Interesting. Our investigation in the Bharatrum system has stalled. We shall follow up this lead. Well done, Captain."* He lifted his chin a little, nodding tersely at Henderson. *"Anything else?"*

"We received a threatening message. Did you see it?"

Kromm growled affirmatively.

"Then I don't have to tell you how worried everyone here is. We need to find these fanatics and fast."

"I do not require you to remind me of that, Henderson. I'm still

here fighting for the safety of both our nations, the Empire and your Federation. It's Adams who disappeared on a fruitless errand."

Henderson had no intention of getting involved in *that* discussion. He had read Adams's report and knew what he hoped to achieve with his trip to the Taurus Dark Cloud. Henderson couldn't say that he would have decided to do the same, but that was none of Kromm's business.

"We appreciate your effort, Captain," he said instead. "Good luck. *Venture* out."

Kromm disappeared from the bridge screen and was replaced by the Theris system's primary star.

Loos turned around to face Henderson. "Captain, the transporter room reports that all personnel have been beamed over from the Renao ship."

"Thank you, Lieutenant." The solar-jumper had served its purpose. The dead had been retrieved and were waiting for their transport to the Renao embassy on Lembatta Prime. All relevant technologies had been stored in the *Venture's* cargo holds.

Henderson touched a button on his armrest, activating the intercom. "Henderson to Admiral Gepta."

"Go ahead," the Chelon's voice said.

"Admiral, we're done with the solar-jumper. What should we do with it? Do you want us to take in tow back to Lembatta Prime?"

"Negative," Gepta replied. *"We're not going to burden ourselves. Scuttle it. And then we will continue our patrol."*

"Aye, sir." Henderson closed the channel. He got up from his chair, turning to face Lieutenant Commander Kraalbat. "You heard the admiral. Load a photon torpedo and target the Renao ship."

"Right away, Captain," the Tellarite at tactical said.

A yellow glowing projectile hurtled from the bottom of the bridge screen towards the ship drifting in space. The torpedo hit the solar-jumper right in its center. The vessel ceased to exist with an impressive but noiseless explosion.

Satisfied, the captain rubbed his hands. This part of their mission was definitely a resounding success. "Commander Makzia, plot a course for the next system. Warp five."

"Aye, sir."

"And, Mr. Loos, get in touch with the *Bougainville* and arrange a rendezvous somewhere along our route. Captain Stern will want his Bynars back."

"Will do, sir."

Henderson knew Rebecca Stern as a charming and generous person. But when it came to her ship or her crew, she was like a mother hen.

"Captain!" shouted Kraalbat. "Two dozen ships are closing in at warp speed!"

Alarmed, Henderson turned around to his tactical officer. "Where are they coming from?"

"From the Lembatta Cluster. That's why we didn't spot them until now."

The captain whirled around to the bridge's viewscreen and watched countless small and large spaceships drop from warp.

"Yellow alert. Shields."

A warning signal sounded, and the computer called yellow alert. At the same time, signal panels across the bridge started to blink.

"Mr. Kraalbat, scan the fleet. How many ships are we talking about?"

"Twenty-three, sir."

"Armed?"

"Some, not all. But they're not activating any tactical systems—no shields, no weapons."

Henderson stood up, walking toward the viewscreen. Once he took a closer look at the newly arrived fleet, he realized what a motley bunch they were. He saw several large and bulky freighters, but most of the ships were small passenger transporters, courier vessels, and possibly patrol ships. All of them seemed to be of Renao design—and none of them looked even remotely like a solar-jumper.

"Mr. Loos, open hailing frequencies," he said.

"Hailing frequencies open," the ops officer confirmed.

"This is Captain Henderson from the Federation starship *Venture*. You are in an exclusion zone that has been set up around the Lembatta Cluster. Please identify yourselves and state your intentions."

Loos looked at his console. "We're receiving ten replies at the same time. There's also constant communication among the ships. They seem pretty agitated."

"Can you identify some kind of leader among them?"

"Most of the communication seems to center around one of the large freighters. That ship is also the only one attempting to establish a visual link with us."

Henderson nodded. "Fair enough. Open that channel."

A slender Renao in simple brown clothing appeared on the viewscreen, sitting in a confined but functional cockpit. The skin of his face showed deep wrinkles. His long black hair with some silver streaks had been braided and hung over his left shoulder. His violet eyes glowed only faintly, and it seemed as if he hadn't slept in days.

"Federation ship, this is Captain ak Mhanib of the space freighter Boudhani. *We… Please excuse us trespassing in your exclusion zone, but we had no other choice. We need your help.*

Our ships are not designed for long-term space travel. Many of them are damaged, and the Renao aboard them are risking their lives if they stay there. Please, help us."

Bewildered, Henderson stared at him. "Captain, we'll be happy to help, of course. But why did you leave the cluster?"

The old Renao grimaced, and a shadow of sadness fell on his face. *"Because we had no choice. The home spheres are in flames. Madness is spreading farther and farther. We're refugees, Captain Henderson. And we have no idea where to go…"*

Space freighter *Boudhani*

"That alien ship is huge," Alyys whispered, staring out of the small porthole in the cargo hold of the algae transporter, her eyes wide with awe. And, Brossal was certain, with fear, as well.

"They won't hurt us," he said, not only reassuring her but himself as well. "I'm sure they don't mean us any harm."

But strictly speaking, he didn't know that. He had heard rumors among the other refugees who were crammed into the large cargo hold with them. Allegedly there were all kinds of sphere defilers. Some—the *Klin-goons*—acted with terrifying brutality. They abused and abducted citizens, threatening to destroy their arcologies with their disruptor weapons if the Renao didn't hand them the fanatics of the Purifying Flame on a silver platter… or so it was said.

But that's absurd, thought Brossal. *How should we hand over believers of this movement? Officially, no one belongs to them. But half of our people identify with their hatemongering about fighting against the sphere defilers from other worlds.*

Personally, he hadn't met a single Klin-goon yet. He

didn't know what their ships looked like, or whether the stories about them were even true.

But he prayed fervently that their small, broken fleet had fallen into the hands of the other side—the Federation. They were peaceful. He remembered that there had been a contract between the Renao and the Federation many years ago. They had traded and taken the first steps to get to know each other better. Brossal hadn't been keen on these efforts. The Federation was a vast, multicultural star empire that expanded further and further into space, penetrating sphere after sphere in the process. The Harmony of Spheres didn't mean anything to them. Any Renao living by the ancient traditions weren't to mix with such people.

Still, the Federation was definitely the lesser of two evils, compared to the Klin-goons. Their philosophy might be thoughtless and blasphemous, but at least they were peace-loving. *But is that really the truth?* he asked himself. Flyers from the Purifying Flame came to his mind. They had told stories about the terrible wars that had raged beyond the borders of the Lembatta Cluster in recent years. And why exactly had the government canceled the agreement with the nations of the Federation? He felt the cold chill of fear spreading through his entrails. *Is it possible that they are just as dangerous as the Klin-goons, after all?*

"They're coming closer," Alyys whispered, "Iad's enemies."

"Be quiet, Aly! I don't want to hear about Iad or the Son of the Ancient Reds!" Brossal shook his daughter, perhaps a little too fiercely. But he was so terribly exhausted. Kynnil was dead, Hisk had disappeared. Madness had torn them away from Brossal. Alyys was all he had left, his only purpose in life. She was the only reason he carried on. She was the only reason why he had fled from Xhehenem, leaving the home sphere behind. And even if it stood in contrast to everything that had ever been important to him—for her, he would be willing to live in foreign nations, on a world and in a sphere that wasn't home.

Above them, the loudspeakers of the ship's internal communication system crackled with the voice of the captain, relief evident in the tone of his voice. *"Attention, everyone. The Federation starship* Venture *has agreed to take us aboard. We will receive food and accommodation. The injured will be treated. They will take us to safety."*

Some people started cheering. But most of them just glanced at each other, insecure. Brossal ak Ghantur was one of the latter. *They will take us to safety.* These words lingered like a promise, sweet and menacing at the same time. *Where will we end up? Where lies our future?* Not within the Lembatta Cluster, that much was certain. Not at home. But would he really be able to live in a foreign region; he, of all people, who had never in his life traveled further from home than to Kharanto's offshore algae growth station?

"Where are they taking us?" asked Alyys, who apparently had similar thoughts. Anxiously, she looked at him.

Brossal pulled his daughter close, embracing her reassuringly. "I don't know," he whispered in her ear. "But wherever it may be—promise me that we both manage to live on. We must. For Mother and Hisk." He looked at Alyys solemnly.

She remained silent for a moment. In her eyes was a flicker, a hint of a child's fury. He was scared to ask what she was thinking in that moment.

"Yes," said Alyys finally. "For Mother and Hisk."

20
NOVEMBER 30, 2385

U.S.S. Prometheus, in the Taurus Dark Cloud

A huge purple energy discharge flickered across the viewscreen on the bridge. It hit the *Prometheus*'s shields, fraying out into countless small branches. Adams could hear crackling and pattering all over the outer hull.

"Shields down to sixty percent," Carson said.

"Engage polaron modulator," Adams said. "Auxiliary power to the regeneration routines."

"Aye, sir."

During a battle situation, these precautionary measures would have been premature. Sixty percent was still more than enough shield strength for the *Prometheus* in combat. But the chaos zone they were crossing was more treacherous than a phaser or torpedo. Abruptly appearing radiation fields or gravimetric shear put a lot of pressure on the three ship sections. Fortunately, the adaptive radiation filter and the regeneration routines that Kirk and Mendon had improved worked as perfectly as they had hoped.

So far.

With their modified sensors, Mendon had managed to detect a source of psychic radiation deep within the swirling energies that was similar to the Son's emanations. Adams and Spock agreed that it was worth a look, so they had been heading toward it for five hours now at full impulse speed.

The captain looked left where Winter and Spock were busy trying to work out a method of communicating with the White Guardian, or whoever else they might find. Since these beings consisted of pure psychic energy, their best approach so far involved sending recurrent radiation patterns from *Prometheus*'s main deflector dish in the hope of initiating a basic conversation.

So far, they hadn't exceeded the binary phase of *yes* and *no*. Adams was glad to have the old diplomat by his side. The way things looked currently, they would have to depend on him once again in order to establish contact with the incorporeal being.

Adams wiped his face with his hand. He needed some coffee. He hadn't had more than five hours sleep. *This is not healthy*, he thought. He knew exactly what Doctor Barai would say: "You should trust your crew, Captain, to manage the ship even if you're not present. You chose these people, remember?" *Once this crisis is over, I'll make sure that all of us get two weeks' shore leave.* He, for one, was in serious need of it.

Carson noticed something on her console. "Careful, there's a graviton eruption on the port side."

"Lieutenant ak Namur, turn the ship into the current," Adams said.

"Aye, Captain."

The swirling and lightning on the viewscreen seemed to shift position as the young Renao brought the *Prometheus* about. The board computer controlled both secondary hulls in perfect harmony so that their proximity remained unchanged and the mutual shield bubble stayed at maximum strength.

Only a few seconds later the *Prometheus* shuddered under the impact of graviton particles. Adams experienced a strange sensation of bobbing while the systems tried to compensate for the unexpected lateral gravitation. The hull vibrated so heavily for a couple of seconds that the captain clenched his teeth to prevent himself from biting his tongue.

Just like all phenomena they had encountered so far, this one didn't last long. The stream of gravitons died down and turned into something else. The light flickered once, and the situation on the bridge returned to normal.

"Resume course."

"Resuming course," said ak Namur.

Winter turned away from his comm station, looking at Adams. "Captain, we're ready now to send our general greeting on a wavelength that the energy beings might understand." Since they had entered the chaos zone they had been sending on all frequencies, asking to establish contact. So far, they hadn't received a response.

"I believe our statement should be very specific," said Spock. "We are sending an urgent impulse of sorts, periodically repeated. In order to arouse the Guardian's interest, we are copying the radiation pattern as best we can. Even if the meaning might be cryptic for the entity, we should be able to at least attract its attention."

"That's what we're hoping, anyway," Winter added.

Nodding, Adams said, "Let's give it a try."

Winter touched a keypad. "Sending signal."

A faint *ping* sounded from the communications console, repeating in intervals of two seconds. Adams turned away from the station, focusing his attention once again on the viewscreen. Static noise danced across the screen like dense snowfall. Beyond, green flashes danced in a maelstrom of ionized matter.

"Captain, I'm picking up a widespread field of thalaron

radiation straight ahead," Mendon said. "I urgently recommend we avoid flying through that field."

Adams frowned. "I thought thalaron radiation was artificial... Oh, forget it." There was no point in being surprised about anything in this zone that seemed to defy all known laws of nature. "Lieutenant ak Namur, initiate course correction for all ship segments. Mr. Mendon, keep an eye on that field. Let us know if it shifts."

"Yes, Captain."

The "snowstorm" on the viewscreen increased for a short while before disappearing altogether as they advanced into a region of the chaos zone with less radiation.

Two red glowing dots appeared in the distance ahead of them.

"Captain, we're approaching a twin star system," ak Namur said. "Two red supergiants, spectral type M1 and M2. They're not listed in Starfleet's database as they're right in the center of the chaos zone."

"Fascinating," Spock said. "The Lembatta Cluster is also a concentration of red giants. The Son's appearance in that location might give us a clue as to the preferred habitat of this energy species."

"Are we picking up psychic radiation patterns similar to those of the Son near those stars?" Adams asked Mendon.

"Negative, sir. The main source that we're following is still twelve light hours away from them. However... Hang on!" Mendon took two hectic inhalations from his respirator. "The source is moving. It's approaching us at faster than light speed."

"How fast?"

"Currently approximately warp four, sir. ETA, eight minutes."

"Red alert. Auxiliary energy to shields. Don't ready weapon systems!" Adams swiftly returned to his command chair while the alarm signals for red alert called the crew to their stations. The alarm was more or less unnecessary. Since their arrival at the chaos zone, everyone had been at their stations anyway. But Adams wanted to let the crew know that things were about to turn serious.

"Mr. Winter, shipwide to all three segments."

"Channel open, sir."

"Attention all hands, this is the captain. We have established contact with something that might be another member of the energy-species we encountered on Iad. Please observe your emotions carefully during the next few minutes. Extreme thoughts and impulses will most likely not be induced from within your mind, but could be a result of this being's presence. Please also look after your fellow crewmembers to avoid irrational outbreaks of violence. I trust in you and your exceptional training. Adams, out."

"Captain, look!" Carson said urgently.

Adams shifted his gaze back to the viewscreen. Ahead of them, between the twin star system and the *Prometheus*, a zone of white glistening energy had appeared that was rapidly increasing in size.

Adams looked at his science officer. "Analysis, Mr. Mendon."

"I'm sorry, Captain." The Benzite looked bewildered. "There is virtually nothing I can tell you about this cloud of energy. All I know is that it's approximately twenty times the size of the *Prometheus*, and it's now approaching at warp three. Other than that, it's resisting all our attempts to examine it."

"How strong is the psychoactive radiation?"

"Amazingly, it has drastically decreased. Our shields should easily be able to absorb it."

"Understood. We should remain vigilant, though." Adams looked toward the front again, where the energy life form had grown considerably.

"ETA, one minute," said Carson.

The being looked like a cloud that was fraying at the edges, and its color reminded Adams of pure snow glittering in the sunshine.

"The White Guardian…" Chell whispered at the engineering station.

"That name would, if nothing else, be suitable for such a being," Spock said.

"Do you sense the presence of the being, Ambassador?" Adams asked.

The Vulcan folded his hands in front of his chest and closed his eyes. "I sense an ancient presence," he said slowly. "It does not perceive me, but it has detected the ship."

"Is it hostile?"

Spock remained silent for a moment. "Difficult to ascertain. I do not sense any of the madness I sensed within the Son."

"That's at least something."

"The life form is slowing down," Carson said.

"And so will we," said Adams. "Full stop for all segments, Mr. ak Namur."

The Renao hastily complied.

"Sir, it's still coming closer," Carson said. "Distance only ten thousand kilometers now."

"Ambassador?" Adams glanced at the Vulcan out of the corner of his eye.

Spock's eyes were still closed. Motionless like a statue he stood there, apparently listening for or to the strange presence. "I detect no hostility. Only... curiosity."

Adams squinted slightly, before nodding. "All right. Maintain position. Let's see what the being's intentions are. Mr. Winter, send a greeting."

"Aye, sir."

"Five thousand kilometers."

"Interesting," Mendon said. "The being completely absorbs the chaos zone's radiation. As far as I can tell, there's a complete balance inside its... body."

"The eye of the storm," said Adams.

"In a manner of speaking, yes."

Roaas got up from behind his tactical console and stood beside the captain. "Captain," he said quietly, "what are we going to do if the being doesn't stop but engulfs the *Prometheus* instead?"

With a weak smile, Adams looked up to his first officer. "I guess we better hope that such an event won't bring any harm to either party."

"One thousand kilometers," Carson reported. "Five hundred."

The energy entity now covered the entire viewscreen— glittering white, blanking out the chaos zone behind.

"Reduce magnification factor," Adams said.

The image sprang backwards but less than ten seconds later the glittering cloud filled the viewscreen again.

"One hundred kilometers," Carson said. "Fifty. Ten. Contact!"

All the crackling noise along the outer hull of the *Prometheus* stopped instantly. The slight but permanent vibration they had been experiencing since entering the chaos zone had stopped. It seemed as if they were floating through a glittering bank of clouds.

"Shield energy is rapidly decreasing." Carson's fingers danced across the console. "Ninety percent. Eighty percent."

"Switch polaron modulator to full output."

"The loss of energy is slowing down—but only marginally."

"Ambassador Spock?"

"It is not a malicious attack, Captain. I believe the being is attempting to get through to us, and it is confused by the energy barrier."

Adams rose. "Fair enough. We're going to chance it. Mr. Chell, power down the shields."

"Right away, sir." The Bolian engineer touched some of his sensor buttons.

"Mr. Winter, relay those orders to the hull sections."

"Understood."

Immediately, the bulkheads, the deck, everything on the bridge took on a white glow.

At the same time, Adams felt a tingle spread through his legs as if high electric voltage flowed through the deckplates. The others seemed to feel it as well because they uttered noises of surprise and astonishment.

He turned to face his science officer. "Mr. Mendon, what's going on?"

The Benzite tried to touch his console for an analysis but he jerked back when he touched the sparkling light aura. "I… I'm not sure, sir. I believe the energy being has swallowed us. It seems to permeate through the entire ship."

"Mr. Chell, is there any imminent danger to the *Prometheus*?" Adams was particularly concerned about the antimatter containment field in the warp core.

The Bolian glanced back insecurely before he reached out into the light aura to begin a query. Squinting, he tried to read the results. "Negative, sir. The phenomenon... it seems to be purely optical. Neither the bio-neural circuitry nor the computer core nor the secondary engine rooms seem to have any issues."

"Engine room to bridge." Kirk's voice came from the loudspeakers.

"Adams here."

"Sir, something weird is happening here. We're noticing an intense energy phenomenon."

"I know, Commander. We have established contact with the energy life form. According to Lieutenant Chell, this hasn't led to any problems so far. Can you confirm that?"

"Uhm, yes, it seems as if our instruments are not affected. I still don't like it. We can neither locate nor analyze this light phenomenon."

"Understood, Commander. Stay vigilant and watch the readings. If we run into trouble, we will attempt to break free from the being."

"Yes, sir."

"Captain, careful!" Zh'Thiin's exclamation made Adams whirl around. He winced when he found himself facing an almost head-high flickering light tentacle. Zh'Thiin rushed to his side, her phaser raised and pointing at the sparkling fog apparition.

"No, leave it." Adams raised his hand defensively and looked at Spock. "Do you think that's another attempt to make contact?"

Spock had opened his eyes, curiously regarding the wriggling energy phenomenon. "I believe we are about to find out." Slowly, he walked towards the tentacle, cautiously reaching out with his hand. Adams had the impression of someone approaching a shy dog, allowing it to take a sniff.

Much to everyone's surprise, the flickering light column shifted away from him, across the bridge towards Carson and ak Namur. Both watched the apparition with wide eyes.

Sarita Carson stiffened. "Hey, don't you get too close to me, I'm allergic to energy columns—even if they sparkle as beautifully as you do."

"Don't move," Adams said sharply. "We don't want to scare it. So far, the being has not done us any harm. Let's assume it's just curious."

"I hope it knows how much electrical charge the human body can take before the synapses snap," Carson said dryly.

Adams had also thought about that. Peaceful intentions or not, during first contacts there was always the danger of a misunderstanding or simple ignorance being lethal.

Behind him, he noticed the familiar humming of a tricorder. When he looked over his shoulder he saw Mendon, who had pulled out his device and was trying to analyze the energy life form.

Frustrated, the Benzite shook his head. "I simply can't get any decent readings."

The tentacle hesitated between Carson and ak Namur, swaying to and fro undecidedly. Finally, it slithered away from them.

"It would seem our friend here has the same problem we do," Roaas said. "It wants to talk to us but doesn't know how to."

Winter at the communications station snapped his fingers. "Of course!"

"Ensign?" Adams looked at him quizzically.

Excited, the communications officer turned to face him. "Sir, Lieutenant Commander Mendon's tricorder gave me an idea. How about if we call Trik to the bridge? Maybe he can serve as some kind of communications interface."

The captain looked around. "Lieutenant Chell, Lieutenant Commander Mendon—opinions?"

"I think that's an interesting approach," the Benzite replied. "However, I'm uncertain how the being would get along with the programmed personality of the EMH. Trik has no emotions, and this species seems to define itself for the most part through psychoactive radiation."

The Bolian shrugged. "Well, it can't do much harm. We've got backup copies of Trik's personality matrix."

"Let's try it," Adams said. "Computer, activate Emergency Medical Hologram."

Trik materialized less than three meters beside the light phenomenon. "Please state the nature of the medical— What is *that*?" Perplexed, the doctor stared at the glittering energy tentacle. He pulled out his tricorder instinctively, pointing at his opponent.

"That's a resident of the Taurus Dark Cloud, and we wish to establish contact with it," Adams said. "Whatever it does, please let it proceed."

"What it does?" the EMH echoed. "What could it possibly—"

With the speed of a pouncing predator the tentacle shot toward Trik, piercing his chest. Of course, there was no wound. Except for a brief flickering of Trik's holomatrix at the point of entry, no immediate effects were noticeable.

Stunned, Trik stared at the glistening energy current that connected him like an umbilical cord to the light aura that hovered above the bridge.

"Oh," he noted, confused, "that feels extremely weird…"

Suddenly, his body stiffened, and his face became completely void of expression. His body started to glow, and his eyes turned into two small points of light, glistening and glittering.

The EMH slowly circled around, regarding all those present. Finally, it opened its mouth and spoke in a tone that was most definitely not Trik's. "WHO ARE YOU AND WHY ARE YOU DISTURBING OUR SPHERE?"

Spock raised his eyebrow. "Fascinating."

21
NOVEMBER 30, 2385

U.S.S. Prometheus, in the Taurus Dark Cloud

"I'm Captain Richard Adams of the Federation starship *Prometheus*," Adams said. "We come in peace, and we need your help."

"We can hear your words but we do not understand them," replied the being with Trik's voice.

Spock said, "It might be beneficial to upload data about the Federation into Trik's memory. He needs to not be a doctor, but rather a diplomat."

"Good idea," Adams agreed. "Computer, delete medical database from the EMH and load general information about the Federation. Keep it to college level, and do not include armed conflicts. Concentrate on peaceful research missions and first contacts." He didn't want to take any risks. The events of recent years didn't paint a good picture for someone who didn't know the ins and outs.

The computer confirmed with a chime. *"Deleting medical database. Transferring educational material of selected Federation history."*

Tilting his head, Trik stared at the ceiling for a moment, which made him look alarmingly like one of the living dead.

"Can you access the information we are making available for you?" Adams asked.

The EMH blinked twice before staring at him again. "We

CAN SEE MANY IMAGES. WE DO NOT UNDERSTAND EVERYTHING. BUT WE SEE THAT YOU TRAVEL ACROSS THE GREAT VOID IN ORDER TO MEET OTHER LIFE FORMS AND LEARN FROM THEM. THAT IS A DESIRE WE CAN RELATE TO." Trik tilted his head again, this time curiously. "WHY DO YOU REQUIRE HELP?"

Adams heard Mendon breathe heavily behind him. It sounded as if the Benzite was close to collapsing with excitement. During all the years they had been serving aboard the *Prometheus*, they had never been in a first contact situation. Being at this exotic location that seemed to defy all laws of nature and speaking to a representative of an entirely alien species was an extraordinary moment. *This is the reason why Starfleet was founded*, Adams thought, overcome by a mixture of awe and melancholy. But then he realized that this being was waiting for an answer, and he cleared his throat.

"We have discovered a being in another system that is very similar to you. It is stuck on a planet, and its presence is making the inhabitants on adjacent planets sick. We need to remove that being from there." He hesitated briefly. "Wait, we will show you." He turned to Mendon. "Commander, transfer our sensor recordings about Iad and the Son into the doctor's memory. A picture is worth a thousand words."

The Benzite needed two seconds before he realized that someone had spoken to him. He nodded eagerly. "Yes, sir. Right away."

Again, Trik seemed distant, while the energy being sifted through the information it had received. When the EMH's white glowing eyes stared at Adams again, it seemed concerned. "WE KNOW THAT ONE. HE IS ONE OF OUR YOUNG."

"It is said he came to that space region that we call Lembatta Cluster some ten thousand years ago," said Adams. "He caused a lot of devastation among the inhabitants there, before a White Guardian came to lock him away."

"ALL THAT IS TRUE," replied the being. "BUT YOU MUST NOT JUDGE THE BOY. HE DID NOT INTEND TO CAUSE ANY HARM. NONE OF US WANT TO CAUSE ANY HARM TO ANYONE."

"But why does your companion provoke hatred and violence?" zh'Thiin asked. Her antennae stretched forward belligerently. "If he's as intelligent as you are, he must know how much pain he is causing. He is the reason for thousands of deaths."

Adams silenced her by raising his hand. "Commander, leave this to me, please."

"WE REGRET WHAT HAS HAPPENED IN THE PAST AND WHAT IS HAPPENING NOW," the energy being said. The aura surrounding Trik flickered slightly. "THE BOY IS CONFUSED AND ILL. HE DOES NOT KNOW WHAT HE IS DOING."

"Could you elaborate?" Spock asked. "We do not wish to cause harm to the boy, but we require a solution for this predicament before any more lives are lost."

Trik turned away from Adams, facing the ambassador. "WE ARE CURIOUS. WE WANT TO TRAVEL THE STARS. IN THAT RESPECT WE ARE SIMILAR TO YOU. ESPECIALLY THE YOUNG ONES SOMETIMES RISK TOO MUCH WHILE DOING SO. THEY TRAVEL TOO FAR AWAY—AND THEN THEY DO NOT FIND THEIR WAY HOME."

"So the—the boy had lost his way back then?" Adams asked.

"YES. BUT THE VOID IS DANGEROUS FOR US. WE CANNOT SURVIVE FOREVER WITHIN IT. WE NEED OUR SPHERE IN ORDER TO FIND NOURISHMENT. WE WILL STARVE IN THE VOID. THE BOY WAS STARVING. HE WAS WITHERING AWAY. AND THEN HE FOUND THE RED SUNS THAT LOOKED LIKE HOME. AND HE FOUND NOURISHMENT HE HAD NEVER TASTED BEFORE, STRONG AND INTOXICATING."

"The emotions of the ancient Renao." Spock nodded as he began to understand. "Their joy, their love, their anger."

"THEY DID NOT DO HIM ANY GOOD. THEY MADE HIM ILL, CONFUSED HIM. HIS HUNGER GREW UNTIL HE COULD NOT HELP HIMSELF, AND HE HAD TO CONSUME INCREASING QUANTITIES OF THIS NOURISHMENT."

"And that way, he became insane." The old Vulcan briefly exchanged a knowing glance with Adams. "That would explain what I sensed in the Son's presence."

"That's all well and good," Adams said, "but can we focus on the Guardian again? A second being arrived at the red suns... white, just like you are. And it locked up the boy."

"YES. WE BEGAN TO MISS OUR BOY. SO WE SENT AN OLD ONE TO SEARCH FOR HIM. HE LISTENED INTO THE VOID FOR THE BOY'S CALLS AND FOUND HIM AMONG THE RED SUNS. BUT HE COULD NOT TAKE THE YOUTH BACK WITH HIM. HIS ILLNESS HAD PROGRESSED TOO FAR. WITHOUT THE EMOTIONS THAT HAD BECOME HIS NOURISHMENT, HE WOULD HAVE WITHERED. BUT THE OLD ONE SAW WHAT HAPPENED TO THE LITTLE PEOPLE OF THIS WORLD AND HE FELT COMPASSION FOR THEM. HE LOCKED UP THE BOY AND RELOCATED THE LITTLE PEOPLE FAR AWAY TO THE EDGE OF THE RED SUNS IN ORDER TO PROTECT THEM FROM THE BOY'S HUNGER."

"The transfer that Councilor ak Mousal mentioned during our talks on Onferin," Spock said to Adams. "Fascinating that the Renao's memory about the legend of Iad has prevailed with such precision."

"Yes, who would have thought that the myth actually tells the story as it was," the captain said. He turned back to their alien visitor. "What your Old One did back then saved the entire Renao race. But unfortunately, your boy has been freed from his prison by accident. Since then he's been sitting on Iad, wreaking havoc. We would like to ask you to send another Old One to rebuild the prison around the boy. We're asking for the welfare of all Federation people and their adjacent realms."

"WE CANNOT SEND ANOTHER OLD ONE," the energy being replied.

Adams hadn't expected that answer. "Why not?"

"IT IS TOO FAR AWAY. THE ONE YOU CALL THE WHITE GUARDIAN STARVED ON HIS WAY BACK. HE HAD OVERESTIMATED HIS STRENGTH."

"He starved? How did you find out about the events in the cluster then?"

"HIS LAST CALL STILL REACHED US. HIS ESSENCE WITHERED, THOUGH, BEFORE HE WAS ABLE TO REACH THE PROTECTION OF THE SPHERE AGAIN."

"But we can't subdue the boy on our own." Adams raised his hands, pleading. "Thousands may die if you don't help us. Is there no way to give the Old One enough nourishment for his journey? We have extraordinary technologies at our disposal. Maybe we can invigorate him while he accompanies us." Adams had the *Prometheus*'s deflector dishes in mind. Mendon would surely find some form of energy that he could inject into the glittering white cloud in order to keep its strength up. The Benzite's adaptive radiation filter was able to neutralize the dangers of the chaos zone. Maybe they could reverse the effect to make a tasty cocktail from rotating energy frequencies for these beings.

"WE BELIEVE THAT YOU ARE EXTRAORDINARY CREATURES," the being said. "YOUR HISTORY PROVES THAT IN MANY IMAGES. WE TRULY REGRET YOUR SUFFERING BECAUSE WE KNOW HOW VALUABLE THE EXISTENCE OF EACH INDIVIDUAL IS. THAT IS ALSO THE REASON WHY WE CANNOT SEND ANOTHER OLD ONE.

It is impossible. The loss of the boy and the Old One has dealt us a devastating blow. We are few; we must not lose another one of us."

Adams sighed. He didn't know what else to say. He had no way of estimating the exact numbers of energy life forms. But they said that they could not risk the life of one of their own, even if it might save thousands of others, and he had to accept that decision. He didn't have the right to judge them for it.

Is that it? he asked himself, downhearted. *Did we undertake this journey in vain? Is our only option at the end of the day to deprive the Renao of any spacefaring capability in order to avoid the threat from the Purifying Flame? Or do we need to evacuate the entire Lembatta Cluster and declare it a quarantine zone?*

"You also need to consider this," the being in front of Adams continued after a brief pause. "Even if we were to lock away the boy again, the prison might be destroyed once more. Or could you guarantee that it would last longer this time than the time span you call ten thousand years?"

That was something Adams had indeed not considered yet. Of course, Starfleet would declare Iad to be an exclusion zone once the crisis was over, but Starfleet had only existed two hundred years so far, and who was to know whether it would still be around in two hundred more? Besides, there were always men and women with a hunger for knowledge larger than their reason. And the Son's influence was tempting and dangerous even when he was imprisoned, as the *Valiant's* crew had established.

"No," he admitted, "we can't."

Jassat ak Namur got up from his chair. "Requesting permission to speak, Captain."

Adams eyed the young Renao. He didn't believe that his

words would make a difference, but he understood why ak Namur had to try. This was about his home, his people. "Permission granted."

Ak Namur approached Trik and stood right in front of him. "My name is Jassat ak Namur. I belong to the people resident in the Lembatta Cluster—near the red suns, as you call them. They are my people, and they are dying because your ill boy is making them ill as well. And there are not only old people dying—men and women—but also young people… children, many children. Can you really allow that? Can you really stand by and say, 'Their death does not concern us'?"

He hesitated briefly, pressing his lips together as if he was trying to fight back some more drastic reproaches that were on the tip of his tongue. When he continued, his voice was quiet but determined. "Listen to me. There must be a solution. I am not only talking about saving my people but also about saving your boy." He paused, apparently searching for words. "You say that he is ill. The truth is, he has completely succumbed to madness. His mind is destroyed. What he used to be doesn't exist anymore. He's merely craving hatred and violence while being stuck on an alien world far away from his home sphere. I don't know how old the likes of you can grow to be, but do you want to condemn him to that kind of existence? Shouldn't he be… released?"

The energy being stared at the young Renao for quite a while. Adams began to wonder whether it was conferring with the other Old Ones—who apparently existed within the chaos zone—or whether it was simply stunned at the suggestion.

"You are talking about terminating the boy."

Ak Namur straightened. "Yes. It would be… the compassionate thing to do. The boy wouldn't have to suffer any longer. And the Renao would regain their freedom."

Their visitor fell silent again. This time it took so long that Adams glanced quizzically at Spock.

"I sense upheaval," the ambassador answered the unspoken question. "I believe the Old Ones are debating the issue."

"So there are really several of them?"

"It would appear so. I am not able to ascertain how many presences are participating, but there are at least half a dozen of them."

The captain looked at ak Namur. "That was an unusual attempt, Lieutenant."

"Forgive me, Captain. But it had to be done."

Adams shook his head. "There's no need to apologize. As awkward as this subject might be, it was the right decision to consider the death of the being as an option. I would have preferred to lock it up with the help of the Old Ones; however, your suggestion may well be the more compassionate one. To be perfectly honest, I hadn't even considered the way this being must feel in its eternal prison. And we have learned that rescuing it is out of the question."

"IT CAN BE DONE." Trik's voice abruptly rejoined the conversation.

Adams turned back to him, hope budding. "You can help us?"

"WE BELIEVE SO."

"How?"

"WE CAN FILL A VESSEL WITH ENERGY FROM WITHIN US. THE VESSEL NEEDS TO DISCHARGE THAT ENERGY JUST AS SOON AS IT IS FACED WITH THE BOY. THE DISCHARGE WILL LET THE BOY WITHER."

"This vessel," Spock said. "Am I right in assuming that you are referring to one of the small people... someone among us?"

"Yes. The vessel must be alive. Otherwise it cannot contain our energy."

A very bad feeling spread in Adams's stomach. "And how difficult is it for this vessel to discharge the energy on Iad? Will it also wither, like the boy?"

Trik's eyes fixed those of the captain. Sadness reverberated in his voice. "Yes."

Jassat ak Namur felt an excitement he hadn't felt since his return to the Lembatta Cluster. Once the Son—the boy—was gone, the Renao all over the cluster would return to their old selves. Soon after, the Purifying Flame would be no more than an embarrassing memory.

Unfortunately, this hope came at a price. Someone had to accept their death willingly. *Who, if not me, could carry this burden?* went through Jassat's mind. The Renao were his people. He could hardly ask anyone else to sacrifice their life for him.

He didn't want to die. If there had been any way to avoid it, he would have been all too happy. But since he had joined Starfleet he had vowed to help those in need, even if it cost him his life. The crisis in the Lembatta Cluster was his very personal *Kobayashi Maru* test, he suddenly realized. His only choices were thousands of deaths… or his own death.

There was no way to win this scenario. This was all about him handling death as an officer. And how much he was willing to sacrifice in order to make the galaxy a little better.

Jassat made his decision, took a step forward, and addressed his captain. "Sir, with your permission I would like to volunteer to take in the energy of the Old Ones. I am offering to be the vessel that will overcome the being on Iad."

Adams raised one hand. "I'm not ready to have one of my officers walk to his certain death." He looked at Trik, still possessed by the white glittering energy being. "Death is inevitable for the vessel? There's no other option?"

"WE CANNOT SPEAK WITH ABSOLUTE CERTAINTY," the being replied patiently. "NEVER HAS ANYTHING LIKE THIS BEEN ATTEMPTED. BUT WE HAVE EXAMINED YOUR BODIES AND OUR MINDS, AND WE HAVE DETERMINED WHAT IS NEEDED IN ORDER TO TERMINATE THE BOY. ALL INDICATIONS ARE THAT THE VESSEL WILL WITHER AS WELL."

"I'm ready for it," Jassat said intently.

Adams ignored him. "Give us a little time to think about it. I need to confer with my officers." Turning around, he touched a button on the armrest of his command chair. "Bridge to engine room."

"*Kirk here,*" the chief engineer replied.

"Commander, please come to my ready room."

"*On my way, Captain.*"

"Lieutenant Commander Mendon, Lieutenant ak Namur, you're with me also. Commander Roaas, you've got the bridge."

With determined steps, Adams marched toward the door to his ready room. Jassat followed him dutifully.

Even in the captain's small office, the energy being's white light aura emanated from every surface. It was a strangely dreamlike sight, as if they weren't on the plane of reality any longer.

When Kirk arrived at the ready room, she found Adams leaning against the edge of his desk. Mendon and ak Namur stood at parade rest facing the captain.

In a few words, Adams described the encounter with the energy being on the bridge to Kirk. He told her about the possible solution for the crisis within the Lembatta Cluster, including the catch. "Mr. ak Namur is willing to act as the vessel. This decision is to his credit; however, I have no intention of agreeing to it unless we have explored and dismissed all other options. Jenna, Mendon, I require your input."

The Benzite put his arms behind his back. "I'm afraid, Captain, the problem that we're facing is that we know next to nothing about the life form on Iad, and we also don't know much about the life form we have encountered here. The energy this being consists of defies all analysis. Just like the chaos zone, it does not seem to correlate with the laws of nature existing in this dimension. Now, undeniably, both exist, therefore it is we who are lacking the capability to understand what we call reality."

Adams sighed. "In other words, we have to trust the word of this Old One because we simply don't have the means to verify any of it."

"That is… erm, more or less correct, sir." The Benzite looked uncomfortable.

Kirk ran her fingers through her hair, shaking her head. "I can't really contribute anything from the technical side of things, Captain. An analysis of the white energy is impossible, so I could only offer some basic advice on how to store and transport energy. If you want, I'll ask our host to run a few trials with various energy storage devices. But there's a strong psychoactive aspect where these beings are concerned—mind and energy seem to be connected somehow. So I doubt that a purely technological approach would do us any good. What's more, it would still leave the question of how we should manage the intended discharge. Also, we shouldn't overextend the duration of our stay in this zone. You might not notice it on the bridge but we're in a cold sweat trying to keep the ship systems afloat. The *Prometheus* is not designed for this place. The longer we remain within the chaos zone, the more we risk some spontaneous radiation damaging or destroying important systems. The slipstream drive in particular is a delicate piece of experimental technology. If we lose it, it will take three or four months for us to return to the Lembatta Cluster."

Jassat saw Adams frown. He obviously didn't like what he was hearing. The captain turned his head, staring out of the window, which showed only glittering white energy.

Finally he sighed, turning back to his officers. "All right then. The way things look, we don't have any other choice but to accept the Old One's offer. Lieutenant ak Namur, you will *not* be the vessel. Since I am the captain of this ship, I will sacrifice myself."

Surprised, Jassat's eyes widened. "Captain, no! I mean… please, sir, don't do that. I have already volunteered to carry this burden."

"I know, but I can't allow it. I'm the captain of the *Prometheus*. It's my duty to protect my crew. If a life is required to resolve the Lembatta crisis, it should be mine. It's my duty."

"With all due respect, sir, I must disagree," Jassat said. "Your duty lies with your ship. The *Prometheus* and her crew need you more than they need me. My duty, on the other hand, lies with my people."

"Mr. ak Namur… Jassat—" Adams began, but Jassat dared to interrupt him.

"No, please, sir, let me explain."

The captain bit his lip, looking as if he intended to reprimand him. Instead, he nodded tersely.

Jassat composed himself, choosing his words carefully.

"Captain, I know that I always gave the impression of being different from most Renao, and that I'm an outsider in that society. That is basically true. Most Renao just look inward to their community. I always wanted to look outside, and get to know the wonders that exist between the stars. But despite them thinking differently from me, we're all Renao—and I feel connected to them."

He made eye contact with Jenna and Mendon. "Imagine your homeworld was ravaged by a major disaster that resulted in thousands of deaths. It might even be millions if the Son's power keeps increasing, driving all Renao mad. Wouldn't you voluntarily give your life in order to save your people?"

Jassat turned back to Adams. "Besides, this is also about the Federation, my second home. If we don't stop the Purifying Flame, it will continue to commit atrocities. And there's only one way to stop them—stop the source of their madness. How much death and pain could be avoided for the price of just one life? I willingly give it if I can save both worlds I belong to."

He was expecting further argument, but after a moment of silence, deep in thought, Adams nodded slowly. He pushed himself off the desk's edge, straightening himself. "Very well, Lieutenant. For the benefit of the Renao and the Federation I give you my permission to act as the vessel for the energy of the Old Ones. I just hope these beings know what they're doing."

Jassat fervently hoped so too.

22
NOVEMBER 30, 2385

Mining colony Kobheni, Yssab
Shaool system, Lembatta Cluster

The factory siren relieved Jonah ak Seresh from his ordeal. Comparing inventory lists for ten hours was a task that could drive a person mad. He finished inputing the last entries into the table on the monitor of his terminal before switching the device off. With a long sigh, he leaned back in his work chair. White dots danced before his eyes, and his neck muscles felt so hard that a freight transport could have driven over them without breaking his neck.

Three more days, he said to himself. *And then it's done.* Jonah was a logistics expert in the metal processing plant in Kobheni, and the tables were his everyday business. But the biannual stocktaking was not only boring, it also took up valuable time that he would have preferred to spend on his usual daily chores. If his assistant Shamar had been here, everything would have been much easier. But Shamar had had an argument with the new owner of the factory and had been fired two weeks ago. Jonah didn't know what the argument had been about. In any case, the atmosphere had been very hostile. Strictly speaking, the atmosphere had been very tense for a while now, which had ruined the enjoyment he usually got from doing his work.

Just as well that I'm done for today, Jonah thought. Grunting, he got up, grabbed his shoulder bag, and left his office above one of the factory halls. He heard agitated voices down in the hall. Two people were having an argument. Jonah walked faster. He didn't want to get involved.

Hear no evil, see no evil; that was his motto.

That way he also managed to ignore some of the stock losses that he kept noticing on the cargo lists. Initially he had alerted the new owner to them, who had told him with friendly but firm words that he shouldn't bother him a second time with this matter.

"If you don't like the numbers, change them," he had said. "Just do your work, ak Seresh. And don't concern yourself with matters that are none of your business."

Yet another reason why he didn't enjoy his work any longer.

With a lowered head and swift strides Jonah left the factory complex. A cold wind blew—as it did so often—through Kobheni, bringing dust from the adjacent strip mine. Jonah coughed, pulling his hood over his head.

Another scribbling from the Purifying Flame had been scrawled on one of the outside walls. You could find them everywhere in town by now—in the arcologies as well as in the industrial area around them.

The graffiti was not as bad as the recruiters, though. They appeared everywhere—in the taverns, the assembly halls, the markets. Aggressively, they attempted to convince people to participate in the battle against all sphere defilers. Sometimes they just distributed flyers, sometimes they gave rousing speeches. Rumor had it that they sometimes even abducted Renao and forced them to fight. Such things only happened at night, though, in abandoned arcology corridors.

Jonah snorted. *Life here is getting worse.* He had to admit that he was frightened; not just for himself but also for Laali, his female companion. If they came one day to get him, what should he do? They would threaten Laali, and he would follow the fanatics on their ill-fated raid against the rest of the galaxy. No one could stop the Purifying Flame anymore. Even the sphere custodians of Kobheni were powerless against the spreading blight, unless they made a pact with the fanatics.

He heard muffled thuds and clanks on his side of the road. Someone laughed maliciously. Jonah turned his head inside his hood and caught a glimpse of three men, about fifty meters away. Two of them were hitting a vehicle that was parked by the roadside with metal tubes, while the third one was finishing a fresh batch of graffiti that said *Outworld lover!*

Jonah quickly averted his eyes and hurried on. *It has come to that already.* Jonah loved Kobheni, his home sphere, the same as every Renao loved theirs. But recently, he kept wishing that he could leave the arcology, and all this idiocy that was happening here, behind.

I need something to drink. In his agitated mood, he would only scare Laali. She knew as well as he did that Kobheni's society was increasingly deteriorating. But even more than him, she closed her eyes before that fact and covered her ears, singing loud songs that reminded her of better times. *We're also going mad*, Jonah thought. *Just in a different way.*

His favorite tavern was at the base of the arcology. The windows were small, and the view out onto the ore mines south of Kobheni was only beautiful when the full and red evening sun sent her last beams across the landscape. But the *bri* was good, and the guests, tired from their day's work, left each other alone while they were staring at viewscreens where generally some dancing or singing shows with young, popular local artists were broadcast.

Today was no different. When Jonah came into the bar, only a handful of other guests sat in there. Judging by their clothing, they were all laborers from the metal processing plant or the adjacent smelter. Two colorfully dressed women danced on the three screens to driving rhythms. The sets' volume was turned down to avoid disturbing people. Those who wanted to watch could look at them; those who didn't simply stared into their glasses of *bri*.

Jonah waved at Banuk, the bartender, to order his drink. The men knew each other and not many words were needed. He sat down by the counter, nodded politely at the man next to him, and waited for his *bri*.

Banuk placed the glass in front of Jonah, who grunted in return.

"Work?" the bartender asked.

Jonah nodded. "Work. The Flame. It's getting worse."

This time it was Banuk's turn to grunt in agreement.

The image on the television sets abruptly changed. The dancers vanished and a sinister alien face appeared. His hair was black and came down to his shoulders, his eyes were glowing menacingly, and he had a ridged forehead with numerous bony humps.

Jonah's hair stood on end. "Banuk, what is that? Isn't that one of these strangers from the worlds beyond our home spheres?"

Confused, the bartender turned around. "You're right. What in Bharatrum's name is he doing in that broadcast?" He grabbed the remote control and changed channels, but the stranger was also on the next channel. And on the next.

"*Citizens of Yssab,*" the man began speaking with a booming voice. "*This is Captain Kromm from the Klingon battle cruiser* Bortas."

"Turn the volume up," one of the customers shouted. "I want to hear what the Klingon has got to say."

Reluctantly, Banuk obliged.

"I come with a call to arms against the Purifying Flame. They are a malicious group who have made dozens of honorless attacks on several worlds and bases within the Klingon Empire and the United Federation of Planets. Thus, they have challenged us, and our answer of choice would be to crush them." He raised the index finger of his gloved hand. *"But… that is not our goal. During our search for the Purifying Flame, we have learned that the madness that is spreading across all worlds within the cluster is not yours! The hatred the Purifying Flame is displaying toward us is nothing but deception. You're all being manipulated by a demonic being from the depths of space that has settled on Iad."* He leaned forward, staring imploringly at his audience. *"The elders among you might recall the legends of the Son of the Ancient Reds, the White Guardian, the transfer. All that is true. Everything! But the Son, who had been imprisoned for millennia, has awakened again. He intends to lead the Renao into disaster. He feeds you with his poisonous thoughts, because the hatred and the violence he incites are his food. The Purifying Flame is just the beginning."*

His voice lowered and took on a menacing tone. *"Do you not feel the fury and desperation within you? Do you not observe the violence in the streets of your very cities? This will only get worse—much worse, because the Son is greedy for murder, and destruction, and hatred. We are the only ones who can save you. We are warriors, and we fight against this being with all our considerable might. But we need time; time which the cowards of the Flame might use to attack more of our worlds in their rage. That must not happen! Therefore we need to find their headquarters, their secret shipyard where they are constructing the weapons of war to be used against us. We need to destroy this shipyard and take the Purifying Flame's weapons away from them. Only then can we concentrate on the final battle against the being that intends to throw your worlds into an era of darkness. So, by the hand of Kahless, help us, if you don't want to face your doom. Save your damn spheres, which are so important to you, before they perish during the war!"*

He leaned back, folding his arms in front of his chest. *"The* Bortas *is in orbit. We expect to hear from you soon."*

Stunned, Jonah stared at the viewscreen even as the image changed and another music group appeared. *Iad? The Son of the Ancient Reds? And all the fury, all the viciousness, all the fanaticism is only the result of being manipulated by a mythical being?*

"Either this guy is the biggest liar among the suns," Banuk said, "or there's a lot more going on between Onferin and Catoumni than we ever imagined."

Jonah nodded slowly. "Yeah, it looks that way."

The Klingon had asked for help to stop the Purifying Flame until the Son had been defeated. Jonah remembered all those incidents in his factory. He would never have dared to investigate them on his own. But suddenly, powerful allies offered their help, and he didn't need to be afraid with them by his side. *It's a chance*, he thought. *A chance for a new beginning.*

Quickly, he emptied his glass of *bri*, before getting up to pay his bill. He urgently needed to find a public comm cabin in order to make an extremely dangerous call.

I.K.S. Bortas

"I should be granted a seat on the High Council." With a satisfied grin, Kromm leaned back in his command chair, once the transmission to Yssab had ended. "Do you agree, Ambassador?" He looked over at Alexander Rozhenko, standing beside him.

Now that they were no longer broadcasting, the Federation's representative to the Klingon Empire came closer. "Your performance was indeed not too bad," he admitted. "I thank you for being *benevolent* enough not to threaten them with brute force, and for letting me write the draft for the speech." Alexander had had a dispute about this with Kromm before the speech. But in the end, the impulsive Klingon captain had realized that it was more prudent to pose as someone who would help the Renao rather than someone who was their enemy. Because enemies were what the Purifying Flame needed in order to recruit soldiers for their cause.

At least he listened to me for once, Alexander thought. Apparently Adams's words about all of them being in the same boat, and about Kromm's chance for glory, had hit home. *I wish he had said them earlier. That might have spared us near disasters like Xhehenem.*

Had it been up to Alexander, he would have taken over command aboard the *Bortas* a long time ago. But despite being Martok's eyes and ears during this mission, his status as Federation diplomat was no more than that of a guest. Doubtful as Kromm's abilities as a commander might be, the majority of the crew stood behind him. That wasn't at all surprising, as the *Bortas* crew—with very few exceptions—consisted of warriors whose careers had reached a dead end one way or the other. No one on Qo'noS or at high command cared much about these men and women. This blemish of being an outsider bound them together.

"Now we need to wait," L'emka said. Although she was

present, she had distanced herself so far from Kromm that she seemed to be merely an observer on the bridge.

That rift will never close again. Alexander hadn't missed the increasing hostility between captain and first officer. If L'emka was as smart as the ambassador thought she was, she would ask for a transfer as soon as the *Bortas* finished this mission.

And Kromm would gladly fulfill that request.

The captain stood up from his command chair. "We can't possibly expect these fools to pick up their comm devices straight away. I'm going to eat. Perhaps someone will have gotten in touch by the time I've finished my *klongat* leg."

"Captain." Klarn turned away from his communication station, looking at Kromm. "I have a Renao who claims he has important information for us."

Stunned, Kromm stared at his communications officer. "That was fast."

Alexander frowned. "Could it be a trap? Perhaps one of the terrorists wants access to us."

The Klingon captain grinned menacingly. "We simply beam him aboard. If he carries weapons or explosive charges he'll find that he won't be able to do any harm with them here. Klarn, tell him to stand by."

"Yes, Captain."

Kromm returned to his chair, hitting the intercom button. "Bridge to transporter room."

"Brukk here, Captain," the *bekk* on duty responded.

"Is it possible to beam someone up from the surface of Yssab? There is no atmospheric interference?"

The *bekk* fell silent for a moment before replying, *"No, Captain. There are heavy storms and bad weather fronts, but nothing the transporter can't handle."*

"Very good. Lieutenant Klarn will provide you with the coordinates of a Renao man. Lock on and beam him directly to the bridge. Be sure to neutralize any weapons or explosives before he materializes."

"Understood, Captain."

With a grim smile, Kromm settled back into his chair. "Rooth."

The gray-haired security chief stepped down from the tactical station in the back of the bridge. Pulling his disruptor out, he stood next to Kromm. Chumarr remained at the weapons station but also looked straight ahead. The second officer folded his arms in front of his chest. L'emka stood with her hands on her hips.

Alexander shook his head. The poor Renao would be faced with a terrifying welcoming committee. He turned to the captain. "You should leave the conversation to me."

"Why should I?" Kromm asked.

Because you're going to scare the poor man so much he probably won't say anything after all. Rozhenko was not foolish enough to voice that thought, however, instead saying, "Because you're the captain. It's beneath you to talk to some low-life informant. That's why you have men like me who are your voice in these situations."

Kromm rubbed his bearded chin. "Very well," he replied, placing his arms on the rests and leaning back in his chair. He gave the impression of a relaxed but very present sovereign on his throne.

With the characteristic reddish flicker of the air, a man materialized in front of them. He was of average height and weight with an oblong face. He wore a black hooded robe that reached down to his ankles. He appeared on the bridge slightly bent forward, the way he had been standing at the comm device.

When he saw what had happened, his eyes widened and he gasped. "What by all the spheres...?"

Alexander approached him, spreading his arms. "Welcome aboard the *Bortas*. I'm Ambassador Rozhenko, and this is Captain Kromm." He made half a turn, pointing at the Klingon.

Kromm just growled, glaring at the Renao.

"I'm on the spaceship?" The Renao swayed, looking as if he was about to lose consciousness in shock.

Alexander quickly stepped toward him, supporting him before he fell. "Don't worry, my friend. It's all right. You called us and we thought it best to bring you here where it's safe." Recalling that the Renao had little experience with transporters, he added, "We have beamed you up from Yssab using our transporter. You don't have to be scared. The process is completely safe."

"I... I understand." Insecure, the Renao looked around. The dark metal architecture of the *Vor'cha*-class cruiser seemed to spook him. Then again, it might have been the half-dozen grim-looking Klingons.

"What's your name, my friend?"

"I... My name is Jonah ak Seresh. I'm a logistics expert in a metal processing plant in Kobheni."

"A man with an overview. Very good." Alexander smiled encouragingly at ak Seresh, before looking serious again. "You called us because you wanted to give us some information."

The Renao nodded shyly. "Yes. You know, I... I'm not a traitor. But... but you said that you wanted to help us. You want to cure us from this madness, right?"

"Absolutely." Rozhenko put his hands on the Renao's shoulders. "And Klingons are a people who hold honor in the highest respect. Captain Kromm spoke only the truth in his broadcast. But only people who follow their conscience have honor. If your conscience tells you that your people are sick, you will not blemish your honor by helping us do something about it. Instead, you'll be proving that you have a vision. Because your information might help us in our campaign to end the needless violence and suffering."

"Just talk," Kromm said with a growl. He was obviously growing impatient with the diplomatic approach. "That's why you're here."

"Yes… yes, you're right." Ak Seresh cleared his throat. "As I said, I'm working as a logistics expert in a metal processing plant. The owner has changed recently. The new boss is a radical, I'm sure of it. We used to produce all sorts of items in our plant before. But since he's been there, all we produce are plates for ship hulls. That… that in itself isn't odd. The majority is being delivered to Onferin, since our only shipyard is there. But I constantly check the cargo lists; that's my duty. And I've noticed that containers keep disappearing."

Alexander's ears pricked up at that. "Containers with plates used for starship hulls are disappearing?"

Ak Seresh nodded. "I'm a good employee, so I pointed it out to the owner. After all, it might be organized theft. But they told me in no uncertain terms that I should keep my nose out. The… the boss even ordered me to adjust the cargo lists in case I noticed inconsistencies."

"Now *that* is suspect," L'emka said.

The Renao briefly glanced at her, nodding. "That's what I thought as well. So I dug a little deeper and found out that *Kranaals* are taking those containers away at night. That happens every two or three days now. I have no idea where they're taking their cargo, and eventually I became too scared to investigate further. I have a wife, you know. I don't want anything to happen to her—or me."

"Can you tell us when and where these *Kranaals* will be next time?" Alexander asked.

"I believe the next shipment will be loaded tonight after midnight. I can tell you where, but you have to promise me something first."

"What?"

"You must take me and my wife away from Kobheni. We're not safe there any longer."

Kromm grumbled something from his command chair.

Alexander shot him a quick look of warning before focusing his attention back on ak Seresh.

"That shouldn't be a problem. Just name a location on Yssab, and we will transport you and your wife there."

Ak Seresh looked disappointed. "Can't we stay under your protection while madness rules down there?"

Now Kromm leaned forward. A grim smile played around the corners of his mouth. "You don't want to be here with us, Renao. Because if your information is worth anything, we will be going immediately into glorious battle."

23
DECEMBER 1, 2385

I.K.S. Bortas, in orbit around Yssab

The *Bortas* lay in wait, invisible thanks to its cloaking device. Kromm was pacing his bridge, feeling the frustrating combination of the anticipatory thrill of glorious battle with nagging impatience for the battle to actually start. By now, it was the middle of the night on Yssab. Kromm waited with bated breath for something to finally happen on the perimeter of the container storage area outside the space port in the south of Kobheni.

As promised, they had taken their Renao informant and his mate to a hidden refuge on the other side of the planet that they both recalled from the early days of their courtship. Once he was safely there, ak Seresh had provided the exact location where the *Kranaals* would be loaded with stolen containers every few nights. During their next orbit, Raspin at ops had had no difficulty locating the small landing area next to the container storage area with his sensors.

If it had been up to Kromm, they would have beamed a company of troops down there in order to break up the secret loading. Rooth had argued convincingly that they would only catch the most insignificant link in the chain of smuggling. It was far better to track the *Kranaals* to their destination, which had to be somewhere on Yssab considering that the flying vessels were not capable of space travel.

"And if they take the containers to a ship somewhere in the wild beyond Kobheni, it would also be better to follow that ship instead of striking," Rooth had said. "After all, we're interested in the destination of these hull plates."

"Why not simply capture the smugglers and torture them until they talk?" Kromm had asked.

"Why waste time and effort, and possibly only obtain false information, when we can defeat these farmers using strategy?" Rooth had replied.

His plan had convinced Kromm. First, they had sent a second planetwide transmission with Kromm complaining about the lack of cooperation. "You all will regret this!" he had thundered. "We will return!"

After that, the *Bortas* had left orbit and had gone into warp. Then they had dropped from warp on the periphery of the system, far away from any satellite observation by the Renao, cloaked the *Bortas*, and returned at full impulse speed.

And now they were in orbit again, not detectable by the Renao's backward technology, a predator stalking its prey.

Tension lingered in the artificial atmosphere of the *Bortas*. All warriors were at their posts, keeping a watchful eye on the sensors and communication frequencies, so they wouldn't miss the terrorists of the Purifying Flame when they finally appeared. Kromm was the only one who didn't have anything specific to do, so he paced and kept glaring at the viewscreen, where a slightly blurred image showed the nocturnal container park.

But there was no movement.

"I hope this Renao didn't lie to us," Chumarr said from the gunnery station. "We could be watching a location with no significance while the fanatics on the other side of the planet frantically clear out their secret base."

"If a ship leaves the planet, we will know about it," L'emka said. "The Renao have so little space travel that every vessel should be detectable."

"What's more, they don't know that the *Bortas* is able to cloak," Rozhenko said. "As far as they're concerned—and that goes for all their satellites and possible observation ships—we were furious and left their system. We want them to feel safe. Besides, ak Seresh seemed genuine."

Kromm grinned. "He seemed to me like someone about to soil himself. Cowardly red-skin."

Klarn, Chumarr, and Mobok, the new pilot, laughed approvingly.

"He didn't betray us," Rooth said. "If he did, he will spend the rest of his life in fear. When we beamed him down to the surface, I told him that I might have marked him with a radionuclide, and that we would find him, no matter where on Yssab he might hide. And if it became necessary for us to find him because he'd betrayed us, we would be very furious." The security chief cackled. "He very hastily assured me that everything he told us was the truth and nothing but the truth."

Now it was Kromm's turn to laugh. It felt good to be in action again, and not having to attend any briefings and talks. Finally free from Federation restrictions, everything suddenly felt much easier, which reflected in the mood among his bridge officers. The only one who wouldn't join the general good mood was L'emka, but that was to be expected. But her sentiments didn't bother Kromm anymore. *We will fight, and we will be victorious.*

"Sir, something's happening down there," Raspin reported from ops.

Kromm turned to face the viewscreen. A slender vehicle

that seemed to consist only of a frame of welded steel beams and a cockpit that had been placed on top appeared among the containers. The driver didn't use any external lights, but *Bortas'* sensors showed him using infrared tracking lasers to maneuver his vehicle in between the containers.

He maneuvered above one of the containers, and a magnetic gripper snagged the cargo. Cautiously, the driver moved his vehicle backward. He placed the container on the flat ground a few meters away from the storage unit.

The driver repeated this process twice until the container stack had been taken down, and the three big metal boxes stood in a line with approximately a dozen meters' distance between them. Finally, the cargo worker disappeared with his mobile crane-transporter back into the darkness of the night.

"There's our stolen material," Kromm said. "Presumably, the thieves will be here soon."

Chumarr asked, "Why don't we beam a signal buoy into one of those containers? We could follow it easy enough, and I really don't think that the Renao would notice it. They won't expect anything like that—especially since the containers will still be sealed on the outside."

"We shouldn't take the risk," L'emka said. "What if their sensors pick up the subspace signal? Even if they don't know what it means, they might become suspicious and search their containers. Also, what if they open the containers to transfer cargo to other containers? It's best if we simply observe."

It pained Kromm to admit that his first officer was right. "We do not need a tracking signal. Either it stays on Yssab and we watch from orbit, or they load it onto a ship and we follow. And if they use a shuttle to fly to a solar-jumper... well, then we'll have to strike fast and hard. A solar-jumper must not escape under any circumstances."

Three winged *Kranaals* appeared on the screen, coming in from the plains.

Kromm rose and stood in the center of the bridge, hands on hips. "Here they are." These *Kranaals* did not have a passenger cabin like most flying vessels. Instead, they had a large recess in their hull that would hold exactly one standard container. With precise steering maneuvers, the pilots brought their vessels above the three lined-up containers, before landing. The flapping of the wings slowed down when they switched the engines to neutral.

Cockpit doors opened, and some Renao climbed up. With well-practiced movements of men and women who weren't doing this work for the first time, the thieves strapped the containers into the mounting frame of their *Kranaals*. When they were done, they climbed back aboard, and the three flying vehicles took off into the night. Each one of them had a stolen container under their belly.

"Raspin, stay with them!" Kromm said.

"Yes, Captain," the ops officer said. The image section enlarged slightly. Tactical red symbols were placed over the *Kranaals* so it would be easier to follow them visually in the darkness.

"And now, we have to wait again." Rozhenko folded his arms in front of his chest.

"You need not remain on the bridge, Ambassador," said Kromm. "The flight might take several hours. Go back to your cabin. I'll call you as soon as something happens." *If I remember to.*

Doubtful, the young Klingon looked at the viewscreen. The *Kranaals* flew in convoy formation over the dark, rocky wasteland.

"You're right," Rozhenko said. "I also have other things to do. I'll be in my quarters." He walked past Kromm and disappeared through the door at starboard.

Satisfied, Kromm watched him leave. One person less he didn't want present on his bridge. He had an idea and looked at his first officer and security chief.

"L'emka, Rooth, I have a task for you. Look at General Akbas's record of battle regarding the capture of a solar-jumper in the Theris system. Sift through everything and come up with a plan to capture one of these jumpers ourselves, without the entire crew committing suicide. We need their crew alive to be interrogated—which means we must be faster and better than Commander Koxx's people. You should also assemble an attack team for me to lead. Only the best warriors."

L'emka grimaced, then nodded. "Yes, Captain. Let's go, Rooth." Together, they left the bridge.

With a comfortable sigh, Kromm returned to his command chair, settling down. "Finally, we're among true warriors again."

Chumarr growled approvingly, and Mobok grinned at him with two rows of crooked teeth.

"What about him?" Klarn asked, scowling at Raspin.

Kromm looked at the Rantal who had his back turned towards him while working at his console. "Yes, what about you, Raspin?"

The white-skinned *bekk* turned around. His face was quiet, the expression in his large black eyes inscrutable. Unless Kromm was mistaken, the Raspin seemed more confident since the incident above Iad.

"I live to serve the Empire," the Rantal said.

"Don't we all?" Kromm barked a laugh, and then leaned forward in his chair. "Tell me, Raspin—if I stood in front of you, gave you my *d'k tahg*, and said 'stab,' whom would you kill? Me or you?"

After a moment, Raspin said, "Neither. I would never dare to kill my captain. And I would never dare to deprive him of his best ops officer."

His words made Kromm laugh boomingly. If he hurt the Rantal with that laughter, he didn't show it. On the other hand, Kromm could never really tell what Raspin was thinking. This androgynous white face sometimes seemed to be as stiff as a Vulcan—if he wasn't squirming like a Ferengi in fear.

"Captain," Chumarr said, "the *Kranaals* are landing."

Instantly, Kromm put the banter with Raspin out of his head and focused back on the mission. "That happened quickly." Curiously, he watched what was happening on the surface below.

In a valley between two mountain ridges, the flying vessels landed. When Raspin adjusted the image they saw that a box-shaped ship was hiding between the rocks.

"That looks like a carrier of sorts," said Chumarr. "I'm not picking up any antimatter or traces of a singularity drive, or any other indications of faster-than-light travel. Merely standard impulse-engine emissions."

Kromm nodded. "They must be meeting up with either a solar-jumper or a warp ship within the system somewhere."

"Or the shipyard is somewhere in this system," Chumarr said.

Kromm nodded. "That would be the first thing to go right since this mission began."

Silently, they watched from orbit as the containers were loaded into the carrier. Shortly after, the *Kranaals* were on their way again. The ship fired up its engines and took off.

"And now things get interesting," Kromm said. "Mobok, Raspin, stay close to the ship. Lose it, and I will personally throw you both out of the nearest airlock."

"We're right behind the thieves," Mobok said.

Kromm touched the communications button on his command chair. "Kromm to Rooth."

"Rooth."

"We're following the suspects across the system. Is the task force ready yet?"

"Yes, Captain. We also found the mistake that Commander Koxx's warriors made."

"What was it?"

"They didn't set their disruptors to the lowest setting. That's the only safe method to capture enemies alive who are willing to die."

Kromm snarled. "That sounds as if we're in Starfleet."

"Do you want prisoners or not, Captain?"

Another snarl. "Do whatever is necessary for our success." He terminated the link.

"The carrier is flying toward the sun," Mobok said. "They must be meeting a solar-jumper."

"Must be? I prefer surety. Raspin, is there a solar-jumper or not?"

Frantically, the ops officer worked his console. "Yes, Captain. There's a ship hovering right in front of the sun. Difficult to pick up but I have detected it. The ship…" Surprised, the Rantal turned to face Kromm. "It's the solar-jumper we've already encountered in the Onferin system. The one that escaped Adams and his people."

Kromm rubbed his hands grimly. *"We* will not let it escape. Once the carrier has docked, we shall strike."

"Captain, I don't think the carrier will dock," Chumarr said. "The containers are too big to move without special loading gear from one ship to another, and I read no gear like that on either vessel."

Kromm looked at him, confused, even as the door to the bridge slid loudly open. "So, how do they intend to bring their hull plates aboard the jumper?"

Rooth, L'emka, and four troops entered just then. Rooth answered the captain's question: "The same way they got their people out on Onferin. They will beam them. And afterwards, they'll jump. We will have to be swift." He handed Kromm a disruptor. "On the lowest setting, Captain."

Disgusted, Kromm stared at the weapon, tightened his grip, and got up. "That's your team? Only one squad?"

"Another squad is standing by in the transporter room. We will strike in two places simultaneously. On the bridge and in the cargo room."

"Send another squad to the carrier," Kromm said. "The more prisoners the better."

"Yes, Captain." Rooth spoke into the communicator on his wrist and gave that order.

"The carrier has almost reached the solar-jumper," Raspin said. "Transport in progress."

"Commander L'emka, you have the bridge. Decloak for transport and then destroy the solar-jumper's drive."

"Right away, Captain." L'emka went to the center of the bridge. "Disengage cloaking device."

At least this time she's doing as she's told, Kromm thought. He spoke into the communicator on his wrist. "Kromm to transporter room. Beam all units to the hostile ships!"

A veil of flickering red light engulfed Kromm. When the light faded, he and the four troops were in a narrow chamber covered with consoles and displays. Two red-skinned men were working on them.

One of the Renao saw the transporter effect, and unholstered an energy weapon, firing it and taking down one of the warriors next to Kromm the second they materialized.

Without hesitation, Kromm fired back. The green disruptor charge hit the Renao in the center of his chest, hurtling him against his console. Without a sound, he collapsed. The other Renao launched himself at Rooth, but the old Klingon greeted him with a thunderous blow with the back of his hand, sending him whirling around his axis. Another troop stunned him as he fell.

"Rooth, Klakk, secure the bridge," Kromm said. "You two are with me." He waved at the other two warriors, darting out of the room. Further shots could be heard from the depths of the solar-jumper from the other squad.

At the same time, the hull shuddered from the disruptor strikes by the *Bortas*. Kromm's heart hammered in his chest as he led his troops into glorious battle. *This* was what he lived for!

They came upon a turbolift, but Kromm moved past it. You could hardly be in a more disadvantageous position during a fight than standing inside a lift. Instead, he yanked open a maintenance hatch, taking the service crawlway leading downward.

With a kick, he opened the hatch one deck down. Three standard containers almost filled the cargo hold behind it. With a quick glance, Kromm assessed the situation. One of his people was leaning against the bulkhead, clutching his abdomen, in pain but alive. Two Renao in simple coveralls lay motionless on the deck. In the back between the containers, the whine of energy blasts was still audible.

The deck shuddered briefly, and the lights flickered. A

strained howl came from the engine section and then the constant background droning of the ship's systems—which you only realized was there when it stopped—died down.

"The engines are down—the *Bortas* has destroyed their drive! Victory is ours!" Kromm gestured with his disruptor. "You two go left, while I walk around the containers to the right. Shoot at everything with red skin."

Even as he said those words, a Renao ran out of the gap between the containers at the back. He screamed like mad, firing two energy weapons in his hands.

One of Kromm's warriors was hit in the shoulder and grunted in pain. *We have enough prisoners*, the captain decided, furious. With his thumb he adjusted the disruptor to the highest setting and fired.

The Renao disintegrated into a red cloud of atoms that dispersed in the cargo hold's artificial atmosphere, a sight that gave Kromm great satisfaction.

Lieutenant B'Tarka appeared from behind one of the containers. He looked around in confusion for a moment.

"I shot the Renao," Kromm said.

B'Tarka lowered his disruptor and nodded. "That was the last one, Captain. Another is lying between the containers back there. The ship should be secure."

"Make *sure* it is secure, Lieutenant. Take all warriors who are fit for battle, and comb this vessel from front to back."

"Yes, Captain."

Kromm put his wrist to his lips. "Commander Rooth."

"*Rooth.*"

"Send another squad to the solar-jumper to salvage everything useful. We will beam back to the *Bortas* with all our prisoners. The interrogation will begin immediately."

"*Understood.*"

Kromm permitted himself a grim smile. They had captured another solar-jumper and taken at least five prisoners. One of them would talk! He would make sure of it.

24
DECEMBER 1, 2385

Somewhere

The cell was tiny, and there was no furniture except a metal bed and a retractable toilet. The light came from a small panel behind a grid in the ceiling, and from the reddish glimmer of the energy field that kept occupants from leaving the cell.

Samooh ak Lahal squatted at the bottom end of the extremely uncomfortable bed, staring into the distance. It was all over. The sphere defilers had imprisoned him, his holy mission could not be continued, and his life had also come to an end. His ship had probably been destroyed, and he didn't know where his fellow members of the Purifying Flame—Musaan, Shaomi, and the others—were being held. He had called for them, but had received no reply. Desperation and pain were his only companions in this dark hour.

The Klingons had said they wouldn't kill Samooh and his companions. They wanted to know where the Purifying Flame's secret shipyard was, where the fighters for the Harmony of Spheres built their lethal cloaked attack ships. In order to get this information out of Samooh, they had beaten him, burned his skin, and tortured him with painstiks. He had screamed until his throat felt like raw flesh—but he hadn't given anything away.

Never would he surrender to these monsters. Never would he betray the holy mission.

That was why Kromm, the leader of these butchers, kept him alive and denied him a painless death and freedom. They had offered both those things if he were to talk. But Samooh would elude them; he would choose a long, painful death over betrayal, like all the brothers and sisters who had already sacrificed themselves for the spheres. The Klingons didn't know the Renao physiology very well. They didn't know how much a Renao could bear before his body capitulated. And Samooh was determined to mislead them until it was too late. If he died under the torture of his enemies, he had won, because they would continue their search for the location of the Purifying Flame's base from where they were waging their war against the depraved empires of the galaxy for all eternity. It was well hidden in the depths of the Lembatta Cluster.

He could only pray that his companions were able to muster the same strength as him.

Samooh's gaze fell on the narrow corridor outside of his cell. It lay quiet, bathed in dim red light. Samooh had no idea where he was. Had he been imprisoned aboard the large Klingon battle ship that had been flying across the cluster for weeks? Or had other defilers penetrated the home spheres, and he had been taken to one of their ships?

The last thing he remembered clearly was the sudden appearance of his enemies on the bridge of the solar-jumper. Musaan and he had just taken the latest shipment of hull plates for the construction of more cloaked attack fighters on board, when the Klingons had appeared. Samooh had struck down one of the intruders with a quick shot. Afterward, he had been hit, and blackness had engulfed him from one second to the next. When he awoke, he was already in the torture chamber of his tormentors.

Somewhere to his left, a massive metal door opened noisily. Someone walked in with heavy footsteps. "Food!" a bestial voice boomed. Samooh wasn't at all surprised that he was able to understand them. He knew that the sphere defilers had automatic translating devices in order to talk to him and other Renao.

A moment later, a huge Klingon came into view on the other side of the red force field. His dark clothing made of leathers and metals, the crooked teeth, the shaggy hair, the bony brow—everything about him disgusted Samooh. The warrior, who carried a weapon in his right hand, was accompanied by a strange being, walking in a crouch and carrying a tray with a bowl full of greenish-brown glop. The being was very slender, didn't have a hair on its body, and probably used to have white skin. Now it was so dirty that it seemed gray, and the shabby clothing looked as if it hadn't been washed for weeks. Another prisoner? A Klingon slave?

"Go on, *jeghpu'wI'*, give this maggot its food," the Klingon said. "We don't want him to die from hunger. We've got plans for him." Laughing, the Klingon touched a control next to the cell, and the energy field collapsed. The white-skinned being trotted forward. Silently, he placed the tray on the floor. Sad black eyes looked at Samooh. And then, the being did something unexpected. When the guard, who was still out in the corridor, couldn't see his face, he looked at Samooh conspiratorially, blinking suggestively with both eyes. A second later, with the deep resignation back on his face, he turned around and left the cell. The guard put the energy field back in place and both disappeared.

Samooh was confused. What was the meaning of that look on the slave's face? Was he trying to tell Samooh something?

He had no idea what—aliens were so incomprehensible. It was why they should have stayed in their home spheres.

Grunting and in severe pain, he pushed himself off the bed, dragging his bruised body to the tray. He lifted it. The food smelled of mashed and boiled entrails.

Samooh didn't want to know what these monsters were serving him. Reluctantly, he took the spoon, stirring the mash.

A piece of paper surfaced. It had been completely soaked but the letters seemed to be water-resistant because they were still legible. The writing was Renao. For a moment, Samooh wondered how the slave would know his language, but then he realized that the sphere defilers probably had enough information about his people by now to have saved their language in their computers.

Take me with you, the notice read, *and I will help you escape.*

Samooh shuddered. Could his situation be much less desperate than he thought? Would the Klingons' brutal attitude and their malicious greed to conquer turn against them now? Something one of the preachers had said ran through his head: *If all those who have suffered injustice stood up together, they would be able to shake off the shackles of servitude.*

Maybe he had found an unexpected ally in the pale, hunched slave.

Samooh stuffed the note into his mouth, chewed and swallowed it. He also forced himself to eat at least a few spoonfuls of that glop in the bowl. Although it didn't taste any better than it smelled, it would hopefully restore some of the strength he would need to escape.

Not much later, the guard and his companion reappeared. When the Klingon saw how little Samooh had eaten, he laughed. "What? Didn't you like it?"

Samooh spat on the floor without saying anything.

His enemy's laughter increased in volume. "You still have some spirit. Good, very good. That means there's something left to break when we continue the interrogation tomorrow." He deactivated the force field, gesturing for the pale man to pick up the tray again. He did as he was told, but the gaze from his black eyes searched for Samooh's eyes. With a barely perceptible nod, the Renao confirmed to his fellow sufferer that they were on the same side. The white-skinned man answered with a quick double blink of both eyes, before withdrawing with the tray. Both men walked down the corridor, and the metal door shut with a loud clang behind them. Samooh was alone again.

Samooh didn't know how long he had waited. Despite the uncomfortable bed and the pain that he felt everywhere in his body, sleep had overwhelmed him after his scarce supper. Fatigue had taken its toll. So he jolted up from a tumultuous dream without knowing what time it was when he felt a hand on his shoulder.

With widened eyes he stared at the figure that loomed over him. Two heartbeats later he recognized the pale-skinned slave who had served his supper. He raised one hand in reassurance, then put three fingers against his mouth while his black eyes stared at Samooh imploringly.

He understood and nodded. Not a sound.

Cautiously, the strange being took a step back. The energy field for the cell had been switched off.

"Come," Samooh's liberator whispered.

I don't have anything to lose, Samooh thought, *and everything to gain*. Nodding, he joined the stranger.

The hairless being led him down the corridor past

empty cells to the heavy protective door that sealed off the prison area.

"Where are my companions?" Samooh asked quietly.

The white-skinned man shrugged with his narrow shoulders. "I don't know. They are not aboard this ship. They only brought you here."

Samooh put a hand on his shoulder, turning him around. "And why are you helping me?"

The pale stranger looked at him with his black eyes. "Because I heard that you're a pilot and navigator. And that makes you my best chance to get away once and for all. There are shuttles capable of warp, but I can't pilot them. That's why I haven't escaped from these monsters yet, although I want nothing more than to get off this ship." In his voice was a bitterness that Samooh understood all too well.

"Very well," he said. "Show me this shuttle and I'll get us out of here."

His counterpart nodded. "I had hoped you'd say that. By the way, my name is Raspin."

"I'm Samooh."

"Here." Raspin handed Samooh a small energy pistol. "You might need it if anyone wants to stop us. I stole it from the guard." He pulled out a larger weapon from under his ripped shirt.

"The guard?" Samooh said, surprised.

Instead of answering, Raspin opened the hatch. The huge guard sat at a small metal table. His head rested on the tabletop, and he didn't move. Beside him was a tankard full of an alcoholic-smelling liquid.

"Is he dead?" Samooh asked.

Raspin shook his head. "I mixed something into his bloodwine. I've been a servant for this crew for so long that they hardly even notice me. Most of all they've forgotten that they conquered and enslaved me, and that I hate them for it. Therefore, I can go virtually anywhere, hear everything, see everything. And I can drug guards if necessary." He grinned menacingly, baring his gleaming white teeth.

"He should die," Samooh said grimly. "He deserves to die. Like all sphere defilers."

Raspin shook his head again. "Shooting will trigger an alarm. We should only use weapons if we don't have any other choice. Otherwise, our escape will fail before it's even begun."

Reluctantly, Samooh agreed.

Raspin gestured invitingly. "Come, quick. Not long now before the night shift is finished. The corridors will be full of people around that time. We need to be gone before then."

Quietly, they scurried through the ship. The deckplates underneath Samooh's bare feet were chilly, but he didn't let that bother him. The humming of the engines came from the depths of the ship, and occasionally they heard laughter in the distance. Otherwise, it was quiet. Most of the crew seemed to be asleep.

Once, they heard footsteps coming toward them. But Raspin quickly opened a maintenance hatch, and they waited with bated breath hidden between energy conduits until the two Klingon soldiers had passed them.

They used a ladder in a vertical shaft to climb two decks down.

"We're almost there," said Raspin. "As soon as we reach the shuttle, you should prepare our departure. I will connect with the ship's computer system from one of the terminals to create a distraction."

"What kind of distraction?" Samooh asked.

"I'll switch off the containment field for the antimatter tank in the engine room."

"I thought you didn't know anything about ships."

"I can't pilot them. But I'm familiar with the technology. I've had to clean up after the engineers aboard this ship for long enough."

They arrived at a long room. Three pressure hatches were along the right wall ten meters away from each other. Raspin went straight for the first one. He touched the control panel, and the hatch hissed open. Behind was a short access corridor that ended at another hatch.

"That's where the shuttle is," the white-skinned being said. "It's not secured. Just board it and enter a course to a place where we're safe. Can you do that?"

Samooh nodded.

"I'll be over there." Raspin pointed at an observation cabin behind a protective glass pane. "I won't be long."

He darted off. Samooh turned around and hurried down the short corridor. The shuttle hatch opened with ease. It revealed a small cabin with a two-seater cockpit and a tiny passenger area. In front of the cockpit window the red nebulae of his home sphere glowed. To Samooh's surprise, the instrument array was not much different from similar space vessels built by the Renao. Although he had some problems reading the alien letters, he soon understood what worked what.

He had just accessed the navigation system in order to program a course when he heard shouts behind his back.

"What are you doing?"

A shot was fired. The ship alarm sounded. Cursing, Samooh turned away from the controls, grabbed his weapon, and ran out towards the exit. When he reached the corridor, Raspin ran towards him.

"Quick! We need to get out of here. We've been spotted."

"Is the distraction in place?" Samooh asked.

"Yes. We should be able to escape with ease. They will be too busy saving their ship to pursue us."

A man appeared at the other end of the corridor, firing his gun. The shot hissed a little too close past Raspin, hitting the frame of the shuttle's hatch. Samooh felt a static electric charge raise his hackles. Their opponent obviously wanted to stun them, not kill them.

Samooh was less scrupulous. He raised his own weapon and fired. The Klingon was hit right in the chest and fell over with a thundering thud.

Raspin jumped back in, hitting the closing mechanism. Rumbling, the hatch closed. He nodded at Samooh.

"Right. Let's get out of here."

"Fasten your seatbelt," said Samooh. "This could be rough." He placed his weapon at his side, returning to the cockpit area where he settled into one of the chairs at the controls. Raspin sat down next to him.

With a quick command Samooh released the docking clamps. He diverted energy to the thrusters and the shuttle shot out into the void. Samooh veered off with the small ship. To their left, the massive cruiser of the sphere defilers came into sight: a bulky dreadnought with two nacelles mounted at the sprawling aft section.

"Quick, go to warp before their crew can nab us with a tractor beam," Raspin said.

"On it," Samooh replied. He typed in a course back into the heart of the cluster. He would have to report to the leaders of the Purifying Flame that they had lost another solar-jumper, and that the secret of the shipyard might have been compromised. Musaan, Shaomi, and the rest of his crew had all known the location. As much as Samooh wanted to believe that none of them had turned traitor, he couldn't take the risk.

"There we go!" he said, activating the drive.

Nothing happened.

"What?" Confused, Samooh hit the start button again.

Again, the shuttle didn't respond.

Instead, something very strange happened. Right in front of them in space a door appeared out of nowhere. Three Klingons walked in, including the leader, Kromm.

"Computer, end program," he said. The surroundings flickered and dissolved—the shuttle, space, Samooh's weapon, everything. Panting, Samooh fell to the ground when the seat beneath him also dissipated. Only a big, empty room with strange grid lines along the walls remained—and Raspin. The pale slave-being straightened, and suddenly he didn't seem haunted or frightened anymore. Instead, something like pride appeared on his features.

"Excellent work, *Bekk* Raspin," Kromm said while one of his subordinates pulled out a weapon, pointing it at Samooh.

Nonplussed, Samooh's gaze wandered from one to the other. "What? What's going on?"

Sneering, Kromm bent down to him. "May I introduce a marvelous piece of technology? It's called a holosuite."

A gruesome understanding washed over the young Renao. "Nothing was real? You fooled me with an illusion?"

"Well reasoned. Since you all stubbornly resisted our torture, Ambassador Rozhenko…" Kromm pointed at his second companion, a young man in a floor-length coat. "…thought it might be a good idea to try something cunning. I'm not too keen on these Romulan methods, but I suppose the end justifies the means."

Samooh felt a chill run through him when it dawned on him what he had done. "No..." he muttered.

"Yes." Kromm's sneer deepened. "You just gave us the coordinates to your secret base."

U.S.S. Venture, on the periphery of the Lembatta Cluster

"We're receiving a priority message from the *U.S.S. Iron Horse*, Captain."

Bjarne Henderson exchanged a quick glance with Di Monti, who said, "The *Iron Horse* is patrolling the narrow corridor of Federation space between the Lembatta Cluster and the border to the Klingon Empire."

"In which case a priority message from them probably doesn't bode well." Henderson finished the thought he and his first officer both apparently had. He turned to his ops officer. "Let's hear it, Mr. Loos."

"Captain th'Clane reports..." Loos turned around on his chair, staring at Henderson and Di Monti with wide eyes, "...that all Klingon forces have been ordered into the Lembatta Cluster." He checked his console again. "The entire Fifth Fleet that has so far secured planetary systems on the Klingon side while the Ninth Fleet was in Federation space is on the move. We intercepted transmissions that the *Bortas* has found the location for the Purifying Flame's shipyard. Apparently, it's located in the system LC-13."

Henderson frowned. "And why haven't we heard anything about that?"

"Let me guess," Di Monti said. "Klingon hunger for glory?"

The captain opened the intercom. "Henderson to Admiral Gepta."

"Go ahead."

"The Klingons are on the move, sir. The *Bortas* apparently found the secret shipyard of the terrorists. But their captain neglected to inform us about that. We only found out by accident when we intercepted transmissions. Generals Akbas and Klag are on their way to the system LC-13 with all available ships."

"To Iad?"

"It would appear so."

The admiral cursed in Chelon. *"That can't end well. I'm coming to the bridge. Assemble the entire task force. We also need to go to LC-13 with everything we have at our disposal!"*

25
DECEMBER 1, 2385

U.S.S. Prometheus, somewhere in the Taurus Dark Cloud

Jenna Kirk had prepared holodeck one for the transfer of the white energy to Jassat. The holodeck made it easy for the energy being to take shape with its photonic body in order to interact with the *Prometheus* crew. They could also simulate any given environment here, for example a long silvery beach under a wide starry sky, where the ocean waves broke while a soft nocturnal breeze made the marram grass rustle.

"It's wonderful here," Kirk said quietly.

"Yes," Jassat replied. "A beach on my home, Onferin, which I used to love."

"The simulation is not entirely correct, though." The chief engineer pointed at the nocturnal sky. "You don't see such stellar splendor on Onferin."

"No," Jassat admitted. "I imported the sky from Earth. While I was a cadet at the Academy we made a field excursion to Australia. I have never seen such a wonderful starry night sky on any other world since. I thought it was suitable for this beach."

Kirk smiled. "It really is." She inhaled deeply, gazing at the six shapes waiting for them several meters down the beach. With their white clothes and the rudimentary human features they reminded her of the legendary ancient species that Captain Jean-Luc Picard had discovered just over fifteen years ago in the Vilmoran system. Apparently, all humanoid life stemmed from them. Another four, smaller figures in red clothes stayed in the background, watching everything curiously. All of them were surrounded by a weak aura, just like the rest of the beach where they stood.

If the species of these energy beings consists of six Old Ones and four Young, I understand why they didn't want to risk another life from their circle, Kirk thought.

Except for the ten energy beings, Jassat, and Kirk, the beach was empty. Adams, Spock, and Doctor Calloway waited outside the holodeck. The rest of the senior officers were at their stations. Kirk would also leave her friend before the transfer began. If the experiment was to be successful there couldn't be any disturbances—the Old One who had become the voice of his people had made that very clear.

While they slowly walked toward the group, Kirk glanced at Jassat from the corner of her eye. "Part of me wishes you wouldn't do this. But the rest of me is so immensely proud of you. You're saving not only your people with what you're doing, Jassat. You also honor the uniform you're wearing. Helping, no matter what the cost, is what makes a Starfleet officer."

The young Renao smiled at her. A warm fire glowed in his eyes. "Thank you, Jenna. It means a lot to me that you're escorting me here."

"Hey, it's the least I can do."

They reached the group and stopped.

One of the white shapes—Jenna recognized a hint of Trik's features—stepped forward. "ARE YOU READY?"

"In a minute." Jassat turned to Kirk. "You were a great friend right from day one when we met. You made sure that I didn't feel alone, and you have always stood by me, even when many turned their backs on me. For that, I'd like to thank you, Jenna."

Kirk felt tears well up in her eyes. "I should thank you. It… it was fun."

For a moment, they stood opposite each other, not sure what to do next. Finally, Kirk spread her arms, walking toward Jassat. "Come here, you." Sniffling, she hugged him and held him close. She wanted to tell him that everything would be all right, that he would survive somehow. Hadn't the Old Ones claimed they didn't know exactly how the discharge of the white energy would happen?

But she remained silent. She didn't want to destroy the moment with silly chatter or false hopes.

Eventually, they let go of each other, and Kirk took a step back. "I'll see you when it's all over," she said.

Jassat nodded quietly.

Clearing her voice, she spoke up. "Computer, exit."

Behind her, a door appeared on the smooth sandy beach. With one final glance, she turned away and left the holodeck.

Jassat stayed behind behind on the beach, alone with the energy beings. The waves rushed, the grass rustled, and the warm wind blew through his hair. If this really was the last moment of his old life, there couldn't be a more comforting place than this one. It felt like home, even if it was a home that only existed in his dreams and the memory banks of the holodeck.

"EVERYONE HAS COME," said the energy being in Trik's shape. "THE OLD ONES AND THE YOUNG. THEY ALL WANT TO HELP YOU DELIVER THE BOY WHO HAS LOST HIS WAY—AND SAVE YOUR PEOPLE." A calm, solemn expression was on his face, and it was mirrored in his voice. To Jassat, he looked like a priest.

"Thank you," said the Renao. "We appreciate your willingness to give a part of yourselves in order to restore peace in our home spheres."

The entity tilted its head. "ARE YOU READY TO BECOME THE VESSEL?"

Jassat hesitated, before nodding. "Yes, I..." He straightened himself and raised his voice. "Yes, I am." His shoulders slumped slightly. "Is it going to be bad?"

"IF YOU ARE ASKING WHETHER YOU ARE GOING TO EXPERIENCE PAIN—WE DO NOT KNOW AS WE DO NOT KNOW PAIN LIKE YOU DO. BUT WE KNOW THAT YOUR BODY IS CAPABLE OF HOLDING THE WHITE ENERGY. OTHERWISE WE WOULD NOT HAVE OFFERED TO TRANSFER IT TO YOU."

"I understand." Jassat breathed deeply. "Let us begin. What do I have to do?"

"NOTHING. JUST COME INTO OUR MIDST AND LET EVERYTHING HAPPEN."

Purposefully, the young Renao walked forward, and the six shimmering white beings encircled him. Jassat turned around once, looking into each of the photonic faces. Three of them had taken the shape of men, three of women. Some looked grave, some with a more friendly mien. *How different they are from the Son of the Ancient Reds on Iad*, Jassat thought. *It's almost unimaginable that he came from their circle all those years ago.* And then another thought from his childhood struck him, one that his father had always tried to drill into him to no avail: *He who leaves the Home Spheres will meet nothing but misfortune.*

No, Jassat objected. *Only those who are frightened think that way! The Son of the Ancient Reds' destiny is tragic, but it's not mine. He was reckless, and when he ran into difficulties he didn't have anyone to help him. I have always leavened my boldness with reason—and I was never alone, even if it sometimes felt that way!*

He turned back to the speaker of the energy beings. Nodding, he gave his permission.

The six figures reached out with their right arms. Their hands touched Jassat's shoulders, back, and chest. The glow of their aura intensified, especially around the arms. A quiet, ethereal chime sounded that reminded him of a transporter. The contours of their photonic limbs blurred until they had changed into glittering, pure white energy currents. Jassat felt a prickling sensation spreading from his torso as if thousands of small four-legged insects crawled all over his skin, below his skin, and in all bones, muscles, and organs. The prickling steadily intensified and became a massive rush, like a waterfall pouring into him.

Jassat noticed pressure building up inside of him. It was a strange sensation that he couldn't compare with anything he had ever experienced. It had nothing in common with the pressure of headaches or an upset stomach. It seemed as if his body had suddenly become fuller and heavier, and that the muscles were bulging under every square centimeter of his skin.

Panic began to spread within him, and he looked down at himself. But his body looked perfectly normal. His hands weren't swollen at all, and the arms and legs still featured their usual proportions. Only a weak light aura formed around Jassat's skin, like the sheen of phosphorescent oil.

The pressure increased while the six Old Ones silently pumped their white energy into Jassat. The strange feeling turned into nausea, and finally pain. Jassat gasped, his heart rate increased, and sweat broke on his forehead. A weak mist that slowly thickened veiled the beach and the ocean. Jassat needed a moment to realize that it was his own light aura limiting his sight.

"How much longer?" He had the feeling that his body was about to explode. Nothing could withstand such pressure for long.

"IT IS ALMOST DONE," the Old One replied. "WE MUST NOT BE HESITANT. IF YOU WANT TO ELIMINATE THE BOY, YOU NEED TO TAKE IN AS MUCH ENERGY AS YOU POSSIBLY CAN."

"I understand." Jassat breathed hectically in and out.

The humming increased, as did the light and the pressure. The world around Jassat ak Namur blanked out.

The door to the holodeck hissed open, and ak Namur stumbled out into the corridor, shaking with apparent exhaustion. His entire body was suffused with a white aura, and his eyes were like tiny suns, they glowed so bright.

"Doctor!" shouted Adams, rushing to the lieutenant's aid. Kirk also moved to help him.

Calloway pulled out her tricorder, pointing it at the young Renao. "His readings are extreme. Heart rate has increased considerably, brainwaves show hyperactivity." Closing her tricorder, she knelt on the floor, opening her medkit in order to prepare a hypospray.

"No," ak Namur gasped. "No… medication. We don't know what that would do… to the energy."

"He is correct," Spock said. He had been waiting alongside Adams, Calloway, and Kirk outside the holodeck. "We must not take any risks."

"But he could die if this condition persists too long." The doctor looked at ak Namur. "Your heart will fail eventually."

To Adams's surprise the young Renao actually managed a smile. "Eventually doesn't… bother me. The main thing is that we reach Iad beforehand."

Adams acted without hesitation. Leaving ak Namur to Kirk, he tapped his combadge. "Adams to bridge."

"Go ahead," Roaas said.

"Commander, set course for the Lembatta Cluster, system LC-13. We're flying straight to our destination in slipstream."

"Captain," Massimo Ciarese, who had taken over Jassat's post, said. *"That's awfully dangerous. The stars there are extremely close together. We would be speeding through an obstacle course with no margin for even the tiniest of errors."*

"Then make sure, Mr. Ciarese, that you don't make any errors."

He heard the young Italian officer gulp. *"Understood, Captain."*

While the background noise of the *Prometheus*'s engines changed, Adams glanced one final time through the open door into the holodeck. The ten energy beings stood on the beach of Jassat's homeworld, staring back at him.

"Thank you," he said.

"MAY YOUR JOURNEY BE A SUCCESSFUL ONE." The light aura around their photonic bodies, the holodeck itself, and the corridor of the *Prometheus* became darker as the beings withdrew.

"Computer, end program," said Adams. The beach, the ocean, and the nocturnal starlit sky flickered and disappeared, returning to the gold-and-black grid pattern.

The captain turned to Calloway. "Take the lieutenant to sickbay for observation."

The doctor nodded. "Come on, Jassat," she said, taking over from Kirk.

"With your permission, Doctor, I would like to accompany you," said Spock. "I believe I might be able to aid the lieutenant with his burden."

"Sure, Ambassador."

"I'll be on the bridge," said Adams. "Kirk, you go back to the engine room and put in a good word with the slipstream drive. We need every ounce of speed we can get."

"I'll make sure we're just as fast if not faster than the *Aventine*," the engineer said with a cheeky grin.

They went their separate ways, and the captain walked to the nearest turbolift. Several seconds later he reached the command center. On the bridge viewscreen he saw that the *Prometheus* had just left the outer regions of the chaos zone behind.

"The course to the Lembatta Cluster has been set, sir," Ciarese said.

"We're awaiting your orders, Captain," Roaas added, getting up from the command chair.

Adams nodded as confirmation. "Give me a rear view of the ship."

He just wanted one last glance at these strange beings who had helped them so selflessly and without asking for any kind of reward.

The screen's perspective changed, and there they were. Ten vast energy clouds—six white, four red—hung at the periphery of the chaos zone in space. They had escorted the *Prometheus* there and had made sure that she steered safely through the radiation inferno that was their home. Now, they stayed behind. Their bodies of light glittered and glistened, while they looked on, watching the small starship fly away. Maybe they were the only ones of their kind, and without a doubt they, and their habitat that defied all known laws of nature, were the most alien that Adams had ever seen in his life.

"I hope we will meet again one day," he said quietly, "and

preferably under better circumstances. There's so much we could learn from each other."

As if they were responding, the flickering in the bodies of the Old Ones and the Young increased briefly, before they darted away. They shrank with unbelievable speed before disappearing in the raging chaos.

Adams nodded. "Return to forward view." It was time to look ahead. He walked to his command chair and sat down.

"Mr. Ciarese, take us to Iad. Maximum speed."

26
DECEMBER 2, 2385

*I.K.S. Borta*s, on the periphery of the Souhla system
Lembatta Cluster

"We're arriving at the Souhla system. Dropping from warp." Mobok's fingers danced across the instruments before his eyes.

The shuddering and vibrating of the *Bortas*, which had been pushed to the limits of her performance, stopped, and the tunnel of red swirls collapsed along with the warp bubble. Dense stardust became visible outside.

"Position?" Kromm asked.

"We have reached the coordinates that Samooh entered into the holographic shuttle controls," Raspin said. "In front of us lies the asteroid belt on the periphery of the Souhla system."

"Begin scanning. Somewhere around here must be this wretched shipyard of the Purifying Flame."

"Yes, sir."

Kromm turned to his communications officer. "Lieutenant Klarn, any news from the fleets?"

"Yes, Captain. General Akbas's flagship, the *K'mpec*, is closest to us. She will be here in half an hour. All other ships will follow within minutes. General Klag's fleet will need another hour. Oh, and, Captain…" Klarn turned to face Kromm, grimacing. "The Federation found out about our discovery. According to a message from General Klag almost a dozen Starfleet ships are en route to this position.

They will arrive at the same time as our armada."

"Captain," L'emka said, "we should wait for reinforcements to arrive. You've seen the multitude of attack fighters waiting for us in the shipyard. The *Bortas* will not be able to defeat them singlehandedly. So far, it would seem that we haven't been noticed yet."

Kromm's fingers clawed into the armrests of his command chair, while he glared at his first officer. "Spoken like a true coward, Commander. Oh no, we haven't come this far to have the glory for the victory over the Purifying Flame taken away from us. The *Bortas* will fire the first shot in this battle—and the last, so help me Kahless. Chumarr, engage the cloak! Raspin, find this shipyard—and by Kahless's hand, I'll make sure that you will have your own verse in the song they're going to sing about us!"

Base of the Purifying Flame

The wailing of the proximity alert startled Koubla ak Yafor so much that he almost fell out of his chair. For nearly sixty days he had been aboard the NA-2812, serving as sensor guard of the night shift in the command center. Not once had any of the alerts signaled.

Right now, though, the most feared alert sounded. Proximity alert meant that a ship was heading toward their shipyard without sending the valid identification code. That had to mean trouble.

Koubla leaned forward, checking his sensors. He felt queasy when he spotted a blinking dot almost above them in space. Within the next second it had disappeared, and the proximity alert stopped.

He blinked in confusion, staring at his instruments.

Mesood ak Aneez, his friend and fellow soldier, came running from the adjacent room where he had just brewed a *Lamat* tea in order to stay awake during the late hours. A wet spot on his dark green jacket bore witness to the fact that the alert had startled him considerably as well. "Koubla, what's the matter?"

"I don't know," Koubla replied. "There was a ship right above us. Now it's gone. Could it have been a sensor malfunction?"

"Open the event log and we'll have a closer look." Mesood had been working twice as long in the asteroid station as Koubla.

Koubla typed in the commands, and the dot reappeared on the sensor screen.

Mesood joined Koubla, propping himself up on the console. "Try to run an identification. Start with the sphere defiler ships that we know to be in the cluster and the neighboring systems."

"Good idea." Koubla's fingers danced across the keys. With a signal the computer confirmed a match. "By the spheres! It's the Klingons. But why have they disappeared so abruptly?"

"Maybe they were able to jam our sensors. It doesn't matter." Mesood turned around to the comm systems. "If the Klingons are that close, they will discover us. We need to inform the Honorable Commander and raise the alarm."

Hamash ak Bhedal was jerked from a bizarre dream by a humming noise. He hadn't slept properly for weeks, and his mood was accordingly bad.

"What?" he yelled into the communication module after pressing the button.

"This is ak Aneez at the base, Honorable," a panicky voice said.

"Why are you disturbing me?"

"The proximity alert has announced a Klingon ship, Honorable, that dropped from warp in the immediate vicinity."

"What?" Ak Bhedal was instantly wide awake. He jumped to his feet, grabbing his pants and boots. "Have we been discovered?"

"We don't know, Honorable. The ship disappeared again. We're worried that it might be interfering with our sensors."

Ak Bhedal cursed openly. "They cloaked. The Klingons are capable of masking their ships from sensors, just like we do with our attack fighters." There it was—the beginning of the end. Where *one* cloaked Klingon ship skulked around, there would surely be more. Now he had to act swiftly, because their holy mission was in grave danger. "Sound the alarm. Everyone report to their ships and attack fighters. I want the Inner Circle to convene in the command center. I'm on my way there."

Without waiting for confirmation, he put on his black tunic and buckled his weapon belt up while crossing his private quarters. He opened the door and made his way double quick down the corridor.

The sirens inside the asteroid base began to wail.

"It's too early. They're coming a day too early." Golaah ak Partam threw his hands up in desperation, while glaring at ak Bhedal reproachfully, as if it was his fault that the sphere defilers had found them.

"Our opponent doesn't adhere to a schedule," the commander said. He could relate to the frustration of the starship engineer from Xhehenem. Just yesterday they had finished the latest batch of attack fighters they had been working on. Fifty *Scorpion* fighters waited for their deployment. But they hadn't uploaded all programs for flight control, weapon control, or propulsion yet, so the ships were useless at the moment.

"How many vessels are ready for deployment?" he asked.

"Twenty-two attack fighters," ak Partam replied. "Plus four shuttles capable of warp flight, one transport ship, and our third refurbished solar-jumper."

"Have your technicians speed up the program transfer, Golaah," ak Bhedal said. "Omit everything that we don't necessarily need. We need those attack fighters in the nebula. Everything has to leave base as quickly as possible."

"Are we going to fight?"

The commander shook his head. "No. A few attack fighters will keep the Klingons busy and buy us some time. The rest will spread out in space. The loss of this base is a setback for our holy mission to reestablish the Harmony of Spheres. But even if this base falls, the Purifying Flame will carry on!"

I.K.S. Bortas

"Fighters are launching from the large asteroid at starboard!" Lieutenant Chumarr shouted from the gunnery station. On the bridge's viewscreen, one of the thousands of rocks that made up the asteroid belt on the periphery of the Souhla system turned red when the gunner marked it.

"We've found our shipyard," Kromm said. "Can you confirm that, Raspin?"

"Not yet, Captain," the Rantal replied. "The asteroid is rich in metals, and they block our sensors out. I'll check visually." He fell silent for a few seconds. "Confirmed, Captain. Look."

The asteroid went into the center of the main viewscreen and Raspin enlarged the image. Artificial structures on the jagged surface became visible. Apparently the Purifying Flame had hollowed the enormous piece of rock, or they used natural cavities for their base inside the asteroid. Only a handful of structures on the surface gave their presence away. It was a good hideout, Kromm had to give them credit for that.

"Battle stations!" the captain said. "Decloak and attack. Fire at will. And don't hold back, Chumarr. We're here to wipe the threat that the Purifying Flame poses from the face of the galaxy once and for all."

27
DECEMBER 2, 2385

U.S.S. Prometheus, approaching lad
Lembatta Cluster

The slipstream tunnel disgorged the *Prometheus* with screaming drive and shuddering hull out into space. Captain Adams had pushed his ship far past its specified limits in order to return from the Taurus Dark Cloud to the Lembatta Cluster as quickly as possible. Every minute counted, because nobody knew how long Jassat ak Namur would survive as a vessel for the white energy—not Doctor Calloway, not Spock, not even the young Renao himself.

Straight in front of them, a cloud of swirling chaos seethed. At first sight it seemed as if the *Prometheus* hadn't moved at all during the past few hours, as their destination looked very much like their starting point.

"We have reached the Souhla system," Carson reported. Relief was audible in her voice. The last part of the way across the cluster had been like a charge through a minefield—but the mines here were super-hot enormous gas globes.

"Shields up," said Adams. "Yellow alert. All stations, report."

"The engine room reports minor damage to the EPS conduits," Chell said at the engineering station, while the signal stripes that were embedded in the bridge walls began to glow yellow. "Additionally, a bank of bio-neural gel packs has burnt through. The ship's readiness for action is not affected."

"Understood. Roaas?"

"I'm picking up ships on the periphery of the system," the Caitian replied. "One of them is the *Bortas*. She's engaged in a skirmish."

Surprised, Adams turned to face him. "A skirmish? Who is Kromm fighting?"

"Apparently, *Scorpion* replicas. I'm also picking up several shuttles and a transport, all taking off from a large asteroid within the Kuiper belt."

"Mr. Winter, hail the *Bortas*."

"Aye, sir."

The chaos zone and the nebula on the viewscreen disappeared and were replaced by the bridge of the *Vor'cha*-class attack cruiser. The ship shuddered; sparks flew from overloaded energy conduits at the ceiling. Still, Kromm—sitting on his command chair—hadn't looked this happy since the beginning of their mission.

"Prometheus, *you're late.*"

"What's going on, Kromm?" Adams asked.

"*What do you think, Adams? We found the Flame's shipyard. A handful of fighters are breathing down our neck, while the rest of these* nuchpu' *try to escape. We could do with some help to stop them before they're gone.*"

"We still have another mission to complete above Iad. But we'll be by your side as soon as possible."

"*More glory for us, then,*" Kromm said with a nasty grin. He terminated the link.

Adams focused his attention on the matter at hand. "All right, let's take Mr. ak Namur to Iad. Computer, call for battle bridges to be staffed. Mr. Mendon, upload the adaptive radiation filter into the deflector array. Ensign Ciarese, synchronize the flight controls of all three ship segments."

A frenzy of activity broke out on the bridge when the officers hurried to put the orders into action. At the same time, the computer's voice called personnel aboard the ship to battle stations.

"Battle bridges report ready for duty," said Paul Winter.

"Very well." Adams touched the intercom button on his armrest. "Adams to sickbay."

"Calloway here, Captain."

"Send Mr. ak Namur into the shuttle hangar. Have him board the *Charles Coryell*. We'll remotely pilot him down to the planet."

"Understood, Captain. Ambassador Spock wanted me to let you know that he's on his way to the bridge. His work here is done."

"All right." The Vulcan had not left the young Renao's side during the entire journey. Adams didn't know what exactly he had done to alleviate his suffering, but he assumed that Spock had taught Jassat some Vulcan meditation techniques.

Not even half a minute later, the turbolift door opened and Spock entered the bridge. The old ambassador nodded at Adams solemnly. "Everything is ready."

"Will he make it?" asked the captain.

"I believe so. Lieutenant ak Namur has displayed impressive willpower. His determination has not faltered."

Ak Namur's voice then sounded over the speakers. *"Charles Coryell to bridge."*

"Go ahead, Lieutenant."

On the viewscreen, the young Renao's face appeared. He seemed much calmer than he'd been outside the holodeck hours earlier. Sitting at the small shuttle's conn, he looked at Adams with white glowing eyes. *"I'm ready for the flight to Iad, Captain. Thank you again… for everything."*

His words referred to a small farewell gathering that

Adams had arranged following Kirk's advice in the Starboard 8 during their flight back. They had only sat together for about an hour—Jassat, the bridge officers, Kirk, and a handful of men and women that the Renao had invited. The young man hadn't had the strength for more. On his shoulders rested the destiny of the entire cluster, after all.

During his return to sickbay at the end of the celebration, a surprise had been waiting for him. The entire crew of the *Prometheus* had lined the corridors in order to salute him, to shake his hand, or just to say, "Farewell, and good luck." Each and every one of them—even those who had been unpleasant to ak Namur several days earlier—knew of the sacrifice he was about to make for the future of his people. And for peace.

"Don't mention it," Adams replied. He smiled at the young man encouragingly. "You've been a role model for your people since you first came aboard as an exchange officer. You leave our ship now as a role model for all of us."

"It's been an honor serving under you, sir."

"The honor is all mine… Jassat. Good luck."

"Thank you, Captain." The young Renao lifted his fist to his chest, saluting Adams for the last time in Renao style, before terminating the connection.

Adams swallowed, permitting himself to feel the apprehension he had kept from ak Namur. Silently, he glanced at the rest of his bridge crew. Their expressions showed him that they were ready for the final battle.

The captain raised his voice. "Computer, initiate separation sequence."

"Separation sequence initiated. Auto separation in ten seconds." The computer began the countdown. *"Separation sequence in progress."*

A blue warning light overrode the yellow alert. Adams felt the familiar rumbling when the three hulls separated.

"Upper and lower secondary hulls, stay in close formation," he said. "Synchronize shield grid."

As before, the three segments of the *Prometheus* assumed a belly-to-belly flight position. Engulfed in their concerted shield bubble and protected by the increasingly effective modifications that Mendon, Kirk, Spock, and Barai had made to the ship, the *Prometheus* penetrated the chaos zone around Iad once more.

I.K.S. Bortas

The *Bortas*'s bow disruptor fired a massive energy blast at the asteroid. Another surface structure disappeared in a soundless explosion. Debris and frozen gas formed a spreading cloud around the base in the rocks. But Kromm's ship hadn't caused any damage worth mentioning so far—except for the solar-jumper that had been almost ripped apart by a full hit from the same bow disruptor right at the beginning.

Captain Kromm cursed. "This rock is as tough as the heart of an old warrior."

The attack cruiser shook under enemy fire.

"Shields down to seventy percent," Raspin reported.

Kromm hit his armrest with his fist. "Get these attack fighters down from the sky. I feel like I'm in a *Zekar* swarm here."

"They are too fast," Chumarr said. "They have improved their strategies since Onferin. Then, they just tried to ram us. Now, they are using their plasma cannons."

"They are farmers!" Kromm shouted. "The former flagship of the Empire must be able to deal with a few farmers."

Inwardly, though, he had to admit that the fanatics handled themselves much better than expected. But he would rather have bitten his tongue off than admit that out loud.

"Firing torpedoes, wide dispersal pattern." Rooth might dally over peace and philosophy, but when push came to shove, he still fought like the warrior he had always been.

On the viewscreen, a small black shadow darted past, firing green energy blasts. Behind it, a red glowing torpedo suddenly appeared. The projectile came around in a tight loop, found its target, and hit the tail of the replica *Scorpion* attack fighter.

A huge detonation tore the small ship apart—much bigger than a ship of this type should have produced. The blast hit the *Bortas* head-on, shoving the battle cruiser aside.

The force threw L'emka, Mobok, and Raspin off their feet. Klarn was the only one who managed to grab his console and stay upright. A beam underneath the ceiling broke with a sharp bang, impaling a grid floorplate and barely missing Kromm's left arm.

"What was that?" the Klingon captain demanded.

Raspin pulled himself up on his console. "Shields down to fifty percent."

Rooth cursed. "These little *taHqeqmey* have bombs aboard."

"Captain, we need to keep them at arm's length," L'emka said. "Otherwise, this will be a very short-lived battle."

Kromm merely growled.

"Captain!" Klarn turned away from his comm station. "Apparently, there are even more of these fighters. I have just intercepted a transmission from the asteroid base. They said that the 'armada' will be ready for battle in two minutes."

"Armada?" Kromm sat up straight in his command chair.

His face became a visage of fury, and he cursed, "*Va!* How many ships do these *petaQ* have?"

"The way it sounds, Captain," Klarn said grimly, "a great many of them."

U.S.S. Prometheus

"We've reached Iad," Ensign Ciarese reported.

"Mr. Winter, pass on the order to launch the shuttle," said Adams.

"Right away, Captain," the communications officer answered. He spoke into his console. "Lieutenant th'Talias confirms the launch of the *Charles Coryell*. Ensign Naxxa has taken over the remote control."

"External view."

The stern of the upper secondary hull appeared on the viewscreen of the bridge. The small, sleek shuttle broke away. It performed a tight loop before descending in a steep angle toward the planet surface.

"Flight altitude stable, no noticeable reaction from the energy being on the planet," Carson reported.

"Good," said Adams. "Mr. Winter, open a channel to the shuttle."

"Yes, sir. Channel open."

"*Prometheus* to *Charles Coryell.*"

At first, there was only static in response, but then ak Namur's voice came through. "*I can hear you,* Prometheus."

"How are you? Can you feel the life form's influence?"

"*Barely, Captain. And I'm not even sure whether the restlessness that I feel isn't my own.*"

Spock stood next to Adams on the bridge. "It would seem

that the white energy is protecting Mr. ak Namur from the Son's influence. Unless the being's attention is being drawn away by the battle on the periphery of the system."

"Commander Carson, can you try to ascertain the being's current whereabouts?"

"I'm on it, Captain," said the ops officer. "The strongest concentration of psychoactive radiation is still within the remains of the ancient Renao city."

"Something is still keeping the Son there," Roaas said, "even if his prison has long since been blown away, and the fury within the cluster is permanently increasing."

"Lucky us." Adams turned to Winter. "Have Naxxa land the shuttle on the edge of the ruined city."

The dark-skinned German nodded affirmatively.

"Coming in to land," ak Namur said. *"Distance to target coordinates: one kilometer. Five hundred meters.* Charles Coryell *has touched down."*

"Understood, *Charles Coryell.* We'll be on our way, then. Once again—good luck, Lieutenant. We will never forget your commitment."

"Thank you, Captain. Good luck to you as well. Stop the Flame. Enough innocent people have died."

"We will. *Prometheus,* out." Adams turned his attention back to the bridge. "Ensign Ciarese, take us out of here. Set a course for the Kuiper belt. Let's give Kromm a hand."

I.K.S. Bortas

The *Bortas* shuddered and shook like a mad *klongat.* Sparks flew from the damaged gunnery station, where Chumarr lay on the ground, a sharp piece of debris protruding from his skull. Nuk had personally come up from the engine room in an attempt to fix the console in a hurry. A *bekk* was assisting him.

"Shields down to nineteen percent," Raspin said.

"Keep firing!" Kromm ordered, glancing over his shoulder at the gunnery station. "We need to break open this asteroid before the armada launches."

Rooth, who stood alone by the secondary weapons control, frantically entered commands. His dark face showed traces of burns and his gray hair had been singed. "Firing bow disruptor and photon torpedoes."

Once again, a thick green energy bolt darted towards the Purifying Flame's shipyard, accompanied by a barrage of glowing light globes. When they hit, stones and structures were hurled into space soundlessly. The little celestial body looked as if it had been in the middle of a meteor shower. Craters had opened all over its surface, and a large piece had broken off. But the shipyard still seemed to be intact.

Klarn was still reporting from his intercepted transmissions. "Crews are boarding the fighters and preparing for takeoff!"

Raspin shouted loud enough that his voice broke. "We have an attacker from behind!"

"All disruptors, fire!" Rooth said.

A Titan's fist hammered into the battered *Bortas*. The stars whirled across the main viewscreen, bodies fell on top of each other.

A moment later, the bridge went dark.

lad

Jassat climbed slowly, gingerly, up the knoll on the edge of the ruined city. Columns and segments of the wall were scattered all over the landscape, witnesses of a civilization long gone. He—he of all people, the eternal outsider—had come to Iad, a world his people only knew from legends but that was the mythological core of their entire culture. At any other time, he would have considered the historical meaning of this area absolutely fascinating. This was the cradle of the Renao people.

Today, however, he barely noticed it.

Thick red fog surrounded him. Up until his landing, he had believed that the white energy that filled his body to the brim would protect him from the Son, who was eternally greedy for violence. But he had been wrong. The Son simply hadn't noticed him before, and had ignored his tiny ship.

Now, however, the ancient entity turned its attention toward the unwelcome guest.

DEATH! the Son screamed at Jassat in a thousand languages and images that penetrated his mind from everywhere and anywhere. HATRED! VIOLENCE! FURY! HUNGER, UNIMAGINABLE HUNGER!

A groan broke from Jassat's lips, and he held his head. What was he doing here? He was about to throw away his life—for what? *The Renao despise me, because I have left the home spheres. That's what they all said: Evvyk, Moadas, everyone. And my fellow Starfleet officers hate me because I am Renao, a people of murderers and fanatics.*

He shook his head as he staggered to the top of the knoll. "They don't deserve it! They don't deserve being freed! None of them! Let them kill each other for all eternity, die and return, and die again. Why should I give my life for them? *Why?!*" He screamed the last word at the destroyed landscape that had been ripped open and devastated by the starships' bombardment. It was a mirror of his soul—devastated and empty.

He sensed that the Son's overwhelming presence was close; an enormous mind, corroded by madness.

BLOOD! WAR! BATTLES! RAGE! KILL! KILL!

But suddenly, he perceived something else amid the maelstrom of screams for destruction. It was a quiet voice, a gentle disharmony in the screaming greed for murder and devastation. Like a child's hand in a storm it tugged on Jassat, asking him to extend his hand and offer comfort.

LONELINESS, DEEP SADNESS, LONGING FOR THE HOME SPHERE...

Trembling, the young Renao raised his hands, staring at them with widened eyes. He saw red skin extending from Starfleet sleeves. And he saw a white glow engulfing both, a weak mist that made the sleeves and his hand look unreal in a way. *I'm here, my son*, he suddenly thought with the strange clarity that replaced all doubts and dark thoughts. *I'm here... AND I WILL REDEEM YOU.*

The gigantic cloud-body of the energy being towered above him like a mountain of glittering red. It bent down to him, swirled all around him, and apparently wanted to swallow him.

Jassat looked up, spread his arms and looked towards the Son, the boy.

And he released.

With a massive eruption, the energy inside his body broke free—and the world around Jassat ak Namur turned white.

28
DECEMBER 2, 2385

I.K.S. Bortas, on the periphery of the Souhla system

"Shields down," Raspin said.

"Weapons systems malfunctioning," Rooth added. "Main power fluctuating."

Squinting, Kromm looked around. He had a splitting headache, and his left arm dangled broken and useless by his side. The bridge was only illuminated by the weak emergency lights. But what he saw was sufficient to let him know that the end was near. Pungent smoke lingered in the air. Flames came from the comm station. Sparks flew everywhere. The *Bortas* shuddered and groaned like a deadly wounded animal.

And the asteroid shipyard was still intact. The bridge's viewscreen flickered with interferences but Kromm believed he could see tiny ships take off.

"Engine status?" he asked.

"Impulse engines functioning normally," Mobok answered, gasping for air. "Warp drive is down." He coughed, wet and rattling. A dark liquid oozed from his mouth, staining his armor.

Kromm straightened. He knew what he had to do. There were no alternatives left. The certainty calmed him—the first time he'd truly felt calm for longer than he could remember. "Today is a good day to die."

L'emka approached him. "Captain, the *Prometheus* is en route, they—"

With a smooth movement, Kromm pulled his disruptor out and fired.

His first officer collapsed unconscious.

He turned toward the gunnery station. "You!" he said, nodding at the *bekk* from engineering. "Take the commander to escape pod five."

"Captain?" Bewildered, the *bekk* just stared at him.

"Do it!" Kromm shouted.

The young Klingon quickly threw L'emka's limp body over his shoulder and left the bridge.

Kromm opened a channel on his chair. "Kromm to security."

"Lieutenant Woch here."

"Go to Ambassador Rozhenko's quarters. Stun him with your weapon, and take him to escape pod five. I want him off my ship, and I don't wish to discuss it with him. The same for the two Renao in the brig. They're to join the ambassador and my first officer in escape pod five. Once all of them are inside, jettison the pod."

"Understood, Captain," Woch said without hesitation.

Kromm terminated the link. The *Bortas* shook again under hostile fire, but this time, Kromm didn't sway.

Rooth limped to his side. The old Klingon looked at his captain with a grim face. He didn't say a word but his look said more than Kromm needed to hear.

"Do you think it will be enough?" Kromm finally asked.

The corners of Rooth's mouth twitched. "Nuk would know that better than me, sir."

The captain turned around to regard his chief engineer with a querying glance.

A lopsided grin appeared on Nuk's wrinkled face. "It will be enough, Captain. I'll make sure of it." The stout engineer went to one of the engineering consoles, typing several commands.

The *Bortas* shook again, but no one cared to give any status reports anymore.

Kromm gazed at all those still present. Klarn pressed his lips together in determination. Mobok stared at him from glazed eyes, blood on his chin and chest.

"And you, Raspin?" Kromm asked the Rantal, seated at ops.

Raspin sat up straight. "You didn't shoot at me, Captain," he said.

Kromm nodded. "That's right, I didn't."

The Rantal straightened his narrow shoulders. His black eyes glittered. "My life never had meaning, sir. May my death have one after all."

Kromm smiled. Maybe there was Klingon blood inside this *jeghpu'wI'* after all. Who would have thought?

An alert flickered on Raspin's console. "Escape pod five has been jettisoned."

That was it. Now everyone was gone who could have blemished this heroic act by Kromm, son of Kaath, with their presence. Now, only warriors remained on the *Bortas*. They would knock on the gates of *Sto-Vo-Kor* together.

Today was a good day to die. Maybe even the best.

Kromm looked up to the viewscreen. "Mobok, set a course for the asteroid base. Ramming speed."

"Yes, Captain."

With an unwilling shudder, the *Vor'cha*-class attack cruiser started moving, to bring the wrath of the Klingon Empire to the Purifying Flame. The *Bortas* could look back on a long, glorious history. She had been Chancellor K'mpec's flagship. Chancellor Gowron had commanded her during the battle for the Klingon Empire. She had escorted the returned Emperor Kahless to Qo'noS. And now, under Kromm, she would protect the Empire from a threat that had cost thousands of lives already, and would have cost millions more if they didn't stop it.

Rooth next to him started hitting his armrest rhythmically. And then he began to sing with a guttural voice. *"Qoy qeylIs puqloD. Qoy puqbe'pu'."*

Behind him, Nuk raised his voice, and Klarn also began to sing.

"YoHbogh matlhbogh je SuvwI'. Say'moHchu' may' 'Iw."

The *Bortas* kept accelerating. The deckplates began to vibrate. The drive howled as it was overloading. The asteroid base came closer and closer.

"Raspin," said Kromm, and the warmth inside of him was like home. "Open all communication frequencies, internal and external. I want everyone to hear us. And I mean everyone."

He also started singing.

"Hear! Sons of Kahless.

"Hear! Daughters too.

"The blood of battle washes clean,

"The warrior brave and true.

"We fight, we love, and then we kill.

"Our lives burn short and bright,

"Then we die with honor and join our fathers in the Black Fleet,

"Where we battle forever, battling on through the eternal fight!"

* * *

U.S.S. Prometheus

The *Prometheus's* three hulls dropped from warp in a bright flash. Adams had ordered a micro-jump to reach the asteroid belt within seconds, where the battle for the base raged with unabated intensity.

"Red alert," Adams said. "All ship segments, break from formation. Upper and lower secondary hull, pursue the escaping *Scorpions*. No one must leave the system. We will help the *Bortas*."

He looked straight ahead. The *Vor'cha*-class cruiser was visible in the center of the viewscreen. The ship was listing, and debris hovered around it. One of the warp nacelles had been half torn off, and plasma fires burned in numerous hull breaches. Kromm's ship wasn't firing any photon torpedoes or disruptor beams. Several fighters circled around it, firing at the battered Klingon ship from their turrets with deadly energy blasts.

"That doesn't look good," Adams said. "Commander Roaas, fire phasers and quantum torpedoes. Get rid of these fighters around the *Bortas*."

"Aye, sir," the tactical officer confirmed.

Amber beams and glistening blue projectiles cut through space toward the small fighters. One of the fighters was hit and blew up in a spectacular fireball.

"That was more intense than it should have been," zh'Thiin said.

"The bombs!" Carson turned around in her seat. "Sir, we need to be careful. The fighters carry critical amounts of trilithium, tekasite, and protomatter."

"Understood," replied Adams. He chided himself a fool for forgetting this additional danger. "Take it into consideration from now on, Mr. Roaas. Only shoot if the fighters are far enough away from the *Bortas*. Mr. Winter, warn the secondary hulls."

"Yes, sir." The young comm officer quickly executed the order.

"I'm receiving a report from the *U.S.S. Venture*," said Carson. "She will be with us in five minutes."

Adams clenched his fists, frowning. "So we need to hang on a little while longer."

"More fighters are launching from the shipyard," Roaas said.

"Captain, what is the *Bortas* doing?" Ciarese asked.

Adams would have liked to know the answer to that as well. Kromm's ship had accelerated. With its impulse engines glowing red, the battered ship was accelerating straight toward the asteroid base.

"Ensign, hail Kromm," he said to Winter. "I don't want him to do anything foolish."

The German's fingers danced over the keys. "No response, Captain."

"His comm system might be damaged," Chell said.

Tense, Adams leaned forward.

"Open all frequencies, Mr. Winter. Maybe we'll reach the *Bortas* that way."

"Frequencies open, sir."

"*Prometheus* calling *Bortas*. Kromm, can you hear me?"

"No answer, Captain."

They watched the *Bortas* pick up speed. There was no doubt where she was heading.

"Kromm!" shouted Adams. "Wait! You don't have to do that!"

"Captain," Winter said, sounding confused, "I'm picking up—well, singing, sir."

"Singing?" Adams asked. "What kind of singing?"

"On audio."

"NaSuv manong 'ej maHoHchu'."

"NI'be' yInmaj 'ach wovqu'."

They heard at least half a dozen voices. They were singing at the tops of their ragged lungs, death-defying and full of pride.

"Batlh maHeghbej 'ej yo' qIjDaq."

"Oh no." Adams slumped back in his chair.

"Vavpu'ma' DImuv."

"Pa' reH maSuvtaHqu'."

The *Bortas* had almost reached the asteroid. The warp nacelles started glowing just like the impulse drives. The Renao hunters realized what was going on, and tried to withdraw. Too late.

"MamevQo'. MaSuvtaH. Ma'ov."

29
DECEMBER 2, 2385

Jassat woke up.

At first, he didn't know where he was or why he was there. *I should be dead*, he thought. *Shouldn't I?* Chaotic bits of memories about a red cloud of fury that had descended on him flashed through his mind. He had felt anger, fear and desperation. Finally, he had let go, had given himself up and sacrificed himself in a massive eruption of white light. He had died—or at least that was what he believed.

But now, he was back. Or, more to the point—he was still here.

Squinting, he looked around. He lay sprawled in the crater that had once been the location of the first Renao city, and had later turned into the grave for the *U.S.S. Valiant*. Shattered columns, blocks of stone, and remains of walls were scattered like toys all over the slopes, and there were deep dips that the torpedoes of the *Bortas* and the *Prometheus* had ripped into the ground.

"I'm alive," he muttered. He hesitated to say the words out loud, but once he had, he was overwhelmed by joy. He scrambled to his feet and threw his arms up. "I'm alive!" he shouted into the silent landscape.

Elated, he looked around again. He didn't see the slightest trace of a red glittering life form. He didn't feel anger, hatred, or the unbridled desire for violence. The pressure that had previously weighed down on him was gone. The white energy seemed to have dissipated completely also. When he looked up to the sky, he experienced another pleasant surprise: along with the Son of the Ancient Reds, the zone of chaotic radiation around Iad had also disappeared! Jassat saw nothing but a pale pink sky, which was typical for the worlds in the Lembatta Cluster.

The shuttle! I need to get back to the shuttle and call the Prometheus. *I hope she's still around somewhere.*

As fast as the rough terrain permitted, Jassat hurried back to the edge of the crater landscape. He found the *Charles Coryell* near a destroyed forest. It looked exactly the same as when he had left it behind. Frantically, he entered the unlock code, opened the hatch, and went inside. He moved into the cockpit area and started up the systems.

The Coryell *is capable of warp flight,* he recalled. *Even if the captain and the others are no longer within the system, I can get away from here.* Still, he would prefer it if the *Prometheus* could pick him up as the flight from Iad to Lembatta Prime on the periphery of the cluster would take more than three weeks in a shuttle.

He established a connection on the *Prometheus's* standard frequency. "*Charles Coryell* to *Prometheus*, please come in."

Nothing happened.

"*Prometheus,* this is Lieutenant ak Namur on the *Charles Coryell*. Please come in."

Static was the only response.

Jassat was just about to begin a pre-flight check to make his own way out of there, when a voice came from the cockpit's loudspeaker.

"Charles Coryell, *this is the* Prometheus." It was Captain

Adams, and he sounded more than just a little surprised. *"Jassat, is that really you?"*

"Yes, Captain. Switching to visual." The *Prometheus* bridge appeared on the small monitor in the center of the dashboard. Jassat saw Adams standing in front of his command chair. Behind him were Roaas and Spock. Sarita Carson and Ensign Ciarese sat in front of him. An incredible feeling of relief and happiness washed over him. "Captain. It's really good to see you."

"The happiness is all ours, Mr. ak Namur. We didn't dare hope that you might have survived."

"But I did. I have just woken up among the ruins. Not a sign of the Son or the chaos zone is in sight."

"Yes, we noticed that the chaos zone had dissolved. Just like all angry emotions have gone." The captain smiled. *"You did it, Jassat. Congratulations."*

"Thank you, sir." Jassat grinned. "Now I'd just like to get out of here."

"Understandable. Get into orbit. We will rendezvous with you in just a few minutes."

"Yes, sir. Ak Namur, out."

One minute later, the small shuttle took off into the clear skies above Iad. Jassat ak Namur didn't look back once.

DECEMBER 5, 2385

Paris, Earth

A hurricane of applause began when President Kellessar zh'Tarash entered the council chamber of the United Federation of Planets. Delegates, diplomats, and other dignitaries of various member worlds rose all over the galleries. While she walked past them toward the dais, zh'Tarash glanced at the faces of the assembly. She saw Admiral Nechayev here and Councilor Kyll there. The Deltan delegation cheered on one side, the Klingon K'mtok nodded at her from the other side. Even Lwaxana Troi, whose selfless effort had been invaluable during recent months, had remained in the city until the crisis was over. The Betazoid also stood on her feet to honor zh'Tarash, smiling cordially.

The president didn't smile. When zh'Tarash reached the dais, Admiral Leonard James Akaar came to his feet as well. The huge Capellan had waited for her, sitting in one of the shell-type seats next to the lectern. Now, he walked toward his president.

"We've got Qo'noS standing by, *Zha* President," he whispered to her while the assembly's cheers still echoed from the high walls. "Whenever you're ready."

Zh'Tarash just nodded. Silently, she took Akaar's hand, walking with him to the lectern where he stood by her side.

She raised her hands to silence her audience, looking at the dignitaries before her. One after the other fell silent and sat down, but joy and enthusiasm remained on their faces.

"This is not a good day for the Federation," zh'Tarash began, just as soon as silence had fallen over the council chamber. Her tone of voice was harsh and didn't sound the way the assembly had expected. "We don't have a reason to celebrate. We haven't done anything."

Incredulity, everywhere. Looks were exchanged, whispering began.

"What happened in the Lembatta Cluster three days ago was no victory," zh'Tarash continued. "Not for reason and not for ethics. It was a rescue operation—one in the nick of time, no less."

"The Renao are free, aren't they?" someone from the stands shouted. Zh'Tarash recognized the voice immediately—the Tellarite Kyll of all people felt the need to object. "The Purifying Flame no longer poses a danger. Why shouldn't we be happy about it?"

It was inappropriate to interrupt the head of the Federation with comments. In this case, no one really seemed to mind, not even zh'Tarash. Quite the contrary.

"We're not happy, because it was we who allowed the Flame to get this far," she said quietly and firmly. "You're absolutely right, Councilor, if you consider the outcome in the Lembatta Cluster as lucky. It is. But make no mistake—I can assure you, I won't—this problem only ever arose because we weren't vigilant. Because we were distracted by other problems. Because we looked away." She paused briefly, waiting for more objections, but none came. "When the U.S.S. Valiant disappeared a hundred and twenty years ago near Iad, we believed to know the reason—technical failure. We didn't ask any questions, we simply mourned our dead and carried on with our daily business. When the Renao closed their borders and severed the thin bonds of cooperation that we had tied with them, we didn't ask many questions, either. We were surprised, yes, and we were sad about losing a prospective partner, but we didn't ask enough questions."

Heads nodded in agreement. Zh'Tarash looked at Nechayev, Troi, Zoona—so many faces, so much regret. Almost all those present had been here four weeks ago when the crisis had begun. Some of them had voiced completely different views from today. Now, they remained silent, and that filled zh'Tarash with confidence.

There's hope for us after all, she thought, and suddenly, she knew that a break in Federation history was possible; the return to peace and research that they all needed and longed for. *There's always hope.*

"Did we have reasons for our ignorance?" she asked her audience. "Of course we did. There were other emergencies, other front lines that demanded our attention. The Borg, the Dominion, the Typhon Pact—you know the list as well as I do. And yes, we can make excuses for our ignorance if we want to. There are enough reasons." She shook her head. "But I don't want to do that. I will not do it, ever. The Renao were a people in distress, and we—the Federation of all organizations, which has been devoted to nobility and altruism since its founding days—were too blind to recognize this distress. Too blind to help. We reacted when we were immediately involved. And that, honorable council members, was far too late!"

Nechayev started the second round of applause. The seasoned female admiral clapped her hands emphatically. One by one the rest of the council members joined her. But this time, the praise was not for the events of the past few days but for zh'Tarash's admonishing words. This time, the praise was subdued, pensive, and clearly more valuable, and the president smiled weakly.

Hope.

"We need to be vigilant, whatever happens," she said when the applause died down. "A wise man once said that the three most important words of his language were, 'Let me help.' The Federation and Starfleet have been committed to these words since day one. *That* is our most important role—as league of worlds and as individuals. We respect the peaceful interests of our neighbors, celebrate cultural differences, and benefit from the strength and the diversity of society. We help wherever it is necessary and where we're allowed to do so. If the destiny of the Renao and the mission of the *Prometheus* and the *Bortas* that lies behind us should teach us one thing, it's this: 'Let me help.'"

"Hear, hear," Akaar whispered at her shoulder. He sounded very pleased—and very relieved.

"Admiral Akaar told me earlier that Chancellor Martok is waiting to join us via subspace communication. We shouldn't let him wait any longer. I'm sure he has a lot to say about today."

"*Not anymore,* Zha *President,*" a familiar voice came from the loudspeakers in the chamber. Surprised, zh'Tarash turned around, just as Martok appeared on the holoscreen at the wall behind the dais. "*You've already said all there is to say, and I for one can only agree with each and every word.*"

Zh'Tarash was speechless. "Chancellor?"

Martok grinned wickedly. He sat on a throne within the High Council, and a mischievous glint stood in his remaining eye. "*Admiral Akaar patched me through during your speech. Apparently, he thought I should hear your words. And I am grateful. I would not have wanted to miss such profound eloquence.*"

The president glanced at the commander-in-chief of Starfleet with mock annoyance. "It would seem that I need to have a serious word with him."

Akaar lowered his eyes ruefully, but smiled.

"*Not too serious, I hope,*" Martok said, laughing.

"No," she replied, still glaring at Akaar. But then she also smiled. "Not too serious." She looked back at Martok. "In any case, I'm glad to have spoken in your name as well, Chancellor. Let me assure you that the Federation is by your side in this hour. Captain Kromm and the *Bortas* have met a very honorable end. We will not forget their sacrifice."

The old Klingon nodded. *"Nor will we. I did not believe that Kromm had such honor in him. It would seem I was wrong. Sto-Vo-Kor is well populated with heroes today."*

"And the Alpha Quadrant has won another friend, I hope," she said. "I heard from the cluster that the Son of the Ancient Reds' mental influence is rapidly decreasing. According to Admiral Gepta, the medical staff from the *Venture* and the *Bougainville* reckon that all afflicted personnel should make a full recovery. We will help the Renao as best we can during this process, and we would also like to extend our neighborly hand to them once more, should they wish to accept it."

"The Empire will be by your side in that, Zha President," said Martok. *"Let us hope that it will be to all our benefit. Martok out."*

I'm convinced it will be, thought zh'Tarash as his face faded from the holoscreen, and the Federation's star seal with the laurel reappeared.

30
DECEMBER 5, 2385

Auroun, Onferin
Lembatta Cluster

Never before had Evvyk ak Busal seen so many spaceships. There had to have been at least half a dozen in orbit. The sight was majestic and awe-inspiring.

Much more important to her, though, was the world at her feet: Onferin, her home.

She turned away from the large window in the remarkably comfortable lounge in the belly of one of the huge Federation starships, the *Venture*.

"Can we go home now?" she asked the Starfleet man by her side. She had found out that he was the captain of this ship, and his name was Henderson.

"Soon," he promised. "Just this small reception to celebrate the end of the crisis, and we will beam you and your companion back down to your home city." He smiled at Moadas, who stood next to Evvyk.

Moadas smiled back, if somewhat strained. "We don't really feel like celebrating."

Henderson leaned forward. "Between you and me? Neither do I. But hey, there are free drinks and attractive people in uniform. What more can you want?" He laughed, and his gaze returned to a red-haired woman across the room who wore a similar uniform to him. She was talking to a creature that looked like a huge reptile in a barrel-shaped plate. *Admiral Gepta*, Evvyk reminded herself.

There were so many people in that room that she didn't know—so many strangers from beyond the cluster—that she felt uneasy. Ambassador Rozhenko and Commander L'emka were the only ones that she didn't consider strangers. The two Klingons had been stuffed into the escape pod along with Moadas and her and thrown into space before Kromm had steered his battle cruiser into the Purifying Flame's asteroid base. Why the sadistic captain had spared their lives, Evvyk still didn't understand. L'emka had looked pretty angry when she woke up inside the pod, but she had tried to explain it to her. It had something to do with the notions of glory and honor that apparently dominated Klingon culture.

It didn't matter to the young Renao woman. What did matter was that she and Moadas were alive, and Kromm was dead. With his demise, their involuntary journey as prisoners of the *Bortas* crew had come to a good end.

The door to the lounge opened, and another group of Klingons stomped into the room. "General Akbas! General Klag!" Gepta shouted with a booming voice. "I'm honored." He left the redhead behind and marched to the delegation from the Klingon Empire.

"Please excuse me," said Henderson. He walked over to the female captain, taking Gepta's place at her side.

The Klingons and Gepta made quite a racket while introducing each other and their adjutants. Rozhenko also joined the group, but only the one called Klag greeted him with any enthusiasm. The young ambassador didn't seem to mind the chillier reception from Gepta and Akbas.

At that moment, the door opened again, and three more guests appeared in the doorway. Evvyk recognized

Ambassador Spock immediately, as he had truly saved their lives on the *Bortas*. He was accompanied by a human with gray streaks in his hair and a cat-like man. When they entered the room, a fourth man came into sight, a Renao. Her eyes fell on him, and she felt a sharp pain in her chest.

Jassat!

Of course, she had heard about his incredible experience—the rumors about him had spread like a bushfire. Jassat had found Iad, had traveled to the edge of the galaxy to face the White Guardians, and had defeated the Son of the Ancient Reds. They said he had become the White Guardian's sword, and that he should have died during his confrontation with the Son. But somehow, he had survived. If only half of that was true—and it was perfectly obvious that the Son was gone—her childhood friend had made an extraordinary development from outsider to legend.

He saw Moadas and her at the same time. His eyes glowed brighter. But before he could join his old friends, Gepta noticed the newcomers.

"Captain Adams!" he shouted. Apparently he was in a good mood and had the urge to greet every guest at the top of his voice. "The man who solved the riddle of the Lembatta Cluster."

Some of the guests felt the need to interrupt their conversations and applaud cordially.

Adams raised his arm. "I was only one of many who did their best during this crisis in order to prevent an even bigger disaster."

Gepta made a strange, jerky noise that might have been laughter. "Humble as ever, Captain. That's the way I like you. Come on, let's have a drink at the bar."

While Adams and his cat-like companion were led

away to the counter by Gepta, Spock and Jassat joined Evvyk and Moadas.

"I am pleased to see that you are both alive," the Vulcan diplomat said.

"As are we," Moadas replied dryly.

"How did you manage to escape the *Bortas*'s destruction?"

L'emka joined the small group, along with Rozhenko. "Kromm threw all those who were not worthy in his eyes off the ship before he chose a hero's death. I am torn as to whether or not to be grateful or furious."

"Be grateful," Spock said firmly. "Your days under his command were numbered in any event. It would have been wasteful to end your life before you were able to earn your own glory."

"You're probably right." The Klingon smiled. "I am indeed considering a new assignment already."

"Oh really?" Rozhenko seemed interested. "May I ask what?"

L'emka's gaze wandered from Jassat to Moadas to Evvyk. "I wish to learn more about the Renao, their culture, and the Harmony of Spheres. I will be requesting permission to stay in Auroun."

"Maybe we could make this a little more official," the young Klingon said. "I imagine that the High Council would not mind having eyes in the Lembatta Cluster."

"You want to leave a minder behind before you take off?" Moadas asked.

"An ambassador," Rozhenko said. "Someone who takes care of the negotiations between the Renao and the Klingon Empire. I will speak with Chancellor Martok and Ambassador K'mtok and see if they're amenable."

Spock said, "I will add my own recommendation to

yours, Ambassador—if my voice carries any weight with the chancellor."

Rozhenko smiled. "I doubt there's any place in the galaxy where your voice doesn't carry weight, Ambassador. Thank you."

"Klingon ambassador to the Lembatta Cluster." L'emka visibly enjoyed that title. She smiled. "Not bad for a farm girl, eh? I could get used to the sound of that."

"What about you, Jassat?" Evvyk asked. "Will you return to Onferin? Or will you fly away again?"

A shadow darted across his face when he noticed the subtle accusation in her voice. But he answered without any anger. "I will remain aboard the *Prometheus*. She's my home sphere now. But I will certainly not forget Onferin, and will visit as much as possible. Because this world is *also* my home sphere."

"You can't have two home spheres," Moadas said.

"Oh yes, I think you can," Jassat said, and his voice was calm and firm. Evvyk wondered whether he had gained some deeper wisdom during his encounter with the White Guardians. "And once all Renao have realized that," Jassat continued, "a universe full of wonders awaits them."

Later that evening another celebration took part; much less formal and with considerably fewer people.

"To us!" Jenna Kirk raised her glass, which was full of a violet cocktail with synthehol. "To the *Prometheus*, the best goddamn ship in Starfleet! And to her fearless crew, who was able to defy stubborn Klingons, religious fanatics, and ancient, mad life forms. And to the man who freed the Renao and saved us a lot of trouble in the next few months." The chief engineer looked at Jassat.

"Hear, hear," Sarita Carson said, raising her glass as well. Geron Barai, Lenissa zh'Thiin, and Jassat also joined in the toast. The young Renao smiled. It was good to sit here at a corner table in the Starboard 8 with them, and to shake off all the burdens of the past few weeks.

"And who would have thought," Carson joked. "At the Academy five minutes ago, and now the savior of millions. Just watch it, ak Namur, you might command your own ship in two weeks' time."

The others laughed.

"I guess I have extraordinary luck on my side," Jassat said. "Going on a mission that can't be survived and returning home, nonetheless… not everyone can do that."

"I'm glad you did," said Jenna. "It's bad enough losing a crewmate. Having to pay my respects to a close friend would have spoiled the lucky end to this crisis enormously for me."

Barai looked serious when he raised his glass again. "To all those we have lost—Bhansali, Ward, Dilmore…"

"…Loanaa, Atasoy, Kalim bim Gral…" Jenna continued.

"…Losheg and Goran Tol," zh'Thiin finished the list of the casualties.

They drank silently.

A grin crept back onto Carson's face. "But hey, we're here to celebrate. We're still alive! And the last time we all sat together like this was on Deep Space 9 before the Lembatta crisis. Far too long, if you ask me."

"Agreed," zh'Thiin said.

"Good to have you back with us, too, Doc." Jenna nodded at Barai. "Nothing against Calloway, but no one applies a hypospray as tenderly as you do."

The chief medical officer smiled. "Yes, I'm really glad to be fit for duty again. The days in my quarters were… awkward. It felt as if I was trapped in a permanent nightmare. Strangely enough, I always felt as if I heard Ambassador Spock's voice."

"He was there," zh'Thiin said. "Counselor Courmont asked him to stabilize your mind with the help of a therapeutic mind-meld."

"Oh really?" Barai looked surprised. "In that case, I should probably thank him again. An interesting therapy. I wonder if it could heal other mental ailments. Maybe I should take a closer look at the studies in that field."

"Not tonight," the Andorian woman stated with pretended strictness.

"Aye, Commander."

Jassat saw them exchange a look.

"Would you excuse us for a few minutes?" said zh'Thiin suddenly. "I have to speak to the doctor alone."

Now it was Jenna and Carson's turn to exchange a knowing, amused look.

"Sure," Carson said. "You two clear up what you have to clear up. And afterwards, we'll drink Moba's bar dry." As if to stress her words, she raised her empty glass, waving at the Bolian bartender.

"We'll be right back," said zh'Thiin, getting up. Barai followed her. Together, they left the Starboard 8.

"I bet two holodeck time sessions that they will be at least an hour," Carson said with a wicked smile.

Jenna grinned. "Leave them be. We've got time, we've got drinks—I'm not in a hurry to get out of here."

Jassat agreed with her wholeheartedly.

"What do you want to talk about?" Geron asked when they reached Lenissa's quarters.

Lenissa walked into the dimly lit cabin. Her antennae swayed to and fro. Geron didn't have to use his telepathic talents to sense that she was nervous.

"Geron," she said, turning to face him, "we need to talk about us, about our... relationship."

His face changed to a resigned expression. "I was worried that this moment would come eventually. Great timing. The mission is finished, life goes on."

"Wait." She raised her hand. "Listen to me first."

He nodded. "All right."

Lenissa chewed on her lower lip and looked as if she was trying to find the right words. "You know how difficult things were between you and me during the past few weeks. Especially after I was kidnapped by the Flame."

Cautiously, he tilted his head in confirmation. "I admit that I sometimes didn't know how to treat you properly. You seemed... torn inside. Sometimes you showed me the cold shoulder, sometimes you pulled me between the sheets. And after every time we were together I was worried it might have been the last time."

Lenissa turned away, walked to the bulkhead, and looked into the mirror that was mounted there. "I really did have my doubts. You know, back then, when I came aboard, I began having an affair with you because you didn't demand anything, the same as me. You didn't have any hidden agendas. That was fine by me because that's the way it had been for me on the other ships as well. I looked for a man, we had fun; that was all."

She turned back to him, leaning against the wall next to the mirror with her hands behind her back. "But eventually I realized that you... felt more for me. More than you should. More than I wanted. And once I got away from the Renao fanatics…" She shrugged. "I was completely confused. I wanted you close to me, but your care annoyed me."

Geron cleared his throat awkwardly, rubbing his chin with his hand. "Well, you know, as far as the care is concerned… I'm probably guilty as charged. I really was worried about you when the Flame abducted you and Jenna. And once you were back, I thought I had to look after you—which, honestly, was pretty stupid. You are the security chief, not me." He grinned at her. "I'm sorry."

"I'm also sorry that I was so… ambiguous." She sighed, shaking her head and looking at the floor. "When the Son got you, and I didn't know whether you would ever recover, something stirred in me." She looked up again, regarding him with shimmering eyes. "I realized that you… are more to me than just someone I'm taking to bed. I went to see Courmont—and believe me, that wasn't easy for me—and we talked. Thanks to her I could see that I was scared, that I could allow proper emotions, and… well, it was all pretty complicated. The important thing is—she advised me to leave the past behind me and to look to the future. And she told me to be courageous and take a risk… with you."

A wonderful warmth spread inside Geron's chest when he heard those words. That sounded a lot different from what he had expected to hear. With a smile on his lips, he walked towards Lenissa, putting his hands on her slender waist. "Does that mean I'm allowed to love you?"

A mischievous sparkle was in her eyes when she looked up at him. "Would you stop it if I forbade it?"

He shook his head, grinning. "I'm afraid not, Commander."

"In which case, I'm obviously powerless, Doctor." She pulled her arms out from behind her back, putting them around his neck. Her fingers stroked the back of his neck.

"And what about you?" he whispered. "Do you think you could love me back?"

Affectionately, she looked at him. "You never know. Everything is possible. *Now*, everything is possible." She pulled his head down to her and kissed him.

Elsewhere, in the captain's ready room, two other people enjoyed each other's company, though they were old friends, not lovers.

"Jamaican Blue Mountain blend," Adams said when he handed his first officer a cup of coffee.

"Captain, why are you wasting your special coffee on me?" Roaas asked. "You know I'm not capable of distinguishing good coffee from bad."

"Oh, stop whining, Roaas. I feel like celebrating, and you don't celebrate with a standard blend from the replicator in the mess hall."

"As you wish." Dutifully, the Caitian accepted the cup.

Adams had dimmed the lights, and outside the window the first streaks of passing stars appeared in the red warp swirl. The *Prometheus* was approaching the periphery of the Lembatta Cluster. It was a reassuring sight. The crisis in the Renao home spheres had been overcome, and they were heading toward a two-week shore leave. Of course, there was damage to the *Prometheus* that still required repairs. And once again, Adams would have to write letters of condolence for the families of crewmembers who had lost their lives during the battle for the shipyard of the Purifying Flame. Fortunately, only a handful of men and women had fallen, but every loss hurt. Not to mention the thousands who had died in or outside the cluster. They would need to be remembered—at an appropriate time.

But not now, he reminded himself. *Not tonight.* He took a sip from his coffee, enjoying the wonderful flavour that unfolded across his palate. Slowly, he walked toward the window, looking out.

"Oh, the irony," he said, lost in thought.

"What?" Roaas joined him by the window.

"We were so close to losing the peace with the Klingon Empire. We were on the verge of war against the Renao. And we regarded the energy being on Iad as the root of all evil." He shook his head. "It's so easy to make enemies or regard others as the enemy. But in the end, they were all victims one way or another. The Klingons, the Flame, us—we were all victims of the Son's madness. And the Son was a victim, too. He fell prey to his own inquisitiveness, of his wish—that we know all too well—to boldly go where no one had gone before."

"According to your reasoning, the Renao would be right after all," Roaas said. "All this wouldn't have happened if we had all remained in our home spheres—in the space that nature has defined for them."

Adams shook his head. "That's not the answer. In fact, I think it's more important than ever to question one's actions and their consequences consistently. Recklessness, bigotry, greed for glory, hubris... These traits blind everyone's sight for the greater good, whether they stay home or not."

"So, according to you, the Federation suffers from hubris?" Roaas looked at him curiously.

"In this case, yes. We regarded the Renao as a backward people and neglected the Lembatta Cluster. How much sooner might we have noticed these difficulties if we had taken their problems seriously?"

Roaas shrugged, taking a sip of his coffee. "I believe the Federation had simply reached the limits of its capabilities. You know the crises of the past few years as well as I do, sir. We simply *had* to lose sight of the galactic sideshows eventually."

"Yes, maybe. So it's even more pleasant to have one problem less than before. And with L'emka on Onferin, the first step has been taken to bring the Renao and their neighbors closer together."

"That sounds like a toast to raise your cup to." Roaas's whiskers twitched in amusement.

"You're right." Adams smiled faintly. "Talking about events worth drinking to—I have received pleasant news from Starfleet."

"You mean other than the permission for two weeks' shore leave?"

"Yes, other than that." Adams walked to his desk, picked up a padd, and handed it to his first officer, who scanned the contents. His furry ears pricked up in surprise.

"Starfleet is beginning a new science program?"

"The most extensive for ten years," Adams said, nodding. "With everything you would expect from such a program—deep-space missions, the search for alien life, exploring unknown regions of space. It sounds like a true new beginning. And the first ships have already embarked on their missions."

"The *Enterprise*-E under Captain Picard, the *Robinson* under Captain Sisko." Roaas read the rosters of those ships participating in the new program. "That looks huge. If they send out famous captains like these on research missions, the fleet and the Federation are sending clear signals. The decade of war has ended. Hail a more peaceful future."

Adams raised his coffee cup, toasting Roaas. "To the future—and all the amazing things it may bring us."

APPENDIX

1. *U.S.S. Prometheus* Personnel

1.1. Alpha Shift

Commanding Officer Captain Richard Adams
First Officer/Tactical Commander Roaas
ConnPilot/Lieutenant Jassat ak Namur
Second Officer/Ops Lt. Commander Sarita Carson
Communications Ensign Paul Winter
Security Chief/Environmental Lt. Commander Lenissa
zh'Thiin
Chief Engineer Lt. Commander Jenna Winona Kirk
Science Officer Lt. Commander Mendon
Chief Medical Officer Doctor Geron Barai

1.2. Additional Crew members

Commanding Officer Beta Shift Lt. Commander Senok
Commanding Officer Gamma Shift Lieutenant
Shantherin th'Talias
Deputy Chief of Security Lieutenant John Paxon
Deputy Chief Engineer Lieutenant Tabor Resk
Deputy Chief Medical Officer Lt. Commander Maddy
Calloway
Transporter Officer Chief Wilorin

Counselor-Isabelle Courmont
Barkeeper-Moba

MHN-II (MHN-XI) Doctor Tric
2. *I.K.S Bortas* Personnel

Commanding Officer Captain Kromm
First Officer Commander L'emka
Second Officer/Tactics Commander Chumarr
ConnPilot/Lieutenant Toras
Ops Bekk Raspin
Communications Lieutenant Klarn
Security Chief Lt. Commander Rooth
Chief Engineer Commander Nuk
Science Officer Lieutenant K'mpah
Chief Medical Officer Doctor Drax
Transporter Operator Bekk Brukk

ABOUT THE AUTHORS

Christian Humberg is a freelance author who has written for series including *Star Trek* and *Doctor Who*. His works have so far been translated into five languages and won German-language prizes. He lives in Mainz, Germany.

Bernd Perplies is a German writer, translator, and geek journalist. After graduating in Movie Sciences and German Literature he started working at the Film Museum in Frankfurt. In 2008 he made his debut with the well-received "Tarean" trilogy. Since then he has written numerous novels, most of which have been nominated for prestigious German genre awards. He lives near Stuttgart.

STAR TREK
PROMETHEUS

The Root of All Rage

A dangerous evil is flourishing in the Alpha Quadrant. In the Lembatta Cluster, a curious region of space, fanatics who call themselves the Purifying Flame are trying to start a galactic war, and the warlike Klingons are baying for blood. The Federation have sent the *U.S.S. Prometheus* to settle the crisis, and the crew must contend with both the hostile Renao: the secretive inhabitants of the Cluster, and the Klingon captain of the *I.K.S Bortas*, who is desperate for war.

TITANBOOKS.COM

For more fantastic fiction, author events, exclusive excerpts, competitions, limited editions and more

Visit our website
titanbooks.com

Like us on Facebook
facebook.com/titanbooks

Follow us on Twitter
@TitanBooks

Email us
readerfeedback@titanemail.com